Title: Patriot Royal
Author: Russ Pottle
Publisher: Chestnut Hill Publishing
P.O. Box 2225
Williamsburg, VA 23187
(Ph) 804-220-8527; (Fax) 804-229-2324
Classification: Historical Novel
Price: $22.95 US; $29.95 Canada
Binding: Hardcover, smythe sewn
No of Pages: 360
Finished Size: 6" x 9"
ISBN: 0-9646664-0-5
Publication Date: September 1, 1996

For additional information, contact the publisher at the address/phone/fax above.

PATRIOT ROYAL

PATRIOT ROYAL

Russ Pottle

Chestnut Hill Publishing
Williamsburg, Virginia

ISBN 0-9646664-0-5
Library of Congress Catalog Card Number 95-68667

Manufactured in the United States of America

First Printing: February 1996

~ *Introduction* ~

All the world's a stage,
And all the men and women merely players;
They have their exits and their entrances;
And one man in his time plays many parts...

As You Like It
William Shakespeare

Welcome!

The stage before you is hidden now, yet captivating with the muffled sounds of voices and movement emanating from behind the drawn curtains. Slivers of bright light escape from above and below as you await with anticipation the opening act.

The characters are taking their positions. Some will be familiar to you; old dear friends perhaps. Others you will be meeting and getting to know for the first time.

There are villains as well as heroes here; the bold, the occasionally bold, and the downright cowardly. And a few who will make you laugh right out loud.

At times you will reach with the players for the higher ground — placing honor and duty and the well-being of others above your own fear of danger. You will also confront the wretches who readily succumb to greed and base self-interests. And you will come to know the common folks too, trying to succeed, or just survive, amid monumental events for which no one was prepared.

There is love here — unrequited and requited. There is loyalty, betrayal, and redemption.

There are formal set-piece military engagements involving thousands of soldiers in uniformed pageantry. There are bloody skirmishes too, and intensely personal battles that are waged within.

You will soon go into line of battle where you will face down a terrifying bayonet charge (more than once). You will be expected to endure all the formidable allies of armed conflict: illness, starvation, bitter cold, blistering heat, loneliness, and despair. You will meet the enemy, come to know him well — but you will never learn to hate him.

Having said all this, you may be surprised to learn that this is *not* a tale of war, but of people. Some from the living past. Others imagined representatives of people whose lives and times beg for telling. All are with us again, with us here, on the stage before you. They are ready and anxiously waiting to escort you to a different, exciting, turbulent, history making, history shaping era.

The stage is set. The players are in position. The lights are coming up. The curtain is about to rise. So take your seat. Get comfortable. The performance begins.

You are now in the time just before the outset of the American Revolutionary War. The War for Independence. By the end of your journey the war will be over. But the Revolution will continue. It continues still. May it always be so.

Chapter 1

December 15, 1774

Charles Royal hurried along Beacon Street, drawing his cloak tightly about him against the cold, knifing wind that blew off Boston Common.

Though it is his 21st birthday, Charles is in a state of anguish. Earlier that evening while celebrating with friends at Robinson's Tavern on King Street, he had foolishly lost his late father's victory sword in a wager with a stranger. Even to a careless youth like Charles the loss of such a prized possession, which his father had bestowed on him for his 16th birthday, brought feelings of regret and self-recrimination.

Perhaps the stranger was a vile scoundrel who tricked me out of the sword, Charles thought. As he staggered forward he paused momentarily and considered returning to the tavern and perhaps reclaiming his property. No, he realized that the stranger had undoubtedly left and the sword was lost. He decided not to tell his family and hoped that no one would notice.

Charles turned left onto Joy Street and climbed the narrow cobblestone passage until he reached his family's residence at the crest of the hill.

Swinging open the great oak door, Charles was greeted by the sight of birthday bunting everywhere and the smiling faces of his two younger sisters — Sarah, who is four years his junior, and the effervescent Sally, who exudes all the promise of a budding debutante of fourteen.

"Happy birthday, Charles!" Sarah beamed as she embraced him warmly.

"Smithson!" The valet appeared and took Charles's cloak and hat.

"Happy birthday, Charles!" Sally added excitedly. "The others are waiting for you in the drawing room. Are you surprised?"

"Very pleasantly surprised, Sally," Charles replied while turning his head so that she would not detect his earlier revelry from his breath.

Taking his arms, Sarah and Sally led Charles past the other rooms to the large drawing room that had been the scene of many a festive gathering in earlier days. It is not to be so this evening.

"You are late as usual, Charles," said Robert Royal who glanced at his gold watch disapprovingly.

"Oh pooh, Robert," Sarah interjected. "How can a person possibly be late for his own *surprise* party?" Robert merely frowned and shook his head.

"Happy birthday, Charles," said his mother in a cold, obligatory way. She crossed the room and kissed him dispassionately on the cheek. "I suppose you've been drinking rum again with those idle friends of yours." Turning to Robert she continued, "None of whom could earn his keep if his very life depended upon it."

"Yes Mother," Charles replied wearily.

"Well, your father would certainly not approve of such behavior. But as it is your birthday, we shall speak no more of it. Sarah, ask Mrs. May if dinner is ready."

"I have, and it is."

Mrs. Royal and Robert led the way into the main dining room followed by Charles with Sarah and a giggling Sally clinging to his arms. Just as they were seated, brother Joseph hurriedly entered the room, still trying to tie his cravat. Absent-mindedly he bumped into the table, rattling the water glasses.

"Joseph!" Robert admonished. "Watch where you're going!"

"Sorry Robert."

"And just look at yourself!" added Mrs. Royal. "Coming to dinner while still not fully dressed!"

"Sorry Mother."

Joseph smiled and sheepishly offered his hand to Charles as Sarah worked to straighten his cravat. "Happy b-b-b-birthday, Charles," he stuttered.

"Thank you, Joseph," Charles smiled as he accepted his hand.

Sally began a jibberish on the latest fashions in London as the first course was served. Robert sat solemnly at the head of the table in the place that had been the purview of the late Colonel Joshua Royal, the King's Chief Magistrate in Boston and one of the richest sea merchants in all the colonies.

Robert was only 33 years of age, but had always struck Charles as being much older. A largely humorless and stern man, he ran the family's enterprises well and assumed the many roles expected of one of the patriachs of the city. He was a Loyalist to the core, as was his mother. He had never married, or for that matter shown any interest in the ladies. His efforts were directed toward enhancing the family's wealth and position in society. Robert and Charles could not have been more different.

Joseph, on the other hand, was a simple and likeable fellow, unpretentious and with a kind word for everyone. Robert had thought at one time that a clergyman's life might best suit Joseph.

But Joseph failed at his studies, as he did at most every undertaking, to the consternation of both Robert and his mother. Except for the keeping of a lovely family garden, Joseph showed little aptitude for anything but good cheer.

As the plates for the main course were being set upon the table and the wine poured, Robert rose with glass in hand. Charles thought that it was to toast his special day, but instead Robert looked straight ahead and intoned, "To the King!" All about the table drank to the health of King George III. All except Charles.

"You do not honor your Sovereign, without whose beneficence we would not enjoy the blessings of this table!" Robert said to Charles in a challenging tone.

"Please Robert, not today, it's his birthday!" Sarah pleaded. Both men ignored her.

"It was my understanding that we owe our blessings to God," Charles countered evenly. "And to the toil of our own hands."

"Toil? Ha!" Robert shot back derisively. "The toil of your hands, *dear brother,* would not feed a sparrow for a day. Indeed, the only *toil* I recall from your hands was when you joined with those common vagabonds to dump your family's own tea into Boston Harbor!

"Such noble toil cost your family more that twelve hundred pounds, which, I am quite certain, we shall never recoup. And made the Royals the very laughing stock of Boston!"

"Praise God that your father never knew of your involvement in that heinous act," added Mrs. Royal.

A tense silence fell upon the table, interrupted only by the sound of knife and fork on plate. Finally, Charles could endure it no longer.

"I readily admit to my many shortcomings," Charles blurted out. "I don't have the skills at commerce that Robert possesses, or even the inclination to develop them. I lack focus as to an occupation and yes, dear Mother, I have a taste for hard liquor and the company of coarse people.

"But there are questions that I ask myself, for which I cannot find answers. Such as why should we live with such riches while so many must suffer? Would we truly be less well off with one less silver spoon or sailing ship? And why must we pay to support a government across the ocean that determines our fate, yet we can have no say in it?"

"Since you have obviously struggled with these questions for long hours, I am surprised that their solution has not become clear to you, because it is quite obvious," Robert replied in an imperious manner. "In a word, it is service. Men are forever in service to other men, and the better men are rewarded by their Creator with more possessions. Just as the liveryman and the dock workers serve us, we in turn must serve the King, who is ordained by God to rule over us. What you question is the natural and eternal order

3

of nature.

"Now that that has been made clear, let's move on to more practical matters. It is becoming exceeding evident that hostilities between His Majesty's forces and the rabble of Boston will commence in earnest shortly. I have commissioned the refitting of one of our packets, the *Westwind*, into a frigate to serve in His Majesty's American Fleet. It has been renamed the *Vulture* and Charles, I have secured for you a position as third officer. She will be ready for duty the fifteenth of next month."

"But Charles knows nothing of sailing," Sarah protested.

"Then he shall learn!" Robert replied firmly.

"If hostilities commence in earnest, I shall take my place on the American side," Charles announced.

"You would draw your sword against your King!" Robert stated with mounting anger.

Charles paused and then answered, "Yes."

"And against your own brother?" asked Mrs. Royal in a rising voice. Robert was an officer with the Loyalist militia.

To this Charles remained silent.

Robert finally threw his napkin on his plate in disgust and rose abruptly, his finger pointed directly at Charles, his voice in a rage, "By your own admission you have been a disappointment to your family and now a traitor to your Sovereign King! As you have thrown off all the advantages that this life has brought to you and now visit despair upon your mother, you must certainly accept the fate that you yourself have cast — Go from this house! Go now with only what you wear! From this day hence place your fate in the hands of God, for you have surely turned your back on all else!"

Robert stormed out of the room, followed shortly by his mother. At the base of the stairway he shouted back, "Joseph!"

Joseph rose quickly, but before leaving he thrust his hand out to his younger brother. "G-g-g-good luck and God be with you, Charles." A second harsh call from Robert and Joseph vanished from the room.

Charles was alone now with his sisters. Without saying a word they stood and walked slowly to the door where Sarah handed Charles his cloak and hat.

"You must let us know where you are and how you're doing. We'll bring you clothes and whatever else you need."

Charles smiled weakly and placed his hand on Sarah's cheek. "It would be too dangerous, Sarah. If Robert found out his anger for me would fall upon you."

"Robert doesn't frighten me."

"I doubt if anyone frightens you."

Charles turned his attention to Sally who was now crying uncontrollably. "I love you, Charles," she managed to say between sobs.

"I love you, too, my dear sisters."

Charles kissed them both tenderly and then turned to the door. In a moment he was out on the street, without money and with no idea where he would spend the frigid night. As he pulled his cloak tightly about him, a gentle snow began to fall.

As Charles shuffled along his thoughts tumbled one over the other. Perhaps he could pass the night at a friend's house. Or maybe at the old Puritan Mission. Or at one of his family's warehouses — surely the man on watch would recognize him and let him in.

Suddenly, from out of the shadows of an alley, a woman emerged and stood directly before Charles, who was taken aback. He did not recognize her, but she apparently knew him. Her eyes, life-worn though they appeared to be, spoke of a gentleness as they fixed upon his. She was a beauty who, nonetheless, showed the hard lines of a wordly life. Charles took her for a prostitute and attempted to pass.

"Young sir, you'd be Charles Royal would you not? Son of the late Colonel Joshua Royal?"

"I am madam, but—"

"I thought so. I have something for you."

She reached beneath her coat and brought forth a magnificent sword and sheath. It was the very sword Charles had recklessly parted with earlier in the evening.

Charles gasped in astonishment, "The victory sword! How did you come by it? I'd pay you any amount you asked for it, but I have just now been turned out by my family and am penniless."

The woman smiled ever so slightly and shook her head. "I only wish to return this sword to its rightful owner. It's what your father would have wanted." She paused a moment longer, reached and gently brushed aside a strand of hair from Charles's forehead, then turned and hurried back down the alley.

"Thank you, dear lady!" Charles called after her. Then, "Wait! I don't even know your name." But the woman was gone.

Putting aside his other problems for the moment, Charles was overjoyed at his good fortune in regaining the sword. It immediately conjured up memories of earlier, happier days spent with his father fishing off the docks and watching the great ships pass, trekking through the forest, and fencing.

As a lad, Charles adored his father. In later years he could scarcely imagine that the loving, patient father he knew was the hardened business-man and strict father that Robert and his mother so admired. Had they fabricated a man to suit their own ideal? Had he?

Joshua Royal had come from the humblest of origins. An orphan moved with his sister Ophelia from relative to relative, he was apprenticed at twelve to a distant cousin who was a Philadelphia printer, but subsequently took his leave and eventually worked his way back to Boston where he survived by his quick wits and strong back.

As a Massachusetts militia captain, he gained some notoriety for his part in the successful conquest of the French fortress at Louisbourg on Cape Breton Island in 1745. By the time of the French and Indian War, he had begun to amass a very comfortable living, primarily as a sea trader. Despite the demands of commerce and his growing family, he accepted a colonel's commission with the militia and joined an expeditionary force sent to the Pennsylvania and Ohio frontiers.

Against overwhelming odds, Colonel Royal led his small army in coop-eration with the militias of other colonies on a daring attack on the French stronghold at Fort Duquesne. By successfully bluffing the size of their force, the Colonials captured the fort without firing a shot. At the capitula-tion ceremony that followed, the chagrined French commandant presented the commander of each militia regiment with a sword signifying his surren-der.

Upon his return to Boston, Colonel Royal became the celebrated toast of the town. He wore his victory sword proudly during his triumphant march into the city at the head of his troops. And in short order he and his family were accepted into the upper echelons of Boston society.

In addition, his military accomplishments (and some well placed gold) earned him one more honor — the title of Chief Magistrate for the city.

Like many men who rise to prominence so rapidly, Colonel Royal had his share of enemies. That he could drink any man under the table and was a skillful gambler was common knowledge. Also that he was popular with many a lady, although he was a married man (there were rumors that he actually died in the arms of a longtime mistress). But the most frequently asked question about Colonel Royal was how could a penniless orphan ever acquire such a vast fortune.

None of the scandalous stories that surrounded his father diminished him in Charles's eyes. On the contrary, he admired his father all the more for meeting life head-on; asking no quarter while drinking fully from life's many cups. For most importantly of all, Charles knew that his father loved him. Just a week before he died, the two were walking along Tremont Street when the old man turned and said, "Son, you are the joy of my life." At the time, Charles attempted to joke the matter aside. But now, nearly three years later, his father's words rang as clearly in his ears as the moment they were spoken. And Charles was warmed by them.

Up ahead, at the corner, Charles could distinguish a familiar figure. It was the infamous rabble-rouser, Samuel Adams.

"Mr. Adams!" Charles called out.

"Ah! Young Mister Royal. What would cause you to venture out into such a night as this?"

"Well, sir, it's quite simple. At dinner at our home earlier this evening I expressed my heartfelt sympathies for the American Cause and made known my position that should hostilities take place, I would side with the Patriots. Because of this admission, my elder brother Robert had me put out. And so I find myself wandering the streets aimlessly until my path becomes clear.

Adams was moved by the young man's experience. "Come," he said to Charles.

Chapter 2

With the help of Sam Adams, Charles secured a job as a barman at Robinson's Tavern where the Sons of Liberty sometimes met. Charles served drinks at many of their gatherings and found his own social consciousness grow as he listened to the rebel leaders of the day — men like James Otis, Dr. Joseph Warren, Paul Revere, John Hancock, and of course John and Sam Adams debate, often heatedly, the latest events and what course of action should be taken.

Henry Robinson, the proprietor of the tavern, was a gregarious old gentleman with a ruddy round face and a warm smile for all. Henry's wife Maude did the cooking. In her day she had served as head chef for three royal governors. Arthritis had crippled her hands, but her mind was nimble and as time went by she passed her vast culinary knowledge on to Charles who, surprising himself, showed a remarkable talent for the craft.

Sarah and Sally learned of Charles's employment and paid him a visit one afternoon. They met on the walk in front of Robinson's.

"We were so worried about you, Charles," Sarah said. "Thank heaven you've found work. Where are you living?"

"Here. In a small room in the back. Aunt Ophie took me in for a few days, but I didn't want to cause a rift between her and Robert. Besides, in the tavern business you have to work quite late sometimes. It's convenient if you don't have to trudge off somewhere in knee deep snow at 2 a.m."

"We brought you some of your clothes," Sarah said, handing him a small bundle. "And Sally has some food for you."

"Here."

Sarah leaned closer and pointed to the bundle. "There's twenty pounds and some change in the pocket of your brown breeches."

"Twenty pounds! Where'd you get that kind of money?"

"Never mind."

"She sold her bracelet."

"Sally!" Sarah scolded her sister.

Charles tried to decline the money. "No, I can't—"

"Yes you can!" Sarah admonished him. "You'll need money, Charles. That bracelet meant *nothing* to me."

8

"But it was a gift. From Phillip."

"So?"

"Won't he be upset?"

Sarah went into her coy act, "Why Phillip, I don't know *where* I've misplaced your lovely bracelet. I do declare, I'd lose track of my head if it weren't fastened on." She fluttered her eyelashes and Charles smiled.

"Thank you. Thank you both."

"Is there anything else you need?" Sarah asked.

"I'm fine. Don't worry about me."

Just then a group of Charles's old friends crossed the cobblestone street and were about to enter Robinson's. At the door they caught sight of Charles.

"Hey there! Barmaid! Step lively now! You have four thirsty paying customers here. Move it or you'll receive a swat on the fanny!" Charles glared as the laughing ne'er-do-wells went inside.

Sarah was unamused. "Why do they taunt you, Charles? I thought they were your friends."

"So did I."

"They can't treat you that way!" Sarah bristled with anger as she started for the door, but Charles grabbed her by the arm.

"It's alright, Sarah. Really. They're just having a little fun is all."

Sarah fumed nonetheless. "It's *not* alright! Just because they're wealthy and don't have to work at all is no justification for making fun of a man earning an honest day's wage."

"Yeah!" Sally added.

"What can I do?" Charles asked plaintively. "If they cause trouble for me I could lose my job. Then what? Begging in the streets in the dead of winter?"

"You could come back and live with us," Sally suggested hopefully.

"No, Sally. That's not an option for me. Robert made that quite clear."

"Maybe he's changed his mind."

Charles and Sarah looked at each other. Sally was so young and innocent. They understood far better the permanence of the breach.

Charles spoke gently, reassuringly to Sally. "Robert and Mother have their way of thinking, Sally, and I have mine. We're not the same and never will be. Every bird must leave its nest one day. Some fly out, some are pushed out, but the result is the same — they must learn to make their own way in the world as best they can. That's what I'm doing now. Do you understand?"

"Yes."

"And I don't want you to worry about me at all. Everything's going to be fine."

"Can we still come visit you?"

"Of course."

"And you'll always be our brother?"

"Oh Sally," Charles said hugging her. "There's nothing Robert or Mother could ever do to change that."

"Good. I *hate* Robert."

"No you don't."

"Yes I do!"

"He's just angered you. He works very hard to provide a quality life for you and the family. Now that I'm working I have a new respect for the sweat and personal sacrifices he's made."

The church bells rang three times. Sarah stood on her toes and kissed Charles on the cheek.

"It's time to go. We'll be back on Thursday with more of your clothes."

"And your Christmas presents!"

"Sally!"

"Oh please, that's not necessary. I . . . I have no gifts for you."

Sarah looked at her brother, shaking her head. "You just don't get it, do you Charles? Come along Sally."

"Bye Charles!"

"Goodbye. And thank you," Charles said holding up his bundles. He watched his sisters go around the corner toward home, then turned and went back to Robinson's

"Ah! There you are maid! Ales for my friends and myself and be quick about it!" shouted Phillip Overton, the son of a leading Cambridge and Harvard physician and one of Charles's regular drinking companions in his carefree days. Overton was also one of the herd of young swains calling regularly on the lovely Sarah Royal, thought by many to be the finest catch in Boston.

Charles fetched the drinks and placed the tankards down on the table. As he turned to leave, Overton grabbed his apron.

"Here now! You've spilled some."

"Where?"

"Right there!"

"I don't see anything."

"Are you blind? You don't see that pool of spilt drink? You all see it, don't you lads?" Grinning, they all professed to the phantom spill. "Do I have to call the proprietor over? Where is the old fool? Saucy wench! You'll pay for your imputence!"

"What do you want?" Charles asked stern-faced.

"Well-l-l-l, I'd say a round of free drinks at your expense might ease the offense. What say you gentlemen?" Overton's cohorts readily agreed. Without comment, Charles went and drew four more ales, handed payment for them to Mr. Robinson, returned and placed them on the table.

"And what is the charge for *these?*" Overton asked with a mocking crane of his ear.

"No charge," Charles replied.

"Well then, off with you! And see that your clumsy ways upset no more customers."

Charles moved toward the bar with the derisive laughter of his tormentors trailing behind him.

"Don't let the likes of them get to you, lad," Mr. Robinson advised Charles who was wiping the bar down with unusual force. "In my book, you're a better man than the lot of 'em."

"Thank you, sir."

"There's a, er, political meetin' if you catch my drift in the upper chamber tonight at eight. I'll be attendin'. I'll need you to serve drinks and to keep a watchful eye for, as we say, gentlemen of a differen' political persuasion."

"Of course."

"That's a good boy. Now, Mrs. Robinson's preparin' her famous veal stew. Would you like to learn the art of it, son?"

"Indeed I would!"

"Run along then. I'll take care of things out here."

"Barkeep!" Overton barked across the tables. "What does a man need to do to get a drink in your roach-infested establishment?"

"Act like a human bein' fer starters," Mr. Robinson muttered. "Thanks for your kind patience, sir! I'll be over directly."

That evening virtually all the local leaders of the Sons of Liberty filled Mr. Robinson's upper room. Tensions seethed with the British occupiers and threatened to boil over at any time into open conflict far more serious than the Boston Massacre. Some of the more radical members even spoke of a general armed rebellion.

Committees of Correspondence sent letters with news and views flying up and down the Eastern Seaboard. The closed port of Boston was now center stage in this epic drama, and all eyes — including those of the King and Parliament in London — were focused there.

The Intolerable Acts, pushed through Parliament by Lord North with the full support of King George III, were specifically designed to punish the unrepentant Boston rabble and their rebellious leaders after the Boston Tea

Party and other brush fires of blatant defiance against the Crown's authority.

But throughout the colonies, Parliament's retaliatory acts had the unexpected result of rallying support for the beleagured Bostonians. In every colony orators spoke out against the heel of Britain that pressed down upon the necks of their brethern to the north. Prayer vigils on behalf of the Bostonians were well-attended. In pulpits from New Hampshire to Georgia clergymen denounced the harsh measures of Parliament in terms that left no doubt where their (and God's) sympathies lied.

The plight of Boston, many feared, would one day be their own. A subtle, unifying sense of sharing in a just protest against a common antagonist was spreading across the land. But was the general population ready to fight? No. In the finest English tradition, most people thought that the way to redress their grievances was to petition London. Even the most widely recognized radicals, men like Sam Adams and Patrick Henry of Virginia, hastened to profess publicly their loyalty to Great Britain and their willingness to, in Henry's words, "shed my last drop of blood for King George III."

It was the King's Prime Minister, Lord North, and his henchmen in the House of Commons who were portrayed as the arch villains. America actually had staunch friends in Parliament — Chatham, Burke, Conway, Fox, Johnstone — but the followers of North and the King were more numerous. To them, America would acquiesce to the rule of the Crown — willingly if possible, by force if necessary. None in the corridors of power in London (and few in the scattered governments of the colonies) doubted that Great Britain, now the most dominant nation on earth, could enforce its will.

While serving drinks and bussing tables, Charles listened attentively to the discussions. To Robert and his mother, Charles appeared to be a seditious firebrand. But to these Patriot leaders, many from families of wealth and influence equal to the Royal's, Charles would have seemed politically moderate. After the meeting, Charles summoned up his courage and approached Sam Adams.

"Mr. Adams, sir."

"Yes Charles."

"There's a question which puzzles me."

"And that is . . ."

"Well sir, you appear to support mob violence to achieve your ends. How, sir, can this be consistent with the wish of every fair-minded man to seek all peaceful means first for resolving differences?"

Some of the more narrow-minded radicals were disturbed by the young upstart's question. But Sam Adams was a broad-thinker who welcomed open discussion of sensitive issues.

"A contradiction does appear to exist, Mr. Royal. Do you not agree gentlemen?" He did not wait for a reply before continuing. "You were at the dumping of the tea in the harbor weren't you Charles? And on the unofficial visit to Governor Hutchinson's mansion, the night his wonderful library was burned?"

Charles looked about the room before answering. To admit his involvement in these acts of vandalism within earshot of a British spy might one day mean an appointment with a hangman's noose.

"I was . . . an observer, sir," he said guardedly.

"And what were your impressions?"

"That private property was wantonly destroyed by a frenzied mob."

"Hmmm. On one level you're entirely correct. But you must understand that the goal was not to destroy the petty belongings of wealthy men. It was to send a message — loud and clear — that the people are moved to action by their grievances and cannot be long ignored. It is the *symbolic* act that's important."

Charles considered the explanation. "With all due respect, sir. Can it be said that these 'symbolic acts' achieved their ends? The port of Boston has been closed. Redcoats are quartered in private homes. And we live in constant apprehension that the Royal Navy will appear in the harbor and fire the city."

"The stakes have been raised, it's true," replied Adams, "But what course is left open to us? To kneel and submit as slaves before the Tyrant? Or to stand tall and defiant, claiming the fair and just treatment that is the birthright of every Englishman, including Colonials?

"If a fight is to come, Charles, it is the young men of your generation who will decide its outcome. When the tide of history forces you to choose, will you stand up for your rights?"

Charles's answer came from the heart. "Yes."

"Good," Adams said placing his hand on Charles's shoulder. "I promise you that you won't be alone."

The next day Charles decided to join a provincial regiment being formed in Boston under Colonel William Prescott. He waited patiently in line as a stream of men from all walks of life — from sailors to preachers to town drunks — pledged their allegiance, made their marks in the book, and moved on to receive their military accoutrements.

When it was Charles's turn the sergeant asked without raising his head, "Name?"

"Charles Royal, sir."

"I'm not an officer. You address me as sergeant, not sir," came the clipped response. Then the name sank in.

"Royal you say? Of the well-known Royal merchant family?"

"Yes, sir, ah Sergeant."

"Well now, Mr. Royal, it would appear that you are in the wrong recruitment depot. I'm sure there's an officer's rank and a soft bed awaiting you with His Majesty's Loyalist brigade." Many of the men hooted scornfully and hurled harsh comments in Charles's direction.

"I have come to enlist as a private and serve my country," Charles stated in his own defense.

"To *spy* on her you mean!" growled the sergeant, rising to his feet.

"Just one moment, Sergeant!" came a deep voice from the back of the room. Men parted to let Sam Adams step forward.

"I will vouch for the worth and convictions of this young man. He has already sacrificed much for the Cause. He has foresaken family, friends, and fortune. Let him be known to all as a true patriot."

The sergeant harrumphed and resumed his seat. He slowly dipped his quill in the inkwell and, casting a last skeptical look at Charles, entered in the roster, *Patriot Royal.*

When the winter weather permitted, militia drills were conducted on Boston Common every Saturday. Charles took part brandishing a stick for a musket. These Yankee Doodle soldiers were a comical lot, stumbling and bumbling through the baffling marching drills wearing pieces from a hundred different unmatched uniforms. Their officers and sergeants — elected by the soldiers themselves — tried to maintain what they thought was a proper military bearing, but more often than not the stupidity of the men in formation got the better of them and they resorted to shoving and cursing. One militia captain got so upset that he started throwing snowballs at his men, which resulted in a fist throwing free-for-all.

British Regulars watching these martial displays howled in amusement. There was nothing illegal about local militia practicing the military arts, in fact it was a hallowed Colonial tradition. To the eyes of seasoned veterans of European wars, though, these farmers and shopkeepers were rank amateurs *playing* at being soldiers — much like children. It was while enjoying these Saturday militia revues that many Lobsterbacks developed their haughty disdain for the fighting ability of American troops.

During one militia exercise, while standing in line of attention, Charles spotted his brother Robert walking across the field about a hundred yards distant. With him was his general manager, Maxwell Chessman, carrying a portfolio overflowing with papers under his arm. Robert did not appear to notice Charles, who remained silent.

That evening Charles went to his Aunt Ophie's home on Beacon Hill for dinner. She was his father's only sister. A headstrong, politically active woman who had never married, she was one of the most powerful socialites in Boston, counting among her many confidants such disparate characters as Royal Governor Hutchinson's wife and Abigail Adams, wife of John Adams.

Ophelia, who insisted everyone call her Ophie, endured the poverty and uncertainty of an orphan's childhood, just as Charles's father had. Even though Colonel Royal saw to it that she was financially secure, she never turned away from her roots, often circulating petitions and even leading marches to the statehouse in support of bills to help the poor and unrepresented.

Aunt Ophie also possessed the heart of a romantic, and when Charles accepted her invitation to dinner, she arranged to have a special surprise waiting.

Celeste Bradford was a rare and delicate beauty. Light golden angel's hair fell in full and gentle waves below her shoulders. Her eyes were light blue and her skin was soft and without blemish. She smiled easily and with a youthful shyness that men found irresistible. Her father was the rich and powerful businessman Winthrop Bradford, an old-money pillar among Boston's elite and a devout Loyalist. Celeste, his only child, was the apple of his eye and he spoiled her shamelessly. In his mind, Celeste could lay just claim to any of the best sons of Boston's finest families, or London's for that matter. In most instances Celeste was the model of a dutiful and obedient daughter. But when it came to the issue of love, she chose from her many suitors the one who her father liked least — Charles Royal.

"It's me Aunt Ophie!" Charles called out as he hung his cloak and hat on the pegs by the front door.

"Come on into the parlor, Charles."

Entering the room, Charles's eyes immediately fixed on Celeste who wore a low-cut pink dress with white lace. She smiled at him nervously.

"Are you happy to see me Charles?"

"Oh yes! Yes! I wasn't expecting . . . Oh it's wonderful to see you."

With a cunning smile Aunt Ophie made an announcement. "Oh me! I've just remembered. I promised Mrs. MacPherson that I'd drop by to discuss plans for the new . . . orphans' shelter. Yes. Well, I'm off then. I may be quite late." Then adding privately to Charles, "In fact, I seriously doubt I'll be home at all.

"Dinner's by the fire, children. Enjoy!"

With a quick wave she grabbed her coat and hat and was out the door. Charles and Celeste had the house to themselves. There was an awkward moment when neither one seemed to know what to say.

"Quite a matchmaker, my Aunt Ophie," Charles said as an icebreaker. Celeste smiled slightly, nervously scanning the paintings on the wall. Charles picked up a curio from the table and fumbled with it.

"Charles."

"Yes."

"I know what happened with Robert. Your friends told me everything. I'm so sorry."

Charles shrugged.

"Every family has its disagreements," Celeste went on. "Sometimes father is even cross with me. But then it passes. This will pass too, don't you think?"

Charles shook his head slowly. "I just don't know."

"Perhaps if you sit down and speak with him. Apologize for your rash behavior. He'd forgive you, I know it! Then everything could go back as it was."

"Celeste . . . you're so beautiful. But the world isn't."

"You told me you loved me, Charles."

"I do!"

"And that one day soon we'd marry. You said that we could announce our engagement at the Governor's Ball in May."

"Yes, I haven't forgotten."

"But I'm confused. If you've been disowned by your family — cast out without a penny — then how can we possibly wed? Oh Charles, I'm so afraid!"

Charles took Celeste in his arms. She buried her face in his chest as he gently stroked her silken hair.

"I don't know what to say to you. It's true my position and fortune are gone. I scarcely earn enough money now to support myself, much less a wife and family."

"But all is *not* lost," Celeste said anxiously. "Don't you see? Beg Robert's forgiveness. Your wealth will be restored and we can be married. Think how happy we'll be. Father says my wedding will be the social event of the season!"

"Your father hates me."

"No. He just doesn't love you as I do. I'm sure in time you'll become fast friends."

Knowing their political differences better that Celeste, Charles seriously doubted it.

"Come here," Celeste cooed, pulling Charles down on the couch with her. "It's been so long since we've been . . . *together.*"

She touched Charles's face softly with just her fingertips. They drew closer together and began to kiss. Soon the kisses became more intense as warm passions rose in each of them. Perhaps Celeste was right. Perhaps everything could return to the way it was. Did anything matter except this? Locked in a hot loving embrace Charles's attentions focused on but one thing, and it wasn't politics. He reached down and freed Celeste's breast from her bodice. He caressed it and kissed it and wanted more. At first she welcomed his warm touch. She craved physical affection as much as Charles. Maybe more. But then with a sudden thrust she shoved him away.

"What? What?" Charles stammered between panting breaths.

"You *promised.*"

Slowly regaining his composure, Charles nodded.

"Don't worry my darling. When you've made everything right with your family and we're happily wed, there is nothing I possess that I won't willingly share with you."

To Charles, at this moment, that prospect had enormous appeal.

"Come on," Charles rose and offered Celeste his hand. "There's a craving in both of us that *must* be satisfied."

Celeste looked at him puzzled and a little afraid, then Charles smiled, "Let's eat!"

In a vain effort to somehow earn enough money to keep Celeste's affections without having to grovel to Robert, Charles took on every part-time job he could find. He taught fencing to young aristocrats and started a small catering sideline at Robinson's Tavern. He also became an occasional coachman for John Hancock. Hancock's Patriot leanings were common knowledge and rumors abounded that he and the other known leaders of the Sons of Liberty would soon be arrested by the Crown's authority — or worse, simply disappear. Charles was felt to be a trusted driver who would not betray Hancock to this enemies for a few pieces of silver.

On Thursdays, Sarah and Sally religiously visited their brother. They always brought something, if only an item they'd sewn or a jar of preserves. Charles gave up asking them not to bring gifts. They were both blessed with generous spirits and to deny them their offerings would only hurt them. And Charles would never do that.

On one visit, Charles's former friends repeated their boorish taunts in Sarah's presence. The mean-spirited grin fell from Overton's face when it met Sarah's icy glare. No words were spoken, but Overton realized his enormous loss. His cruel shenanigan's had just cost him forever his place in line for the affections and possible hand of Miss Sarah Royal.

When Charles returned to work, he noticed Overton brooding with his cohorts at a corner table. Things had been going a little better for Charles lately and he certainly wasn't looking for trouble.

"Hey barmaid! BARMAID!" Overton stood and bellowed. Charles turned around. "Yes you. Bring us a round of ales and good cigars. Be quick about it!"

With a deep breath Charles did as he was told. Placing the drinks around the table, Charles could almost feel Overton's foul mood rising to the surface.

"Well that cuts it! I'll not take any more of your insolent ways!" Overton jumped to his feet and hurled the full contents of his tankard into Charles's face. For a moment Charles stood dripping in shock. Then he let forth a gutteral roar and flew across the table, grabbing Overton by his skinny throat.

Over with a crash went the table and chairs as the two men grappled to the floor. One of Overton's cronies smashed a chair over Charles's back which gave Overton a momentary advantage. He pummeled Charles with the side of his fist, but with little effect.

Old Mr. Robinson shot out from behind the bar in a flash swinging a menacing wooden mallet over his head. Terrified, Overton's companions scrambled out of harm's way and raced out the door, abandoning Overton, who was now clearly getting the worst of it.

Charles sat on his chest pinning both arms with his legs. Clenching his fists in rage, Charles was an instant away from pounding him into the floorboards when Overton cried out in a high squeeky voice.

"Please no! Don't hurt me Charles! Don't hit me I beg of you!" He closed his eyes tightly and squinched his face in anticipation of the blows he was certain would follow.

But Charles, revulsed by the vile coward beneath him, chose instead to be merciful. Slowly he climbed off Overton and stood glaring above him. Overton, with a frightened look, snaked his way across the floor on his back before scurrying to his feet.

"Get outta here ya damn sissy!" Mr. Robinson yelled with his mallet poised for damage. "And you can take ya business elsewhere from now on!"

Overton quivered like a shaken animal, blood flowing from one nostril, his shirt torn. It took only a flinch from Mr. Robinson's mallet-filled hand to send him stumbling out the door to safety outside.

When he was gone, Charles surveyed the damage. "I'm sorry for all this, Mr. Robinson. I'll expect you to take the cost out of my wages — if I still have a job."

"Charles, if ya *hadn't* stood-up for y'self I would've been angry. You did the right thing, lad. Damn their blackened eyes! You've done me a service. We're well rid of that lot I say."

Mr. Robinson took note of Charles's battered right hand. "Best have the missus take a look at that."

Charles left to find Mrs. Robinson, rubbing the back of his neck where he had been clubbed by the chair. Mr. Robinson looked after Charles, chuckling to himself. He had been a tavernkeeper in Boston for thirty years and had witnessed far worse that this.

"A little fight every now and then is good for the soul," he told a nearby patron. Then looking about the room added ruefully, "But not for the furniture."

Several busy but uneventful weeks passed quickly for Charles. The demands of his various jobs and militia training left little time for a personal life. He had just finished counting the meager contents of the leather money pouch he kept stashed beneath his bed when an unexpected letter arrived.

Celeste had taken a bold initiative that she could never have imagined herself doing with any other suitor — she sent a note to Charles asking him to meet her at a tea room around the corner from Robinson's Tavern. On a sunny afternoon, with the early spring thaw turning snow and ice to rivulets on the street, they met.

"I've missed you Celeste," Charles said with longing in his voice.

"Have you Charles? So much has happened since I last saw you."

"I know. The Redcoats are everywhere and the countryside is up in arms—"

Celeste interrupted, "I meant with *me* silly!"

"Oh."

"Charles," she continued, shaking her head slowly, "Father has forbidden me from seeing you. He demands that I break off our relationship and choose another."

". . . Is that what you want?"

Celeste's eyes shifted to her lap. "I don't know. I'm so confused. We can't even announce our engagement at the Governor's Ball. It's been cancelled!"

"I know."

"Have you spoken to Robert?" Celeste asked intently. "Apologized?"

"No."

"Charles! You promised!"

"No I didn't."

"How can I possibly marry you now? You're poor. Look at you! You're no more than that cursed rabble that's filled the streets with terror and absolutely *ruined* the spring parties."

"Then you share your father's belief . . . that it would be best if we part?"

"Oh Charles, what can I do? If I disobey Father he may turn me out too — then I'll be no better off than you are."

"At least we'll have each other."

"And to what end? To beggar side by side in the street?"

Several moments of uneasy silence passed before Celeste spoke. "I can't just not see you anymore."

"I love you, Celeste. I want you to be my wife."

"Why did I have to fall in love with the crown prince of fools! With all the eligible men in Boston standing outside my door, why were you the one I let in?

"Tell me what to do, Charles."

Celeste peered innocently, helplessly into Charles's eyes. He could have told her what to do. It was what she wanted. But something inside him said that this time she would have to make up her own mind.

"Do what your heart tells you," he said softly. "I have to get back to work."

When he reached the door he heard a cold clear voice behind him. "Goodbye Charles." He had her decision.

Over the days that followed, Charles kept as busy as he could, trying to block out the heavy loss of Celeste from his mind. Evil thoughts kept creeping in telling him that his life was now an utter shambles. It didn't help at all when a week later he passed by the same tea room and glanced in. There, seated with Overton and his former friends, sat his beautiful, beloved Celeste. When Overton caught sight of Charles he quickly threw his arm around Celeste and kissed her on the cheek, shooting Charles a wicked smile. Charles looked at Celeste. She didn't pull away, but he thought he noticed a sadness in her downcast face that he had never seen there before.

All in all it had been a rough few months for Charles Royal. He had no way of knowing, but it was about to get a whole lot worse.

Chapter 3

On April 19, 1775 the real fighting began on Lexington Common and at Concord's Old North Bridge. Though many in the streets of Boston celebrated the smart spanking inflicted by the local militias on the Lobsterbacks during the skirmishes and on their harrowing trek back to the city, the more seasoned heads realized that this was not a true victory in a military sense, only the raising of the curtain on the great conflagration that all now knew was inevitable.

"We have tweaked the nose of the British Lion," Sam Adams announced as he gazed out of the window of Robinson's Tavern at the weary Redcoats trudging back along the cobblestone street. "Now, I fear, we shall hear him roar. Pray God, gentlemen, that we are equal to the task before us."

The first response to Adams would not be long in coming.

In early May Charles said goodbye to Mr. and Mrs. Robinson and joined the American troops massing in and around Charlestown. Days were spent in drill and foraging, with liberal amounts of gambling, drinking, and enjoying the company of camp followers. The joyous spring weather and the heroic engagements at Lexington and Concord invigorated the men and made them anxious to once again face the enemy.

Many boasted of the courage they would show in battle and the laurels they were certain to claim. They quickly wearied of the dull routine of camp life, itching to get on with the business for which they had come; namely to shoot Redcoats.

Surprisingly for one who had until recently enjoyed every comfort of the wealthy, Charles readily took to the rugged life in the field. He became company cook and took his turn in every detail without complaint.

Late one afternoon while stirring a kettle of stew over an earthen campfire, Charles looked up to see a tall, powerfully built man towering over him wearing frontier buckskin with Indian bead embroidering. A huge reddish beard and long unkempt hair falling beneath his cap framed radiant blue eyes that gleamed with either merriment or mischief. Grinning, the man pointed to Charles's stew.

"It smells like an old moccasin and looks like a beaver's entrails, but as I am not a man of harsh judgment, I will honor you by partaking of it." He reached down to the kettle with his tin cup.

Charles rapped him sharply on the knuckles with his wooden spoon like an old shrew. "You'll wait like the others, about an hour or so."

"But I'm not *like* the others!," the man bellowed. "I'm Rainbow Samuels! Famous Indian fighter, devout Patriot, and lover of more women from here to the Ohio than any ten men *you'll* ever meet!"

"Impressive though all that is, you'll still take your place with the others and wait."

"An affrontery!" cried Rainbow Samuels. He turned to the small group of coarse militiamen around him. "Gentlemen, my honor has been trod upon by this poor excuse for a charwoman. Tell me, how shall I avenge myself?"

"Cut off his balls!" shouted one.

"And his pecker!"

"No, a duel! You must fight a duel!"

"A duel! A duel! A duel!" the men chanted in unison.

"So be it!" pronounced Samuels, raising his arms. "A duel it is. But since the firing of arms within camp is punishable with fifty lashes and I posses no skills with the sword, it must be a special duel fought with special weapons.

"Sir," he said turning to Charles, "Choose the manner of your death — drink or women!"

The men howled their consent as Charles contemplated his fate. He had no intention of backing down.

"You have chosen most dastardly tools for a duel, sir," Charles began. "Whereas a ball through the heart or a sharp blade promises a quick death, both hard liquor and soft flesh can lead men to a long and agonizing demise. Nevertheless, I accept your challenge and your weaponry. As I have seen many of the women about camp and heard the cries that they bring forth from the men, I must assume that drink would be the less painful way to die."

"Drink it is then, sir! Tonight, after tatoo, we shall go to the Iron Horse and let Justice Grog hold court!"

That evening thirty men stole out of camp and stumbled down the path that led to the Iron Horse Tavern. Many had been drinking already and all were up for a night of revelry. At the Iron Horse the rules of the contest were quickly agreed upon. Ale would be the drink. Each man must empty his tankard in a single draw and must then place it on top of his previous tankards. If the stack tumbled, or if a contestant passed out, the other man would be declared the winner.

"And to raise the stakes to a level worthy of sporting men such as ourselves," Rainbow shouted from atop a table, "The winner shall enjoy the company of the lady of his choosing at the expense of the loser." He swept his arm across the room in the direction of the serving maids as the men cheered.

Many a side bet was placed that night. The contest soon became a test of wills as tankards were drained and placed precariously one upon another. The boisterous crowd of onlookers was reduced to hushed whispers as each man emptied his eighth, ninth, and tenth mug. By now both Rainbow and Charles were standing tipsily on chairs to reach the top of their stacks.

The tavern was eerily silent as each contestant carefully added another level to his spire, then, as hands slowly pulled back with the stack still standing, a thunderous roar swept the room. Fourteen, fifteen, sixteen rounds and still neither man had faltered.

As Rainbow rose to his full height to place his twentieth tankard at the top, his chair, rocking under his unsteady feet, tapped the table once, then twice, and on the third time his stack gave way sending the pewter tower caterwalling off the wide planked floor.

Rainbow fell back off his chair with a stream of blasphemies that would have done the devil proud. Fortunately, friends reached out to break his fall.

Now it was up to Charles, whose stack, though jutting out ominously in several places, was miraculously still standing.

Charles raised his last tankard to his mouth and slowly emptied it as men leaned forward to bear witness. When he finished, he paused for a moment and gazed upward. *Surely the walls of Troy looked less high to the Greeks than the pinnacle of this evening's work looks right now,* Charles thought to himself.

Nevertheless, he rose to his feet and called for a second chair. This he placed on the first, shook it to check its stability, and began his ascent. Once on top the chairs began to sway like a crow's nest in a nor'easter, but Charles somehow managed to steady himself.

Ever so slowly, with the gentleness of a mother placing her infant in a cradle, he stretched his hands out and placed his twentieth tankard atop the stack. As he drew back, for an instant, the room was as quiet as a Shaker church, and then Charles threw his arms up in triumph and the tavern exploded in cheers and laughter.

Two burly men plucked Charles off his perch and paraded him around on their shoulders as the fiddler struck up a merry tune. Several others thrust drinks toward him, but these Charles declined.

Rainbow managed to stand upon the table of the competition and motioned for quiet. "A battle fairly won, good sir. And now, to the victor go the laurels. Which of these excellent prizes will you put in your sack?"

The men called out their favorites as Charles was placed before the women of the tavern. With a look of serious contemplation he sauntered along the line, checking each woman's attributes. He paused before a young flaxen-haired beauty with green eyes and exceptionally large breasts.

"Hello, my name is Charles Royal," he said, bowing before her in the manner of a gentleman. "I'm pleased to make your acquaintance."

"Well how do you do, Mr. Royal," she replied in a distinct Scottish brogue. "I can see that you're a gifted drinker, but tell me, what *other* talents might you posses?"

"Ooooh," the men moaned in unison

Charles motioned the woman to a small table in the corner near the fireplace. As the evening drew on, Charles did his best to impress her with the witicisms and repartee that had so impressed the better ladies of Boston in his previous life. But this earthy wench was slow on the uptake and growing visibly bored.

Rainbow Samuels, who was by this time cradling two well-travelled wenches of his own, saw Charles's plight and came to his aid.

Calling him aside he said, "Charles, you're obviously a person of some refinement and culture. But you must keep in mind that that young lovely of yours is not. See, even now her eyes wander. She wants a man of action, not words."

"I thought I might enlighten her," Charles replied plaintively.

"Enlighten her? The only thing you want to enlighten her of is her dainties! Charles, if you want to make beautiful music with the ladies, you must learn to *play* them as they are *tuned*."

Rainbow slapped a heavy hand on Charles's shoulder and grinned as Charles nodded his understanding. Then he added in a low voice, "How much money do you have?"

Returning to Charles's table Rainbow said, "Miss, my shy friend here finds you a most beautiful woman and he desires to know you, shall we say, intimately, as he has known no other. And as a token of his deep affection and respect for you he has expressed his willingness to offer you a gift of, I believe, three Spanish Reals." Samuels snapped his fingers to the mesmerized Charles, who then produced the coins. "Please accept these in the spirit intended," Samuels said as he placed the money before her.

The tart looked at the gleaming coins, then at Charles. She swooped up the money with one hand and thrust the other out to Charles with a smile. "Come."

As Charles followed her up the stairs he looked back and gave Rainbow a small shrug. With a wide grin, Samuels made a quick screwing action with his finger in the air.

Just before sunrise the men trekked back along the footpath to camp. There were groans and curses from the groggy soldiers as they stumbled over rocks and stumps hidden by the darkness.

"Keep it down you fools. Do you want to alert the sentries?" one called out.

"Oh hell, they're probably drunker than we are," replied another.

"Rainbow? Such an odd name. How did you come by it?" Charles asked Samuels.

"It's my true Christian name. My mother once told me that she chose to call me Rainbow because my birth was a beautiful act of God, just like a rainbow."

A voice shot up from behind, "More likely she claimed his birth was an act of God because she had no idea who the *father* was!" All the men, including Samuels, laughed loudly, though many quickly grabbed their throbbing heads as laughs turned to moans.

As the men fell on their blankets in their small tents, they had barely a moment to rest their blood-shot eyes before the clear, crisp strains of reveille pierced the air, signaling the dawn of another day.

Chapter 4

As word of the opening of hostilities in Massachusetts spread after Lexington and Concord, both sides flew into a heated frenzy of preparation.

Fresh militia companies soon arrived from New Hampshire under the command of the celebrated Indian fighter, Colonel John Stark. From Connecticut, General Israel Putnam and his second-in-command, Benedict Arnold, brought 3,000 men to the lines now forming outside Boston, including the elite Governor's Foot Guard. And from Rhode Island came a column of well provisioned troops led by a young, handsome asthmatic and former Quaker who walked with a limp, Nathanael Greene.

These hastily raised soldiers (known as "8 month men" since that was the term of their enlistment) joined with a hodgepodge of local militia companies to form a loose arc around the port of Boston. Virtually without discipline or military experience, the men elected their own officers and rarely listened to them. They were mostly shopkeepers, laborers, and small farmers.

Some came to defend their freedoms and stand for their principles, but most came for the adventure, or simply for love of a good fight. Although they were men who barely knew the rudiments of marching in formation, let alone tactical battlefield maneuvers, they were, for the most part, men of daring and courage who, in an entrenched defensive position, would hold their ground.

Having grown-up with firearms and the knowledge that a single missed shot might mean the loss of their meal — or their scalp — they were deadly accurate marksmen with their long flintlock rifles. These weapons were accurate to two hundred yards or more, but had the decided disadvantage of being unable to be fit with a bayonet. At close quarters the American used his rifle like a club, or wielded his tomahawk or hunting knife.

Overall command of the troops surrounding Boston fell to Massachusetts General Artemas Ward, a respected veteran of the French & Indian War and many other engagements, but who was now old and weary and "sick of the stone." His second-in-command, Dr. Joseph Warren, was not a military man at all, but a distinguished Patriot. He was given a commission as a major general by the Provisional Congress just three days before the

Battle of Bunker Hill.

General Ward took direct command of the efforts to fortify the heights of Charlestown north of the city. The battlements were suppose to be erected on the highest point, Bunker's Hill, which was out of range of the guns of the British warships lying in the harbor. However, through ineptitude or simple missed communications, the American position was established on the smaller, less defensible Breed's Hill. Working at a furious pace, the Patriots threw up an impressive line of defensive earth works that took the British by surprise when they first viewed them on the morning of June 16th. Unfortunately for the Americans, though, they had made no provisions for relief; specifically, no food or water was sent out and, even more incredibly, there was no way to move more ammunition to the lines if necessary.

It was within these earthen barricades and behind a fortified split-rail fence that stretched for 600 feet, nearly to the Mystic River, that the Patriots took their positions. And waited.

Charles tried to wet his parched lips to no avail as he knelt in line of fire behind the fence on Breed's Hill. From his vantage point he could see clearly the British troops disembarking from their barges and forming on the beach. The far-off covering fire flashing from the cannons of the great British armada could not quite reach the massed American militia, but they did guard against an attack that would pin the Redcoats by the water's edge.

As the act played out below him, Charles felt again for his cartridge pouch. As his fingers touched lightly on the twenty rounds he felt a bit more secure. He glanced to his left and saw a scene that was the very fabric of this new American Army — men and boys, farmers and merchants, some in makeshift uniforms, most in homespun and buckskin. Armed with hunting rifles that could not be fitted for bayonets, even if they had them, and brandishing knives and tomahawks at their sides, these citizen-soldiers knelt at the ready for the advance of the veteran British Regulars that was to come.

To Charles's right crouched a stoic Rainbow Samuels.

"How do you think we'll do?" asked Charles.

"Well enough if we only have to maintain our position for three or four rounds. After that, if the Lobsterbacks are still advancing, they'll be upon us and most of these first-time militia boys will cut and scatter."

"What then?"

"Our officers will shoot the first men who run." Charles looked disbelieving until Samuels motioned back with his thumb. "Why do you think they're positioned as they are?" Charles turned to see lower grade officers and sergeants with halberds several paces behind the line eyeing their own troops rather than the slowly advancing enemy.

A sudden feeling of panic swept over Charles as he realized that there was no turning back, and the soldiers in red uniforms with sharply pointed bayonets were drawing near.

Even as the enemy began their determined march up the hill, shovels continued to throw dirt into the air in a feverish effort to improve the earthen breastworks. A few of the plowboys noticed that their company's precious kegs of rum were outside the fortifications. More fearful that some harm might come to their delightful refreshment than they were for their own safety, they sauntered out to retrieve them.

Cheerfully jogging alongside one another they paid little heed to the wave of red-clad soldiers rolling toward them. Cannon fire had been filling the air for an hour, but it seemed more flash and noise than danger. That is until a perfectly placed shot decapitated one of the lads, a farm boy named Asa Pollard. For a single, horrifying moment he stood upright among his comrades, head gone, blood spurting out of the severed neck. Then he fell backward dead.

Suddenly the shocking reality of this adventure struck home. The twisted, anguished faces of the simple country youths told the tale. If this was war, they'd already seen enough. One fell to his knees vomiting, the rest turned on their heels and ran.

Their flight might have triggered a wholesale rout if at that moment Colonel William Prescott hadn't arrived on the scene. A rock-hard veteran of the Louisbourg campaign and the French & Indian War, he was the perfect man to steady the troops.

Prescott eyed the corpse dispassionately.

"What should we do with him?" a sergeant asked in a quivering voice.

"Bury him," Prescott snapped.

"Without prayers, sir?"

"Without prayers," came the blunt reply.

Prescott saw the agony in the men's faces. He knew he had to stiffen their resolve immediately before their shaking legs got the better of them.

"There's a whole breastwork waiting to be finished down there on the other side of the hill!" he shouted. The soldiers slowly took up their shovels and picks and resumed their efforts. Colonel Prescott drew his sword, hoisted himself above the protective walls, and calmly strode across the ridge of the works in open defiance of the enemy. In a loud voice necessary to be heard over the booming cannon and the rifle fire that hissed around him, he told the militia, "It was a million-to-one shot. See how close they come to hitting me!"

Prescott's display of bravery had the desired effect. Men were soon back to their duties, making dirt fly with renewed vigor. Only now there was a lack of any merriment. Grim, silent faces were evident all down the line. Private Asa Pollard had sent a wake-up call to the American soldiers on Breed's Hill that all had heard.

"Steady men," ordered a tense militia captain, leaning over Charles's shoulder to assess the situation. "See that mulberry bush eighty yards out? No one fires until the first Redcoat passes it and I give the command. Then aim for their belt buckles and take out the king birds first." Nothing more was said. The men half-cocked their muskets and waited.

As the moment of battle approached, two or three skittish soldiers threw down their arms and bolted. One was grabbed by the shoulder and thrust rudely back into position.

"Steady men, steady."

The sergeant poised directly behind Charles eyed him sternly. Charles felt something warm running down his left leg. Firing had already commenced further down the hill. Slowly the sergeant raised his halberd, held it high as men took deadly aim. Then suddenly the captain cried out, *"FIRE!"*

A deafening roar of galling shot flashed out and dozens of British soldiers in ordered formation fell to the ground dead or screaming in agony.

"RELOAD AND FIRE AT WILL!" ordered the sergeant as the Redcoats filled in the gaps in their lines and continued their methodical march with drums and fife keeping time and standard bearers following behind.

Charles didn't know if his first shot was accurate, but Rainbow Samuels' self-satisfied grin said that his had hit the mark.

Hurrying to reload, Charles tore away too much of his cartridge and threw it to the ground and grabbed for another. Despite the roar of musketry and sporadic cannon, the British were close enough now that their officers could be heard to order the front line to advance with the bayonet. To an inexperienced and ill-trained soldier, the sight of a veteran foe charging with bayonets flashing can prove totally unnerving.

Charles aimed his musket but jerked on the trigger, sending the ball high and dislodging the bearskin cap of a grenadier.

Now the British were closing fast through the acrid smoke and the American line began to melt rapidly despite the calls, curses, and occasional fire and jabbing swords of their officers.

Charles stood almost transfixed as a screaming British infantryman with a look of madness in his eyes thrust his bayonet toward his chest. At the very last instant a hand on Charles's right shot out and knocked the steely blade off target and the long menacing hunting knife of Rainbow Samuels plunged into the soldier's side.

As the man fell dead, eyes still wide open, Charles stared at him for a moment, and then felt a sharp tug on his sleeve. "C'mon!" Samuels implored, "We must fall back or be slaughtered!"

Charles and Samuels scurried back with the last remaining Americans through pricker bushes to a position nearly at the crest of Breed's Hill. There, hiding behind trees and rocks, the men regained some of their courage.

Had the British pressed their advantage at the old fence immediately, the Americans would surely have been routed from that sector of the battlefield. But in textbook military fashion, the British officers paused to reform their badly mauled lines and advanced in a slow, orderly march that gave the militiamen the time they needed to regroup.

From his high vantage point on the hill, Charles could look down over the entire field, and what he saw was appalling. Amid the smoke he could see the fighting continuing everywhere, often hand-to-throat. The bodies of the dead and dying were strewn about, with a great concentration of Redcoats lying at the point where they first received the hot lead from the American lines, and along the American flank by the water's edge where Stark's brave New Hampshiremen continued to hold off every assault.

Like a great snake slowly coiling and uncoiling, the two sides exchanged ground grudgingly and at a frightful price.

Charles could see that the Americans were falling back, but he noted with pride that they did so in good order, showing the closing enemy their tomahawks and rifle butts, not their backs.

General Israel Putnam stood on a stump not twenty yards from Charles calmly drawing on his pipe; seemingly impervious to the musket balls that whizzed by as he surveyed the scene. Officers hurried up to Old Put, received orders, and hurried off.

As late afternoon came on, the order was given to fall back along the neck to Charlestown. Ammunition was running low and the veteran American officers feared the affects of darkness on still green troops who had just received their first taste of action. With little artillery and no sea support, they knew that they had done exceedingly well to give the King's troops such a stern bruising. Better to abandon the field and live to fight another day. Little did they know that they were setting the pattern that was to mark the Continentals' strategy throughout the war.

By traditional convention, the British had won the Battle of Bunker Hill since, when the smoke cleared, they were in possession of the ground. But at what cost? Of the 2,400 Redcoats engaged, 1,054 had been casualties (including 226 killed). The Patriots losses were 140 killed and 310 wounded. So devastating was the day that British General Sir Henry Clinton wrote in his diary, *A dear-bought victory, another such would have ruined us.*

Over the next few days the American companies began to reform as these farmers and merchants were reunited with their friends and neighbors. There was not as much boasting as there had been the night before the battle. The carnage and, perhaps, self-doubt touched even the boldest man. This was war — an heroic and humbling and life-altering experience. And while some had shown that they had no stomach for it, most were resolved to remain in the service; so long as it did not interfere with tending their crops.

After fiercely debating whether to offer the olive branch or the point of a sword to London, the Continental Congress voted to press ahead with armed resistance (but to keep the door to reconciliation open a while longer). The fledgling nation adopted the remnants of the ragged Massachusetts, New Hampshire, Connecticut, and Rhode Island militias to form the first Continental Army.

For the troops the change in title meant little at first. Provisions, especially uniforms, were in very short supply if they came at all. Even then, they were sent directly from the state governments, not courtesy of the new national assembly in Philadelphia.

Men's loyalties were to their local communities first, and many took up arms only when they felt directly threatened. At other times, it was the mantle of farmer and provider that was foremost in their thoughts.

For Charles and a growing number of men like him, though, the dawn of a new and broader consciousness was rising. They began to see the larger struggle and the need to sublimate local interests and rivalries in order to overcome the seemingly indominable might of the greatest power on earth. It was by fire and the sword that the new nation would be forged, and there would be long years of darkness and suffering before they would know the great warmth of that distant dawn.

As Charles stirred his cookpot one evening, a trooper from his company snatched the ladle from his hand. "No more of that for you!" he said.

"What do you mean?" asked Charles.

"Well," said another man grinning, "We have some good news and some bad news."

"What's the good news?"

"We decided to elect you corporal!"

"Yeah," another chimed in. "That means when we're all captured by His Majesty's troops, you get to be the first one hung!"

"That's the *good* news?" Charles replied, "What's the bad?"

"Samuels stole your horse, sold it, and lit out for the Berkshires."

~~~ **Chapter 5** ~~~

With the arrival of the famous Virginian, George Washington, to take over command, many of the men expected another pitched battle for Boston. Instead, a sort of dormant siege ensued.

Washington realized all too soon that he had not the manpower or materials to launch an assault on the fortified city. The troops at his disposal were poorly trained and more interested in working their farms than forming an effective army. In addition, jealousies were high among the officers who competed shamelessly for rank and honors. And before any assault could be considered, Washington would need cannon.

General Gage in Boston had his own host of problems. The Royal Fleet protected his position and offered a means of escape if necessary, but that was unthinkable. A British Army had been mauled badly by a rabble on the field of battle. Unheard of! Already Parliament was at each others throats, with recriminations hurled in every direction. Gage was under intense pressure, while King George's position was perfectly clear — *crush the rebellion.*

But this was easier to order in London than execute in Boston. The rebels surrounded the city. And while Gage knew that in a conventional European battle his army would surely triumph, these damned Colonials fought like Indians — crouching behind trees and stone walls — appearing, firing, vanishing, only to appear again. There were no rules to fight this war.

So the two sides held their positions and waited through the summer and fall. All the while, Washington's new Continental Army melted away. "When there's more fighting we'll be back," was their attitude. And nothing that Washington or his officers could say or do could hold them. Indeed, many were secretly glad to see the soldiers depart, for there was little food, less clothing, and no money to pay them.

Who would win this stalemate? Washington did not wish to find out. Many in Congress still did not grasp that reconcilliation with the Crown was beyond hope, and rather than leave the fate of his country in the hands of politicians, Washington hungered to take decisive action. Enter Colonel Henry Knox.

The corpulant, jovial Knox, whose military acumen came entirely from reading the texts in his Boston bookstore, approached Washington with a bold plan. The army needed cannon desperately. There were guns aplenty at Fort Ticonderoga in New York, which had fallen to Ethan Allen and Benedict Arnold and was now, for the moment, in American hands. If those guns could be brought to bear, then Washington would have the advantage he needed to force the action.

Washington listened to Knox attentively. He then brushed away the naysayers on his staff and gave Knox orders to attempt the transport.

Unfortunately, neither man new the terrain. All the navigable rivers in New England run north-south. So the heavy cannon would have to be hauled overland through the mountains, where roads were nonexistent and winter's heavy snows and ice had already set-in. It is well that they did not know the odds against success.

Corporal Royal was among the first to volunteer for the arduous journey. Unlike the others, he had no family or farm to tend to. Camp life had grown exceedingly tiresome and he yearned for adventure.

With a detachment of handpicked men, wagons, and draft animals, Knox set out. At Fort Ticonderoga he was delighted to find 59 guns intact, but he quickly grasped that the effort necessary to transport them to Boston would be nigh on impossible. Yet he must try. And overland was the only way. The British controlled all water routes. In fact, they were probably moving up the Hudson toward Ticonderoga at that very moment.

With all haste Knox set his woodsmen to work fashioning great sleds for the journey back. Charles worked side-by-side with his men from dawn to dusk, but the weather was bitterly cold and the work slowed to a crawl. *We need more men,* thought Charles, *but whom in this country can be trusted?*

And then it struck him. He ordered two of his men to backtrack to the town of Deerfield beyond the Berkshires and find the man named Rainbow Samuels. "Tell him this: 'Bring thirty men with axes and strong backs. The fight for Boston is not yet won. Your country needs you.' And if that's not enough, add, 'Charles Royal waits to attend you with his famous stew, strong grog, and three women for every man.'"

Within five days the booming voice of Rainbow Samuels could be heard hailing the fort. He had brought not thirty, but over seventy men, many of whom had stood the lines at Breed's Hill. They all joined in the work almost without breaking stride.

"Well young Royal! I see you've taken up the carpentry trade," Samuels bellowed. "It is well, says I, for I've tasted your stew!"

"You stole my horse, you bastard!"

"It followed me home."

"And you *sold* it!"

"And for a *disappointing price* I might add. I should be angry at you for neglecting the care of your animal!"

"You're hopeless," Charles said shaking his head.

"That's what two of my wives say," Rainbow replied slapping him on the shoulder. "That's why I prefer the others."

With the additional labor the work renewed at a brisk pace despite the numbing conditions, and within a week the cannon were underway toward Boston. The men of Deerfield knew the best of the Indian trails through the Berkshire snows and though the trip was grueling, they guided Knox's troops safely all the way to the Lexington Road.

Standing outside his Cambridge headquarters in mid-January as the artillery procession passed by on hissing runners, General Washington doffed his hat and smiled incredulously, overjoyed to see what Knox had accomplished. "You've done it Knox!" he cried. "By God you've done it!"

Working through the night the Americans placed the guns from Ticonderoga on Dorchester Heights with a commanding view of Boston, and with first light Henry Knox was given the honor of firing the first salvo.

It was a rude awakening indeed for the British and their Loyalist supporters lying snug in their beds. Gage quickly summoned a council of war with his top advisors. The enemy fortifications must be scaled at once was the initial reaction. But Generals Howe, Burgoyne, Clinton and others who remembered Bunker Hill all too well had different thoughts. In the end, General Gage decided to evacuate Boston. Neither he nor any British soldier would set foot in the city again for the duration of the war. On March 17, 1776 the last of the Redcoats and the Loyalist civilians boarded warships in the harbor and made sail for Nova Scotia. Boston fell to the Americans.

Together with Colonel Knox, Charles rode solemnly through the streets of the now liberated city. Debris and the look of chaos were everywhere. Many residents, especially those who had collaborated openly with the British, feared the rebels' retribution and fled with what they could carry on the transport ships.

Charles led Knox into his former home. Anything of value had been "liberated." Charles's family had apparently long since departed as the house had been used as British general staff headquarters. There was still stale bread and empty wine bottles on the dining room table.

Charles sighed. "I've lost my home not once but twice."

"The cost of war is paid in many coins," Knox offered consolingly. "Blood and property are but two."

"What now, Colonel?"

"We shall see. I've spoken to His Excellency. Told him of your invaluable assistance and ingenuity during our recent adventure at Fort Ti. He was impressed. War makes men, Royal. And it is my honor to inform you that it has just made you a lieutenant!"

Charles's eyes widened, "Lieutenant?"

"Lieutenant Royal. Do you like the sound of it?"

A smiled formed slowly on Charles's face. "I believe I shall learn to like it quite well, sir."

↞ **Chapter 6** ↠

Lieutenant Royal was growing decidedly bored with the dull routine of camp life along the Hudson. At least on the march from Boston there had been new country to see, if not the enemy to engage.

He wrote often to his sisters Sarah and Sally of days on end in which the simple meals were the only highpoint. And of the discontent and frequent fights among the men for want of activity. He was doubtful that any of the letters got through, but he wrote them nonetheless.

After the evacuation of Boston the British high command made a change. King George named Admiral Lord Richard Howe to replace Gage as His Majesty's Commander-in-Chief in America, and Howe's brother, Sir William Howe, to head the army. The King and his advisors turned a deaf ear to the Howes' outspoken criticism of the war. In their hearts, the Howe brothers were unabashed American sympathisers.

But for King and Country they put personal feelings aside and took up their mission to bring the rebellious rabble back to the authority of Great Britain.

Prime Minister George Germain (who had succeeded Lord North) and General William Howe agreed on a strategy proposed by Gentleman Johnny Burgoyne that would focus the land war on New York City. If they could gain control of this major port, move successfully up the Hudson and join with General Guy Carleton's force traveling south from Canada, then the radical New England colonies, "that cauldron of sedition," would be cutoff from the more docile (or so most in Parliament believed) mid-Atlantic and southern regions. Pockets of rebellion could then be crushed piecemeal and the Revolution brought to its knees.

Anticipating the British plan (perhaps substantiated by paid informants in London), Washington abandoned Boston and marched his army of five Continental regiments, several militia units, and Henry Knox's artillery brigade over the dusty Boston Post Road toward New York.

Charles was offered an artillery officer's post by Colonel Knox, but chose to take his place with General Israel Putnam's infantry, serving with the 21st Massachusetts.

Once in New York, Washington's forces did what they always did when anticipating a visit from the British — they took to pick and shovel, digging trenches and building earthen breastworks belted with sharpened abatis. They would not have long to wait.

On a balmy day in late June a flotilla of ships approached Staten Island that appeared to one on-shore observer to be "something resembling a wood of pine trees trimmed . . . the whole Bay was full of shipping as ever it could be. I . . . thought all London was afloat."

Howe landed his troops on Staten Island's Lower Bay. There they would languish for seven weeks. Howe still hoped to avoid a fight and he gave diplomats on both sides all the time he could to bridge their differences. His command of 32,000 veteran troops, including 8,000 of the mercenary Hessians, was the largest expeditionary force ever landed by Great Britain.

Opposing him was Washington's ragtag army that had been swelled by local militia units to nearly 20,000 men. Most had never before been asked to withstand the roar of cannon or face down a massed bayonet charge by merciless professional soldiers.

Charles noted with youthful fascination how the New York encampment had brought together for the first time Americans of many contrasting stripes. New England farm boys who had never journeyed more than twenty miles from home in their lives shared their campfires and vittles with strange-speaking men dressed in an assortment of uniforms — plus hunting shirts and backcountry buckskin and beads. Some favored tricorns or broad-brimmed felt hats while others preferred headware made from animal furs — beaver, raccoon, bear, rabbit, squirrel, and wolf being the most popular. Skull bandannas were commonplace too. They kept the sweat out of a man's eyes on a tiring march, and could be easily converted into a bandage or tourniquet when battle came.

While politicians squabbled in Philadelphia, the yeomen of the colonies were united on the field. John Durkee's 20th Connecticut bivouaced alongside Laommi Baldwin's 26th Massachusetts. There were New Yorkers of course, and Jerseymen. General Anthony Wayne's Pennsylvania Line and William Smallwood's sturdy Marylanders standing shoulder-to-shoulder with the "Blue Hen's Chickens," John Haslet's Delaware Continentals. And who else in charge but the planter-soldier from Mount Vernon, Virginia.

Charles commanded one of Old Put's work details, spewing dirt and rocks along the American line established on the coastal plain of lower Manhattan. In the sweltering heat his men largely ignored his orders. They laid about in whatever shade was available — playing dice, complaining about conditions, and telling raunchy camp stories.

The Patriots were still basking in the afterglow of their strong showing at Breed's Hill and their stout defense and rebuff of the British at Sullivan's

Island in Charleston, South Carolina. Those who had tasted battle already were brimming with confidence. The majority who hadn't were hungry for glory. Days spent in menial hard labor clearing brush and building fortifications was not what they had come for.

Washington and his advisors conferred and decided that the most likely points for an amphibious assault were at the southernmost extreme of Manhattan Island and across the isthmus at Brooklyn Heights on Long Island. Washington strengthened his entrenchments in both locations.

His pleas to Congress for more men to meet the impending onslaught proved fruitless — virtually the entire American force in arms was already under his control.

Military stores were so scanty that each soldier was allowed only two rounds for practice. Nevertheless, morale was high. Huzzas rang out and church bells pealed throughout the city on July 8th when the new Declaration of Independence was read aloud. The lofty words stirred the hearts and strengthened the resolve of the men in the lines. They had announced to the King, themselves, and the world that they were ready to take their rightful place among independent nations. Yet each knew that those rights would have to be secured not by lofty pronouncements on parchment, but by fire, hot lead, and the sword. And if any forgot, General Howe across the way on Staten Island was ready to remind them.

In late August Howe made his move. With eighty-eight barges supported by the guns of four frigates and numerous bomb ketches, he transported the first of his troops to Gravesend Bay, Long Island — light infantry, grenadiers, cannoneers, and Colonel Carl von Donop's corps of Hessians who stood menacingly at attention throughout the crossing, their deadly bayonets glinting in the bright sunlight.

Within hours, with military bands creating an almost parade-like atmosphere, 15,000 men had been put ashore. American soldiers entrenched on Brooklyn Heights could see clearly the scarlet jackets and Hessian blue. There was the dashing 17th Light Dragoons sporting their signature purple plumes in their hats riding ahead of the famed and feared Black Watch in dark kilts and the green-coated jagers wearing oversized cockades. It was a superbly orchestrated military pageant that sent more than one new recruit's knees to shaking.

Washington believed initially that Howe was staging an elaborate feint to draw him out of his New York fortifications. With total control of the sea lanes and any action near the shore, circumstances favored the British from the outset. For two days the opposing armies tested each other's strength along the mile long defensive perimeter the Americans had established on Brooklyn Heights.

General Clinton took the van with fast moving dragoons supported by Lord Cornwallis in reserve with grenadiers, two more regiments of dragoons, and artillery. Howe and Lord Percy stayed with the main body ready to move as the situation warranted.

There were four passes through and around Brooklyn Heights. American General John Sullivan on the left wing foolishly left them lightly guarded. At 3 a.m. on August 27th in a wholly unexpected night march, General Clinton's force blew past the five defenders at Jamaica Pass on the American's far left and poured behind the lines, effectively trapping the Patriots in a vice. Quickly British axes flew, dispatching trees to widen the road. Right behind were draft horses pulling field pieces and munition wagons into position.

Meanwhile, the British pestered the American right. Here was the real feint. The Patriots fell for the deception, believing with certainty that the main attack would come there against New Jersey General "Lord" Stirling's troops, and began shifting reinforcements to the right.

At 9 a.m. the British sprang the trap, roaring in on the American left wing from three sides, smashing Sullivan's position and rolling up the line. A signal gun from the lowlands now sent the center and left of the British line flying into action. Everywhere the Americans were in disarray. Their heavy rifles took far too long to reload and they had no bayonets to ward off the yelling, stabbing, swearing swarms of British and German soldiers who fell upon them.

Charles's hand shook so badly from the sight of this oncoming herd of screaming demons that he could not even draw his sword from its sheath. His men literally knocked him to the ground in flight and as soon as he could regain his footing, he turned tail and ran with the best of them.

Further down the line the American right valiantly dug in its heels. William Smallwood's Marylanders and Colonel Haslet's Delaware Continentals fought ferociously, swinging their rifle butts like shelaleighs and hacking away with their hatchets and knives. So inspiring was their resistance that Pennsylvanians and Connecticut Yankees rallied to their side, but it proved too little too late.

Almost surrounded after two hours of bloody battle, Stirling sent most of his remaining command in a hasty retreat across the "impassable" salt marshes into Brooklyn. He himself then took charge of the rear guard defense and with Smallwood and his 250 indomitable Marylanders — who turned to face bayonets with empty muskets — held off the onslaught until the retreating force was safe. Six times Stirling and Smallwood led headlong counterattacks into the red and blue lines, shocking the fur-capped grenadiers and Hessians and causing them to waver and nearly break at one point. Fresh troops were hastily brought up to join the British thrust and the exhausted and overwhelmed Stirling was at last forced to surrender his sword.

By early afternoon it was over. Howe's forces stood alone as masters of Brooklyn Heights with Washington's shattered army dead, wounded, or in full retreat toward the beach.

Howe was slow to follow up on his victory. His men were just as slaked and bone-weary as Washington's under the brutal August sun. Plus they had been rudely manhandled by Stirling's valiant stand. With his brother's warships covering every route of escape, Howe felt confident that he could move on Washington's 9,500 remaining troops cautiously and at his own leisure.

Within the American lines chaos and a mood of desperation were pervasive. Even the greenest private knew that they were trapped with their backs to the East River and no chance of a relief column coming to their aid. Yet Washington's very presence calmed the men. Outwardly stoic and always in control, Washington posted guards and reorganized units. He then sent parties of riflemen ahead to harass and delay the British while he planned for the army's escape.

Fortunately for Washington he had among his remaining force a contingent of skilled Marblehead watermen under Colonel John Glover, and other seafarers from Israel Hutchinson's 27th Massachusetts. As talented as any men alive when it came to steering a bobbing rowboat through choppy seas, Washington took full advantage of their expertise.

On the evening of August 28th, following a day of drenching, unremitting rains, Howe boasted to an aide, "I shall bag the old fox in the morning."

Almost miraculously for the Americans a thick fog settled over the East River that night, the perfect ally for their plans. Washington had ordered up all of the small craft in the area. Quickly and in near total silence his men were put aboard and rowed by Glover's Marblehead men to the far shore. Throughout that tense night, with little rations and no rest, the steadfast oarsmen leaned doggedly into their task, making the two mile round trip more times than any could remember.

As dawn approached, American Lieutenant Benjamin Tallmadge looked behind him to the Brooklyn shore. There he saw a tall, powerfully built officer in a blue and buff uniform being assisted by two Marbleheaders into the last craft and shoving off. Washington had lost the Battle of Long Island, but against all odds, he had saved his army.

Rather than take the militarily correct course and abandon New York City entirely, Washington instead took the politically correct course and strengthened his hopelessly untenable front on the southern tip of Manhattan.

Here at the Battery stood Israel Putnam and Henry Knox with 4,000 men, mostly poorly trained militia, and irreplaceable ordinance and supplies. Many of these defenders were skittish as colts. They, like Charles, had just experienced the terror of leveled bayonets driving towards their chest. There had been no time to regain their courage and confidence. They were beaten and confused, with terrifying nightmares having replaced their recent dreams of glory.

On September 15th under favorable winds, British warships and gunboats opened a deafening offshore barrage against the American positions guarding the East River. Meanwhile, in a flanking maneuver that once again took the Americans by surprise, Howe (with Clinton, Cornwallis and the fearsome Hessians in their tall steel helmets) quickly disembarked 10,000 troops at Kip's Bay on central Manhattan above the American lines. With little effort they routed the green militia there and appeared to have the remainder of the outmaneuvered Patriots trapped.

Realizing his precarious position, Old Put abandoned his precious supplies and began an orderly retreat north along Manhattan's western shore. British frigates on the Hudson and roving units of Tories and British dragoons pummeled his force as it ran the narrow gauntlet to safety. The militiamen finally panicked, chucked their weapons and anything else that would slow their escape to the ground, and literally ran for their lives — through marshes, woods, cobbled streets, and open fields. By nightfall hundreds of officers and men, including Lieutenant Charles Royal, had reached the newly formed American lines on Harlem Heights.

A more active Howe might have bisected the island and cut off the retreat, but he saw no need to take any unnecessary risks. The Americans would exhaust themselves in due course and surrender. He rested his men, reformed, and continued his unimpeded march up through Manhattan.

At Harlem Heights the British encountered their first stiff resistance since Stirling's courageous stand. A Connecticut infantry regiment commanded by Lieutenant Colonel Thomas Knowlton, a veteran of Breed's Hill, collided with British light infantry. Unlike most of their brothers in arms, Knowlton's men stood firm, exchanging musket fire and giving no ground in fierce hand-to-hand combat. Washington ordered up Rhode Island and Massachusetts brigades to join in the fight and the British advance began to falter. Reazin Beall's Maryland militia and Joe Gourd Weeden's rock-hard 3rd Virginia Rifles sprang to the fray and suddenly it was the British and Hessians who turned heel and ran, kilts and bearskin hats flying through a nearby apple orchard with New Englanders, Marylanders and Virginians in cheering pursuit.

For the moment, the American line had held.

A devastating fire of mysterious origin gutted much of New York City on September 21st. With little left to fight for and less means to do so, Washington finally acquiesced to the pleas of his top military advisors, Charles Lee and Nathanael Greene, and evacuated his last toehold in the city. The first step in Germain and Howe's grand scheme had now been accomplished. The British had taken control of New York City.

Washington's force drew-off from Harlem Heights north into Westchester County. The order of the day was chaos. Some men had no ammunition. Others no rations. Lost units blundered here and there like befuddled children in a marketplace, or simply deserted altogether — war not having been at all what they expected. There was no glory here. Only mud, blood, sickness, death, and food that they wouldn't feed to their livestock back home.

Charles had failed in action on Brooklyn Heights and in Putnam's retreat. His men, those who survived and had not scattered to the wind, would not take orders from him anymore. If they had humorously or grudgingly accepted him before, now the rules had changed. Every man became his own general. Circumstances didn't just dictate the movement of the army, but the individual actions of each soldier. Trust no one except the man to your left, the man to your right, your musket, and (if the enemy got too close) your feet.

By late October the Americans had regrouped in and around the tiny village of White Plains. There, on the 28th, a skirmish began when the British advance of light infantry and jagers ran into and was roughed up by General Joseph Spencer's Connecticut Volunteers. This quickly grew into an unplanned full engagement.

The Patriots held three hills, the highest of which, Chatterton's on the far right, was inexplicably the most weakly defended. Howe saw his opportunity to gain control of the high ground and took it. He plunged headlong through the New York and Connecticut militia units who were still traumatized from their whipping on Long Island. But behind them stood the formidable Delaware and Maryland Lines, the backbone of the American Continental Army.

Howe sent the best troops he had on their position, backed by the Royal Artillery's accurate and devastating fire. But when the smoke cleared, it was the Hessian blue and British red who were falling with terrifying screams and retreating down the slippery slopes of Chatterton's Hill.

Before the Patriots could launch a counterattack, the signal of pounding kettle drums sent the mounted 17th Royal Dragoons charging into action, plumes flying, sabres extended at a deadly angle. Since before the time of the Egyptian Host, the ability of a thundering cavalry to unnerve troops had been established. This was the first such charge of the Revolution and its impact on the militia was predictable. They sprinted for the woods. And the Americans were swept from White Plains.

Following this debacle the American Army broke into three separate commands — Lee at North Castle, General William Heath at Peekskill, and General Washington falling off to the southeast with the largest contingent. A series of posts were established to delay the British advance, but each of these fell in turn, continuing the overall refrain for the Americans since Brooklyn Heights — defeat, retreat, repeat.

General Greene confidently advised Washington that Fort Washington on the eastern shore of the Hudson was defensible. Washington was skeptical, but Greene had reconnoitered the fort's battlements personally and his upbeat assessment pursuaded his commander to leave the garrison intact.

On November 16th Howe's infantry overran the American's perimeter defenses outside the fort and pressed hard upon the troops now trapped. Colonel Robert Magaw rejected Howe's demand for his surrender with a grand pronouncement, "Give me leave to assure his Excellency that activated by the most glorious cause that mankind ever fought in, I am determined to defend this post to the last extremity." The Englishmen were not impressed. The next morning they attacked simultaneously on several fronts — General Percy hit Lieutenant Colonel Lambert Cadwalader's Pennsylvanians from the south, General Edward Matthews, supported by Cornwallis, routed Colonel Baxter's militia from the east, and Hessian General Wilhelm von Knyphausen's bear-hatted hussars took on Lieutenant Colonel Moses Rawling's Maryland and Virginia regiments who put up a fierce fight, but eventually gave ground.

In just three hours, all American lines had collapsed. Magaw, inside Fort Washington's palisades, saw the hopelessness of his situation and surrendered that afternoon.

The British forces, particularly those under von Knyphausen, had suffered heavy losses (nearly 300 killed) but for the Americans the day's reckoning was catastrophic — 54 killed, 100 wounded, and 2,858 captured, plus the heart-rending loss of all their precious supplies, artillery and ammunition.

Within three months of their initial assault on Long Island, the British had smashed the American Army in a succession of battles, taken control of New York City and the lower Hudson, and were now in all-out pursuit of the shattered Revolutionary forces as they fled before them into New Jersey.

Thomas Paine captured the moment perfectly for every Patriot when he wrote, *These are the times that try men's souls.*

Chapter 7

Even before he marched with the Continental Army out of Boston, Charles was aware that he had problems leading his men. Many had known him as their lowly camp cook, or viewed him contemptuously as the privileged idler who had been brought down to their level. They may have grown to like him — Charles never put on aristocratic airs — but now he had leapfrogged everyone and been made a lieutenant. An officer. *Their* officer. And they resented it bitterly.

These were blunt, uneducated, coarse laborers in many cases, with a life of drudgery behind them and a future that promised much the same. They fought for themselves and their comrades and held authority of every rank in contempt. In their hardscrabble world, a man who had tasted the lash for standing up to an officer was a man respected.

Charles tried to be tactful, cajoling, understanding, compromising — all of which his men read as weakness. He could never bring himself to order corporal punishment no matter how obvious an offense, so his more bellicose malcontents seized authority with the result that Charles was openly snubbed. A part of Charles wanted to remain "one of the boys." He didn't grasp what his men knew instinctively — that their relationship had changed irreparably. Charles was an outsider now, and because he was weak-willed, he didn't command even grudging respect.

Adding to his woes, Charles felt inferior to certain of his men who had performed bravely at Breed's Hill and in the New York campaign when he had not.

This dysfunctional relationship between officer and men could only prove disastrous on the field of battle. Charles was in over his head — and men were dying because of it.

"Lieutenant Royal," said the sentry looking straight ahead, "Colonel McVee orders you to report to him in his tent without delay."

Charles rose from his cot, pulled his cloak tightly about him to fend off the bitter November night's chill and followed.

"Lieutenant Charles Royal reporting, sir!" Charles snapped a salute.

Lieutenant Colonel Temple McVee, temporary commander of the depleted Massachusetts and Connecticut regiments under General John Sullivan, looked up from his small table, but did not verbally acknowledge Charles's presence. He held a paper in his hands which he read to himself by candle-light. A gnawing sense of foreboding grew within Charles.

At length McVee sighed deeply. "Royal, I have in my hand a document which I am duty bound to share with you:

> *"It has been my observation and opinion that over the many confrontations with the enemy beginning on Long Island and including engagements at Brooklyn Heights, Kip's Bay, White Plains, and Fort Lee, Lieutenant Charles Royal of the 21st Masschusetts displayed an appalling lack of leadership and personal fortitude. Time and again he has wavered before the foe and failed to direct his troops in a stout defense that would have brought them honor and glory. As a result of his ineptitude, which at Brooklyn Heights and Kip's Bay bordered on cowardice, a dispro-portionate number of his men have been killed; many bayo-neted in the back as they fled the field.*

> *"Lieutenant Royal has proven himself to be, at the very least, an incompetent officer, and it is my opinion and conviction that he should be courtmartialed at the most expedient opportunity and dishonorably discharged from the Continental Army."*

Charles stood dumbfounded as the accusations were read. Had he been the only one to buckle at the charge of the British Line? Had he not done the best he could, often acting without any clear direction from *his* superiors?

"What do you say to these charges, Lieutenant?"

Charles started to speak, but he didn't know what to say.

"Come now man, speak up!"

"I . . . I . . . I do not fully agree with them, sir. I did the best I could—"

McVee exploded, "*The best you could!* The best you could got the men entrusted to your care *slaughtered* by the wagon-full! Do you wish to tell their widows and children how well you performed? Do you!"

Charles's jaw tightened.

"Dammit Royal! If the greenest private deserts his post and flees in the face of the enemy his punishment when caught is to be placed before a firing squad! Why should your fate be any less?"

McVee, red-faced with anger, stood no more than in inch before Charles, who said nothing in his own defense.

Finally McVee barked in disgust, "Get out of my sight! Consider your-self under house arrest until a courtmartial can be convened."

Once outside the tent, Charles took three steps, then nearly crumbled to the ground.

It was if he had been shot — no, that would have been far better, inflicting honor with the pain. The pangs of despair he felt at this moment tore right at his soul. He hated Lieutenant Colonel Temple McVee. He hated everything he said. But most of all, he hated that every charge was true.

Charles didn't sleep at all that night. Didn't even try. He just laid on his cot staring up at the dark billowing canvas above. In that gloomy darkness he forced himself to painfully relive every failure of his life, real or imagined.

If he were not so overwhelmed with self-loathing, Charles would have realized that he had received no military leadership training, or civilian training for that matter. He was thrown into the breach like so many other raw recruits and forced to learn how to command soldiers in the very heat of battle. An impossible task.

At 4 a.m. he arose trancelike. He slipped his boots on and strapped his father's sword around his waist. Eyes fixed with resolve, he stepped outside his tent into the deathly frigid night air. He left his cloak behind.

A light snow swirled about him as he walked slowly but purposely toward the far edge of the encampment. He passed the last sentry and headed up the narrow path of a wooded hill. Near the top, well away from every person who might interfere, he drew the sword slowly from its sheath; a long steel snake hissing metal against metal. He placed the sword against a large boulder and sat down, lips tight, staring blankly ahead.

Did five minutes pass, or was it thirty?

Charles took up the sword again and casting about saw a gnarled juniper tree that would serve his purpose. He wedged the hilt firmly into a low lying crook in the branches. Then he tore his shirt open and gazed hard at the sharp point of death bare inches before him. Even in the chilly darkness it seemed to twinkle invitingly. Here was the quick solution to all his problems. An end to every failure.

Charles leaned forward, his chest now pressed against the solution. The point indented the flesh before his heart, but had not yet pierced it. And there he remained, suspended. A sudden impulse, a slip on the frozen earth, any forward movement at all and he would be free.

How long he stood there transfixed, God only knows.

Off to his left, a razor of light slowly caught his eye. He turned to see the dawn breaking on the horizon. *It was still not too late. Just a distraction, nothing more.* But his inner voice of destruction was growing fainter with the growing brightness. With a blow of visible breath, Charles backed off

There was a rustling on the path and a high-pitched voice, "Who goes there?"

Charles shook his head at the sight of the private, a smallish lad of maybe sixteen. *Now they're enlisting children to fight.*

"I am Lieutenant Charles Royal, late of the 21st Massachusetts, currently assigned to General John Sullivan's brigade. And whom do I have the pleasure of addressing?"

The soldier fumbled his musket trying to salute and it clanked on the frigid ground. Attempting to retrieve it he fell victim to the slippery slope and dropped to all fours. He saluted from there. "Private Jonas O'Hare of the 12th Pennsylvania Rifles, sir."

Charles picked up the musket to demonstrate a point. "Well Private Jonas O'Hare of the 12th Pennsylvania Rifles, before you announce your presence to an unidentified person in a remote area such as this, you would do well to half-cock your piece and draw a mortal bead on him." The young trooper was visibly nervous as Charles put the muzzle of the rifle directly against his chest.

"In this way, if he's a friend, then you need only draw off and none will take offense at you for doing your duty. But if he's a foe . . .," Charles pulled the trigger causing O'Hare to flinch, "Then you'll be alive with a thrilling tale to tell your friends. Got it?"

"Yessir."

"Good! Let's eat. Damn cold out here." Charles started down the path.

"Sir," O'Hare motioned to the tree. "Your sword."

Charles looked at him, then without a word walked over and pried his sword free and returned it to its sheath. "C'mon."

In the days that followed, Charles was somber and kept to himself as much as possible. Solitude was impossible in the cramped encampment, but he avoided contact and idle conversation, preferring to dwell with the personal demons within.

He drank more than ever before, every evening and sometimes during the day. It was not gaiety he sought from the liquor, but its numbing effect. His humor was gone. He rarely offered even a faint smile. He drilled his men austerely and his temper was short. Even the big dogs sensed the change and backed off.

In the recesses of his still conscious mind, Charles expected to be called from his tent every day to face the graven panel of senior officers — the mere formality preceeding his being cashiered out of the service. But Colonel McVee, for some unknown reason, didn't act.

Eleven days before Christmas McVee came down with a vicious strain of camp fever and was carted off with other sick and wounded soldiers to the army hospital in Danbury, Connecticut. Most would have considered this a stroke of good fortune, but not Charles. Whether McVee was there or not, whether a courtmartial was convened or not, Charles had already held his own trial — and the verdict was guilty as charged.

On impulse on the evening following McVee's departure, Charles borrowed a quill, some ink and paper from another officer. He pulled his candle close as he dipped his quill in the small dark bottle. For several minutes he hovered over the paper composing his thoughts. He had not written or received a letter in more months than he could remember.

Newtown, Pennsylvania
December 15, 1776

Dear Father:

I am writing to you from a place I never expected to be, in a soldier's uniform I never imagined I'd wear, fighting in a Revolution that will decide the very fate of our nation. At present, it does not go at all well.

As you anticipated and confided to me in my youth, the colonies have banded together in a loose confederation with the purpose of gaining our freedom from Mother Britain and forming our own self-government. And as you wryly suspected, our Mother did not take the news of her child's independence well.

War ravages the land and stalks the high seas. British soldiers, German mercenaries, American Tories, even Indians on the western frontier raise their hand against us. Brother fights brother, father opposes son, widows and orphans grow in number — no one it seems has been spared.

I have sided with the Patriots while Robert, as you would imagine, has cast his fortunes with the Crown. I am comforted by the belief that if you were alive today we would stand side by side in battle for the Cause of Liberty.

It saddens me to report that I have no knowledge whatsoever regarding my brothers or sisters or of your wife, my mother. I left Boston with the Continental Army last spring and have had no word since.

You should know, Dearest Father, that Robert and I had a serious falling out on my 21st birthday. The spark that lit the powder was our opposing views on the present conflict, but the truth is that Robert (and Mother) had long since decided that I was a directionless idler fit for little more than carousing with like minded fellows and charming the ladies. I admit to you freely that I gave them more than ample evidence to support their views. The upshot was that I was cast out with no more than the clothes on my back and your victory sword — forced to fend for myself.

I found employment at Robinson's Tavern as a barman and in time became engaged with the Sons of Liberty who met in secret in rooms upstairs. I joined the local militia as a private and served in the lines at the first major battle of the Revolution on Breed's Hill in Charlestown, not far from your North End counting house.

I fear you would not look with favor upon my showing on Breed's Hill. Like many I expected to give the Lobsterbacks a sharp Yankee spanking. But then the cannon roared and the smoke of spent powder filled the air and darkened our faces and, most terrifying, the British charged us with bayonets and spikes flashing before them. My knees, like those of many of my comrades, took to knocking.

Fortunately our brave officers kept our bodies and minds to the gruesome work at hand. Israel Putnam, whom you knew so well from the French & Indian War, was our general. Old Put stood his ground like an oak, calmly drawing on his long clay pipe. Our goodly physician, Dr. Warren, distinguished himself for bravery in the fiercest fire before he fell, a valiant hero, guarding our retreat.

Shortly thereafter we extended our lines from Cambridge to Dorchester, but the large English fleet lurking in the harbor prevented our storming the city.

His Excellency George Washington of Virginia, whose name and sterling reputation were familiar to you, was selected by the Continental Congress as our Commander-in-Chief. A more perfect choice is unimaginable.

Just before our departure from Boston I was promoted to the rank of lieutenant. I marched off to New York City

*with my new charges brimming with expectations, but never
was a man so unfit for command as I.*

*Whatever measure or strategm I took to instill military
manner in my unit failed. These men, who were so
recently my bosom friends at bar and bordello, soon became as hostile as the foe we faced. My orders and my
person were ignored. And when battle drew upon us at
Brooklyn Heights on Long Island, they showed their mistrust of me by running at the first whiff of the enemy. And
to my utter disgrace, I joined them.*

*There followed debacles throughout Manhattan Island
and into the hinterlands of New York and New Jersey. At
each juncture the enemy drove our forces from the battleground with overwhelming numbers, bolder leadership,
and unshakeable resolve. Of the twenty thousand stal-
warts who stood to meet the British and Hessians at the
outset of this campaign, scarcely 3,000 battered and discouraged men remain; half-naked, forlorn and near starvation.*

*Countless individuals served with distinction, however.
Old Put led his men in an orderly retreat before the guns
on Manhattan, and a courageous Connecticut officer, Thomas Knowlton, fell at Harlem Heights after leading a ferocious rear guard action. His Excellency George Washington himself rode directly into the firing line at Kip's
Bay trying to rally his troops. I turned my face away,
fearing for certain that a sharp-shooter with a taste for
instant immortality would cut him down. Fortunately, his
aide grabbed his reins and led His Excellency to safety
just in time.*

I can report no such valor on my part.

*A beaten man in a beaten army, I have been taken to
task by my superior officer and will face courtmartial. My
defense will be that I have no defense.*

*My failures in this campaign well-up in me, combin-
ing with my earlier litany of disappointments as son and
brother to overwhelm me.*

*How I miss your good counsel, necessary admonitions,
and most of all your strong arm wrapped warmly around
my shoulder. You lit the path, but I foolishly refused to
follow.*

Instead I became lazy and insolent; a child born to every advantage who now sees in the mirror a self-made failure. At night the cries of my fallen comrades — men whose lives were in my hands — ring as clearly in my brain as if they stood like a chorus from MacBeth before me. Would I not trade my sullied life in an <u>instant</u> if but one of those heroes could live again in my place.

Of all my shortcomings, though, the one that I am most ashamed of is that I am no longer worthy to call myself your son. I have brought disgrace upon the family name that your life hallowed. The sword, your sword, that hangs by my side is my daily reminder.

Redemption may be beyond my grasp now, Dearest Father, but I have set upon a plan which will end at last this string of failure. Whatever the outcome, I pray for your blessing and approval. Only by achieving that will I know peace.

*I Remain Your Most
Affectionate and Devoted Son,*

Charles

Chapter 8

Muddy roads and cold weather proved a blessing for the disheveled Americans as they retreated through New Jersey — they slowed Cornwallis's pursuit to a near halt. The closest he came to "bagging the fox" came on December 1st at New Brunswick, but Washington's sawyers cut down the timbers supporting the bridge over the Raritan River. As the structure collapsed into the churning, icy waters, Cornwallis could only stand fuming on the other bank while his prey slipped away.

Howe merged his main force with Cornwallis and they pressed ahead. Beyond Trenton, Colonel Glover's seamen once again saved the day, ferrying Washington and all his men and horses across the ice-choked Delaware River to the Pennsylvania shore, leaving no boats behind for the British pursuit.

On December 14th, with the weather turning numbingly cold and snow falling, General Howe broke off the advance and ordered his troops into winter quarters. As he declared in a dispatch to London: *No army ever campaigned in the winter.* Howe left with the bulk of his command to the comforts of New York City and the waiting arms of his mistress, Mrs. Betsy Loring. General Cornwallis anxiously anticipated his return home to England and the bedside of his beloved and ailing wife.

To the Hessians went the honor of establishing a string of outposts to hold the Americans in check until springtime when a new campaign would quickly and decisively crush the last vestige of resistance to the King's authority.

Washington's situation was even more desperate than Howe imagined. His 3,000 disconsolate, poorly-trained, ill-equiped, unpaid and starving troops began to desert in large numbers. Or froze to death at their posts. And to make matters worse, by December 31st the enlistments of half the men remaining would run out and for all practical purposes the American Army under Washington would dissolve. Then Howe would not even have to launch a springtime offensive — the fight for independence would be lost.

Across the bleak Delaware the enemy's well provisioned force numbered over 10,000 strong.

For the morale of his troops and to keep alive the flickering hope of the people that the Cause could yet be saved, Washington decided to risk all on a surprise attack against the Hessians at Trenton. Not a single one of his staff officers supported the idea. The odds against success were incalculable. But Washington knew what the others failed to grasp; that the fate of the Revolution itself hung in the balance.

Bolstered by reinforcements from Lee's former battalion near New York (once Lee was captured by the British, his men marched to Washington's banner), 500 men sent by General Gates from Ticonderoga, Colonel John Cadwalader's 1,000 Philadelphia Associates, and Nicholas Haussegger's Pennsylvania Germans, Washington could number his command at nearly 6,000 soldiers, though no more than two-thirds were fit for duty.

On Christmas Day the Delaware River was at full flood levels with great blocks and sheets of jagged ice bobbing menacingly through the current. Anyone could tell at a glance that the river was impassable.

Yet that evening Washington's daring plan began to unfold. Sixty foot long flat-bottomed Durham boats were lashed to the water's edge. Once again Washington turned to an asset that the English and their Hessian allies had not bargained on — the unique talents and courage of Colonel John Glover and the men of Marblehead, Massachusetts.

Down the slippery embankment they came, the sons of New Hampshire, Connecticut, New York, Massachusetts, New Jersey, Pennsylvania, Rhode Island, Maryland, Virginia, and Delaware — strangers united in the common cause. They held their pitiful rags against their faces with one hand to ward off the biting cold. In the other hand they held their muskets. The snow where they passed was tinged red from the blood of many a cut, shoeless foot.

Quickly, quietly they boarded the boats and shoved off. Icy sleet lashed every face on this darkest of nights. Cascading ice flows were pushed away with bare frozen hands while Glover's men skillfully rowed and poled with all their might. Back and forth this forlorn flotilla went, carrying troops, ammunition, horses, even General Knox's heavy guns.

By four the next morning, in what could only be called a miracle in military transport, Washington's army stood shivering on the New Jersey bank of the Delaware. Not one man, horse, or cannon had been lost to the river.

But there was no time to rest. Nine long miles still needed to be covered on foot. And surprise meant everything.

Washington's elaborate plan of battle called for a carefully coordinated two pronged attack. General Nathanael Greene's column took the inland Pennington Road. With him were hastily realigned brigades under Adam Stephen, Hugh Mercer, Lord Stirling, and the French officer Roche de

Formoy.

Approaching Trenton along the river highway was General John Sullivan's column which included the troops under Arthur St. Clair, Paul Sargent, and the indefatigable John Glover.

Charles was temporarily reassigned to Glover's brigade. The two knew each other through the Royal's shipping interests in Boston. Colonel Glover asked Charles to assume the point position, a high honor which Charles readily accepted.

The storm intensified as the men marched on Trenton at the quick step. The slick footing claimed many, but they either scrambled to their feet or were hauled aloft by their comrades without breaking stride. There was no talking in the ranks and anything that rattled was held tight.

Greene's men were first to reach the outskirts of the town, where 1,700 enemy troops were, for the most part, still groggily sleeping off the rum-soaked revelry from Christmas Day. A seventeen man guard first spotted Greene's advance, which fanned out in the sparse woods and blew past them. Hessian Captain Weinhold ordered his men to race back to town and sound the alarm which they did running down King and Queen Streets crying, "Der fiend! Heraus! Heraus!" (The enemy! Turn out! Turn out!).

Greene's men fell upon the foreign mercenaries as they rushed from the houses in various states of dress. Meanwhile, Sullivan's force hit the lower part of town to the south, rolling up resistance almost as quickly as it appeared. Glover's men spearheaded the attack, with the tip of the point being Lieutenant Charles Royal.

Charles sprinted directly toward the enemy line now forming, a plug bayonet in his musket. The weather had turned for the worse and the gale-force sleet carried he and his men forward. Some paused to try and load their weapons, but Charles yelled over his shoulder, "No time! Press on! Press on!" The men fed off Charles's steely determination. For the first time he appeared utterly fearless and the sight inspired them. This was the day Charles had waited for.

The instant he reached the enemy Charles charged headlong into two Hessian grenadiers wearing huge black bear hats and brandishing muskets with fixed bayonets. The first fired at Charles from point blank range, but only got a flash in the pan. Charles parried with him musket to musket and fortunately for Charles his foe slipped on the ice and fell hard.

Suddenly the second Hessian clashed muskets with Charles. He was even larger than the first and the force of his initial blow sent the plug bayonet flying from Charles's weapon. The two locked muskets and pushed for all their worth. Slowly Charles began to turn to his left under the immense pressure. The Hessian leaned into his advantage and smiled menacingly as his blade drew closer and closer to Charles's face. About to be overwhelmed, Charles loosed his grip and instinctively reached for his sword. In one flashing motion he whipped it from his sheath and straight across the Hessian's belly. A cry and both men staggered back a step. The shocked Hessian dipped both hands into the blood and entrails pouring from his abdomen. He glanced up at Charles with a look of horror, then collapsed dead in the snow. Charles hovered for a moment over the first life he had taken in the war. Then he waved his sword over his head and called above the roar of battle, "Press on!"

The Hessian commander, Colonel Johann Rall, burst upon the scene. He had paid no heed to warnings of an American advance the night before. Now the advance was here on King Street, raging with the clash of metal and the cries and curses of the wounded. Rall's superbly trained grenadiers tried to form into lines but the Patriots were everywhere, slashing and clubbing their defenses to pieces in a scene more reminescent of a no-holds-barred street brawl than a classic battle.

Several of St. Claire's men rushed the nearby houses, cleared any opposition and clambered to the upper floors where they poured a withering crossfire into the enemy below.

While rushing about valiantly trying to rally his troops, Rall was struck once, twice, and then fell from his horse to the ground mortally wounded.

On the north side of town, Greene's column drove hard against the stout-hearted forces of von Lossberg's brigade. At one point the advance of Continental troops led by Sergeant Joseph Martin appeared to stall. Up galloped a frantic looking officer.

"Why the halt!" he demanded.

"Our powder is wet, sir," responded Sergeant Martin. "We cannot fire."

"General Washington has said we *must* take Trenton at all hazards. Use the bayonet!" He spurred his horse onward.

The men looked quizzically at the muzzles of their rifles, then at each other. Not one had a bayonet.

Martin shrugged, lowered his musket and ordered, "CHARGE!" His men took up the battle cry and they all rushed forward.

Henry Knox's field pieces commanding the high ground to the north unleashed a galling fire of round shot into the enemy's flank. The grenadiers attempted to overrun Knox's position, but were turned back reeling into the maelstrom.

Directing movements from Princeton Avenue, Washington threw in all his reserves — Stirling's brigade, Captain William Washington and Lieutenant James Monroe, St. Clair's infantry, Joe Gourd Weedon's 3rd Virginians, and the veteran John Stark with his New Hampshiremen.

Glover's force finally sealed off the desperate Hessians' retreat over the Asunpink bridge and the contest was about up. Every breakout attempt was foiled as the trap rapidly closed. With escape now impossible and the prospect of total annihilation at hand, the last of the Hessians finally grounded their arms and surrendered in a nearby orchard.

The Battle of Trenton was over scarcely an hour after it began. For the Americans, the surprise had been total and the victory complete. The Hessian losses were 22 killed, 83 wounded, and nearly 900 taken prisoner. The American casualties — four wounded.

Charles stood bone-weary, his sword hanging limply in his hand, as he watched his men load valuable supplies and weapons onto wagons for the hazardous trek back. As he moved to join them he passed a burning caisson. Pausing, he withdrew a folded letter from an inside pocket. He fingered it for a moment, and then with a wry look he tossed it into the all-consuming flames.

Chapter 9

The smashing victory at Trenton electrified the American Army and gave hope to the infant nation.

For the British command, the news came as a shocking blow. Howe and his German allies had been caught napping and now, wintery weather or not, they were itching for a fight.

General Cornwallis was immediately called back to active duty just as he was boarding a ship in New York harbor bound for England. To him went the task of carrying out General Howe's order, "Find the rebel army and crush it. Let no man stand in New Jersey who will not bow before his Sovereign King!"

Of the 14,000 British and Hessian troops in New Jersey, the energetic Cornwallis took control of about 8,000 hardy and well-provisioned men in Princeton on January 2nd and began marching without delay straight on Trenton.

After successfully renegotiating the treacherous Delaware following the Battle of Trenton, Washington had no time to bask in his success. Enlistments were about to run out. Henry Knox and Thomas Mifflin along with other senior officers pleaded the case for staying-on in front of every campfire from unit to sullen unit. But the men were hungry, sick, and unpaid for months. Despite their recent victory at Trenton they worried about their families with winter coming on and most had been marking the days until they could leave with honor (many, of course, had already deserted). Why should they remain? "When the fighting starts up again in the spring, we'll be back." The officers knew better.

Congress offered the promise of a ten dollar bounty for every regular who agreed to reenlist. The troops hooted and laughed scornfully as the proclamation was read. They held out their greatest mistrust and contempt for those "damned politicians wining and dining by their warm hearths in Philadelphia." Truth was that the Continental Congress was broke. So broke that it had to pass the hat among its members to come up with enough money to pay the poor courier who brought the news of the "bonuses" to Washington.

Finally, the only person who could touch the hearts of the men humbled himself before them. Washington personally called upon his regulars' un-failing courage and determination in the face of every adversity. Would they not hold fast a little longer for the Cause of Liberty — for themselves, for their loved ones, for posterity? The future of a nation hung on their reply.

Grudgingly men turned toward one another. "I'll stay if you will." And through the grumbling ranks moved a slow nodding of heads. With nothing more to offer than cold, misery, and the prospect of a slow or violent death, the Commander-in-Chief had somehow managed to hold 3,000 of his band together for the additional term of six weeks. Why they stayed, each man would have to answer for himself.

On December 31st Washington and his men recrossed the Delaware, hooked-up with Cadwalader's Pennsylvania and Rhode Island militia, and took up defensive positions in and around Trenton. The combined American force of 5,000 soldiers waited grimly by their arms, each peering out across the bleak winter fields for first sight of Cornwallis and his 8,000.

American Colonel Edward Hand harassed and hampered every step of the British advance from Princeton — felling trees, contesting creek cross-ings, placing snipers in trees with instructions to "aim for the epaulets."

As the regiments of British and Hessians maneuvered the icy, rutted road toward Trenton, the American line fell back against overwhelming numbers across the Asunpink. A cannonade flew across the creek in both directions as night came on.

The advantage lay with the British. They had more men and materiel and could cut off any American retreat except back the way they came. And if the rebels tried to slip across the perilous Delaware, they would inevitably be trapped on its barren shore. His advisors pressured Cornwallis to finish the job that evening. "If Washington is the commander I take him to be," offered General William Erskine, "He will not be found there in the morn-ing."

But Cornwallis was physically spent from the torturous march and the day's fighting and so were his men. "The old fox is trapped. Morning will be soon enough to bag him." Washington, as on Long Island, had a different plan.

In a move as daring and unexpected as his crossing of the Delaware to attack Trenton just one week before, Washington didn't hold or retreat. At midnight he divided his smaller force and flanked the British lines.

Leaving 500 militia behind to stoke the campfires and "amuse the en-emy" to cover the ruse, Washington tiptoed the bulk of his makeshift army unnoticed around the British left — their destination: Princeton.

Over tree stumps, thickets, ice patches and hidden frozen pools they stumbled through the starless night, wagon wheels and horses' hooves sheathed in sackcloth to muffle the noise. When dawn's first light twinkled off the hoar frost that hung from bare branches and men's beards, the American breakout was complete — the British stood bewildered and incensed in a ghost town Trenton.

Ahead in Princeton, Lieutenant Colonel Charles Mawhood was preparing two of the three regiments under his command to join Cornwallis, loaded with supplies that Washington desperately needed.

The march had scarcely begun when, at Stony Brook, Mawhood's 17th Regiment of Foot and 55th Borderers literally ran into Hugh Mercer's brigade at the van of Washington's column coming up Quaker Road. Both commanders, seizing the moment, spotted a nearby hill that held great strategic advantage and ordered their men to take it. The two armies sprinted for the high ground. Mercer's men were closer and swifter and they immediately went into line of battle by a rail fence on the hill's crest.

The British halted and fired a volley that went high. The Americans returned the fire, leapt over the fence, and charged screaming down the 100 feet of snow covered ground into the British line. With the bayonets (and the skill to use them) on their muskets, the British soon had the best of it. Continental platoons, remnants of the celebrated Maryland and Delaware Lines, plunged into the fight, but panic-stricken militia companies withered away. Huzzaing and racing ahead, Mawhood's men burst over the rail fence, muskets crackling, and swarmed in on the Patriots. Mercer was bayoneted and Colonel Haslet of the Delaware regiment was shot dead.

With Americans giving ground and apparently about to be overrun, Washington galloped up on his great chestnut horse and rode with reckless courage between the opposing lines. Miraculously unhurt, he then called out to his men who, stiffened by his bold action, dressed ranks and mounted a countercharge supported by Henry Knox's guns now booming across the frosted meadow.

Just then Colonel Daniel Hitchcock's Rhode Island and Massachusetts brigades arrived and smashed into Mawhood's center, sending it reeling backward. Now it was the King's soldiers' turn to throw off their weapons and packs and run for their lives — all the way to Trenton.

With little opposition left, Sullivan's column stormed into Princeton. On the college campus a few British diehard infantrymen barricaded themselves into Nassau Hall intending to prolong the fight. But a perfectly aimed cannon shot by Captain Alexander Hamilton's battery decapitated a portrait of King George in the prayer hall and the soldiers decided they'd had enough and waived the white flag.

Washington claimed the priceless magazine at Princeton and spoke long-ingly of moving on New Brunswick where the huge British supply base and bulging treasure chests for all New Jersey were stored. But after two straight days of grueling march and battle, this tantalizing prize would remain out of reach. Cornwallis was by now aware of the attack on Princeton and un-doubtedly on the quick march. To avoid being overtaken and wiped-out, Washington had no choice but to escape with his tattered army toward the western hills — to Morristown and winter quarters.

At a humble dinner the next evening, Washington could enjoy with his fellow officers the amusing account of General Knox imagining Cornwallis and his troops arriving too late at Princeton "in a most infernal sweat — running, puffing, and blowing and swearing at being so outwitted."

What Cornwallis and Howe, and indeed all of the British military lead-ers failed to grasp was the amazing resilience of this new American people. They could be beaten, and were time and again, but always they rose once more like new leaves in springtime to take the field and fight on.

Through the long, bitter months that followed at winter quarters in Morristown, Charles embarked on a self-imposed course of study. If the skills of an effective military commander didn't come naturally to him, he reasoned, then, by God, he would learn them by observing others.

Picking his mentors carefully, Charles slowly learned how an officer leads by strength of character. How to gain the confidence of men, yet maintain a necessary distance. How to administer discipline and the neces-sity of it. And most importantly, how to lead men who trusted him into the jaws of death.

"There is a moment in the midst of every furious battle when your men will either die for you or turn on you," Captain Jacoby of the Maryland Continentals said pensively one evening as they huddled around a campfire. "If they see fear in your eyes, if they think you will flinch at the prospect of accepting their fate as your own, then all is lost. Let each man know through your words and your actions that you will ask them to take no step forward that you yourself will not take. That your life's blood will mingle with their's on the ground before you retreat in dishonor. If they believe this, then they will believe in you. And they will follow you through the gates of hell itself. Cheering and waving their hats to raise the dead."

Charles made it a point of taking on his most belligerent and lethargic troopers, to send a message to them all that he would no longer be intimi-dated or brushed aside by them. In one case he lay in wait for a brutish former farmhand named Foley to step out of line. One day while conducting field drills, Charles got his chance.

"Private Foley! There is no talking in ranks!" Charles barked. With a sneer and a huff, Foley continued his conversation with the soldier beside him.

"Foley, shut your mouth, that's an order!"

Charles drew himself up eye-to-eye and glared into the man's rough stubbled face. The gauntlet had been dropped, the challenge must be met.

Punctuating his remarks on Charles's chest with his forefinger, Foley replied, "I'll talk to who I want, when I want, whether any of you damned officers likes it or—"

In a flash Charles had hold of Foley's offending finger twisting it violently behind the man's back and hurling him headlong into a muddy puddle. Foley lurched around in a rage to find the point of Charles's sword pressing firmly under his chin. Scurrying backward on his rump, terror replacing his combativeness, Foley was quickly subdued.

"Sergeant!" Charles called out.

"Sir!"

"This man is under arrest for insubordination. Take him to the blockhouse and place him in irons."

"Sir!" The sergeant motioned for two soldiers to bring the beaten Foley to his feet. Foley offered no final act of defiance, or even made eye contact with the stone-faced Charles as he was hauled-off. From then on, drills took on a new level of precision.

As he became a hardened military man, Charles kept mostly to himself, preferring to read what books were available or simply sit for long periods emersed in his own thoughts. The gregarious youth who sought friends by being easy-going and carefree was dead and gone. In his place was a man who took responsibility deadly seriously; who no longer craved the approval of subordinates or superiors; who found his only peace in solitude. His statement of a soldier's purpose that he gave to every new recruit assigned to him was the same, "Kill the enemy before he kills you." Charles had become a one man war machine.

Chapter 10

Late in the summer of 1777 a select detachment of soldiers was reassigned to General Daniel Morgan's brigade with orders to march in support of General Gates's army on the upper Hudson. Lieutenant Charles Royal was included among them.

Here was an opportunity that Charles relished. He had admired the rough and tumble Morgan, the "Old Wagoneer," from the moment he arrived in Morristown after being swapped in a prisoner exchange. Rarely shaven, preferring buckskin to buff and with a perenial chaw wedged into his lower cheek, Morgan was the antithesis of the ordered parade ground officer. Charles knew he could learn much from this legendary backwoods pioneer.

Morgan's 200-odd Virginia riflemen were, for the most part, tough as leather frontiersmen and Indian fighters like himself. It was said that Morgan's men would as soon shoot an American officer as a British one, but in a wilderness skirmish they were nigh on unbeatable. What the British command, use to the ordered alignments of European battles, would call abominable conditions, Morgan's men called home.

Center stage of the Revolutionary theatre had now shifted to upstate New York where General John Burgoyne was attempting to carry out his grand scheme by marching his army down from Canada to join with Howe's forces in New York City and effectively cutting off New England.

Overall command of the American troops poised along the Hudson to intercept Burgoyne belonged to General Horatio Gates, an overrated former British officer who had as little respect for the rabble under him as the Redcoats.

Gates's objective was clear and simple — to stop Burgoyne and his 10,000 troops (including Hessians, Tories, Canadians, and nearly 400 Indian allies) from reaching New York City. With a force of about equal size, Gates had tustled and sparred with the enemy throughout the summer before settling in September on the site for the major engagement — a small clearing near Saratoga known as Freeman's Farm.

Many of the men in Charles's company were napping in the midday sun when a messenger galloped in shouting orders, "Prepare to break camp, we march at sundown!"

A night march, Charles though as he packed his haversack. *Weeks of inactivity and now we must rush off in the dark?* It could only mean one thing. Troops marched at night to conceal their numbers and intentions from the enemy as they moved like growing storm clouds into lines of readiness. Battle, and a major one, was in the wind.

Freeman's Farm was one of untold hundreds of small freeholdings hacked from the wilderness by pioneer families and defended from the Indians. On this day, September 19, 1777, and one to follow nearly three weeks later, it would rise from anonymity to assume an unimaginable role as the pivotal point in the war of the North. If Burgoyne could smash through the Continentals here and march triumphantly into New York, the already teetering morale of the Americans would almost certainly collapse and the war would be lost. This could well be the Patriot's last stand. They needed a victory.

For the first time since Bunker Hill the tactics and terrain favored the Americans, who invariably fought best from a concealed, defensive position. Burgoyne's plan was to march the cream of his seasoned troops toward the middle of the American lines, with the battle-hardened Hessians and Indians guarding his flanks and the river paths.

From the deep woods across the clearing, Morgan's 500-man Continental Rifles could make out the shifting and stumbling of the large British force moving into position. Morgan's troops (signaling one another with their trademark turkey calls) were on the American left, while the Continentals under General Benedict Arnold anchored the right. General Gates, as was his usual course, was nowhere to be found.

Unfortunately for the British, there was not enough open field for them to properly form ranks for battle out of range of American fire. But the proud yet reckless Burgoyne would allow no other strategy, so his courageous soldiers dutifully moved onto the edge of the field where they provided easy targets for the backwoods sharpshooters who rapidly mowed them down.

With his movements severely restricted, Burgoyne gallantly led his infantry in a charge straight into the hellish American fire. Charles and his men poured hot lead into the swarming red-clad wave until the smoke was so thick that individuals could not be singled out. When the advance finally broke off and the King's troops began to recede back into the protective woods, the Americans mounted a countercharge and swept onto the field. But the diehard British, with the timely aid of General von Riedesel's fresh German hussars, held their ground, rallied, and repulsed the American attack.

Throughout the long, blood-soaked afternoon and the entire next day the great armies pushed and pulled like two giant wrestlers back and forth over the small, worthless patch of clearing. No quarter asked for. None received.

As the dusk of the second day drew near, Burgoyne hastily called his remaining officers together for a council of war to determine what course to take. The British and their allies had lost over 600 men to less than half that for the Americans. Rather than risk another attack, Burgoyne elected to dig-in, fortify his position against an anticipated American assault, and await reinforcements from New York City that never came. Many of the Tories and Indians, and a fair number of Hessians, simply melted away until only 6,000 discouraged soldiers remained to continue the fight.

Meanwhile, across the way, fresh militia units arrived by the hour as farmers up and down the Hudson River Valley grabbed their muskets and rushed to the colors, swelling the American ranks to over 11,000 men.

Ever the gambler, Gentleman Johnny staged one last frantic rush at the enemy lines on October 7th, but the Patriots held firm, and sent the British reeling back under a hail of deadly fire. It was time for the British command to face the unthinkable — they must retreat to their supply base and the protection of the warships up the Hudson at Fort Ticonderoga. And they must move fast.

Abandoning his artillery, baggage, wagons, and wounded, Burgoyne began the desperate race northward, but the relentless pursuit by Generals Learned, Morgan and Poor, and the timely intervention of General Stark's militia and the Green Mountain Boys (flush from their decisive victory at Bennington) further upriver caught the elusive Burgoyne in a vice-like trap from which there was no escape. Reluctantly, he asked for terms. For the first time in the Revolution, the Americans had won a clear-cut victory against a regular British army. And all Europe stood up and took notice.

Near the end of the second battle at Freeman's Farm, Charles witnessed a band of Loyalist troops in green waistcoats cut down almost to the last man. Their officer, who led them bravely to the end, was struck cleanly in the chest and carried from the field just ahead of an American countersurge. The officer, Charles knew in a frightful instant, was his brother Robert.

After Burgoyne surrendered the remnants of his shattered army to Gates at Saratoga, Charles received permission to enter the encampment of the vanquished enemy to find Robert. He made his way to the large makeshift field hospital; more a waiting place for the dying as doctors were few and medical supplies virtually nonexistent.

Charles stopped a passing British surgeon. "Sir, I'm looking for a Tory officer named Robert Royal who received a chest wound and was carried from the field."

The surgeon stared straight ahead. "British officers first, German officers second, Tory officers last."

Charles searched tent after tent until he finally found the one where Robert lay. Kneeling by the coarse blanket that covered his brother, Charles gazed down upon the ashened face that he had not seen up close since that fateful night in Boston nearly three years before.

"Robert?" he said softly, touching his brother's hand. "Robert it's me, your brother Charles."

Robert's eyes fluttered open slowly and looked in pain as they focused on Charles.

"Charles . . . Charles . . . Charles, is it really you?" came the almost whispered response.

"Yes Robert, it's me. I saw you fall and searched until I found you. Praise God you are alive."

"Scarcely, Charles. My time on this earth grows short."

Charles began to protest, but Robert raised his hand and shook off any denial. "It's all right, Charles. In fact, death may be the only true peace that any of us may know. And I thank God that at the moment of my passing I may ask forgiveness of you, my dear brother, whom I have so grievously wronged. More than you know."

"You have not wronged me brother. Nor I you. We just chose to walk different paths."

"If that's true, I do confess that it is you, Charles, who has chosen the wiser path to follow."

Robert, in halting passages, told Charles of the degradation that the Loyalists suffered at the hands of the British; of their lowly status within the military and the loss of every dignity.

Robert also informed Charles that he feared that the Royal family fortune had been lost. The ships and warehouses had undoubtedly been confiscated by the British in the final frantic days before the evacuation of Boston, and the great house on Joy Street was left for the rebels thereafter. The family was permitted to take only what meager items they could squeeze into a few small trunks. Robert had left instructions with Maxwell Chessman to guard what remained of the Royal's interests as best he could. To safeguard his family, Robert had paid outlandish bribes so that his mother, Sarah and Sally would be placed on a schooner bound for Nova Scotia. Joseph was to follow by land with a small train of what possessions he could salvage. Robert had no way of knowing if any of them had gotten through.

After arriving in New York on a British transport, Robert was unsuccessful in securing a commission in either the Royal Army or Navy. Instead, he was made a captain with the King's Loyalist Rangers and subsequently shipped off to join Burgoyne's troops on the upper Hudson.

"So you see, brother, since our rude parting so long ago in Boston because of my arrogance and foolish pride, I have lost all, all except my life. And so the thought of moving on to a finer world is not fearful or distasteful to me. It is a blessing."

Charles could feel the life slipping from his brother when, suddenly, he shot his head up, eyes wide open.

"Charles, you *must* promise me something!"

"Anything," Charles replied.

"When this damn war is finally over, whatever the outcome, you must go and find what's left of the family. We have not lost all if we still have one another. Promise you will do this thing, Charles. *Promise.*"

Charles had never imagined his brother capable of such sentiment. "I swear, Robert. I will not rest until I have been reunited with what remains of our family. You can count on me."

Robert looked into Charles's eyes and smiled weakly. "It is well done then," he said in a gentle voice. "You're the head of the family now, Charles. The burden is yours. You will bear it well enough . . . God's peace upon you."

Charles knelt for a long while beside his now still brother. A lifetime, a hundred lifetimes, had passed in such a short while. And now a new world gone awry was his to put right. He began to sense for the first time the "burden" Robert had spoken of. Father was gone. Robert was gone too. The family and its future, as utterly hopeless as it now seemed, rested in his hands. How, Charles wondered to himself, would he ever be equal to the task.

A hand fell softly upon Charles's shoulder, waking him from his self-absorbed trance.

"He was a good man, your brother. He cared more for the well-being of his men than any officer I have known."

Charles looked up into the face of a beautiful young woman with dark, loose-fallen hair and striking green eyes. She moved her gaze from Robert to Charles.

"Were you his nurse?" Charles asked.

"Yes."

"Did you know him well?"

"No, but several of his soldiers both in and outside the hospital asked about his condition. That speaks volumes about the way the men loved him."

There was a moment of silence before Charles spoke in a soft voice. "Thank you."

The young woman smiled slightly then returned to her duties attending a junior British officer in the next cot. Charles watched as she gently mopped his fevered brow and thought how fortunate Robert had been to know her caring touch.

Outside the tent Charles noticed a camp cook dumping vegetables into a large iron cookpot.

"Did you wash them properly?" he asked with a studied eye. "And why haven't you sliced them at an angle, it enhances the flavor."

The astonished Tory private gave no reply.

"Here." Charles took up a knife and began peeling a turnip. "Remove the skin thusly and take care that the tip of your thumb doesn't season your stew. What seasonings do you have?"

Soon Charles was lost in this menial work that was so familiar to him. Until a voice behind him spoke up.

"You have a talent for the domestic arts, sir." It was the nurse, who now revealed a broad and radiant smile.

"It was my first assignment in camp. When you can do absolutely nothing else, they make you the cook."

"May I?" She dipped a wooden ladle into the simmering broil and tasted it. "Could use some parsley and thyme."

"Do you have any?"

She chuckled, "Our camp is as poor as yours. We all just make do as best we can."

"Have you been a nurse long?"

"No, just since the outset of this campaign. That officer in there is my cousin Nigel."

"But you aren't from England."

She shook her head, "Montgomery County, Maryland. I was on an extended visit with my aunt, Nigel's mother, on their estate near Wembly when the war broke out. My father feared for my safety and called me home. But when my ship reached New York, the fighting was fierce and travel outside the city was impossible. So I stayed with family friends for several months. There were many wounded and nurses were in short supply, so I volunteered."

"Here, try it now," Charles offered her a sip of his brew.

"Better."

Charles took a taste and concurred. "A while longer I think."

While the cauldron bubbled, Charles decided to try his hand at clever small talk. "I'll wager the Redcoat officers in New York showed the American ladies a good time."

"If your meaning is that they displayed the courtesies of gentlemen, I would agree!" came the terse reply.

"I meant no offense madam," Charles hastily added. He had almost forgotten how to speak to a lady. "Please forgive my boldness."

"Since we are apparently to share a meal together and there is no one here to make proper introductions, it is I who shall appear bold and inquire as to your name, Lieutenant."

"Charles Royal. And yours?"

"Caitlin Serling."

Over dinner these two new acquaintances revealed much about themselves to one another. Placed together under the most unlikely circumstances, they warmed to each others company and the escape, if ever so brief, from the horrors of war that engulfed them, and the circumstances that cast them on opposing sides.

But all too soon, against Charles's heartfelt wishes, the sun began to set. "I'm afraid the time grows late. I must be back through the lines before dark."

"Go in peace, Lieutenant Royal."

"Charles."

"Charles . . . And may God's angels watch over you."

"And you." Charles rose, kissed Caitlin's hand, and gave a comically flourishing bow that brought forth that all-consuming smile on Caitlin's face that he had already grown so fond of. In a moment he was mounted on his horse and trotting off toward the American lines.

A week after returning to his camp, Charles received a dispatch like none he had seen before. It had come from the British side, not by a military courier, but from a farmer who had stored it inside the heel of his boot.

My Dear Lieutenant Royal:

It is vital that I meet with you without delay to discuss a matter of our mutual interest.

I may disclose no more here. Please meet me by the abandoned flour mill near the Great Ravine on the morrow evening at 8:00 p.m. All will be revealed then. Please burn this letter.

Your Most Obedient Servant,

Subaltern Nigel Serling

A trick? Tempting officers into intrigues that would compromise them or picture them as spies was a favorite pursuit of both armies, though a lowly lieutenant was hardly a worthy target for such a charade.

Charles was about to pitch the letter into the fire when he read the signature again: Nigel Serling. *I know that name,* he thought. *Yes.* He fingered the letter loosely. What was he to do? He decided to seek the advice of his friend and noted scoundrel, Rainbow Samuels.

Samuels had fought with General Stark's force at Bennington and joined in the chase that eventually cut off Burgoyne's attempted breakout to Ticonderoga and sealed the American victory.

Charles read the brief letter to Samuels as he sat leaning against an elm tree massaging his sore feet.

"What do you make of it?"

Rainbow appeared thoughtful. "Hard to say. Could be a trap. But hell, they already had you behind lines. If they wanted to keep you they would've then. Makes no sense at all. Battle's over. Both sides'll be movin' out in a day or two. It's a puzzler."

"What do you think I should do?

"You say this fella —"

"Nigel Serling."

"Nigel Serling — he was in a fever?"

"Yes."

"Then he couldn't have recollected you?"

"No. We never met."

"And what's this girl's name again?"

"Caitlin Serling."

"She must've told him about you. So it stands to reason it's her who wants to see you, not Nigel."

"I guess that's true, but why?"

"Don't know. But I suppose if you show up at that there mill you'll find out."

"So you think I should go?"

"I can't tell you that, Charles. There's danger here. I can smell it. Was this girl pretty?"

"Very."

"Hmmm. Well then here it is: You can take the smart, cautious route, burn the letter like you never saw it, and be done with it. You march off with Morgan. I head back to Deerfield. And by God that's the end of it.

"Or . . . we could *borrow* a couple of horses and check 'er out. There's danger here, son. But there's also a certain romance to it."

Now it was Charles who was thoughtful. There was something about this young woman that aroused his curiosity. He glanced at the note once more.

"You can get us horses?"

"Oh, I think I can handle that."

". . . Make 'em swift ones. God knows we may be riding straight into hell."

Charles and Rainbow rode casually out of camp at 7:00 the following evening. With the battle concluded security was loose and no one challenged them. Riding quietly along the Hudson River Road they turned up the path that ran alongside the Great Ravine.

Nigel Serling was already at the mill when Charles and Rainbow arrived. Charles came armed and in uniform, but Nigel was not. He had assumed the disguise of a clergyman. Samuels, as usual, wore his colorful frontiersman's clothes.

"Thank you for coming, sir," Nigel said before Charles and Rainbow had even dismounted. "I am most frantic with worry and knew nowhere else to turn."

"Calm yourself, sir, and tell me the purpose of our rendezvous."

"First, who is this man?"

"He's a friend."

"Can he be trusted?"

"I'd trust this man with my life. Now, tell me, what is the purpose of our meeting?"

"It is to save the life of my cousin, sir, Caitlin Serling of your acquaintance."

"Her life! What is it that threatens her?"

"In a word, sir, documents have been discovered in her possession that mark her as a spy! A spy for the Americans!"

"A spy! Your cousin? How can this be?"

"I don't know, except she has apparently been funneling sensitive intelligence to agents on your side for some time. Detailed information on troop movements during the most recent campaign. General Burgoyne is looking for a scapegoat. He claims that these smuggled documents may have been the decisive factor in his defeat."

"And what does he propose to do to her?"

"The punishment for espionage is hanging."

"He would hang a woman? A lady?"

"Indeed so, sir. An example must be set."

"Who is the American officer who received the secret intelligence."

"I don't know."

"But we must find out! Perhaps an exchange can be worked out."

Nigel's face turned grim. "Sir, if any official attempt were made to intercede on Caitlin's behalf she would be spirited away, or simply vanish."

Charles realized the truth of that. The British, like the Americans, were always on their guard against spies. Both sides used them, but both sides detested the fact that the other side used them too. Once discovered, a spy must be publicly executed, sending a message to any other would-be turn-coats that the price if caught would be paid in full. Prisoners were often exchanged. Spies never. There could be no exception.

"Where is she now?" Charles asked.

"Under guard in an abandoned woodsman's cabin near here. She's to be evacuated north to Canada in the morning. Tonight's our only chance to free her.

"Sir, she's my cousin and I will risk all to save her, but to ask you and your friend to assist is too great a favor. Please, consider the consequences."

Charles turned to Samuels, who nodded. "Come quickly," said Charles mounting up. "There is no time to lose."

As they rode down the moonlit cart path toward the log house, Nigel revealed his plan. He removed his cleric's disguise as he spoke and tossed it into the woods. Beneath he wore the scarlet tunic of a British subaltern. "I will offer relief to the guards outside. Ply them with liquor. While they're distracted, you two can slip in the back and escort Cailtin out and make your escape."

"Will you not escape with us?" Charles asked.

"There are only three horses. Besides, I'm a British officer. I will save my cousin if I can, but I must accept what punishment is deemed warranted."

"Even a firing squad?"

Nigel looked over to Charles and nodded.

At the cabin Nigel, Charles and Rainbow noted with satisfaction that there were only two soldiers assigned to guard duty, though British patrols were certainly nearby.

Nigel waited behind some bushes until he was certain Charles and Rainbow had made their way around to the back of the cabin with the horses. He then put his plan into motion.

"Halt! Who goes there! Advance and be recognized!" one of the guards called out.

"Rest your arms, gentlemen. I come to be sure that all is quiet," was

Nigel's calming response.

"Quiet as the grave, sir."

"It is well then. Here, I've brought you a gift to pass the time."

"Ale sir? No we cannot while on duty."

"Ah! Good lads you are. But let's assay the situation. You are sent to guard a sleeping lady who poses no threat to escape. The night is chill. Wouldn't you be wise to stay warm at your post?"

The two guards looked at one another. Then the one who had been silent thrust his hand out to take one of the offered bottles. "If ya say so, sir."

"I do! Here," Nigel handed the second bottle to the other guard. With that, he took two steps back and spoke in a louder voice. "It is indeed a damnably cold night!"

That was the agreed upon signal. Charles and Rainbow quickly, quietly removed the timber bracing the back door of the cabin and Charles entered. Through the dimness he spotted Caitlin seated on a bed writing a letter by the light of a lone candle that stood upon a poor table before her. She had not heard his entrance.

"Shhh!" Charles silenced her as she first glimpsed him. He motioned with his hand for her to come quickly. Caitlin threw on her shawl and was at the door and outside with Charles in an instant. She glanced at Rainbow but neither dared speak. As they hurried to the horses their movements started one and it whinnied loudly, reared up, then bolted riderless down the road. Rainbow, now without a mount, sprinted for the dark woods.

"What ho!" cried one of the guards who dropped his bottle and lunged for his musket. Nigel sent a crashing blow to the man's head and he dropped to the ground. As he wheeled about to confront the other guard, the butt of a musket came up full on his chin and he fell back unconscious.

"Halt! Halt or I'll shoot!" yelled the guard as he raced around the cabin in time to see two shadowy figures on horseback galloping for the open road and freedom. He leveled his musket and fired. But his ball flew wide of its mark and in an instant the prisoner had escaped.

For nearly an hour the two fugitives flew headlong into the night. It wasn't until Charles was certain that they were behind American lines that he brought his horse to a stop. He dismounted and helped Caitlin down.

"The horses must have a moment to breathe before we push on."

"Charles, how did you know?"

"Your cousin Nigel revealed everything to me. The escape was his plan."

"Where is Nigel?"

"He was creating the diversion out front so I'd have the opportunity to free you."

"Then he was captured."

"I'm afraid so."

"I must go back!" She immediately whirled about but Charles caught her firmly by the arm.

"To what? To be hung? You cannot help Nigel now; nor he you. He knew the risks. His only thought was for your safety."

". . . And you?"

Charles said nothing. Their eyes met for a long moment. Finally he took the reins of Caitlin's horse and handed them to her. "Come. We had best move on."

Chapter 11

Two days after his return to his company, Charles received a message that he was to report to General Morgan immediately. Charles presented himself to the guard outside Morgan's tent and was escorted inside.

"Lieutenant Charles Royal, sir!" the guard announced. Then, with a sharp salute, he turned and stepped outside.

"Jus cain't get use to all this fancy soldierin', Royal. Care fer a Virginny ceegar?"

Charles gladly accepted the luxury and Morgan lit both his and Charles's tobacco with a taper by his writing stand. As the men puffed, Morgan pointed to a rough parchment map pinned to his tent post.

"See here? That's where we was. We shore gave those Redcoats a taste of country lead didn't we? Got to admit though, them fellas ain't afeared to scrap. Lucky for us they warn't use to fightin' in the woods."

General Morgan stood staring at the map for several moments. Finally he turned his attention to Charles.

"I reckon you're wonderin' why I sent for you," Morgan said pointing the mouthpiece of his cigar in Charles's direction. "Fact is, many a man shewd a good fight in this encounter, but few better'n you, Lieutenant Royal."

"Thank you, sir," Charles replied, snapping to attention.

"Relax son. I've been sizin' up what comes next and I reckon that General Washington will be wantin' troops sent on to him in the Jerseys now that Gentleman Johnny's fit and tied. Problem is, old Granny Gates don't think much of His Excellency and is likely as not to drag his feet. That's why I'm sendin' on a detachment of my men to join Washington now — about 200 or so — under Major Wainwright. I want you to be Wainwright's second-in-command."

"Yes, sir. But in truth, I've never commanded more than two dozen men at one time."

"Hell, boy, you think I had before all this started? In the last war I was a damned mule skinner. Fact is, you couldn't get an easier assignment. You don't have to concern yourself with commanding these men. Damn their devil-hearts, they don't never follow orders anyway!" Morgan let forth a bellowing laugh that quickly changed into the near debilitating cough that was his constant companion.

"Collect your things, Royal, and report to Major Wainwright at the southwest corner of camp. You march at daybreak."

As the troops trudged south along the bumpy road, Charles thought how little they resembled soldiers. More like a motly band of hunters. The men wore buckskin coats and pants with fringe on the sides. Often beads were embroidered in patterns in the Indian fashion. Boots were also Indian-style and pulled above the knee to ward off low brambles and snake bites.

Only Charles and Major Wainwright were on horseback. There were several wagons bringing up the rear. Two carried supplies, the rest sick and wounded soldiers whose homes lay to the south.

Charles worked his way forward to where Wainwright led the column.

"Does this road improve, Major?" Charles inquired.

"Nope," Wainwright replied with a squirt of tobacco juice, "Gets worse."

"The wagons barely have clearance now."

"They made it in, they'll make it out."

The two rode in silence until Wainwright broke it with another squirt of tobacco. "Lieutenant, we have some special cargo along that I want you to take personal charge of."

"What is it, Major?"

"In the wagon with the wounded. Green hunting coat. The Old Wagoneer said I was to pay particular attention. He's a close friend of the family in Maryland. 'Anythin' happens, I'll skin your hide myself,' he says."

"If General Morgan placed his trust in you, why are you turning over responsibility to me?"

"Simple, boy," the Major replied with a brown-toothed grin, "I'm a married man."

Charles was baffled, but Wainwright just looked ahead. "Go back and make your 'how dos'."

As Charles approached the wagon he spotted the person in the green coat hunched over a young wounded soldier.

"You there, sir. I am here to inform you that you have been placed in my care."

When no response was forthcoming, Charles reached over and swatted the stranger's butt with the flat of his sword. "You will please turnabout when I address you!"

Suddenly the mysterious figure spun around and with a harsh glare replied, "This soldier needs my attention more than you!"

Charles was taken aback in astonishment. "Caitlin?"

"Charles!"

"What are you doing here?"

"Tending to this wounded man and the others as best I can."

"But why are you wearing men's clothes?"

"In my present station, would the skirts of a woman be more fitting?"

"I can see now why General Morgan was concerned for your safety. What is your destination?"

"Maryland. My father's plantation."

"That's a long journey. And a hazardous one."

"You needn't concern yourself too much with my safety, sir. I've traveled far already as you know and I've learned how to use these pretty well." She brandished two long pistols.

Charles grinned, "Where'd you get those?"

"From your friend, General Morgan. He told me 'If any of my boys give you any trouble, shoot 'em. If they meant no harm, you can always apologize later. They'll understand.'"

"I'll be sure to keep that in mind."

"Now if you will excuse me, my attention is required here," Caitlin said as she returned to her patients.

Charles fell in at the back of the column. *So much for an uneventful journey,* he thought to himself with a chuckle.

As the days past, Charles noted how untiringly this young, strong-willed woman cared for the stricken soldiers, without regard for their rank or for which army they had served. Through three nights of constant fever she attended many a deranged man, offering what comfort she could. *What would I not give to have such a woman care that much for me,* Charles thought.

One evening, while the march was passing through New Jersey, Charles sat by a campfire holding a cup of coffee when a gentle voice behind him said, "That certainly looks inviting." He looked up to see Caitlin smiling down upon him.

"Let me pour you a cup."

She accepted the steaming brew with a smile and sat down on a small log beside him. "I want to thank you, Charles, for all you've done for me and to apologize to you for not confiding in you earlier about my covert activities. My father told me to be very wary of whom I place my trust."

"Your father is a wise man."

Both Charles and Caitlin laughed at the secret now revealed. And as the evening passed they began to share more about their family backgrounds and how they had arrived at this place in the wilderness. The Serlings owned Oakmont on the Potomac, one of the largest plantations in Maryland with over 7,000 acres, planted mostly in wheat and corn.

Well before the first crackling of muskets on Lexington Common, Caitlin had expressed her sympathies for the Patriot Cause in letters to her father from England. Abraham Serling, known to all as Judge, also stood by the Americans and spoke out sharply for independence at the Maryland General Assembly in Annapolis. It was because he knew the outspoken nature of his daughter that he implored her to return home immediately when hostilities broke out.

"Your loyalties were clearer to you than mine were to me early on," Charles confided.

Caitlin gazed into the fire then offered reflectively, "Were I a man, I would surely have fallen at Freeman's Farm, swinging a sword and charging ahead . . . with the Patriots."

"And, I do suspect, uttering every blasphemy imaginable!" Charles added with an impish grin.

"Undoubtedly so!," Caitlin laughed. "You know me all too well already, Lieutenant Royal."

"How I wish that were true . . . Caitlin."

Charles noticed with delight how the flickering campfire radiated off Caitlin's long shining hair. Dark reddish wisps would fall around her lovely, pale face and she would gently brush them aside. Her deep, seductive green eyes could both attract and melt any man and Charles fought the urge to simply gaze into them.

The two sat and talked and laughed throughout the night, which seemed to pass so quickly that each was surprised when the world once again began to grow bright.

By late November, Morgan's detachment had joined Washington's army — or more accurately his skeleton of an army — in a cold, desolate clearing alongside the Schuylkill River, twenty miles outside of the warmth and comforts of Philadelphia. The place was named Valley Forge.

Charles was appalled at what he saw. Virtually every disease known to humanity called Valley Forge home, and no less than one half of the men were deemed unfit for duty. Food was scarce, housing shabby at best, and sanitary and medical facilities woefully inadequate.

Still, there was something special about this camp that Charles sensed from the outset; a feeling of resiliency and stoic courage among the men that was severely tested, but never faltered, in the miserable winter months that mercilessly fell upon them.

Soldiers complained constantly, of course, but desertions were surprisingly few given the inhuman conditions. This was the hard core of the rebellion. Those who had committed their all to the Cause, throwing aside human reason and self-interest, and never accepting defeat as anything but a prelude to ultimate victory. And their leader, the very embodiment of their ideals and courage, was the great General himself, George Washington.

Many were the days and nights that Charles saw the General walking through camp, like an oversized apparition from a Greek tragedy; sometimes with aides, often alone, stopping to talk with the men, listening to their grievances, sharing their lot.

Many an officer of lesser rank and bearing under similar circumstances would have holed up in his warm command house, whiling away the hours with other senior officers and the company of fine ladies, but not Washington. He was, at once, the unquestioned leader and a common soldier. No wonder these pitiful and forgotten men — lacking food, clothing, and warm shelters — held onto this frozen ground against all reason. They stayed for the great affection they felt for their General, who, for many of these weary soldiers, *was* the country.

Twelve grown men were assigned to each drafty, hastily constructed fourteen by sixteen foot log cabin. Lacking windows and with a crude, amateur-built chimney at the rear belching smoke through the confined space, these huts became fertile fields for a long list of communicable diseases.

During that bleak gray winter virtually every Continental soldier suffered from illness. Hundreds died. Innoculations against smallpox were given, but every other affliction — from dysentery to fevers to rheumatism to pneumonia to the dreaded typhus — was simply free to run its debilitating course.

Yet, throughout the worst of miseries, the toughest strain was the men's own spirit of determination. As Washington wrote with admiration, *To see men without clothes to cover their nakedness, without blankets to lie on, without shoes . . . without a hut or house to cover them until those could be built, and submitting without a murmur, is a proof of patience and obedience which, in my opinion, can scarcely be paralleled.* Perhaps the men were inspired by Washington himself who refused to move out of his tent and into a house until every one of his men had a cabin to call home.

One bitter cold day in late January as Charles hobbled along in rags he had tied about his feet in place of boots, he heard a boisterous, familiar voice at the campfire of a Delaware company. He quickened his pace in the direction.

"And, oh, you should have seen the faces of them boys when we came upon 'em. Fresh scrubbed from school they looked and, I wager, nary a-one having ever placed his posterity in the care of a willing maiden."

Occasional bursts of laughter came from the huddled group as Charles confirmed that he did indeed know that voice; that unmistakeable figure.

Charles stood unobtrusively in the back as the speaker regaled his audience with magnificent tales of his derring-do. Many offered the grand orator a portion of their precious corn whiskey which he graciously accepted and always consumed in a single draw.

Finally, over the protests of his entourage, the speaker begged his leave and prepared to adjourn to a small log cabin for a brief respite. It was then that Charles stepped forward.

"Do I actually have the priviledge of addressing that fearless Indian fighter and unquenchable lover of women, Rainbow Samuels?"

Rainbow's eyes grew wide and his mouth opened into a wide grin of happy recognition.

"Why if it isn't that old bayonet-dodging gentleman of Boston proper, Charles Royal! May the saints or the devil be praised for sparing your hide. So you and that lovely miss of yours made good your escape, eh? Here, let's have ourselves a sit-down." Samuels motioned to a rough log bench beside the cabin door.

"Ay, Charles, it is a strange twist of fate that finds our feet once again upon the same path." Rainbow lit and drew on his clay pipe. "Many a man has warred against his fate and lost, Charles. But I, being among the great enlightened, readily embrace life's joys and sorrows and surprises as the plan that the Great Creator has mapped-out personally for my benefit and ultimate redemption."

"You should have been a preacher."

"Was once. Grand occupation. Just couldn't abide the piety of it."

Charles mostly listened as Rainbow poured forth the panorama of his wartime adventures — some true; all embellished. One story in particular caught Charles's fancy.

"Our position at the West Point was shakier than a grizzly on a willow tree. So the order comes down that we're skeedadlin' without further ceremony.

"Now you know that ol' Anthony Wayne himself plucks me out and says, 'Mr. Samuels, I have a hazardous job for you to do. In all the army, you're the one man with the wit and grit to pull it off.'

"Seems Mad Anthony wants to leave a small group behind to destroy all the stores in the fort and leave the enemy no more than cinders for his dinner. Right away I sized up the situation and looked the General straight in his good eye and said 'General, since this mission packs surefire danger and only the most cunning fox alive could see it through, I'm your man.' And you know, Charles, I do believe I saw a tear of gratitude in the old man's eye.

"So next day, Wayne marches the army down the north slope leavin' behind me, Harry Caruthers, and Pricker Bush Jones to tend to business. We had just commenced the mayhem when ol' Harry says, 'Well, will you lookee here!'

"Seems that there was three kegs of fine British ale just a-settin' there pretty as you please. Now the boys looked to me as their rightful leader and I considered the situation carefully. My judgment to the boys was that since no man can work while plagued by thirst and the General's strict orders were to leave no comfort behind for the enemy, it was entirely fittin' that we kill two birds with one stone and drink the ale ourselves.

"Well wouldn't you know that them boys went and got so damn drunk that they didn't hear them sneaky British a-comin' up the path. When the first Redcoat stuck his nose inside the fort and said 'What merriment goes on here?' I drew my trusty pistol and cried, 'You shall see what merriment you scoundrel!' and sent a ball whizzing by his manly parts.

"I was prepared to take on the entire British Army and save honor with a soldier's death, but the other two, bein' creatures of cowardly temperment, immediately threw down their arms and cried for mercy in the name of the Lord!

"Charles, a man of the world must adjust quickly to circumstances and I asked to see the commanding officer without delay. I told him how I had begged for the assignment of destroying the stores left behind, but that my secret love for my King and Mother Country had led me to get my unwitting conspirators hopelessly drunk so that I could safely transfer the valuable munitions to His Majesty's noble legions upon their arrival.

"The bloody commanding officer seemed well pleased with my story and don't you know that that very evenin' a great banquet was held in my honor! And I drank heartily once again of that delicious ale!

"I was presented with twenty pieces of gold and a fine horse with all accoutrements, and the very next day amid three huzzas from the Lobsterbacks I rode merrily on my way."

Charles laughed as he had not laughed since arriving in this God-forsaken encampment. And although he accused Rainbow Samuels of being the greatest liar since the serpent in Eden, he nonetheless was deeply pleased at having been reunited with this unrepentant rogue.

One afternoon a mysterious package arrived addressed to *Lieutenant Charles Royal, late of General Morgan's Brigade.* Charles turned it over then took out his knife and hastily cut the twine. His eyes lit up as he found inside a new knit cap, a lengthy scarf, three pairs of soft mittens and an equal number of stockings. And, perhaps most welcome of all, a letter from Caitlin.

Whenever he could find a scrap of paper, Charles had written to Caitlin, telling her of his experiences at Valley Forge. He tried to be light and cheerful, although there was little to be cheerful about. He even doubted that any of his letters had gotten through.

Caitlin's brief letter to Charles read:

Dear Charles:

I pray that these small comforts have come to your hands and that they help you to endure the difficulties of your place. As I sat by the warm hearth knitting them for you my heart ached for what you must be going through.

I told my father of your courage in rescuing me and of your great kindness during our subsequent journey and he asks me to invite you to visit us if possible at Oakmont so that he might express his gratitude to you in person. I would add that this is my fondest hope too.

Until then, may the Good Lord protect you and all those who serve with you.

If there is anything you need that I might provide, you need only ask. I wait in hope of your reply.

With Sincerest Affection,

Caitlin

Charles held the letter in his shivering hand, reading it over and over until the gray afternoon light grew too dim. He then folded it carefully, repressed the sealing wax, and put it inside his shirt. Sending a return letter to Caitlin now would be impossible. He hoped she would somehow understand.

In early February Charles came down with the fever that had swept back and forth through Valley Forge all winter. His was one of the worst cases. For several days he was delirious and unable to take even the meager nourishment that was available.

Days passed and several of the men conceded that Charles's end was very near. Food was so scarce that some had taken to eating bark off the trees to fill their aching bellies. If provisions were not forthcoming shortly, the Continental Army would surely starve or fade away, and the Revolution would be lost.

Rainbow Samuels sat stoically in the snow leaning against a large elm tree with Charles bundled up by his side. The ice enshrouded branches of the great elm stretched about and above them, giving a bleak, yet almost angelic character to the moment. It was a good spot to die.

As Charles shook with fever, Rainbow's mind wandered to distant, better times. Then, faintly, there was a light ringing away off in the brush. Samuels listened, but heard nothing more. He was about to admit to himself that he was hallucinating when, wait, there it was again. And louder this time.

Summoning what was left of his strength, Rainbow propped Charles up against the elm and trudged through the knee deep snow to investigate.

What he saw he could scacely believe was true. There, nibbling on a sparse juniper bush, were three plump cows, each with a copper bell tied around its neck! Samuels strode, or rather stumbled forward until he could reach out and grasp the tether of the first cow. He tugged on it twice and the massive head turned and followed him, the other two cows following dutifully behind.

Once back in camp a crowd of men quickly gathered and began to shout for joy. "Quiet you fools!" warned Samuels sternly. "Would you have every man and officer down upon us and taking these prizes for their own?"

The men quickly concocted a plan. They would hide the cows long enough to ensure that they shared abundantly in their milk and cheese. Only then would the word be let out. A few men wanted to conceal the cows indefinitely until a veteran reminded them that to hoard food in camp was a crime punishable by hanging.

Rainbow entrusted the care of the precious beasts to a massive frontiersman named McDowell who was known and respected for his skill as an eye gouger and hurried off to retrieve Charles, turning a deaf ear to the skeptics. "If he's out there," sneered an old scout, "Then he's a dead man already."

Samuels found Charles frozen solid against the elm tree — alive, but only barely. Furiously he hacked away with his tomahawk. Alone, with the fierce wind biting his cheeks and ice caking his beard, he swung with all his might and Charles broke free, falling like a corpse to the ground. Heaving him over his shoulder, Samuels staggered back to camp.

Now, at last, there was wholesome food and the glimmer of hope for survival. Rainbow fed Charles warm milk with a small wooden spoon. In a remarkably short time Charles's fever broke and his strength began to return. Miraculously, within a fortnight, he was up and about and able to resume his duties in the camp.

By mid-February the worst of the winter's trials appeared to be over. The quality and quantity of food and supplies improved with General Nathaniel Greene's appointment as Quartermaster General and a flickering of hope grew that a new spring campaign might be undertaken.

It was at this moment that the fortunes of the American Cause took a dramatic turn for the better with the arrival in Valley Forge of a stout, middle-aged Prussian officer who didn't speak a word of English — Friedrich von Steuben.

Into the midst of the shabby encampment of the Fourth Regiment of the New York Continental Line he strode on the morning of February 24, 1778 wearing a sumptuous blue and buff uniform covered with battle ribbons and stars, a thick fur cloak, and an enormous cocked hat. Projecting a regal, ramrod-straight military bearing that contrasted sharply with the slumped, winter-weakened New Yorkers who huddled around the fire with their morning mush, the mysterious stranger went right to work — fingering threadbare blankets, skillfully examining flintlocks, assessing the physical readiness of these scraggly troops, and testing bayonet points with a practiced thumb.

For the most part, American officers and soldiers shared General Washington's weariness with the steady stream of European born soldiers-of-fortune that Congress felt duty bound to send their way. Seeking inflated military rank and outlandish pay while they sneered contemptuously at all things American, these gentleman generals were a burden rather than a blessing, and the Patriot Cause already had all the burdens it could handle.

But this new fellow was one of the exceptions. He dipped his fingers into the cookpots to taste for himself the soldiers' miserable provisions. He soiled his magnificent boots inspecting the "necessaries." And through his aide Pierre Duponceau and French-speaking American officers (von Steuben spoke heavily-accented French) he conveyed his respect for the Continentals' fighting prowess, mentioning specific engagements such as Saratoga and Germantown.

From Washington and Congress's perspective, this well-credentialed German nobleman who claimed to have held the rank of lieutenant general in the celebrated army of Frederick the Great, King of Prussia, arrived with an even more startling revelation — he offered to serve in the Continental Army without rank or pay and to undertake any duty assigned to him until such time as he had won the confidence of General Washington.

Just who was this enigmatic foreigner?

For one thing, he was a military man to the core. Born in 1730 to a

Prussian lieutenant and his wife, an impoverished member of a noble family, Friedrich literally grew up in the army. Prussia, a poor country with a huge army, was almost always at war, or leasing its soldiers out to other belligerent nations. By age fourteen Friedrich was a volunteer serving beside his father, now a major, at the siege of Prague. The next year he became a standard bearer, followed by steady promotions through the ranks — ensign, second lieutenant, first lieutenant, captain. During the Seven Year's War Friedrich exhibited exceptional ability on the battlefield and was selected along with twelve other promising young officers to form an elite core of future military leaders, the *Freicorps*. Their personal instructor in the advanced military arts was to be none other than the world-renowned master himself, King Frederick the Great.

Friedrich Steuben (he would add the aristocratic "von" later) had achieved the pinnacle of prestige in the Prussian Army. At age thirty-two, his career seemed limitless and assured.

Then the roof fell in. Jealousy among the senior officers of Steuben and his fellow *Freicorps* members combined with various intrigues at Court to seal their demise. In Steuben's case, his temper was used against him. Drawn into a confrontation with the powerful and ruthless Count von Anhalt, Steuben foolishly insulted the nobleman which brought the King's anger down on him.

Shortly thereafter, in 1763, Steuben was summarily relieved of duty. In the blink of an eye he had gone from *wunderkind* officer with twenty years of distinguished service under his belt, to an unemployed, virtually destitute former soldier without even a military pension to call his own.

Over the decade that followed, Steuben wandered over much of Europe with his friend and patron, Prince Joseph of Prussia, seeking, but never securing, a post in the officer corps of one of the royal families. When the prince's finances finally collapsed, he and von Steuben (who had taken not only "von" but added the lofty title of Baron) crisscrossed Germany and France, one step ahead of their creditors.

With disaster closing in, von Steuben met and impressed the French agent Pierre Augustin Caron de Beaumarchais, who put the former Prussian officer in touch with Benjamin Franklin and Silas Deane, America's representatives at the French Court.

Franklin liked what he saw in von Steuben, especially his experience as a drill instructor, and promptly commissioned him on his own authority as a lieutenant general. So the Baron played loose with his credentials and had never held a rank higher than captain. He talked gruffly and looked the part of a tough, storybook Prussian Field Officer. And so, with a glowing letter of introduction and appointment from Dr. Franklin in hand, Baron von

Steuben sailed off to the strange English-speaking land across the ocean, leaving his angry creditors and turbulent European life behind him forever. Whatever hopes he might yet harbor for a better life, they lay to the distant west, across the chilly December seas.

Von Steuben's impact on the American Army at Valley Forge began the first day he arrived. In a breathtakingly short time he revolutionized the way Americans fought. With imagination and panache, writing new rules as he went, von Steuben taught veterans and recruits alike to march in four-man-wide formations (far more effective than the single or Indian-file which was the only technique the Americans knew). He also introduced the soldiers to a streamlined manual of arms that allowed them to fire more rapidly and accurately than ever before, and showed them how to maneuver whole regiments as quickly as the British. Von Steuben also shared his tactics for seizing an opportunity in the heat of battle and shutting off an enemy's advantage. Under his watchful eye the troops soon mastered the secrets of charging en masse and reforming under battlefield conditions that had yielded only chaos and panicked flight in the past. And on an individual level, the Baron taught the men how to employ the bayonet with deadly effectiveness.

In short, he took an undisciplined, loosely structured group of individuals and in less than ninety days transformed them into a formidable fighting force, eager to take on the British Army that had sent them to ignoble defeat time and time again.

Professionally, physically, and psychologically the American Army that stood in proud even rows on the parade field in May of 1778 was not the disheveled group of men who retreated into winter quarters the past December. This Army had risen like a phoenix from the ashes, and the Merlin responsible for the incantation was the fallen military angel who had to order, plead, and curse at the soldiers through an interpreter — Baron Friedrich von Steuben.

General Washington was well aware of the Baron's achievements. He wrote to Congress asking that von Steuben's rank of lieutenant general be confirmed. Congress agreed and also named him Inspector General of the Army.

At long last the Prussian officer whose career had been derailed for fifteen harrowing years was back on track. He had what he always dreamed of — a grateful employer who embraced his particular brand of military genius. But for all his accomplishments at Valley Forge, the career soldier knew that the largest question of all remained unanswered — would this newly invigorated force take its training from the parade field to the battlefield. Could it fight, and defeat, the most powerful army on earth.

Tuesday, May 5, 1778

Miss Caitlin Serling
Oakmont on the Potomac
Montgomery County, Maryland

My Dear Caitlin:

First, let me thank you for your delightful letters and thoughtful gifts. They have illuminated the darkest moments in this offtimes dreadful place.

In the most recent correspondence I received (dated April 15 extant) you inquired as to the daily routine of myself and the soldiery here at Valley Forge. I will most happily respond to the best of my ability — to the extent that my limited literary skills will permit.

As you know, the Army under His Excellency General Washington moved into winter quarters here in mid-December. A few officers grumbled that the positioning of our camp was a poor choice. The region had long since been scoured of food. So barren was the land that even our early foraging expeditions returned with little more than exercise for their efforts.

Yet from a strategic vantage point we are well placed. General Howe and his wealthy Tory sycophants may have been dining and dancing in nearby Philadelphia while we froze by the icy shores of the Schuylkill River, but they were prevented by our poised bayonets from venturing out of the city and rallying the countryside to their standard. And so each side passed the bitter winter months — they in comfort, we in a constant state of readiness.

We certainly could have used your tender ministrations. Virtually every soldier (including your humble scribe) succumbed to the legion of maladies that seem to infest every military encampment I've known. In January, when the fierce northern winds and hip deep snows forced us to remain in our humble cabins, the men suffered most dreadfully. Hungry, ill, bored, wearing rags that would make pitiful adornment for a scarecrow, they passed their days and nights coughing and shivering and wedging dirt and snow into the chinks in the walls.

Against all of these adversities, though, the men's spir-

its and morale remained remarkably high. After the first few weeks, desertions virtually disappeared. There is something unifying in shared misery. Even humorous at times. In one cabin the men wagered among themselves as to who had the largest holes in the soles of his shoes. When that was settled, they turned to holes in their breeches. Soon mass hilarity erupted that brought the curious from other cabins to investigate the source of the mirth. And in no time whole sections of the camp were in competition to see who could claim the coveted title of the <u>King of Decrepit Clothing</u>!

As to more traditional social engagements, there have been occasional gatherings of the senior officers and their wives over a dish of coffee or tea (of course, since I am a junior officer and single I am not invited). Due to the wanting conditions there have been no dances or levees to speak of. Pleasant conversation and the periodic songfest are the mainstays of our social season.

General Washington's lady, Martha Washington, has graciously shared her husband's billeting for most of the winter. Mrs. Nathanael Greene and the wife of General Stirling and a few other ladies have likewise chosen to call Valley Forge home. These courageous women have comforted the sick and dying for days on end at the camp hospital, bringing cheer to the cheerless. Many's the time I've witnessed a lady by the bedside of a stricken soldier composing a letter, perhaps the final letter, to a loved one back home. It is a moving sight that never fails to fill me with respect and admiration.

With the improving weather in late March and April our recreational activities also took a turn for the better. I was introduced to a team game with a bat and ball that my fellow officers called cricket or wicket. On one occasion His Excellency joined in. He hit the ball further than any other player, besting my proudest drive by a good sixty paces. A marker was placed on the spot where the General's ball settled. Over the following weeks every robust man in camp attempted to better it. None did.

Amateur theatrical productions are also available to spice up our evenings. I witnessed several well-performed dramas, the best of which was <u>Cato</u>, which played to packed *and appreciative audiences every evening for a fortnight.*

But the highlight of my stay here was a "banquet" I attended at the quarters of General Baron von Steuben, a distinguished Prussian officer who served under Frederick the Great and who has recently been elevated to the post of Inspector General of the Army.

Perhaps feeling sorry for we single officers, the generous Baron (who is also unmarried) sent his emissary, Major Duponceau, with invitations stating that "None should be admitted that had on a whole pair of breeches." This condition, as you can imagine, was one in which we could all readily comply. And as the wise and whimsical General had surmised, this surprising stipulation became the centerpiece for the gaiety that marked the evening. We "feasted" on tough beefsteaks and potatoes with hickory nuts for dessert.

In lieu of wine we had some kind of mystery liquor with which one of the officers introduced us to "Salamanders" — the spirits were set afire and we drank them down, flame and all! Such a merry crew of ragamuffins as we fellows were never brought together.

General von Steuben's skills as a drillmaster have caused a transformation in this Army that I would have scarce thought possible. He began by selecting 120 men from the line, of which I was one, and infusing us with his vast knowledge of military movements and the correct handling of weapons. He taught us to march together, wheel, deploy, reform, retire in good order, counterattack, and execute all manner of battlefield maneuver with excellent precision.

On the company level, we were taught the correct way to carry arms, stand at ease, present arms, load, aim, fire by platoons, and to charge with bayonets. Along the way he filled us with a soldier's pride and upright bearing.

Once we were thoroughly indoctrinated in his martial techniques, the Baron sent us forth like apostles to train our units in his methods. This was accomplished in short order and the overall results were astonishing.

The Army executed a vast array of precise maneuvers under the critical eyes of General Washington, General von Steuben, and the other officers of the senior staff. All without a flaw. Whole battalions moved with the ease of a single company. Moreover, the pride and confidence of the officers and men in the lines soared. We felt like seasoned veterans; master craftsmen in the trade of war. Everyone seemed eager to test his new skills on the swaggering British host that had snuggled warm, safe, and secure in Philadelphia. We may have endured the cold winter, but they will know the hottest summer!

I shall hold ever dear my vivid image of the Baron, red-faced with anger, straining to come up with a stream of profanities that would convey his wrath at one point in our failure to understand and execute his orders. Finally, in utter frustration, he turned to his subordinate and instructed him to "swear at the men on my behalf in English." Thereafter he would roar his curses in German, translate them into French for the aide, who would then translate them into English for us. Rather than feel ashamed or admonished, these drawn out expletives became a comical farce that we all soon grew to enjoy immensely. At first the Baron was confused by our laughter, but when it was explained to him the good-hearted Prussian joined right in and we all shared heartily in the merriment.

How I wish Congress and the state governments had employed the same vigor in redressing the legitimate grievances of the men that General von Steuben has invested in our training.

Clothing is still in tatters, many weapons have rusted or rotted, the sick die from want of adequate medicines and physicians, and local farmers and merchants grow rich and fat selling their wares to the British and their Tory allies — leaving those who fight for the Noble Cause of American Freedom to search in the woods like animals for something to eat.

And all the while the politicians in every state turn a deaf ear to the very army that stands between their necks and a hangman's noose. I'm certain that many a devout soldier who has remained steadfast throughout this brutal trial — tightening his belt daily, burying beloved friends in the snow — would <u>leap</u> at the opportunity to stretch a Congressman's neck. I would say "A Pox On All Politi-

cians," but I realize that not all are to blame. Your own father is working tirelessly in the Maryland Legislature to relieve the suffering of the soldiers in the field. Still, it must be Divine Wisdom that this Revolution shall be decided by the strength of the men in arms rather than the wits of politicians. For if it were the latter, we would all be wearing chains today.

Soon we will leave this place. Valley Forge. My home and the home of the American Army for six long months. Little will remain to mark our presence here. Our suffering. Our death. Our rebirth. Only the memories of the men, and these we take with us. In years to come I hope people will remember Valley Forge with reverence. Honoring the soldiers who froze here, starved here, but refused to give up the fight. It is their spirit that will remain. And that is enough.

With Warmest Personal Regards,
Your Most Obedient Servant,

Charles

P.S. Wonderful news! Just as I finished this letter there was a major commotion outside. I thought we were being attacked! When I ran outside my cabin, sword in hand, I was informed by a private that General Washington had just received word that the alliance with France has been signed! Already cannons are booming in celebration. Men are hurling their hats (and each other) in the air in jubilation. At last we have an ally with unlimited resources and a navy that can contest the British on the high seas. God Bless the King of France!

Chapter 12

In May of 1778, after a wonderful send off party called The Miscianza, General Howe boarded a warship awaiting him on the Delaware River and sailed with his brother, Admiral Richard Howe, from Philadelphia back to England. For them the war was now over.

Howe's replacement, General Henry Clinton, prepared to evacuate Philadelphia by mid-June and transport his army of nearly 10,000 soldiers and over 3,000 Loyalists to his headquarters in New York City. The Loyalists were sent by ship, but Sir Henry led his troops and a huge supply train of 1,500 wagons full of military plunder by the overland route.

At 3 a.m. on June 18th the sprawling caravan began to move. There were several routes available to Clinton, but to camouflage the movements of so large and plodding a mass would be impossible. He knew the risk he took of ambush. Washington, too, saw Clinton's vulnerability, but to him it spoke not of risk, but opportunity.

In six days Clinton's lumbering exodus managed to cover just thirty-five miles. The weather was favorable and the ground relatively firm, but the wagons were heavy laden and the rutted roads made for slow passage.

Washington, of course, knew every movement of Clinton's army. Over the long bitter winter at Valley Forge he watched his adversaries in Philadelphia, snug, enjoying balls and festivities the likes of which the city had never seen, all the while plotting his strategy for intercepting the British when they were once again on the march.

At a council of his general officers, Washington was surprised and a bit annoyed to learn that most favored nothing more than some minor harassment of the British Column. His second-in-command, the recently released prisoner of war General Charles Lee, opposed even that.

But Washington's army was up to 13,500 strong and all of his instincts said that now was the time to strike. The Americans who had retreated to Valley Forge war-weary and demoralized, and then nearly froze and starved there, were now miraculously transformed by von Steuben into a powerful, disciplined fighting force, itching for revenge. Washington gave the general order. The Army would march.

Lafayette and von Steuben alone favored Washington's plan. The drag of the baggage train, they felt, left the British open for attack. The questions remaining were where and when.

Clinton feared getting caught in a pincer move on the shore of the Raritan River between Washington from the south and Gates, who he mistakenly assumed was marching down from Saratoga. So he veered to the northeast at Allentown in a new route that would take him through the pastoral county seat — Monmouth Court House.

To guard his passage during this narrow and exposed stretch, Clinton deployed the Hessian General von Knyphausen with 4,000 troops at the van, and took personal control of the 6,000 member rear, the cream of the British Army in North America. General Cornwallis stood as Sir Henry's second-in-command.

The particularly brutal summer's heat sapped the energy of the King's men on the march who labored under packs weighing sixty pounds and more and who still wore woolen winter uniforms. Each day a few more would perish from sunstroke or sheer exhaustion. When they reached Monmouth Court House, Clinton mercifully decided to order a day of rest.

Meanwhile, Washington had left his army's baggage and tents at Hopewell and sent General Wayne ahead with 1,000 New Hampshire regulars in a reconnaissance in force. Wayne advanced to Englishtown, about five miles west of Monmouth Court House. From there he sent out scouting parties in all directions to probe the enemy's position for strengths and weaknesses. His remaining troops kept their muskets primed and ready.

Washington marched the bulk of his army through the night to support Wayne should the British turn abruptly and force the action. Once in position, Washington again called his generals together to discuss strategy.

As senior officer, General Lee was offered the command of the assault force, which numbered about 6,000 men. Lee, arrogant and utterly disdainful of the American soldier's ability to fight, had few supporters and no friends. But he had been a commissioned officer in the British Army before the Revolution and there was an aura to that. He also came from a distinguished Virginia family with connections at the highest levels of government. Lee had been received with enthusiasm at Valley Forge after more than a year as a prisoner of war. However, his time spent as a guest of the British high command only served to galvanize in his own twisted mind the conviction held by the majority of His Majesty's officers that the Yankee Doodle army was a hopeless rabble that would cut and run in a set piece European-style battle. "Take them from behind their walls and trees. Make them march into the field in formation to fight like men. And watch them whimper and die like the miserable wretches they are!" Lee heard and believed.

Because of this, Lee vascilated in accepting the command. At first he refused it outright, and Washington turned to Lafayette (probably much relieved since he had as little faith in Lee as anyone else). But then Lee changed his mind and demanded that he be reinstated. Bowing to military protocol, Washington agreed. For the rest of his life he would regret his decision.

On June 27th Washington gave the order to attack the rear of the British column without delay. His intent was to force a major engagement. Early on the morning of the 28th — a blistering hot day — Lee's advance cavalry fell upon the British rear guard under Cornwallis. The terrain was not favorable to a general battle. Pine stands were criss-crossed by lengthy ravines and creeks. With poor communications and no plan of action, Lee's force groped for the enemy along the road. It was nearly noon before the majority of the Americans, numbering 5,000, aligned themselves haphazardly to face Cornwallis's 2,000 infantrymen.

Artillery fire burst from both lines signaling the outbreak of the battle, but from the beginning the Americans seemed in disarray. They clearly had the advantage numerically, but Lee didn't know how to press the action. Units began to shift about in an incomprehensible pattern. General Wayne was exposed on his left, and he pulled back in bewilderment. As General William Maxwell, Colonel Charles Scott, and Wayne began to give ground, the old unspoken fears returned to the men on the line. Was this Long Island and Kip's Bay all over again? Without waiting for orders to withdraw, or even firing their weapons in the enemy's direction, soldiers began to panic and turn tail. A rout looked imminent.

But a portion of the line held firm. Several companies dug in their heels and began returning shot and shell in earnest.

Lieutenant Charles Royal, in the center of Wayne's "flying army," stood atop a rise and directed the fire of his men, his father's sword drawn and gleeming in the bright sunlight. Suddenly a deafening volley from the advancing grenadiers decimated Charles's position and men fell back, cursing and clutching their bodies in agony. Charles lay on the ground as a cloud of gunpowder smoke tumbled over him. As it cleared he felt and saw the warm red pool of blood growing beneath his left shoulder. Quickly he ripped off his sash to stanch the wound and, using his sword as a cane, managed to regain his footing.

"Fall back men!" he cried, "To that knoll and regroup!"

With muskets and powder horns in one hand, knives and tomahawks in the other, carrying the wounded as best they could, the soldiers hurried over the 200 yards or so to the momentary refuge of the small hill. There was a broken fence at the crest and they dove over it and wheeled about on their bellies to face the onrushing, screaming enemy. There was no time to tend to wounds or the wounded. As fast as they could load they fired and fired again.

Much of the American line had by now disintegrated, but here and at several scattered points the fighting continued. From the woods behind, sporatic musket fire helped thin the massed British advance and the artillery was brought back in good order. What had began as a rout now more closely resembled a grudging retreat. The British did not have a sufficient number of fresh troops on hand to pursue the fleeing Americans; not so long as these stubborn pockets of resistance persisted.

Cornwallis chose to regroup and mount a steady advance, satisfied that this sharp engagement had only proven once more the ineffectiveness of these Yankee Doodle soldiers.

On the American side, panic quickly subsided just as General Washington galloped up graven-faced with the main body of the army and began bombarding Lee and other senior officers with pointed questions. There had been no major battle. Lee and his bumbling subordinates had withdrawn en masse at the first skirmish!

Washington was outraged, but it was at moments like this, when disaster appeared imminent, that he was at his best. He summarily dispatched the stammering Lee with a flood of invectives and personally took charge of the battleground. A scout galloped in with the news that the British were but fifteen minutes away and closing fast. Washington hastily organized a line of defense on the east side of West Ravine. Cool and decisive up on his great white mount, Washington inspired the men's spirit to stand fast.

Putting Wayne's brigade directly in the line of march, Washington hurriedly rode back along Englishtown Road and brought up Stirling and Greene's detachments, who set up on a ridge behind Wayne to protect his flanks. As the remnants of the battered army that had now become the delaying force that allowed the Americans to reform fell behind the American lines, Washington called out his congratulations to them. "Well done, boys! Your bravery will not go unrewarded this day I promise you. Reform with your brother soldiers!" When the British arrived, they faced a quite different fighting force.

The vicious battle raged on throughout that afternoon amid temperatures that topped $100°$. Fortunately, the Americans had placed themselves in a strong defensive position on high ground, with a swamp in front and a thick woods anchoring their left flank. On Comb's Hill to their right, Knox's fieldpieces, many of which were those hauled out of Fort Ticonderoga two and a half years before, provided a deadly crossfire.

Despite the obviously favorable position of the Americans, Clinton slowly brought up his main force to press the offensive. In sporadic assaults up and down the line British units rushed valiantly ahead only to be cut down time and again by the well entrenched Americans. Cornwallis himself led a courageous cavalry charge against Greene's position only to see the majority of his horsemen fall beneath a hail of fiery lead.

Men's emotions were at a fever pitch — heart's pounding, faces blackened by spent gunpowder, shirts soaked through with sweat, fire, explosions, the ghastly shrieks of the bloodied men and horses filling the ears while smoke stung the eyes. Hellish carnage lay in every direction and even under foot.

And through the worst of it rode General Washington, shouting orders and encouragement. Resplendent. Fearless. A concerned, but totally controlled countenance. As calm as if he were sitting with Martha on his porch at Mount Vernon gazing out at his grandchildren frolicking on the gently sloping front lawn with the Potomac flowing peacefully beyond.

A huge man on a massive horse making no effort to disguise his presence, Washington was the easiest target on the field. But there must have been something magical in the great man's stature that trancended the roar of battle and entered the hearts of the enemy. Washington, miraculously, was never hit.

At one point, as the Continental line wavered, Charles turned to see Washington sitting majestically in command on his horse nearby. "Look men!" he cried. "The General himself is here for our relief! Hold fast men. Hold fast and this day will yet be ours!" For an instant the two men's eyes met across the battlefield and the General bowed his head in respect. A moment later an explosion sent Charles crashing to the ground again in agony, this time from a log fragment that smashed into his left knee.

By 6 p.m. the British energy was spent and they pulled back in good order to beyond Middle Ravine. His men exhausted and without sufficient reserves, Washington was unable to mount a counterattack. During the night that followed, Clinton borrowed a tactic from Washington and stole a march toward New York. On July 1st the British Column reached Sandy Hook and the protection of the cannon on their men-of-war in New York Harbor.

The Battle of Monmouth Court House was a confused blessing for the Americans. It had begun with promise, turned into a rout, and then re-emerged as a significant victory — with a ringing endorsement of all the drillwork and discipline infused into the army by von Steuben at Valley Forge. The Continentals had endured a furious frontal assault and had not cracked. Indeed, they had thrown the British back with casualties totaling 1,200 men — four times those suffered by the Americans. The tide of the war would now turn. And the direction would be south.

It was General Charles Lee who would be charged and held responsible for the "unnecessary, disorderly, and shameful retreat" at Monmouth Court House. Adding to his woes was the equally serious charge that he had shown disrespect to the commander-in-chief.

Washington called for a courtmartial, to be presided over by General Nathanael Greene. Even Lee's staunchest critics within the army and Congress were distressed at seeing such a senior officer hauled before his peers for judgment.

But Washington would have nothing less, and Lee welcomed the trial as well, seeing it as an opportunity to clear his name. As officer after officer gave his sworn testimony of the events, though, it became apparent that Lee had the support of virtually no one. The evidence mounted while Lee seethed in contempt. The final witness called before the military tribunal was a battered infantry lieutenant from Wayne's command — Charles Royal.

Charles, leaning heavily on his crutch, began by saying he had had no direct contact with Lee during the initial encounter (neither had virtually all of Lee's subcommanders), but it was clear from his vantage point that chaos ruled the day. "I witnessed whole units moved into position, and then uprooted and sent in another direction without so much as firing a volley," Charles testified. "The scene became so tragically farcical that platoons marched directly through one another in utter confusion. No officer or man seemed to know the plan. All the while the precise British formations kept up a withering fire. Is it any wonder that when our foes charged with the bayonet, our men ran for their lives? We had come to fight, not to be slaughtered like pigs!"

"Liar!" cried Lee. "All damn lies!"

"Silence!" General Greene ordered, pounding his fist on the table.

"And damn your impudence, Greene! You Rhode Island—"

Greene exploded, "Shut your mouth this instant General Lee! One more word out of you and *by thunder* I'll have you bound and gagged!"

Lee grudgingly turned away from Greene's burning glare, stewing all the while.

When relative calm had returned, the officer to Greene's left asked, "Is there any additional testimony you have to make, Lieutenant Royal?"

"Only this, sir. The men acquitted themselves as well as could be expected throughout the day. None could say otherwise." And then he added with a stern bearing, "If we had senior officers whose skills at leadership were equal to the courage of those men asked to fight and die in the face of the enemy, then this war would have been won long ago, sir."

Charles knew that his statement was a blanket indictment that included all of the general staff seated before him. But he didn't care. He had seen too many brave Patriots fall because of the ineptitude, drunkeness, or outright cowardice of those in command. *If this be insubordination,* he thought, *then make the most of it!*

A few jaws stiffened, but no one took the bait.

"That will be all, Lieutenant Royal. Dismissed," said Greene.

Charles waited outside with the other witnesses and did not hear the judgment of the courtmartial board, which was issued without delay. Charles Lee was found guilty on all counts and later suspended from the army. For the remainder of his life, this imperious, difficult soldier from one of Virginia's leading families would be shunned in disgrace.

On exiting the courthouse, Lee's wrath fell upon Charles. "You damn scoundrel!" he scowled with an accusatory finger thrust directly into Charles's face. Another officer interceded with a plea that Charles merely spoke the truth on his oath, but Lee berated him, "One man's truth is another's damnable lie! What stands before me is not a brave officer, but a lowly political opportunist; a scoundrel who would rise in the world by defaming his betters! The son of a renowned villain!"

Charles angrily threw down his crutch and drew his sword as Lee went for his, but the guards quickly engulfed them both, pulling Lee away, but not before he could vow an oath. "We shall meet again one day *Mr. Royal.* And on that day, by God, we will both be free to draw our swords!"

Over the days that followed, Charles received what scanty medical attention was available. His wound was dressed and a splint made to support his damaged knee. It would be some time, if ever, before he could comfortably ride a horse. Charles wondered if the end of his military career was at hand.

"You sent for me, sir?" Charles stood at attention, listing a bit to his left, inside General Wayne's tent.

"At ease . . . You conducted yourself admirably during the recent engagement, Lieutenant." Wayne remained seated on his folding stool beside his chest. He motioned for Charles to sit on his cot.

"Thank you, sir," Charles said, grimacing as he painfully lowered himself.

"I have two items to convey to you, Royal. Both of which I believe will meet with your approval."

"Sir?"

"First, your battle wounds need time to heal properly. You won't be marching on to New York with us. As of now, you are granted an extended leave of duty." Wayne expected this would be received as good news by Charles, but he looked more perplexed than happy.

"But where will I go, General? My family and fortune are lost. The army is all I have."

Wayne was blunt. "You're of no use to the army in your present state. Surely there's a friend or safe haven for you somewhere."

Charles thought for a moment. "There might be one place."

"Good!" replied Wayne, without asking for particulars. "And when you are well-mended you will return, but *not* in your current station." His grim countenance told Charles that he was now to pay the price for his conduct at the courtmartial.

"You are no longer known to this army as Lieutenant Royal."

"I understand, sir."

"You are hereby promoted *two levels* to the rank of major!"

Charles's mouth fell open, just as Wayne had gleefully hoped.

"Now don't get too excited, Royal. All this means for the moment is that the pay you weren't receiving as a lieutenant, you won't be receiving as a major. Nevertheless, congratulations son!" Wayne extended his hand to Charles.

Charles was still in a state of shock. "I never expected such an honor, sir. I thought I would be demoted."

"What! Preposterous! A man of your fighting skills who also has the courage to look any man in the eye and speak your mind — hell, boy, we need *more* men like you, not fewer."

Before departing, Wayne asked Charles if he had any money to cover expenses on his trip. Charles reached into his pocket and withdrew the entire sum of his monetary worth in this world — nine cents. The General shook his head sadly, opened his own trunk, and extracted some coins. Charles at first refused them. "Please accept these as a gift from a brother officer," Wayne implored. "You'll need money to eat once you leave camp. I'm fairly sure they will feed me here." Charles thanked his general, hobbled to his feet, saluted, and left.

Charles crutched his way back to his tent and began packing his pathetic belongings in his bed roll. In his mind there was only one place that offered any prospect for peace — and it surely wasn't in Boston. Before he left camp for his first leave in over three years, Charles posted a letter to the single person on earth who he knew would welcome his coming — *Miss Caitlin Serling, Oakmont on the Potomac, Montgomery County, Maryland.*

Chapter 13

Sweeping white gates hung from multicolored brick stanchions laced in ivy garlands offered a gracious welcome to Charles as he passed through them. He looked all about the great expanse as his horse clip-clopped along the broad, hard-packed, tree-guarded drive that led the way into Oakmont on the Potomac. Just ahead stood the great white manor house. Strong, elegant, dignified, bespeaking wealth and taste that carried throughout the generations.

The entry road diverged into a wide circular approach enclosing a lush green lawn with dozens of well-tended shrubs forming hedge rows along a bisecting brick path. Summer flowers burst forth from four large equally positioned beds along the rim of the lawn, with the largest and most vibrant closest to the front entrance of the mansion. Lilacs, daisies, white and red roses, lilies, and several flowers that Charles did not recognize, but whose shocking beauty amazed him, combined in a picture that surely rivaled Eden at the Creation. Never before had he seen any landscape so beautiful, so deliciously fragrant, so lovingly cared for. Certainly nothing in Boston or Cambridge could compare. A paradise on earth. Created and tended by slaves. Human chattel. The contradiction did not escape him.

A stable boy took the reins of his horse as Charles slowly, painfully dismounted. He was parched from the searing heat, his left shoulder throbbed from the jouncing it received on the journey and his left leg was completely numb. He staggered to one of the great white carved pillars supporting the front porch and braced himself against it until his leg regained life.

A large, stern faced man with a billowing white shirt, tan breeches, and knee-length riding boots splattered with mud approached Charles in long determined strides. He spoke without offering his hand or a hint of warmth.

"You would be Charles Royal would you not?"

Charles nodded he was. There was something about this man that told him to be on his guard.

"I'm Fowler, the overseer. Judge Serling's been called away to a neighbor's. He shan't be long. He instructed me to show you in and offer you refreshment."

With a wave of the hand, Fowler directed Charles to enter the mansion.

Before Charles could reach for the door knob, the doors were swung open by two black house servants waiting on the inside. They bowed deeply, but said nothing. Nor did they raise their eyes to meet his.

Charles looked about him. Elaborately crafted woodwork framed every room's passageway in the Georgian Revival manner. Glowing cream paint covered the oak paneling, highlighted by lines of peach, sea green, and white. The entry chandelier hung about twelve feet above the foyer and sparkled with hundreds of translucent cut crystal ornaments. A richly carpeted curved center staircase with a deep-polished caramel stair rail led to the upper levels. Fowler directed Charles to a large sitting room off the main hall.

"You'll be comfortable here until the Judge returns. Cassie!"

A black servant girl appeared immediately.

"Bring our visitor a cool drink and refreshments and anything else he desires."

With a slight curtsy the girl turned and left. Fowler spoke to Charles without emotion, "I have work to attend to. Cassie will see to your needs." And without further ceremony Fowler departed.

Charles sat down in a red velvet chair and dropped his hat and riding gloves on the mahogany table before him and stretched out. It was a blessed relief after his long, arduous journey.

A walnut pantry along the wall held English-style silver pitchers and serving trays and Delph china. Over the fireplace mantel hung a three-quarter length portrait of a woman in a royal blue gown with a plunging neckline wearing a jeweled necklace. She bore a resemblance to Caitlin, except that she was older, perhaps thirty, and had auburn hair. But the eyes were the same — a merry, dancing green that the artist had wisely endowed with a penetrating gaze that was at once all-knowing, yet all-forgiving.

After partaking of some fine Madiera, fresh fruits and cheese, Charles moved to the window and looked out across the northwest lawn to the river beyond. There was a small dock by the river's edge, but the plantation was situated above Great Falls and the water level was far too low for any sea going vessel to reach there. *Those barges alongside must carry the crops down river to Alexandria where they would be packed aboard ships plying the Atlantic trade,* Charles thought. His father's merchant fleet may well have transported Judge Serling's cash crops to markets far away and returned with the excellent furniture and furnishings — and wine — that graced this very room. And so both men had prospered.

Near a small stream that ran down a sloping field, Charles noticed three windmills. *For flour,* he thought, *And cornmeal.* The well furrowed wagon path leading to the mills suggested that Judge Serling had cornered a sizeable portion of this business as well.

Several black field hands stooped to tend the vegetable gardens between the manor house and the path leading to the stables and slave quarters. The men wore straw hats and the women calico bandanas. Most of the children ran about naked as the moment they arrived in this world. The work proceeded slowly, methodically, with thrusting hands plucking weeds and tamping the shoots into the deep brown rows as the small hunched army moved along. Passive conversation seemed to be taking place, but Charles did not discern any laughter, or much interest in the work.

A large open gazebo shaded by two towering oaks offered an excellent view of the river. Surely many a sultry twilight hour was passed by family and friends in genial conversation under that great bell shaped roof.

Charles leafed casually through a few books and pamphlets strewn on a side table. Agricultural publications mostly, but what was this? A well-worn copy of Thomas Paine's *COMMON SENSE.* And a personalized autograph — *To my dear friend Abraham Serling, brother in the Common Cause. — Thos. Paine*

There was a commotion outside. A rider approached.

Charles could hear a husky man's voice. "He has arrived? Good! See to my horse good fellow."

Just as Charles limped into the hallway, the servants opened the twin doors and in strode the master of Oakmont Plantation, Judge Abraham Serling, in a gray riding outfit with a crop in his leather gloved right hand.

"Welcome home Jedge," said the smiling servants, almost in unison.

"Thank you my fellows. It is a grand day indeed for we have a distinguished guest with us. Is it my honor to be addressing Charles Royal, sir?"

"The honor is mine, sir."

The Judge shook Charles's hand firmly and warmly. "Sir, my daughter has told me of your bravery, your daring in saving her life. I am in your debt more than I can express."

"Thank you, sir."

"You no doubt wonder after her. She is well and attending to the wounded at the hospital in Rockville. She is the head of nursing there. What with most of the doctors off to war, her skills are much in demand. Though she would be cross at me for telling you, she is frantically training two women to stand in for her so she might return home to spend time with you. We will be off to retrieve her Saturday next. Until then, my home is at your disposal."

With a wide smile the Judge slapped Charles on the shoulder and motioned him ahead to his study down the hall. "Come, my boy. We have much to discuss. How goes the war?"

The oak lined walls and inlaid bookcases of the study framed a large marble fireplace. Books were everywhere. And to a height where ladders were placed on both sides of the room to reach the upper shelves. Leather upholstered Chesterfield couches and chairs were placed around the oriental rug in the center of the room. There were writing and work desks with swivel chairs, a magnificent globe on an oaken stand, and portraits of family members of past generations. Charles's eyes fixed on an object by the window.

"Are you a man of science, Major Royal?" Charles wondered how the Judge knew about his promotion when he remembered the insignia General Wayne had pinned on him just before he left his tent.

"Hardly, sir. My studies at Harvard were all too brief."

The Judge pulled a chair over to his telescope. "Searching the heavens at night is a hobby for me." He flipped open a large book. "See here. Here are the planets, stars, constellations. On a clear night with this device you can fairly well see them all. See Saint Peter himself at the Eternal Gates! If you like, we'll look together one night."

"I should like that very much, sir."

"Done then! Cassie!"

"Yessir, Judge."

"Is dinner on the make?"

"Oh yessir. Mutton, carrots, sweet potato, and that cherry cobbler you so fond of. Mammy say it be ready soon."

"Excellent! You've met our guest?"

"Yessir."

"Off with you then." With a smile and quick curtsy Cassie disappeared.

Charles noted how differently the house servants behaved with the Judge than they had with the overseer Fowler. But he had just arrived, a guest, and decided it was not his place or time to comment. Until now slavery was little more than an abstract to him. A peculiar institution. He had known several northern gentlemen in Boston and elsewhere who kept black slaves as body servants. But in the South, slavery was far more pervasive. It went to the very soul of society and dictated the lifestyle of the family that owned them. Caitlin had told Charles, almost in passing, that her father owned nearly 200 slaves. They performed all of the menial chores on the plantation, but were also skilled craftsmen — blacksmiths, coopers, tailors and seamstresses, bootmakers — trades that earned free whites a comfortable living and status in their communities. Here these artisans were just slaves; the property of their masters, who could do with them, to them, whatever they wished.

Caitlin, and the Judge, did not refer to them as slaves, though, but rather as "our people." Almost as if they were employed of their free will. Truth or rationalization. A benevolent working and living arrangement, or simply another form of tyranny; one far more insidious and cruel than any the British might impose. For now Charles would keep his own counsel on this sensitive matter. He would watch and learn.

Over dinner Charles told the Judge about the events at Saratoga. About his and Caitlin's narrow escape in the night. About the Judge's brave nephew Nigel who probably paid for his selfless act of chivalry with his life. The Judge sat like a child, spellbound, absorbing every word, never interrupting. Charles went on to discuss the battles he had participated in, plus his opinion of the current state of the American Army and its prospects for the future. The Judge proved very sympathetic to the plight of the common soldier. Charles was certain he saw the Judge's eyes moisten as he learned the details of the terrible ordeal that the men endured at Valley Forge. "God bless and preserve our heroes," the Judge finally said softly.

When Charles finished, the Judge raised his glass in a toast. "To the Great Cause and all who serve it!"

"To the Cause," Charles responded, and they drank deeply.

"And to His Excellency, General George Washington," the Judge added. "Our Moses who will lead us to the Promised Land."

"To His Excellency, General Washington."

"I envy you, Major Royal. I do. Despite the great adversities under which you labor, you have taken an active role in this great struggle. And when we emerge victorious, as we surely will, it will be the men of your generation who will shape the future of this great land." The Judge raised his glass once more. "So to you, good sir, and victory!"

Charles bowed his head in humble acknowledgement and the two men emptied their glasses.

"Your son, sir, he serves in the South?"

"Master Randolph, Rake to all who know him, does indeed serve in the Southern Campaign. Are you familiar with a South Carolina partisan colonel by the name of Francis Marion?" Charles replied that he was not.

"Letters are so few. The last I received is now nearly five months old. Rake and what's left of his men have taken to the swamps with Marion. They live on snakes and berries and fight British, Tory, and alligators. It does not go well I fear . . . not well," his voice trailed off.

After dinner that evening and over the days that followed, Charles learned much about the Serlings.

Judge Abraham Serling, squire of Oakmont on the Potomac, was the present standard bearer for one of the oldest and best connected families in the colony. The tract that eventually grew into the plantation was bequeathed by Leonard Calvert, Second Lord Baltimore to the Judge's direct ancestor, Aaron O'Dale, in 1645 and had been in the family for six generations.

The Judge had served as a colonel of militia in his day and had distinguished himself at the Battle of Falling Trees during the French and Indian War where he was wounded. To this day he carried several pellets in his left breast.

The title of "Judge" was somewhat honorific. He had no legal training whatsoever. But when the county court met he was called upon to preside because of his lofty standing in the community, his wealth and bearing, his wisdom in all matters, and his uncorruptibility, which none would ever question. Judge Serling was also Montgomery County's elected representative to the Maryland General Assembly.

He was a planter by vocation and avocation, experimenting liberally with crops and rotations. Also trees and flowers. He kept extensive gardens that would be the envy of any English country lord. His cash crops were primarily wheat, tobacco, corn, and, by the Potomac watershed, rice. He also had the largest cattle herd in four counties.

But his passion was horses — or more particularly, horse racing. As a lad and young man he was widely acclaimed for the way he sat a horse and his fearlessness in competition. He crossbred his stock with meticulous detail and developed a string of stallions that won the annual races in Maryland virtually every year. His winnings from the bets he placed on his animals did much to augment his fortune. It was the only gambling he believed in.

"If you know your horse and those of your opponents, then it's not a wager, but an investment. Any man who places his hard earned money on the chance turn of a card or roll of the dice is a damn fool!"

One spill too many, coupled with his war injuries, forced Judge Serling to retire early as a horse racer. He trained his man servant Junius to ride in his place. During the racing season the two horse lovers would travel throughout Maryland, up to Pennsylvania, and through much of Virginia, preferring regions where the Judge was less known so the betting odds would be more in their favor.

Junius became as skilled a horseman as his master and the Judge beamed with unabashed pride at his slave's accomplishments. Through a generous share of their winnings, Junius had long ago earned enough money to buy his freedom, but he never thought seriously of it. In his heart, he and the Judge were a team, and the sporting life was as much a thrill to him as it was to the Judge. The money was good, the work was fine, and he got to whip the white boys fair and square.

The Judge loved Caitlin. She physically resembled her mother, but was more vivacious, impatient, and headstrong. Rather than rein in his daughter, the Judge saw to it that she received an excellent formal education. If a subject interested her, she soon excelled at it. Caitlin spoke both French and German fluently and was so proficient at mathematics that her father had her audit his books once a year. Her free spirit would be her downfall in the more ladily arts, however, and she was turned out of both Mrs. Hoarsley's School for Girls in Baltimore and the Langley Finishing School in New York. The Judge didn't mind a bit. He had sent her there because it was the fashion for girls of Caitlin's standing and expected. But the Judge had no understanding and even less interest in the demure manners and coy talk of the tea room. The fact that it had equally small appeal to his daughter the Judge took as a plus.

After his wife Sarah's death, the Judge was approached by every dowager in the county on behalf of a daughter, granddaughter, niece, friend, friend of a friend, or friend of a niece of a cousin's acquaintance. The Judge found it all amusing, if the good ladies of the colony did not. A man of Abe Serling's fortune and prominence should not go long unwed, they thought, so they set upon him at every social gathering, church service, and civic affair. As the Judge confided to Charles, half in jest, "If there's one thing a woman can't abide, it's a happily single man."

Once, when the court was in session in Rockville with Judge Serling presiding, a bold woman brought her case before the magistrate.

"I am here, Your Honor, to seek redress for a great wrong perpetrated by yourself, Your Honor, on the ladies of Maryland Colony."

"What is the charge against me," the Judge inquired.

"Failure to take a new wife!" the woman replied defiantly.

The Judge hid his wide grin in his hand until he regained his most regal demeanor. "Unweddedness is not a crime in this jurisdiction to my understanding."

"It is if you but view the scalawags and ne'er-do-wells who make up the present crop of husband material hereabouts!" the woman retorted. "Your Honor would be a fine catch, but you won't take the hook! And we, the poor fisherwomen, must go hungry! How do you respond to this charge, sir?"

The Judge paused, Solomon-like, before offering his answer. "It is true I am not wed. And I will not contest your assertions as to the poor quality of marital prospects, as I am sure you are more expert than I in this matter. But in my defense, I may yet take a bride, and in so doing negate the charges against me. I beg, therefore, for a continuance."

Hands on hips, the woman cast a squinty-eyed skeptical look. "Very well, Your Honor, but don't be too long about it!"

Judge Serling roared with laughter at the telling of the story. "I should have proposed to her on the spot! Though I generally prefer women with a few more teeth and a few less warts. By God, I hope she's found a man for her own. One who appreciates her pluck and character."

The Judge's son Rake was as wild and passionate as any man alive. He rode, lived, loved, fought, gambled, whored, drank, and laughed as if today was to be the last day of his life. "He'll be a millionaire by thirty — or destitute," the Judge had said when the lad was not yet ten.

Rake cared little for what he saw as the bucolic life of a planter. A purgatory of years spent seeding, fertilizing, harvesting, and praying for more rain — or less. One area in which he, his father, and his sister agreed on was their detestation of slavery.

To Rake, a soldier's life, with its fanciful allure of travel, glory, battle, and colorful uniforms, was the pathway to heaven. He would gladly leave Oakmont and its responsibilities to Caitlin, or the devil for that matter.

When war broke out, Rake found the nearest recruitment depot (which fortunately was forming a Patriot brigade) and promptly offered his services to the first officer he met. He brought thirty men with him and agreed to pay for all of their military and living expenses out of his own pocket. With this he was immediately commissioned a Lieutenant of Dragoons in the Maryland Line.

A valiant (if reckless) cavalry officer, Rake was promoted to captain and participated in countless skirmishes throughout southern Virginia, Georgia, and the Carolinas. He became a hardened veteran of the South's merciless brother against brother partisan war. Like Robin Hood of old, he and his men took to the dense woods and swamps — living off the land and striking when they could.

Charles also learned about the overseer, Henry Fowler. A stern, humorless man, he was left as a foundling on the steps of Oakmont. The Serlings took him in and saw that he was well cared for and received a basic country education. Even as a youth, though, a cruel streak was evident. He was punished often for the pain he seemed to enjoy inflicting on the livestock.

As an adult he proved to be a firm, sometimes harsh taskmaster. But with so many men off to war, the Judge reluctantly gave him the job of overseer. Fowler was known as a mean drunk who had fought (and beaten) most of the young toughs in the county.

Strangely, though, he had a tender heart when it came to Caitlin. They had played together as children. As they matured, Caitlin and Rake drew further apart from Fowler, but this only served to fan his infatuation with her. In his mind, her cool attitude was only her deceptive girlish way of stoking the fires of his passion. And it was working. No one, certainly not Caitlin, knew to what depth.

Chapter 14

Charles rose before dawn on the day he and the Judge were scheduled to travel to meet Caitlin. A rain was falling, and from his bedroom window Charles's mind returned to other rainy nights. Cold, crowded tents without enough blankets or dry wood to burn. The coughs, snorts, snores of soldiers, punctuated by the occasional cries of the wounded or sick or scared. Some of the smells were the same, of wet leaves and soaked earth, but the stench of unwashed bodies, refuse of all manner, beasts of burden, and, worst of all, the dead and the dying; these, mercifully, were not here.

How long a time it had been since Charles had taken for granted a full belly, a warm home, a comfortable bed, a peaceful night's sleep. Had it been just four years, or was it four lifetimes ago?

After breakfast Charles and the Judge, assisted by the slaves Damien and Big Leo, finished packing a supply wagon for the hospital. Along with sacks of fresh vegetables and three recently slaughtered pigs, there were lint bandages and several cotton shirts and fresh bedsheets. The Judge also added two casks of rum and several bottles of spirits to be used to numb the pain of the soldiers who went under the surgeon's saw. With two milking cows tied to the back, Big Leo climbed up into the wagon, took the reins, and flicked the large draft horses into motion. Charles and the Judge rode a bit ahead.

By mid-afternoon the tiny caravan arrived at the hospital. The Judge and Charles stood just outside the doorway and peered into the old rambling farmhouse that had been converted to serve the needs of Maryland's fallen heroes.

Inside they saw Caitlin hurring about giving brisk orders and directing the attending nurses and single physician on duty. She paused by the outstretched hand of a bandaged soldier who wanted someone to write a letter home to his wife in Cumberland County. As Caitlin called a nurse over to help the man, she glanced up and her eyes locked onto Charles's. She paused for a moment as a smile slowly, sweetly lit her face. Wiping her hands on her apron as she walked she called out to the physician, "Dr. Young, I'm stepping out for a moment."

"Charles."

"Caitlin."

"Judge."

"Daughter. . . . Now that we've dispensed with the formalities, why don't we have a sit down under yonder shade tree. Can a man get a cup of coffee around here?" The Judge realized with quiet satisfaction that his words fell on not one, but two sets of deaf ears.

Over the weeks that followed at Oakmont, Charles's wounds healed to the point where he could enjoy long, leisurely rides with Caitlin over fields and dales alive with flourishing crops, lush grass and clover, trees with full green leaves, and wild flowers of every vibrant color and intoxicating fragrance. In the evenings they would stroll near the mansion, and sometimes by the cool river's edge where they would enjoy the rythmic roiling of the gentle rapids and hear the high-pitched chorus of the cicadas.

As Charles had imagined on his first day, many a leisurely conversation with Caitlin and the Judge in that lovely white gazebo by the water would mark the end of a pleasant day. Somewhere the war was being fought. Desperate men with weapons of destruction stood facing each other in fields of mortal combat. But that was far, far away. Not here. Not now. This was a time for healing wounds seen and unseen. Of laughter and gentle touches. Amid the whirlwind of war, Charles and Caitlin had found a moment of peace. And they held it dear.

In late September, with much of the harvest completed, Judge Serling announced at dinner his plans to travel to Annapolis to take his seat at the provisional legislature. "I think you should join me, Charles. The other delegates would be interested to hear your first hand assessment of the army. Your experiences and opinions could prove invaluable."

Charles was a bit taken aback. "I'm no politician, Judge. And as a junior grade officer I fear my opinions would be given more weight than they deserve. And let's not forget that I'm not even a citizen of this colony, er, pardon me, state."

"Nonsense!" said the Judge, dismissing Charles's arguments with a wave of his hand. "They didn't ask if you were a local citizen when you fought for the freedom of those in New York or New Jersey, did they? It's a new age, m'boy. An *American* age. And, by God, you've earned a fighting man's right to speak. If any man says otherwise, he shall answer to me! So what is your answer then? Will you come with me to Annapolis?"

Charles turned to Caitlin for advice, and her look said that she concurred with her father. Thus encouraged, Charles acquiesced. "As you wish." The Judge was visibly pleased.

"Splendid! Once the crops are in we'll be on our way. We'll take Junius of course, but travel light. I'll write the appropriate letters tonight to secure our lodgings." With all the enthusiasm of a child hatching his secret plan, the Judge hastily excused himself from the table to begin his preparations.

When he had left the room, Caitlin, her hands clasped before her, turned her attention to Charles, displaying that gentle smile that he treasured so.

"He is very fond of you you know."

Charles turned his head to the door. "And I of him."

"I think he sees this as a way of keeping you in Maryland. At Oakmont."

"But surely he knows that I must shortly return to my unit. I am a soldier." Charles spoke more rapidly with each point. "And when the war ends I must make every effort to find what's left of my family, wherever they are, and then there's my family's fortune and reputation. I must return to Boston."

Caitlin nodded calmly at every juncture as if Charles needed to offer no explanation to her. "I know. I know. Perhaps coming to Oakmont has not made your life simpler, as you had hoped; only more complex."

"I believe you're right," Charles replied.

"And how do you intend to resolve these issues?" It was a leading question.

Charles thought before answering. "I really don't know." Caitlin waited for more, but more was not said.

For the first time since his arrival, Charles did not sleep well that night. It was the first cool evening after a long hot spell, but it was not the weather that kept him awake and tossing. With the dawn came the crowing rooster and an aria of bird songs heralding a new day. A day like many others, but different.

Much had to be done in preparation for the journey. Charles spent most of his time down on "Mercantile Row," the lane near the mansion that housed the many workshops — weavers, tanners, creamery, cooper, livery, shoemaker and the rest — that transformed Oakmont into something resembling a medieval fiefdom. He oversaw the work that must be completed before the Judge could take his leave. The Judge and Fowler discussed the final harvest and arrangements for the marketing of the cattle and crops. Charles had little contact with Fowler during his stay, but still sensed that the overseer resented his presence more and more as the length of his visit grew.

For her part, Caitlin caught up on her correspondence to friends and family, supervised the house staff and some minor repairs to the south portico and cook house, and audited the plantation's books. She also planned for her return to the hospital in Rockville.

When Charles did see her, usually at dinner, he thought Caitlin was a bit detached. The Judge dominated the conversation with animated talk of who they would meet and the likely topics of debate in Annapolis. Charles tried to remain attentive. Caitlin was more reserved.

As the days grew short until their departure, Charles grew more and more anxious. He longed to speak to Caitlin at length about his feelings for her. To take her up in his arms. To risk all in the crushing fear that she did not share his deep affection. But the time never seemed right. And soon he would be off to Annapolis. And then back to the war. And to what outcome would that lead? Damn the war! Damn it to hell! If not for this infernal war he could allow his feelings for Caitlin to develop in natural course, unrushed. But, then, if it were not for the war, he would not have come to know Caitlin at all. His sleep only worsened.

Finally the day he had been anticipating, dreading, arrived. Charles was not even sure if Caitlin would be there in the early morn to see them off, but she was. The final baggage was strapped in the wagon and the Judge was mounted on his great bay stallion, with Junius on his horse by his side.

Charles took his hat from Caitlin's hand and started out the door once, twice, but paused. Each time he turned to Caitlin, started to speak, but the words would not come out. How simple was battle when compared to this!

Caitlin knew instinctively what Charles wanted to say, but she would not help him out of his dilemma. In the time honored tradition, this was one task that he must do for himself.

"Thank you," Charles said absently as Caitlin brushed off the front of his shortcoat with her hand.

"Caitlin."

"Yes."

"Caitlin."

"Yes Charles."

"Caitlin . . . I must leave now. I must leave now and return, later, to the army."

"Yes, I know." She could all but see his anguish. And she was secretly reveling in it.

"Caitlin, there's something I've been meaning to ask you. A question. A question. A very important question."

She raised her eyebrows in anticipation. But Charles could proceed no further. And finally the moment seemed to have passed.

"Perhaps you should be off. They're waiting," she said at last, a look of disappointment and sadness that Charles had never seen before covering her face and glistening her eyes.

"Yes, perhaps so." He started to leave, but wheeled back to her one final time and blurted out, "Caitlin, will you marry me?"

She paused for the sweetest moment and searched his face intently to be sure of his sincerity. Then with a squeal of delight she flung her arms around his neck and kissed him for the first time on the lips, pushing him right out the door. Charles pulled back. "But you must understand that I have *nothing;* that I have *no right* to seek your hand."

Caitlin threw herself upon him a second time and pressed her lips hard to his. Charles stumbled backward down the steps.

Once again Charles pulled away. "I may not even survive this war. Have you thought of that?"

With tears streaming down her cheeks and a smile that could light up heaven, Caitlin placed her hands firmly on either side of Charles's face, gazed deeply into his eyes and said, "Damn you Charles Royal, kiss me this instant or I'll die in your arms!"

With his defenses shot, Charles lifted Caitlin right up off the ground as their lips met and the two turned slowly, deliciously, locked in each other's loving embrace while the Judge threw both of his arms in the air and cheered his loudest cheer.

The lavish wedding that would follow months later was but a formality. It was at this very moment, when they joined together, that they were wed.

Chapter 15

In Annapolis, Charles stepped for the first time into the world of politics and politicians. In Boston, while serving as a barman at Robinson's Tavern, the talk of politics was always in the air. But there it was with a tankard in one hand, a long-stemmed clay pipe in the other, and a wary eye always on the door. Most nights any tradesman, dock worker, or village idiot could compete for the floor with men of distinction like Sam Adams and James Otis. And fists or knives rather than artful persuasion often settled a point at issue.

Here in Annapolis were duly elected representatives from throughout Maryland. Rich, distinguished, well-bred gentlemen for the most part with tailored coats, silver buckles on their shoes, and powdered wigs. The General Assembly met in the imposing State House on a hill with a magnificent view down Francis Street, with its prominent shops that stretched to the Severn River and the Chesapeake Bay. The Assembly usually met in October after the harvest and ran until business was concluded, but rarely more than three months. Each day when the legislature was in session, a sentry was posted at the waterfront with a spyglass and a signal flag to warn of the approach of an enemy convoy. The King's Navy controlled the entire coast from Maine to Florida and a surprise attack up the Chesapeake was always a possibility.

The State House itself was built more in the classical Southern tradition than in the Puritan blockhouse style of Boston's Faneuil Hall. Its great white entryway was graced with magnificent paintings and ancient armaments arranged in patterns on the walls. The wide-planked floor was polished with linseed oil weekly and was so highly reflective that a man could almost shave by it. Great multi-paned windows with heavy velvet curtains drawn back offered elegance and light. The Assembly Hall where the delegates met featured individual writing tables with full ink bottles and new quills always at the ready.

Judge Serling raised a few issues that were of importance to his constituents during the session, but for the most part he listened to the debates rather than participate. He was a senior statesman, known to all, and he felt no need to try to impress anyone, or to be noticed. Instead, he would hear all sides of a question and then cast his vote with his conscience.

It was at the nightly political gatherings at the ubiquitous inns and taverns that surrounded the State House that the Judge held court. More comfortable with informal dialogue than Parliamentarian rules and procedures, the Judge would lead the way till the wee hours, whether the conversation involved thorny political issues of the day, prominent political figures, or bawdy stories and tall tales. Both entertaining and informative, Charles too came to enjoy the comraderie of these evenings.

Without trying to draw attention to himself, Charles soon found himself in the center of many discussions. At first it was because of his front line battlefield experiences. All had heard of Bunker Hill and Saratoga, of White Plains and Monmouth, of Valley Forge. Charles had been there.

But as time went on his opinion was sought on other matters — the spirit of the men in arms, the qualities of various generals, the prospects for the coming year's campaigning. Without knowledge of any man's political leanings or history, Charles was free and open with his observations and opinions. His innate modesty endeared him to every faction and by the end of the session all of the delegates were familiar with Major Charles Royal. Indeed, he was invited to dine with several distinguished men of the state, and asked to correspond on developments in the war after he returned to his unit in the field.

The Judge was highly impressed. Rake, he knew, was not made for the give-and-take world of public life. Charles, though, was a young man of action who could also converse with men of power. Speaking plainly, yet with force and conviction. A man who was already earning respect from people whose opinion carried weight. Perhaps this Massachusetts castaway would one day emerge as a man of influence in the South.

With a flurry of activity, the fall session of the Maryland Legislature adjourned on the 18th of December, allowing just enough time for the delegates to return home for Christmas.

On the long ride back to Oakmont, Charles was startled by a question the Judge asked out of the blue. "Charles, you do not approve of the institution of slavery as practiced in the South, do you?"

It was too direct a question to avoid, but Charles tried to nonetheless. "Well, sir, it's a foreign institution to me, growing up in Boston as I did. I'm new to the local customs. I'm uncertain—"

"Please, sir, if you will," the Judge interrupted. "Your answer."

"No, Judge. I can't say I'm in favor of it."

"Good!" the Judge said, casting a side glance at Charles to guage his reaction. "For I positively *abhor* it. And so do my children."

Charles was baffled. "Why then do you keep them?"

The Judge collected his thoughts before answering. "Any Christian man must detest slavery on every moral ground. To justify owning a fellow human being by convincing yourself that they are not people at all, but mere animals like sheep or oxen, is an argument too ridiculous to even warrant debate."

"So why, Judge, do you own slaves?"

In a weary voice he replied, "It is but economics. On a plantation as large as mine, to pay for labor would mean certain bankruptcy as long as my neighbors, my competitors, utilize them. And once I was forced off my land by creditors, another man — with slaves of course — would take over.

"But I tell you Charles, with God as my witness, I would gladly see *all* slavery abolished, and I will vote for such when the new American government is formed."

Charles was surprised that the Judge would express such strong convictions to him, especially in the presence of his slave Junius who rode along silently on his other side. "You certainly know that your views on this matter are not widely held. The South will never willingly part with slavery."

"Yes, too true."

"What then will be the answer?"

"Perhaps the day will come when it is no longer sensible to keep slaves. Just not worth it economically. Then it will fade out on its own. Failing that though . . ."

"Failing that?"

The Judge slowly shook his head. "Then I fear for the future even more than I fear for the present.

"God visited terrible plagues on the people of Egypt for holding the Hebrews in bondage. I suspect He hears the cries of the blacks now in the fields. Feels the sting of the taskmaster's lash on their backs. And when the time is right, He will once again send his avenging angels among us. And the land will run red with the blood of the just and the wicked alike." The three men rode a good many miles before another word was spoken.

Caitlin was overjoyed that two of the three most important men in her life would be home for Christmas. Normally the holidays meant an endless round of dinners and dances given and attended, but with the war in full progress, and so many families missing or mourning their male members, this Christmas was celebrated quietly. The one social event marking the season was a large sewing bee at Mrs. Darby's home, which Caitlin, as the woman of the house, took part in. All items sewn by the ladies were sent off to General Washington's suffering army, settled outside Morristown, New Jersey.

Charles wanted to give Caitlin a special gift for their first Christmas together, but he had no money except for a few Continental dollars, which merchants were loathe to accept. He settled on a few yards of Irish linen and a small sketch of himself for her locket.

Caitlin surprised Charles with a magnificent new blue and buff uniform, complete with great coat, vest, and purple sash. She had sewn most of it herself during the quiet times at the hospital. She purposely left off the officer's epaulets. They would mark Charles as a prime target for every marksman on the British side. Naturally, Caitlin did not see the disparity in their gifts, which only made Charles feel all the worse.

In a dark corner of Channery's Tavern late on the night of New Year's Eve a sinister figure of a man sat drinking alone, a bullwhip strapped to his side and a loaded pistol tucked under his belt.

Henry Fowler had been brooding there since mid-afternoon. He began in an angry mood that had only grown more morose and belligerent with each passing hour. Caitlin was lost. That *bastard* from Massachusetts had poisoned her mind and stolen her away. *Damn* that Royal for ever showing up. It is only right that he should meet some terrible end. Then Caitlin and one day all of Oakmont would be his.

As he drained yet another tankard of ale, Fowler looked up to see a group of young British officers drinking across the way. In the dark recesses of his soul a plan began to take form.

"Good evening to you gentlemen!" he called over, as cheerily as he could.

Looking over and thinking Fowler just another loudmouth drunk, the Redcoats did not respond.

"You there!" Fowler pressed on, pointing his finger and rising awkwardly to his feet. "Will you not toast the King's health with me on New Year's Eve?"

Drunkard or not, His Majesty's loyal subjects could not decline this toast. They stood without emotion and raised their glasses.

Fowler bellowed, "To His Royal Majesty, George the Third. May he reign forever over all of his dominions. Including this one!"

"To His Majesty the King," they replied without enthusiasm, took a quick sip of their drinks, and returned to their seats and conversation. Fowler, bumping chairs and other patrons as he went, joined them.

"We are loyal servants of the Crown all, are we not brave sirs?" Fowler's rancid breath caused the officers on either side of him to turn their heads away in obvious disgust. "But we must be cautious. Our enemies are everywhere. Everywhere! Even in the home of my own employer, the honorable Judge Abraham Serling."

Now the soldiers had no idea who this lout was, but the name Judge Serling was quite familiar to anyone who served in Maryland.

"His Excellency the Judge is known to side with the rebels at present," sneered one of the officers. "But he is the descendant of a long line of noble and loyal British subjects. When this insurrection is crushed, he will be welcomed back to the fold. I, for one, do not wish to make trouble for him."

"Good sir," Fowler persisted, "You miss my meaning. Under the roof at Oakmont Plantation at this very instant Judge Serling houses a major in the Continental Army!"

The officers looked at one another. They all knew the serious risk involved in harassing a leading citizen of the community; one who they hoped would see the error of his ways and switch his allegiance. But if this wretch spoke the truth, if there was an enemy officer within their grasp, then they would be in jeopardy of severe punishment if they did not act on the information.

The senior officer among them, Captain Ambrose Jenkins, sized-up Fowler for a moment, then he turned to his subordinate. "Lieutenant Nicholson, at first light take twelve men with you and ride with Mr. . . . ."

"Fowler."

"Ride with Mr. Fowler to Oakmont Plantation and check out his story."

"But Captain," Fowler implored, "By dawn the bastard may have made his escape!"

Jenkins was blunt. "I am not about to send men out riding through the hostile countryside on a damnably cold night, perhaps into a rebel trap, on the word of a drunkard like you!" Fowler bristled, but in a flash the point of the Captain's knife leaned on Fowler's throat.

"You would be wise to get some sleep *Mister* Fowler. Dawn comes early. And I warn you my good man, if you are lying, it will be the *devil* to pay for you!"

As the British officers got up to leave, Captain Jenkins called out to the barman, "Innkeeper, no more liquor for this man."

Lieutenant Nicholson was mildly surprised when he arrived with his detachment the next morning and found Fowler up and already in the saddle. Perhaps there was some truth to this sinister character's story after all.

It was the panting Junius who burst through the front doors of Oakmont to sound the alarm, "Soldiers comin'! . . . 10, 15, maybe more! . . . Comin' fast!"

Charles cried out in a panic, "Where's my sword!"

"What good would that do you," said the Judge by the window, "There are too many of them to fight. Quickly! You must escape!"

"What! And leave you to face them alone! Never!"

Caitlin grabbed Charles's arm and spun him about. "Think Charles think! You're out of uniform. They could hang you as a spy! On your love for me, you must escape *now!*"

For a moment Charles didn't know what to to, then he nodded to Caitlin.

"Quickly, this way," said Caitlin. She took Charles by the hand and rushed him out of the room while the Judge and Junius hurried to the front door to intercept the intruders. Caitlin led Charles into the study where she pulled a hidden lever alongside the fireplace. She pushed a large bookcase and it swung away, revealing a narrow staircase. "Take this down to the wine cellar and outside. Don't reveal yourself until they have departed no matter what!" Charles paused, but Caitlin was adamant, "*Hurry!*"

Just as she was closing the bookcase behind Charles, the Judge nodded at Junius and the two of them strode out onto the front porch nonchalantly and unarmed to greet their visitors.

"Why gentlemen, what brings you way out here on this chilly day?" the Judge smiled as if this were a pleasant surprise. "Cassie! Some hot coffee and biscuits for our guests!" He acted as if he didn't even recognize Fowler.

"Your Honor," began Lieutenant Nicholson from his saddle, "We have been informed by this man, who claims to be your overseer, that you are harboring a rebel officer, one Major Charles Royal. Is this true, sir?"

"Lieutenant, many a wandering soldier comes aknocking on my door. And to all who come in peace, I make welcome."

"That is all well and good, sir, but I must respectfully ask you again, on your word as a gentleman, does this Major Royal presently reside beneath your roof?" As Nicholson finished, Caitlin appeared and cast a knowing smile to her father who immediately caught her message.

"Lieutenant, I give you my word that this Major Royal you seek is not at present beneath my roof." In truth, Charles was under the bright blue sky, crouched behind some dogwood shrubs near the river. "Ah, the coffee is ready!" said the Judge. "Won't you join me inside, Lieutenant? Cassie will see to your men."

"Thank you, sir," said the Lieutenant who began to dismount.

Fowler, silent to this point and still feeling the effects of the previous night's binge, suddenly flew into a rage. "You lyin' old bastard! You've let

Royal steal my woman and my rightful inheritance!" With that he drew his pistol and leveled it at the Judge's heart. Just as the hammer hit the pan, Junius threw himself in front of his master and slumped to the porch with a groan as the ball ripped into his chest.

The horses spooked at the unexpected crack of the pistol, giving Fowler just enough time to wheel his horse about and shout in a voice that reached Charles's ears, "Charles Royal, one day you'll pay with your life for stealing the heart of my woman!" And with a quick "Hyah!" he galloped toward the main gates. The British patrol was able to get off two shots in his direction, but they missed their mark.

"After him!" ordered the Lieutenant. His men thundered off in pursuit, but Fowler knew this country far better than they and he made good his escape.

Lieutenant Nicholson sputtered an apology, which the Judge dispensed with a solemn, "Just leave us in peace, Lieutenant."

The Judge hoisted Junius in his arms and carried him upstairs to his own bed. Tearing open his shirt, Caitlin said, "I don't believe he was struck in a vital organ. It appears the ball passed clean through. Cassie, there are cotton bandages in my chest, bring them quickly. And the whiskey!" she called after her.

"Judge," said Junius in a steady voice.

"Be still, Junius. Everything's going to be all right."

Charles burst into the room. "What happened! I heard a shot!"

"It was Henry Fowler," said Caitlin as she hunched over Junius, binding his wound. "He brought the Redcoats. He tried to kill the Judge after he told them you weren't here, but Junius stepped in at the last instant and took the shot instead."

Charles was taken aback. "What an incredibly noble act. One worthy of a loving son."

The Judge and Junius looked at one another, and then the Judge reached out for Caitlin's hand. "There is something you should know, my dear."

"No Judge!" Junius protested, but the Judge rested a reassuring hand gently on the young man's good shoulder.

In a soft, reflective voice he proceeded to tell Caitlin about a beautiful and artistically gifted slave named Rebecca and what she had meant to his life. As children they played together on the plantation. When they grew older, as was the custom, Abe was forbidden to spend time with Rebecca, except as her master. He honored his father's instructions. In time he met, courted, and married "the most wonderful woman I would ever know." Caitlin's mother, Sarah. Their's was a fairy tale romance, but it ended all too soon when she was taken at a young age by scarlet fever. With a heavy heart and the burdens of raising two toddlers bearing upon him, the Judge turned to his dear childhood companion for comfort. And their closeness soon kindled something more.

While it was commonplace for plantation masters and other whites to take black women when they wanted, the Judge would never have done so with Rebecca. No man would. She had a quality about her that was very special — somehow majestic — and she commanded respect. Their relationship matured into a true and mutual love — though one which no one could ever know. Junius was the result of their love.

Rebecca died giving birth to a second, stillborn child. Three years ago the Judge had told Junius the story of his birth and Junius had kept the secret. His feelings for the Judge were such that he would have taken it to his grave.

Caitlin immediately accepted the truth of all she heard. It explained alot. Junius had been taught to read and write and kept those self-same plantation ledgers that Caitlin audited. Junius was never far from the Judge's side, whether checking progress in the fields, hunting in the forest, or traveling to horse races. Most folks thought Junius was merely the Judge's personal valet. Caitlin now knew the truth.

When all was said, the Judge turned to Charles who hovered in the doorway. "So you see, Charles, you were correct. What transpired here today was truly the act of a loving son."

Almost absent-mindedly Charles said to Caitlin, "Your brother . . . a slave?"

Caitlin glared back at him, "My brother, by God!"

She leaned over as she sat on the bed and kissed Junius on the forehead. "Thank you for saving our father's life."

Chapter 16

Much of the tranquil year that followed found Charles engaged in a more subtle form of the military arts — recruitment.

The first order of business for any army is to secure the services of men to fight in it. Love of country and dreams of military glory brought the first recruits rallying to the colors. Others joined who sought a taste of adventure and travel to leaven the tedium of their sluggish lives. For the down and out, the prospect of free clothing and a full belly had appeal.

But once they experienced the cannons' roar and faced bayonets flashing in anger, these idealists, adventurers, and dregs of society were sifted like sand in a prospector's pan. Those who withstood their baptism by fire and lived to tell the tale were too few. Others must be rooted out and somehow challenged, bribed, or coerced into taking up arms for the Glorious Cause.

Every senior officer in the Continental Army shared responsibility for raising troops. Some who were woefully inept as battlefield commanders excelled at selling civilians on the virtues of the soldier's life. The most talented officers, however, were usually stern disciplinarians who turned-off the crowds at recruitment stations because they lacked the "political touch." Charles fell somewhere in between.

Across the dusty back roads of Maryland Major Royal traveled with a company of strong, well-drilled and impeccably-attired Continentals, acompanied by a five-member marching band. Occasionally Charles had a field piece to liven-up the festivities. At every village, town square and country crossroads they would stop and perform their carefully orchestrated routine for the locals.

With the men at attention, shouldering arms, the band of fife and drum would launch into a spritely military tune while a standard bearer proudly held aloft the red, white and blue stars and stripes of the infant American nation.

This simple pageantry would bring the inhabitants from their houses and farms — as well as taverns and brothels — with the prospect of free entertainment and grog. Some cheered, some jeered. Often little boys would take up stick muskets and improvise their own mock infantry line.

When a sufficient crowd had gathered, Charles would solemnly step before his men and the music would abruptly cease. Then, in a commanding voice, he would order the men to perform the impressive manual of arms and close-order drill that he had been taught by von Steuben at Valley Forge. With the full attention of his audience now in his grasp, Charles would unleash his show stopper — a full line bayonet charge, complete with fearsome looks and blood curdling battle cries — directly towards the unsuspecting civilians! With screams of fright they would jump back as Charles's men halted just shy of them. Nervous laughter and hands over pounding hearts followed as Charles ordered his men to stand at ease while, smiling, he addressed the crowd.

"Friends! Brothers and sisters in the great cause of freedom! It is my honor and distinct privilege to speak to you today of that thing that we all cherish most dearly — liberty!

"We are engaged, as you all know, in a glorious struggle to establish on this continent a free and honorable nation that can take its rightful place among the Christian powers in this world — no less their equal.

"The rights and freedoms, the bounty and blessings that you will receive under your new government will make you the envy of every foreigner who visits our shores. The American Paradise they shall call it. And you, and your children, and your children's children will drink from its fountain!

"There are those, however, who would deny you this paradise, as Satan and the Serpent sought to deceive Adam and Eve, but heed them not! You will know them by their fanciful red coats or their Tory sympathies.

"Theirs is the path to ruination! Chains and the overseers cruel whip on your backs! Destruction of your homes and death to your children! Is that what you want? Will you be seduced by their forked-tongued lies?"

"No! No!" several in the crowd would call out.

"Then you stand for liberty?"

"Yes."

"For riches and happiness for you and your loved ones?"

"Yes!"

"For your homes, your honor, and for the Glorious Cause of America?"

"Yes! Yes!" they would shout, thrusting fists in the air.

"Then stand now and show your true mettle! The Maryland Continental Army needs you! Step forward all brave men of (whichever) county and add your mark to the list of heroes!"

At this point some in the crowd might waver, until Charles rolled out his piece de resistance. Reaching into his vest pocket he would withdraw a gleaming gold coin and wave it high for all to see.

"As a token of appreciation from your grateful country, *twenty dollars in gold* for the first recruit, and ten for all who follow!"

That always opened the floodgates as men fought to be first in line and claim the prize.

"Sergeant Novoski!"

"Sir!"

"Welcome these fine gentlemen to the ranks of soldiers." Novoski's quill moved like lightning before any of the "fine gentlemen" could have a change of heart.

Occasionally Charles would be approached by a lad who asked if he might go home and ask his parents' permission before enlisting. From experience, Charles knew that most of them would not return. Still, he always nodded his approval. Whether out of compassion or from the harsh schooling he himself had received, he didn't want a skittish boy whom he couldn't depend upon when the bullets flew. The army already had too many of them.

And then there was the ten dollar signing bonus to consider. The Continental Army was always at a financial disadvantage when it came to recruitment. The state militias offered more, while the Tories and the British regiments paid the best — and in British gold and silver, not in the suspect paper currencies and promissory notes that the poor Continental Congress issued (only the twenty dollar gold coin that Charles held aloft was hard currency; every enlistee after the first man received ten dollars in Continental paper, which was virtually worthless).

More than once a bizarre confrontation took place when two or more recruiting detachments visited the same village at the same time. This promised to be great entertainment for the local bumpkins who turned out enthusiastically as if it were a hanging. Some brought their earthen jugs of corn squeezin's. Whole families spread out a picnic lunch.

Best of all was when there was a Continental or militia unit and a British or Loyalist contingent involved. Then there might be some actual fighting! But rarely did the rabble have its way. Even if the opposing forces inadvertently found themselves on the same common, they had come to persuade, not demonstrate the gorier side of military life. Slashing and shooting and spilling of blood would certainly not induce civilians to sign up. Better to state their cases civily and let the people choose.

As summer turned to gentle autumn and autumn to the outset of winter, Charles could write to his superiors with pride that he had enlisted close to 500 men. He now had the nucleus of his own regiment. Daily he and his junior officers drilled the raw recruits on the modern techniques and battlefield movements of the new Continental Army. Many groused about the poor food or the crowding of four to six men to a tent, but Charles would have none of it. Deprivation? This man had stood the lines of Breed's Hill, Brooklyn Heights, Trenton, and elsewhere, oftentimes without a bayonet, or even gunpowder, to thwart a bloodthirsty enemy who had both. Complaints about marching on a brisk autumn afternoon amid the palette of falling leaves with birds singing above? *Try spending a day patching the shabby cabin walls at Morristown with leaves in a futile effort to fend off the bitter winter wind,* Charles thought, *Or stand alone on guard duty, starving and half-naked in hip deep snow at Valley Forge. Then, my lads, we shall talk!*

Had he ever been that young, Charles wondered as he looked into the faces of the youths struggling to learn formations. Had he ever been so innocent?

Clearly the most pleasant feature of this momentary respite from combat was that he could spend cherished days with his beloved Caitlin.

Rarely was Charles more than a day or two's ride from her side and he took advantage of his independent command to slip away and enjoy her loving company. At the hospital in Rockville he marveled at her organizational skills, working near miracles in recovery despite a chronic shortage of medical supplies. It was well-established lore in the army that a wounded or sick man was better off discharged home than sent to a military hospital where the attrition rate was appalling.

But here in Rockville, under the knowledgeable and compassionate care of Mrs. Caitlin Royal, the men recuperated. Indeed, many achieved the most robust health of their lives and created every imaginable excuse to remain in her charge. Charles delighted in imagining how many of these men must secretly despise him for marrying their personal angel of mercy.

On leave together at Oakmont, Caitlin and Charles were like children at play. They raced across the open pastures laughing and teasing one another until their sides ached. Or they would lay together for hours in a fragrant meadow talking softly and musing about the clouds that floated by on the great blue sky above.

In the evenings and on rainy days they would amuse themselves with indoor activities. Caitlin attempted to teach Charles to play the piano (an abject failure) while Charles impressed Caitlin with his special talents in the culinary arts. Mostly, though, they read to one another from the classic and romantic novels lining the walls of the Judge's study. Acting out Shakespearean plays was a particular favorite (especially *Romeo and Juliet*). They thought themselves excellent thespians, though deep down they knew no one else would.

Sometimes the Judge would join them, but mostly he would think up some pressing business that would allow him to decline their invitations. With the wisdom of a life well-lived, the Judge knew that this was a special time for the young lovers, the young newlyweds, to discover one another. He also knew on a different level that it marked the passage of a new generation at Oakmont — and in his heart he gave it his blessing.

One glorious Indian summer afternoon Charles and Caitlin strolled arm-in-arm along Pear Tree Lane which ran beside a pasture where sheep were grazing contentedly. They had been walking silently for some time, enjoying the soft autumn breeze and the multihued leaves that danced merrily down on them from the cathedral of branches above, when Caitlin decided to bring up a topic they had never discussed.

"Charles."

"Hmm."

"Where will we live when the war is over?"

Charles thought for a moment. "That's a good question. If I survive the war —" Caitlin's sharp rap on his shoulder caused Charles to abruptly alter his response. "As I am *certain* I will survive the war, I suppose we should give some thought as to where we'll settle down . . . You love Oakmont, it's your home."

Caitlin's response was gentle but firm. "My home is with my husband."

"Just like Ruth?"

"Just like Ruth."

Charles chuckled, "It's funny. At the risk of you hitting me again, I'll confide that I haven't given much thought to the future. Any really. Until I met you I was certain I had no future, and based on my past was well rid of it."

"And now?"

Charles grinned broadly, "Now it's a world turned upside down!"

They walked a few steps further before Charles continued. "It's just that the army has filled my whole adult life. I may not be much of an officer, but it's the only trade I know. I doubt that I'm fit for anything else."

Caitlin would have none of this. "Charles Royal! You are a man of immense gifts and talents. You need only focus your energies into a productive course and you will succeed in it."

"You are certain of this?"

"Certain as certain can be! And I'll thank you not to use that teasing tone. We happen to be talking about my husband and the man I love!"

"Yes ma'am." Charles knew when he was outflanked.

As they rounded the far corner of the fence and turned back toward the mansion, Caitlin moved on to another unresolved issue.

"There is also the matter of your family."

"Yes. If they're still alive."

"Oh don't say that! Of *course* they're alive. Alive and well and wondering when you will come to them. We must find them when this war is finally over. I have sisters!"

"Yes you do, and a brother Joseph too." Then, for a moment, Charles's face lost its light. "And of course, there's Mother."

"I shall love them all," Caitlin said cheerily holding firmly to Charles's arm. "We are all one family now." She turned to look into her husband's eyes, "Our family."

Charles nodded in agreement, "Our family."

"Where do you suppose they are?"

"Robert told me they were evacuated with the other Loyalist families to Nova Scotia."

"Will we find them there do you think?"

"Hard to say. They couldn't return to Boston, and it's unlikely that they would sail on to England; we have no close relations there."

"Then we will begin our search in Nova Scotia."

"Yes. As soon as my enlistment is up. It could prove to be a perilous adventure," Charles added.

"More dangerous than facing the gallows as a spy at Saratoga?"

"Good point."

With the flower gardens and towering pillars of Oakmont looming ahead just up the lane, it was Charles who raised a final point. "There is also the question of our family fortune, or rather what's left of it," he said staring blankly ahead.

"I thought all your properties were confiscated by the British, or by the Patriots when the city was evacuated?"

"I honestly don't know. As I told you, my brother disowned me on my 21st birthday and thereafter my only contact with the family was through Sarah and Sally, and that only for a brief time. I haven't so much as set foot in Massachusetts for over three years."

Caitlin paused on the porch before the great doors. "It seems we still have much left to resolve."

"Yes," Charles agreed. "And of course there's still the war."

"Oh yes," Caitlin replied wearily, "Always there's the war."

Chapter 17

On a mild and peaceful day the following May as Charles sat alone sipping a lemonade under a stand of spruce trees, his regiment laboring through its drills in a nearby meadow, he was approached by a lone soldier on horseback; a courier's pouch flapping on his saddle hook.

After saluting, the man inquired, "Do I have the privilege of addressing Major Charles Royal of the Continentals, sir?"

"I am he."

"Sir! I have a dispatch for you from the headquarters of His Excellency General Washington in New Jersey." The courier fished through his pouch and handed down a letter wrapped in twine. "Good day, sir," he said with a final salute, turned his horse about and trotted off.

Charles flipped the document over to check the seal. It appeared to be official. He cut the twine and burst the seal and read the sparse message inside.

> *Major Charles Royal*　　　　　　　　　*May 1, 1780*
> *Maryland Continentals*
>
> *Sir:*
> *You are hereby ordered to move with all haste to merge the forces under your command with those of General de Kalb presently on the march from this place to relieve General Lincoln and lift the siege on Charleston, South Carolina. Gen'l de Kalb should arrive at Head of Elk by the end of May. Godspeed and Good Fortune.*
>
> *- Wayne*

The time had come. Charles knew that he could not remain forever in the tranquil eye of the storm — that the war would rage again and he would be called upon once more to do battle. Were his men ready? Through grim experience Charles knew that the answer to that life-and-death question could only be found on the field of fire. Yet he was concerned. Too many of his troops were raw recruits. They had never engaged in even a minor skirmish, and here they were expected to march off gaily, banners flying, to meet a cold-hearted force of trained professional killers who had already sent countless numbers of innocent farm boys to an early grave. War was the cruelest business.

Charles was unaware of the intermingling of pressures at the highest political levels in London that had caused a calculated shift of strategy to concentrate on conquering the southern provinces. The stage was set and the players were in motion to engage in the final great campaign that would settle once and for all the fate of the American Revolution. And Charles, unbeknownst to him, would be marching along with his troops straight into it.

Parliament was by no means united in its support for this war. America, from the outset, had its advocates who spoke eloquently on behalf of their brethren across the water. Many members of the Commons were also bone-weary of war from the nearly one hundred years of on-again, off-again conflicts with France and Spain. The treaty ending the Seven Years War in 1763, they thought, had meant the beginning of a Pax Britania in North America. Great Britain had won unchallenged control of all lands east of the Mississippi. And the Royal Navy's ship of sail was the absolute monarch of the high seas. Their rivals in Europe, particularly the truculent French, might fume in jealousy, but they kept their weapons cased — at least for the moment.

But Britain had been brought to its financial knees by its incessant 18th century warfare, and the louder voices in Parliament, supported by King George III, called for the colonies to pony-up their fair share. Thus the series of taxes and tax protests that sent the Revolution to spinning.

Now, after five long years of fighting, the mood was turning ugly for the British at home. As the rebellion dragged on — and the dead and the debt mounted accordingly — members of Parliament were besieged by angry mobs and faced the constant threat of personal violence. Merchants and manufacturers who had built great family fortunes on the monopoly of trade with their cousins across the Atlantic were ruined. Thousands of working class citizens were thrown out of work and roaming the mean streets of London, Manchester, Liverpool.

And to make matters worse, archenemy France with her ally Spain had declared war on England; less in support of the republican fight for liberty in America than to settle age-old scores. Holland, Austria, even Russia began rattling their sabres in the direction of the English Channel. Suddenly the greatest power on earth was looking small and vulnerable; its only allies the mercenaries it bought from the petty German principalities, and even these were growing shaky. If the rebellion could not be crushed, and soon, then Great Britain itself might be overwhelmed by forces from without and within, and all would be lost; perhaps even the King's head.

Stubbornly, though, George III and his puppet in Parliament, Prime Minister George Germain, clung to the fanciful belief that the common folk of America still longed for the benevolent rule and protection of the Mother Country. In their disillusionment they saw mad, ambitious firebrands turning the docile citizenry into brainwashed mobs bent on destruction of civil authority.

Always they and like-minded leaders in the House of Lords and Commons felt that if they could just reach the majority of sane Americans, offering them the safety of British soldiery against their ravenous neighbors, then untold thousands would flock to the standard of the British Lion, offering their crops, their loyalty, and most importantly, their lives. "Beat the Americans with Americans" became a grand political slogan — but it was never grounded in reality. The King and his ministers never understood the heart of the American people.

Having failed to win support from the majority of the populace in New England, New York, or the mid-Atlantic states, London decided to play its ace card — the South. Here, unquestionably, the people loved the Crown. And there were additional, practical advantages to shifting the focus of operations there. As Germain wrote to Sir Henry Clinton, the commander of His Majesty's forces in North America:

> . . . the conquest of these (Southern) provinces is considered by the King as an object of great importance in the scale of the war, as their possession might be easily maintained, and thereby a very valuable branch of commerce would be restored to this country and the rebels deprived of a principal source for the support of their foreign credit, and of paying for the supplies that they stand in need of, as the product of these provinces (tobacco, rice and indigo) make a considerable part of their remittances to Europe.

Cutoff the rebels source of collateral for credit in Europe, so the argument went, and the Revolution would starve and wither away.

But it was not the bounty of the fields, but victory on the field that brought European gold, munitions, soldiers and warships rallying to the American side. News of the victories and near victories of these strange American farmer-soldiers at Bunker Hill, Saratoga, Trenton, Germantown and elsewhere was music to the ears of the crowned heads of Europe. Here was an unexpected opportunity to tilt the balance of power in their favor, and they seized upon it. "Beat the English with Americans" had a perfectly lovely ring to it.

The first British effort in June of 1776 to seize Charleston, the jewel city of the South, was foiled by the valiant defenders behind their palmetto log bastions at Fort Sullivan. Led by Colonels William Moultrie and Christopher Gadsden, and Majors Charles Cotesworth Pinckney and William Cattell (with a frail, swarthy, almost silent officer by the name of Francis Marion), they rebuffed a fierce but poorly coordinated sea bombardment and amphibious attack by Admiral Parker and General Clinton. The city's church bells peeled the glorious victory as the battered and frustrated British vessels slinked out of the harbor. Four years later the invaders would return, though — and the results would be far different.

In late December of 1778 the British established a southern beachhead, smashing the Patriot forces under General Robert Howe and capturing Savannah, Georgia. From there they unfurled their plan for recruiting Loyalists and, pushing north, eliminating any pockets of resistance. By early 1780, all of Georgia and South Carolina lay at their feet, except for the fortified city of Charleston under the command of General Benjamin Lincoln. And around this pivotal city, Clinton's army of 10,000 hardened veterans (twice the number the beleagured Lincoln could call on) had already begun digging its siege lines.

Chapter 18

Throughout dinner Caitlin had sensed that there was something on Charles's mind. He had been quiet and distant; pleasant, yet occupied with something other than the vegetables and boiled chicken that he scarcely touched on his plate.

Over coffee he announced his news. "I've received my orders. I am to march within a week's time to join General de Kalb's army moving south. Our destination is Charleston and the assistance of the troops there under General Lincoln."

Caitlin nearly dropped her cup on the table.

"De Kalb?" the Judge said quizzically.

"Baron Johann de Kalb. He's a German officer. One of those who Congress received with open arms."

"Does he know his business?" the Judge continued.

"Oh, quite well," Charles answered reassuringly. "He fought in two European wars under Frederick the Great. I first met him at Valley Forge. A giant of a man. His deportment at Monmouth did him great credit. I believe General Washington thinks very highly of him. He also speaks English fluently."

The Judge seemed satisfied, but Caitlin was another matter.

"You must go then?" she asked. A question she already knew the answer to.

"Yes, my dear," Charles replied. They sat silently looking at one another, each trying to mask the flood of emotions within. The Judge sensed the inappropriateness of his presence and, with an unacknowledged "Excuse me," took his leave.

Turning to the cold coffee before her, Caitlin spoke first. "I'll see to your packing in the morning. You'll not need your heavy coat. Not in South Carolina. Linen shirts would be right, and cotton stockings."

Charles broke her protective spell by softly speaking her name. "Caitlin."

"Oh Charles!" she cried, throwing her arms around her husband's neck sobbing. Charles had never known her to weep before, it wasn't her way. He embraced her warmly and stroked her hair as she loosed her heart-felt feelings on his shoulder. "It'll be all right," he said soothingly. "Don't worry." Caitlin nodded and sniffled and slowly pulled away, eyes swollen red and nose running. Charles offered her his breast pocket handkerchief.

"You will be careful," she implored.

"Why I intend to be the perfect coward!" he replied jokingly. It brought a smile and nervous laughter to his wife's beautiful face.

"If anything happens to you . . ." Caitlin began, but Charles cut her off with his hand over her mouth.

"*Nothing* is going to happen," he said. "You know the army. Lots of marching here and there, back and forth. The most I'll probably come down with is sore feet."

Caitlin was back in control now. She nodded, smiled, and then said coquettishly, "Well, if I only have the pleasure of my husband's company for a short while longer, I had best take advantage of it." Offering her hand and a saucy look that Charles read in an instant, they arose, moving toward the door and their bedroom upstairs. "The army may have you in a week's time, my lover, but until then, you're *mine.*"

By the first week in May, with de Kalb's relief force a world away, the prospects for Lincoln and his troops in Charleston were bleak.

Major General Benjamin Lincoln had been a farmer and local politician in Hingham, Massachusetts before the war. He served as a junior militia officer at Bunker Hill and quickly rose through the ranks, becoming one of General Washington's most trusted aides-de-camp. An able if undistinguished commander, he was a frontline veteran of the campaigns in New York and New Jersey, and received a serious leg wound at Saratoga. Appointed Commander of the Southern Army by Congress (with Washington's full endorsement), this was to be Lincoln's first (and last) independent command

Lincoln was outmaneuvered time and again by Clinton and his second-in-command, Lord Charles Cornwallis. And now the only substantial Patriot fighting force south of Virginia was pinned down on the sweltering coastal plain around Charleston. Admiral Arbuthnot's Royal Fleet blocked all sea lanes and issued daily bombardments over the city's fortifications, while Clinton's sappers tossed dirt in the air like killer moles as they drew closer and closer to their quarry.

Military prudence would dictate that Charleston was indefensible. To abandon (and probably burn) the city was the correct course. But the leading local citizens prevailed upon Lincoln to hold fast. Unfortunately, he had no experience in defending a city under siege, and neither did most of his senior officers. Lincoln waivered in his decision until the last possible window for escape was slammed shut and bolted and the issue decided for him.

Surrounded on land and sea by a vastly superior force commanded by professionals who knew everything there was to know about siege warfare, the fate of General Lincoln was as certain as that of the star-crossed band who would one day garrison a dilapidated Spanish mission in San Antonio called the Alamo.

When the trenches of the British and their Tory supporters snaked to within one hundred yards of the American emplacements, a ferocious cannonading opened from both sides, inflicting terror and death both day and night for several days. Solid shot, cannisters filled with 100 bullets each, exploding shells, and schrapnel of every nightmarish variety — rusty nails, broken shovel blades, cut glass — ripped ghastly holes in men's bodies, severing limbs and bringing blood-curdling screams from the wounded with every hideous blast.

Clinton, ever the politician/soldier, hoped he would not have to storm the fortifications. He preferred to capture Charleston intact and win the fallen citizenry over to the Loyalist side. He meant to occupy the city and make it the base of British operations in the south, much as New York City was in the north. It would not serve his purpose to reduce it to a smoldering rubble.

Once the shelling reached the city and began to set houses and businesses on fire, the civilian authorities played right into Clinton's hands. Those same prominent individuals who had pleaded that Lincoln's troops defend their city to the last man, did an about-face once their property was threatened and demanded that he surrender. Lincoln felt the noose tightening.

"General Lincoln. Might I have a word with you," said the unkempt officer who winced in pain from a broken ankle.

Drawn and half lost in his own melancholy, Lincoln nodded slightly to Colonel Francis Marion without lifting his eyes from the table before him.

"Sir, it appears that the city is about lost and we are soon to be taken prisoner. A fair assessment?"

Again Lincoln nodded. "What do you wish of me, Colonel?"

"My men and I would like your permission to attempt a breakout."

Lincoln chuckled ruefully, "A breakout? I wish we could all 'breakout.' I don't think you fully appreciate our position here, Colonel Marion. All avenues of escape have been sealed-off. Over the past seven nights I've sent riders, the best I have, to test every byway and footpath through the enemy lines. Not one has returned alive. *Not one.* A bird flying straight up in a pea soup fog wouldn't have a chance of escaping this devilish perdition. And you propose to lead a *company of cavalry* thundering down the road to freedom? Please, pray tell sir, where is this glorious route?"

"I believe we can escape to the north. By Monck's Corner near the Cooper River."

"What! Past Banastre Tarleton and his Tory Legion! Better sir that you attempt to tunnel straight through hell!"

Marion stood stiffly, silently. A man of chosen words, he had said his piece.

"I understand, Colonel, why you don't wish to be captured. You are the one man among us whose reputation with the Tories would lead you straight to the gallows. But these men you speak of, do they understand the grave risk?"

"Each has volunteered of his free will, General. I would take no man otherwise."

"How many?"

"Fifty."

"Officers, besides yourself?"

"One. Captain Serling."

"Not Serling!" the general cried. "He's the best fighting man in this army — or *theirs* for that matter."

"Sir, with all respect, this army is through. My men wish only to continue the fight, not rot in the hold of some cursed prison ship."

"You speak bluntly, Colonel Marion," Lincoln said forcefully, but then softened. "It is to your credit. Go. Tonight. Take what arms and provisions you want."

"Sir," Marion said saluting.

Lincoln, the beaten soldier, rose slowly and returned the salute.

At midnight, fifty grim, soot-faced men silently mounted their horses behind a barricade on the north side of the city. Each held a musket primed and ready across his saddle, but orders were not to fire unless Marion gave the signal. When all were ready, Colonel Marion led them out. They were quiet as ghosts, fur muffling every metal piece. Above them in the darkness hung a sliver of moon and there was a fog off the water. Their well-honed wilderness skills and the flash from the British artillery up ahead guided their path.

Marion's plan was simple, yet deadly dangerous; a tactic that he had used before and would rely on again — a surprise attack!

Success required that the enemy be caught unaware, but that seemed extremely unlikely. Soldiers on the British and Tory side were just as spooked by the nightly cannons' roar as their militia counterparts. Ignoring strict orders not to load their weapons, nervous soldiers imagining a phalanx of blood thirsty rebels bearing down on them fired at anything that moved — a shadow, debris blowing in the wind, each other. Raw nerves and a snapping twig sent muskets crackling all over the line. Officers harshly chastised the men for their fear and foolishness — only a lunatic would sally forth into this deadly no-man's land.

Marion's scout hooted like a night owl twice, the signal that they had reached the hidden bend in the road where the attack would be launched. Time for phase two of the plan. Cicero Steele, a powerfully-built black member of the company, slipped off his mount and crawled to the top of a small hill about fifty yards from the Tory position along the stone wall at Monck's Corner. Situating himself safely behind a thick tree trunk, he threw some sticks into a nearby bush. Almost immediately came the clicking of cocked hammers and explosions from half a dozen rifles.

"Cease fire!" shouted an officer in a clipped British accent. "Damn you stupid provincials! You should be flogged for disobeying orders! Each man, right now, show me that your firearms are unloaded!" Cicero grinned as the officer strode behind his cowering soldiers, each pulling his trigger to show that his weapon was empty.

Scurrying back to the others, Cicero tapped Colonel Marion on the leg and quickly jumped back on his horse. Marion drew his sword, stood high in his stirrups facing back toward his men, and shouted the first word any of them had uttered since leaving Charleston — "CHARGE!"

Around the bend they stormed, screaming to wake the dead and firing at the Tories who scrambled for their lives. Horse after horse leaped the log barricade across the road and bolted ahead to freedom. The last to cross was a towering figure of a man in a hunting frock with a wide brimmed felt hat turned up on one side with an eagle's feather through the cockade.

Captain Randolph "Rake" Serling, certain that all of his men had passed safely, yelled "HYAH!" and spurred his horse to a full gallop. As he vaulted the barricade muskets flashed and balls came whizzing by him from thickets on both sides of the road. Reaching behind his saddle, Rake grasped his wooden canteen. Pulling the plug and holding it between his teeth he took a deep drink and then pushed the plug back into place, all at top speed without releasing the reins from his other hand. He heaved the canteen at a Tory and caught him flush in the face. "Helluva day to die, eh boys!" he shouted over the crack of muskets and the clattering hoofs, throwing his head back with a laugh so hardy that it almost cost him his hat. Digging his heels into his steed once more he flew off like straw in a hurricane, roaring into the whirlwind, "You'll not kill me today, my lads! Not today!"

The next day, May 12th, General Lincoln capitulated to an unconditional surrender. With the fall of Charleston, nearly 3,300 Continental soldiers and militia became prisoners of war. Also lost were 343 artillery pieces, 6000 muskets, and 30,000 rounds of ammunition. It was the largest and most devastating American defeat of the entire Revolution.

With Charleston secured, the usually ponderous Clinton suddenly became invigorated, sending detachments north, south, and west into the countryside to welcome the hordes of grateful Loyalists whom he was sure would now come out of hiding to joyously embrace their liberators in scarlet and white.

But Clinton would not be around to witness the event. By the end of June he was hearing rumors of a possible French attack on New York City in his absence. Boarding 4,000 troops on Admiral Arbuthnot's transports, he made sail to the north, leaving the imaginative and ambitious General Lord Charles Cornwallis to take his place.

Chapter 19

"Vhere do you believe we are to be, Major?" asked General Johann de Kalb, mopping his brow and squinting into the scorching summer sun.

"Well, sir," Charles replied, pulling a map over his horse's neck, "We left Virginia two days ago, so now we should be nearing this town of Durham."

"Durham? Does this name have a special meaning?"

"None that I am aware of, sir."

De Kalb called out to a man in buckskin, "You dere! Scout! You ride ahead to dose houses. Find out vhere we are."

"Ay, sir!" Returning a few minutes later he informed his commander, "It's a village called Hillsborough, General."

"Hillsborough. Good. Ve shall halt dere, Major Royal. Vhat is dis date?"

Charles had to think. "July the third, I believe."

"Dat is right!" de Kalb replied with a touch of glee. "Und very soon I have de big surprise!"

Secretly, General de Kalb had planned a special holiday feast for his army of nearly 4,000. Most didn't realize the significance of the following day, but de Kalb did. It was the 4th of July. The nation's fourth birthday. And a birthday should be celebrated.

Baron de Kalb himself had been reborn by the events unfolding in this strange new land. An avowed soldier of fortune, he came to America seeking an opportunity to ply his trade and enhance his wealth. But like other European mercenaries — such as the Polish Count Casimir Pulaski who fought and died bravely at Savannah and the mysterious French cavalry leader the Marquis de la Rouerie, who went by the singular name Armand — de Kalb was swept up by the noble tide of liberty and made the American Cause his own. Congress had an unnatural fascination with anyone professing experience as a European military officer, and de Kalb was the real thing. So when he said those magic words, "I intend to serve at my own expense," a happy Congress commissioned him a major general, gave him a horse, and pointed him in the direction of Washington's army.

Pleased at last to be directing an independent campaign, de Kalb wished to show his love for his adopted country and his appreciation to the men who had endured the long, dusty march with him from New Jersey through Pennsylvania, Delaware, Maryland, Virginia, and now into the Carolinas.

That evening he massed his troops and, standing on a stump, addressed them in a loud and exuberant voice. "My brave und good soldiers! As you may know, tomorrow is July de 4, a glorious day in de history of de vorld! It is de day vhen Congress, with de blessing of God above, told England, 'Ve vant no more of you!' To mark de occasion, I order dat ve observe a day of rest und celebration! De quartermaster has provided de grand feast for us. Vit rum und good beer for you to make merry!"

The men cheered the happy news and waived their hats above their heads, while the General basked in their adulation. "I only say to you, do not get too drunk! Ve still have much marching und de fiend . . ." he turned to Charles who translated "enemy," "de enemy to fight. But for now, drink well!" Wagon tarps flew back revealing huge casks of rum. Men shoved their way into line to enjoy the cool, frothy brew.

The following evening, de Kalb hosted a private banquet for his officers. Among them were General William Smallwood and Colonel Otho Holland Williams who, like Charles, commanded the Maryland Continentals.

After toasts to Congress, General Washington's health, the Glorious Cause, and a large-breasted serving wench named Marie, the talk turned to speculation on the situation in the South.

"It is a pity, gentlemen, dat ve are too late to save our poor brothers in Charleston," offered de Kalb. He stood and raised his glass solemnly once more, "To our comrades who fell und to dose who vill revenge dem!" Each man drained his glass.

General Smallwood spoke next. "Now that Clinton has left with nearly half his force, there's every hope that Providence will smile on us and we will regain this land." De Kalb nodded.

"And we're not alone in our struggles," added Colonel Williams. "Even as we sit here, partisan bands are active throughout the region, stinging British and Tory outposts at every opportunity, and keeping alive in the hearts of the people the glow of freedom."

"All good und true, gentlemen," said de Kalb, drawing on his pipe, "But it is to us, I tink, and de men who follow us to rid dis place of Englishmen and Tory devils. De people grow sick of war. Dey vill side vit whoever can give dem peace. I know dis to be true. Ve must vin on de field of battle und drive de enemy into de sea! Only den vill our people know peace."

Late in July as de Kalb's column was fording Deep River, a corpulant officer in a deep blue coat bearing a general's insignia overtook it. Charles recognized the man from Saratoga. It was General Horatio Gates.

Congress, in its strategic wisdom, had decided that it was inappropriate for a foreigner to command the army that was going to liberate the South, so they turned to Gates, whose glowing accounts of his personal performance at Freeman's Farm mesmerized them. Surely here was the perfect man for the job.

De Kalb, always the soldier's soldier, graciously stepped aside and agreed to serve as Gates's second-in-command.

Despite his tendency toward self-promotion, Gates was a man of simple ways and the men liked him — he was a loose disciplinarian. But from the day he took control, the American troops became a less effective fighting force.

As a commander, Gates was overrated, lazy, and inattentive to crucially important details for an army on the move. He did not gather sufficient provisions although the rich farmlands his division passed through were ripe with all manner of bounty. As a result, his men had to get by on a diarrhea-inducing diet of green corn, tainted beef and peaches. Weakened and dehydrated, they had no stomach for a fight.

Gates also made no effort to enhance his tiny 18-piece artillery complement or swell his ranks of cavalry, though the flat, open terrain was ideal for both.

And most unforgiveable of all, he failed to send out scouting parties to gather intelligence on enemy movements and numbers. In sheer ignorance, Gates trudged methodically southward, giving his adversaries every opportunity to sieze the initiative.

Lord Rawdon, of Bunker Hill fame, was well aware of Gates's army advancing on Camden — its size, disposition, even the names of its general officers. With a contingent of only a few hundred Loyalists, Rawdon hastily sent word to General Cornwallis in Charleston, calling for reinforcements. Within hours of receiving the dispatch, Cornwallis was personally leading a rapid march on Camden with approximately 2,500 troops.

Not only was Gates unaware of the hornets' nest massing ahead, he grossly misjudged the size of his own force at seven thousand. Otho Williams took an actual head count of effectives and came up with a far different figure: 3,052. Undaunted, believing that nothing more than a reconnaissance unit stood in his way, Gates blithely responded to Williams' report, "It is of no matter, three thousand will be sufficient for our purpose."

Hard marching brought Cornwallis to Rawdon's side on August 15th. Taking command of the combined force, Cornwallis decided on a night march, hoping to catch the Americans by surprise.

By sheer coincidence, Gates had elected the same tactic, and on the very same road. At around 2 a.m. that steamy night, the two armies literally ran into each other on the Waxhaw Road just above Saunders Creek.

Sporadic musket fire ensued as both sides hastily shifted into battle formations. The ground seemed to favor the Americans. Impassable swamps on both ends of their lines meant that the green militia troops needn't worry about being flanked. This would have to be a face-to-face battle in a narrow corridor.

De Kalb and the two Maryland regiments, along with the Delaware men, anchored the right side of the road. General Richard Caswell's North Carolina militia were on the left, with Virginia militia units under General Edward Stevens extending the line to the mossy water's edge.

At dawn, Cornwallis ordered a general advance in columns. Proudly he watched his seasoned troops march forward in orderly rows "firing and huzzaing" across the killing field.

Anxiously, the American regimental commanders awaited directions from General Gates, but none were forthcoming. From his position of ignorance (if not cowardice) well behind Smallwood's reserves, Gates decided to "wait upon events."

General Stevens on the far left decided on his own to move his Virginians ahead to engage the enemy. It was a fatal mistake. His virgin troops took a few steps forward into open view, froze at their first sight of fixed and leveled bayonets striding towards them like a moving wall of death, and did what militias from Boston to Savannah invariably did; they threw down their muskets and ran the other way.

"To the quick step!" yelled the British officers who immediately saw the clear path to the American jugular. When the fleeing Virginians rushed smack into the North Carolina militia, panic spread like an exploding grenade and quicker than an officer could scream "HOLD YOUR POSITIONS!," the entire American left collapsed and was in full flight — most muskets hurled to the ground still loaded.

To their undying credit, the stalwart Maryland and Delaware regulars on the American right were unmoved by all the confusion. Holding their emotions in check, they stood their ground, side by side, jaws firm.

Rawdon's North Carolina Volunteers, British Legion, and Irish Volunteers smashed into them with massed fury, their terrifying battle cries ripping the air. It was every man for himself in ferocious, hand-to-throat combat. Bayonets, swords, and knives flashed and burrowed into men's bodies while muskets and pistols fired at point blank range. Whirling rifle butts raged in every direction. And when there was nothing else left to continue the fight, men lashed into each other with their bare fists.

For an hour and more this indominable American 600 fought off attack after attack, formed, charged with the bayonet, and clawed their way deep into the heart of the British horde. In the thick of it, like a human standard, stood the immense Baron de Kalb brandishing a broken sword in each hand. And close by his side, in a sweat-soaked linen shirt, was the major with the odd Boston accent, Charles Royal.

Three bullet holes and two bayonet tears had shreaded Charles's shirt, but miraculously he was unharmed. Unfortunately, the same was not true for de Kalb.

"You are wounded, sir!" Charles called to the General above the battle's roar. "You must retire!" De Kalb, staggering, shook his head violently. Seeing his superior's plight and the dead and wounded falling about him, Charles knew he had to take charge.

The air was so thick with acrid gunpowder smoke that men were coughing and half-blinded, forcing a momentary stall in the action. It was now or never. "Lieutenant!" Charles yelled into the ear of the only American officer besides himself still standing. "Take every unit but the 6th and withdraw." The Lieutenant hesitated, looking bewildered. Charles turned and shoved him. "Now! While there's still time!" Charles called to the men of the Maryland 6th, "Dress ranks as best you can! Form along this line!" He stood before them with his arms spread wide, his back turned to the enemy. Each man knew that Major Royal had cast their lot with his. They were to fight the final delaying action, buying precious time with their life's blood so the others might escape.

With quiet courage that spoke volumes, every soldier took his place, shoulder to shoulder, facing the enemy. They would stand behind their Major to the last man. When the line had formed, Charles drew his sword, picked up a broken rifle stock in his other hand and cried "CHARGE!"

Headlong into the breach plowed the men of the 6th Maryland, clashing bayonets and driving the startled enemy back on their heels with a furious assault. Cornwallis called off the pursuit of the routed militia on the American left and channeled the full force and power of his infantry and dragoons on these diehard Continentals on the right. About to be overrun, Charles turned to see General de Kalb, pierced for the eleventh time, fall mortally wounded to the ground. Suddenly, out of nowhere, a heavy weapon crashed into the back of Charles's skull sending him sprawling face down on the body of a dead Tory. Turning his head in a daze, he looked up into a circle of enemy bayonets poised menacingly over his back. Then he slipped into unconsciousness.

The remnants of the American Army of the South scattered to the nearby hills, swamps and forests after the debacle at Camden, with Tarleton's horse-men hacking at their backs. Many didn't stop running for days. Most shameful of all was their commander-in-chief, Horatio Gates, who mounted the fastest steed he could find when the battle turned ugly and galloped off, covering the sixty miles to Charlotte in record time. There he switched to a fresh horse and high-tailed it to Hillsborough, another 120 miles away.

With an immense haul of prisoners and all the baggage and wagons of Gates's army in his possession, Cornwallis could crow triumphantly to Lon-don, "We are now the masters of Georgia and South Carolina, and the road to North Carolina lies bare before us." If the letter had been directed to Congress, none there could dispute it.

Chapter 20

As the glaze cleared from Charles's vision he found himself lying on his side in fetid hay staring directly into the yellow and black eyes of the biggest rat he had ever seen. "AYH!" he cried, startling the rodent who scurried off, and sending a thundering shock wave of pain through his brain that set the room to spinning.

Slumping back with his arms draped over his face, Charles slowly pieced together recent events — Camden . . . the battle . . .the final desperate fight . . . the . . . his mind went blank.

"On your feet!" barked the voice of a grizzled Tory sergeant with several missing teeth. He spat a stream of tobacco juice on one poor soul. "C'mon y'damn rascals! This ain't no hotel y'know!" Men climbed to their feet groaning. Many looked to be wounded. Charles felt the bandage wrapped tightly around his own head.

"Where are we?" Charles asked a private beside him.

"Prison camp, sir."

"Are there more of us?" Charles continued, scanning the twenty or so disheveled troopers in the barn-turned-jail.

"Don't reckon ah know, Major," came the drawled reply. "Jest seen us'n so far."

The Tory sergeant and four guards rudely shoved the prisoners out the door into the blinding sunlight where a blacksmith in a grungy leather apron fixed each man with leg irons — all except Charles.

"You be Major Royal of the Maryland Continentals?" the sergeant asked Charles. Tobacco spittle matted the black mustache above his brownish teeth. His breath was foul, but Charles answered without pulling back.

"Yes."

"You're to come with me then."

Charles was led to a small wash house where a cake of lye soap and two well soiled towels sat by a basin. Charles washed his arms and face and as he was toweling off, a bewigged British captain approached wearing a smart scarlet jacket with gold thread piping.

"Sergeant, is this the man?"

"Yessah! Jes like you says. I brung um here and cleaned him up real good."

"That will be all." The wretched sergeant attempted a salute, which the haughty captain received with a smirk and didn't bother to return.

"Major Royal, I am Captain Reynald of the Royal Fusiliers. You are enjoined to accompany me this evening to dine at the table of His Excellency, General Lord Cornwallis. Fresh linen will, of course, be provided." Charles looked down and fingered the shredded rag that had been his shirt.

Promptly at six, a mounted guard of six dragoons in tall steel hats arrived with Captain Reynald. Charles was left unbound in return for his promise that he would not attempt an escape.

Riding in the center, Charles began the five mile journey to Camden and dinner with the famous General Cornwallis. Along the way, he realized that he must have been the senior officer captured; why else would he have been chosen for this singular honor.

Dismounting and tying their horses to the hitching post in front of the stately Kershaw mansion that Cornwallis had appropriated as his headquarters, Charles followed Reynald inside, past the liveried servants who stood on either side of the entrance to the main dining room, and all of a sudden there he stood, the military dictator of the South.

"Your Excellency!" Reynald called out. "I present to you Major Charles Royal, prisoner of war, late of the Maryland Continental Army." Snapping a salute, he did an about-face and marched briskly out of the room. The servants closed the doors behind him, leaving Charles and Cornwallis alone.

"Brandy, Major?" Cornwallis inquired, pouring the dark crimson liquid into two crystal glasses before receiving a reply.

Charles took the measure of the man: distinguished, aristocratic, perhaps fifty years old; Lord Cornwallis certainly looked the part of a commanding officer. Charles was well aware and respectful of Cornwallis's skills as a military tactician, and his reputation for personal courage and decisive action on the field of battle.

What he wasn't prepared for was the innate kindness of the man. His benevolent face and his considerate, almost solicitous interest in a mere major and how he was being treated.

Part of developing morale and a fighting spirit among the troops called for portraying the enemy (and particularly its leaders) as merciless, bloodthirsty fiends emanating from the deepest regions of Hell to reek pain and havoc on innocent women and children. Charles had bought the party line. And as a recruiter he sold it. But here, standing alone sipping brandy with General Beelzebub himself, Charles came to see the truth — American, British, Hessian, Tory, they were all just men; with the virtues and vices commen to all men.

"I am pleased that you could dine with me this evening, Major. I wanted to tell you in person how impressed I was with your valiant stand in the recent engagement."

"Thank you, sir. Though I must say that my presence here is hardly voluntary, since I am your prisoner." Charles thought that his words might seem discourteous so he added, "Nevertheless, I am deeply honored by Your Excellency's generous invitation. This is an occasion I hope to share with my grandchildren one day."

"Are you married, Major?" Cornwallis took a seat at the exquisitely arranged dining table and motioned Charles to do the same.

"Yes sir."

"Have you seen your bride recently?"

"Yes sir, we parted company in Maryland scarcely three months back."

"Ah! How I envy you," the general said wistfully. "I'm married as well. To the most gracious and wonderful woman I have ever known. I fear she is gravely ill at present, in England, poor dear. If there is one failing that I would attach to her character, it is that she accepted the proposal of a military man." Cornwallis's words trailed off.

Three black servants entered wearing starched white gloves and carrying ornate silver serving dishes. When they removed the lids, Charles looked wide-eyed at a feast of roast pheasant, boiled potatoes, summer squash, beets, relishes, several savory breads, cheeses, and terrapin soup. The sight momentarily took his breath away.

Cornwallis smiled. "Do I detect that it has been awhile since you've dined in such a manner as this, Major?"

"Sir, we would feed a company for a week on such rations." Charles suddenly looked alarmed at his confession.

"Calm yourself, Major. I am already somewhat informed as to the commissary of the Continental Army. You and your comrades are to be commended for your fortitude. But here we are now. And here are our 'rations' for the evening. So let us partake and enjoy our good fortune, for it never lasts. What was it that the gladiators of Ancient Rome said? 'Eat hearty, for tomorrow we die.'"

The conversation took a more serious turn after dinner as the two men enjoyed tea, a lemon chiffon dessert, and an aromatic cigar.

"Major Royal, I will be direct. You are an officer of courage and merit and I would like to offer you a commission of similar rank and privilege in His Majesty's service."

Charles was taken aback. A major's commission in the British Army would require any Englishman to have high connections at Court and to pay a small fortune. Here he was being offered this coveted prize on a silver platter.

"Sir," Charles hesitated, choosing his words carefully, "I understand and am flattered by the magnanimity of your proposal, but I must respectfully decline."

"May I know your reason?"

"I already have a job, sir. One that I have pursued to the best of my ability since Bunker Hill."

"Surely you must realize, Major, that the crushing defeat of the American Army at Charleston, and now Camden, has doomed the rebellion to failure. You have fulfilled every obligation any man could ask of you."

"There is one still left, General, to whom I hold am obligation."

"And to whom, pray tell, is that?"

" . . . Myself."

Cornwallis was surprised and disappointed by the rebuff, but maintained his composure. It was part of his job to entice American officers and politicians to defect whenever opportunities presented themselves. On several occasions he had been successful. But as he was himself a man of honor and loyalty, he held in contempt any man who would "turn coat."

Later that evening Charles was returned to the jerry-rigged prison. His fate seemed dark, but his character never shone more brightly.

Cornwallis shared Clinton's delusion that the British liberation of the South would allow Loyalists to come out of hiding and roam the countryside safe and free. He was dumbfounded to learn that his victory at Camden had actually touched off the most savage internecine fighting of the Revolution — a veritable civil war within the war.

Brutish partisan warfare is the most repulsive form of conflict for civilians and soldiers alike. There are no rules, and no mercy. Farms and plantations belonging to enemies are plundered and burned to their foundations, sometimes with the occupants still inside. Settling old scores — blood feuds, vendettas — overrides purely military considerations. Spreading terror is the real goal — and both Tories and Patriots quickly grew devilishly proficient at it. The fact that the country was officially at war gave a token legitimacy to this slaughter of neighbors. Without the war, these same Tories and Patriots might be called vigilantes or marauding bands. Worst of the lot were the "outliers" — scavengers, cutthroats and renegades who murdered and robbed either side when they were vulnerable for their own gain.

There were notable exceptions, however, who carried the flickering torch of the American Cause in the South against all odds. Fragments of the shattered armies at Savannah, Charleston, Camden and elsewhere who joined together as volunteers to harass the omnipresent British and their allies. Here were the true freedom fighters. Led by established military officers such as Thomas Sumter, Andrew Pickens, William Davidson, Peter Horry, and the most famous and feared of all, Francis Marion, these Southern Irregulars mastered the art of guerilla warfare, using their meager resources brilliantly as one by one they snapped up the King's outposts so carefully laid out by the British high command throughout the Carolinas.

Collectively, these tough, hard riding saboteurs took so many small bites at the British Lion that it finally roared in pain. Cornwallis sent dragoon units flying all over the countryside with orders to kill or capture these incessant pests. But the task was easier said than done. One British patrol gave chase to Marion and his band only to have their horses sink to their haunches in a soupy bog. Hearing the derisive laughter of his prey as they slipped further into the dark forest, the British captain cried out in frustration, "Damnation! We will never catch that cursed swamp fox!" The name, like the British horses, stuck.

If there was one thing that the common soldier of both armies feared even more than battle, dreaded more than an exhausting march through hostile territory, it was being taken prisoner. Even the greenest private had heard tales of horror about human skeletons lying pathetically in their own waste while their fingers and toes were chewed clean off by vermin. Unfortunately, these stories were often quite true.

The British policy on the treatment of prisoners of war was that they had no policy. Basically, they were unclear as to these prisoners' status — were captured American soldiers entitled to the same general standards of confinement afforded other belligerent nations, or were they British traitors, and thus subject to be hung?

Washington and other senior American commanders made it abundantly clear early on that if Americans captured in the course of performing their wartime duties were executed, then the very next British soldier of similar rank taken prisoner would suffer the same fate. This settled the matter of capital punishment.

Thereafter, for the duration of the war, the British pursued an unofficial plan of culpable neglect of their prisoners of war. American militia were considered play soldiers (Yankee Doodles) by the British and all but the most fiesty were usually paroled after giving their pledge that they would remain neutral for the rest of the war. The Continentals, however, were a different story.

They were carted off to human warehouses, or worse, rowed to rotting cargo ships offshore where they suffered unspeakable deprivations. In just one instance, 800 POWs taken by the British following their victory at Charleston died within a year in the pestilent bowels of the prison ships anchored in the harbor. Better to take a ball or bayonet in the chest, so the common thinking went, than to be taken alive as prisoner.

At dawn on the morning of August 20th a mixed detachment of British and Tory troops began a convoy of about 150 captives from the Battle of Camden along the dusty road that led to their place of detention in Charleston. Throughout the long, scorching morning the Americans trudged southward in sullen lines, bound together by heavy rope. At their head, the only American left untied, walked Major Charles Royal.

At just after noon the column halted for water and a brief rest. But no sooner had the British and Tories brought their canteens to their lips, when out from the swamp burst a screaming herd of wild horsemen, muskets and pistols flashing hot lead from both hands. Panic-stricken, the guards immediately threw up their arms in horror and cried out, "QUARTER! QUARTER!"

Up rode the ragged cavalry, abruptly bouncing off their mounts and disarming the startled, terrified detachment. Not one member of the attacking force wore a regulation uniform. Some had distinguishable odds and ends, but most seemed to favor rugged frontier buckskin. Upon their heads many wore small black leather caps. That was the giveaway — these were Francis Marion's men — some white, some black, others Indian or mulatto.

The commander of the British contingent noted with chagrin that his conquerors numbered only 17 men — to his 45 who had surrendered without firing a shot! Plainly, this would not look good in his report. "My God," he gasped to the oversized auburn-haired man who he assumed was the leader, "You are but seventeen! Why so few?"

Grinning ear-to-ear the man bellowed for all his followers to hear, "Why Captain, I'd say seventeen was more than adequate for the job, wouldn't you?" Boisterous laughter followed, but the downcast British and Tory guards somehow failed to see the humor.

As the Swamp Fox's men quickly slit the bonds of the American prisoners the large man leapt back on his horse and directed the operation. "Move quickly now! An enemy patrol might have heard the shots. You men," he called to the freed prisoners, "Take the Redcoats' weapons and grab your possessions and anything you can carry from the wagons." The Americans were more than happy to trade their squirrel rifles lost at Camden for the magnificent Brown Bess of the British Regulars. And the razor sharp bayonets that fit snuggly beneath their muzzles were a bonus — they could be used to skewer an enemy by day, and roast dinner over the campfire at night.

The three wagons accompanying the convoy were turned over, spilling their contents by the side of the road. Charles fished through until he found his one cherished possession, his father's sword.

Marion's hit-and-run professionals knew that every second wasted lessened their chances of escape, so the large man's next order was "Mount up!" Standing in his stirrups, the leader looked even more formidable. Six pistols, three on each side, dangled menacingly from loops sewn into his white fringed hunting shirt. When his party looked ready, he turned a hard eye on the British commander. "Now Captain, I want you and all your men to *remove your pants.*" Even his own men were startled by the order. But he repeated it. "You heard me! All of you! Drop 'em!"

Afraid for their lives if they didn't comply, the British and Tories did as they were told. Even the Captain reluctantly departed. The tactic may have seemed bizarre, but it was actually clever. Without their pants, the soldiers would feel foolish trailing the escapees. The only alternative would have been to kill the guards, now unarmed men, and where was the sport in that?

While his followers gathered up the clothes the leader shouted out, "You men can regain your dignity at the far corner of that field yonder."

Standing buck naked from the waist down, the British Captain leveled his protest. "This is a base afrontery, sir! If we were in England, the King would have your head!"

The leader cocked his neck to the side in deference, then said, "But as you can see, Captain, we aren't in England. 'Weah in South Ca'lina!' And you can tell your old King George that if he ever comes to 'South Ca'lina', I'll not only have his *head*, I'll have my boot on his *big ol' behind!*"

His boys hooted and hollered their approval.

Four riders trotted off to drop the bundles of pants at the designated spot about half a mile distant. The rest of Marion's men and the escapees moved out in the opposite direction, across the ravine and down a path into the pungent swamp haven that these rough-hewn soldiers called home.

At a fork by a huge weeping willow about two miles from where they entered the swamp, the leader turned his horse about. "I reckon most of you fellas have had your full share of war for awhile, so we're going to part company here." Pointing to the right he continued, "Follow this trail about four miles until you come to three boulders about yay big piled in a triangle. Turn northeast and over a rise you'll see a farmhouse with a blue post in front. The farmer there is named MacGeorge and he'll give you directions to guide you safely into North Carolina."

As the prisoners thanked their liberators and made their farewells, Charles approached the leader. "Sir, you would be Lieutenant Colonel Marion I presume."

"Ha! Not hardly. That's him over there." He pointed to a slight, poorly dressed man who was sitting on a rock massaging his swollen right ankle. The man had been present but silent during the recent breakout. Charles walked before him and saluted.

"Colonel Marion, as the officer in charge of the American prisoners I wish to express my heartfelt thanks on behalf of myself and all the men for your courageous raid today. We owe you our freedom, our lives, and our undying gratitude."

"You're welcome, Major," replied Marion, wincing as he gingerly pulled his boot back on.

"And sir, I would request that I be allowed to remain and serve under you. I have no army to return to and I wish with all my heart to continue the fight."

Marion eyed this stranger with the odd accent from top to bottom. He was not generally quick to accept new volunteers. One spy could mean doom for him and his band. But Marion liked what he saw.

"Welcome aboard Major . . . "

"Charles Royal, sir, late of the Maryland Continentals."

"Royal! Sweet Mother of Jesus!" yelled an excited voice. The man Charles and everyone else had assumed was the leader jumped off his horse and lifted Charles right off the ground, shaking him about helplessly engulfed in a massive bear hug.

Finally dropping the startled Charles to his feet, the man gave the reason for the huge grin that lit up his face. "Charles! It's me! Captain Rake Serling, late of the 12th Maryland Continental Dragoons." Charles's jaw fell open as Rake's beefy arm engulfed his shoulders and he told Marion, "Colonel, this man is my brother!"

At Oakmont Plantation, Caitlin sat alone in her bedroom with the door closed. Outside a cold night wind had crept in, warning of a heavy rain. The curtains blew, but Caitlin did not rise from her writing desk to shutter the windows. By the shadowy light of a single candle she wrote two letters in a shaken hand. They were brief and nearly identical. She folded them slowly and affixed the sealing wax in silence. She addressed them to the last known addresses she had. On one she wrote the name of her husband, *Major Charles Royal*. On the other, *Captain Randolph Serling*.

Chapter 21

After three days of hard riding, mostly at night, Marion's men reached their main camp on Snow's Island in the middle of the Great Pee Dee River.

There were no more than fifty of them in all, and a shifting catalog of characters at that. Over the weeks that followed, Charles came to learn the informal, yet deadly effective tactics of these soldiers of the swamps. With maps drawn with a stick in the sand, Colonel Marion would direct his sparse force in attacks on British and Tory supply trains, ammunition storage places, and undermanned garrisons. Occasionally Marion would ally his troops with the main army, as he had at Charleston, but for the most part they roamed about on their own.

To know these earthy, hard-bitten men was to know the very definition of rebel. They lived by their own rules and answered to no outsiders. They fought who they chose, when they chose, in the manner they chose. Once in a fight, they stood by one another to the last man; their creed: "Victory or death." Attacking by surprise like a frothing swarm of hornets, they would strike blade and terror into the breasts of their enemies, and then vaporize as quickly back into the forest, a gray haunting mist that would rise again.

In Marion's band Charles's imagination saw more than guerillas, mere mortals. To him they were the stuff of Greek legend. *What tales would Homer tell of the adventures of the Swamp Fox and his fearless followers?* he mused. *Where was the chronicler of Ullyses and Helen of Troy while heroes like these strode the woods of South Carolina? Who would write the story that would grant these colossals their rightful place with the immortals?*

Charles joined in on many a raid; not as the leader, but as "one of the boys," which was entirely fitting. It was as if he were back with his first militia unit before his baptism of fire at Breed's Hill. There, Rainbow Samuels and the other more worldly men took charge naturally and Charles went along. This new partisan fighting was as foreign to him as the simple marching drills that he struggled to master with his friends so long ago on Boston Common. But just as he had done in the regular army, Charles paid attention and learned.

Through long, animated, laughing conversations, Charles also learned much about his larger-than-life brother-in-law Rake. (Plus some interesting tidbits about Caitlin's childhood that he tucked away in his memory to spring on her some day when he was in a teasing mood.)

Physically, Rake was an outsized man; like some character out of folklore. Broad-shouldered and ramrod straight, he wore his thick auburn hair pulled back in a loose cue. A red stubbled beard, ever ready grin, and fierce, piercing green eyes that always seemed poised for action completed the picture. And then there was his thundering voice and hearty laugh that could shake the leaves from the trees.

In a hellious fight against overwhelming odds, if Rake was at your side, you felt safe. His towering courage was both reckless and infectious. Time and again he had rolled dice with the Grim Reaper and won. Of all his passionate appetites, and they were legion, the one that he savored most was battle.

Riding back from a successful raid against a Tory supply house where they had liberated, among other things, several pipes of excellent madeira, Rake pulled from inside his shirt a stained letter and began reading it to Charles and the men.

"Listen, Charles, you'll enjoy this." His eyes skipped ahead and he took a long drink of the delicious wine. "Ah! Here it is: 'I made the acquaintance of a gentleman from Massachusetts by the name of *Charles Royal*, a lieutenant serving under Daniel Morgan, during my stay as a guest of General Burgoyne's army at Saratoga. When my cover as an informant for the Patriot Cause was revealed, it was the gallant Lieutenant Royal along with his accomplice and our sainted cousin Nigel who rescued me from an appointment at the end of a rope.

"'Perhaps it was kismet (or an arrow from Cupid's bow) that placed Lieutenant Royal and myself in a caravan shortly thereafter that was evacuating the sick and wounded of Maryland, Delaware and Virginia back home. During our journey he was the perfect gentleman, Rake. We had many a delightful conversation over our humble evening fare — oh, I should mention that he was once a company cook, and an excellent one at that.

"'We parted company in New Jersey — he having to rejoin the main body of General Washington's forces then gathered there. Perhaps we will never meet again, but something in my heart tells me we shall. I have written him two letters, but as yet have received none in return. I am not upset, though. An army on the march has few opportunities to post its mail. I do pray that he proves to be a better correspondent than my dearest brother! (Seven letters sent, no replies received!)'" Rake left off his sister's affectionate close.

"So there it is, boys. It appears that Charles here has been withholding vital information from us."

Charles attempted to plead his innocence, but Rake had the floor. "And what is the penalty for withholding vital information in this man's army?"

"Death!" "Hang 'im!" "Cut off his balls!"

"Gentlemen, please," Rake broke in at the last suggestion. "That certainly wouldn't endear me with my sister. No, we need a more fitting sentence."

"But what is it that I've withheld?" Charles finally pleaded.

"That you're a *camp cook!* And it says here that you're 'a most excellent one at that!'"

"Hear that boys! By the grace of God we've finally got ourselves a cook!" The cheers that followed from the now tipsy men were so vocal that they spooked the horses.

"Charles Royal, it is the judgment of this court that during the duration of your enlistment with the forces under the command of the most benign and gracious Francis Marion, you shall serve as Cook, and apply your utmost efforts and talents to satisfying the needs and desires of the men of this command." Before Charles could say a word, Rake drew one of his pistols and fired in the air, "Court's adjourned!"

That very evening Charles took up his new duties, preparing his Road House Rabbit Stew to excellent reviews. He came to find out that the men were sick to death of Marion's bizarre usual fare of boiled potatoes and water. Nothing Charles could have accomplished against the enemy would have impressed his mates more than a plate of that savory stew.

Experimenting over time, Charles created a varied menu of delectable meals from the foodstuffs available to him. He even came up with a recipe that made leathery alligator meat taste good — marinating it in wine overnight and seasoning it with apple butter and ground chestnuts. The appreciative diners, who dubbed it "Gator au Boston," always scraped the cookpot clean whenever Charles served it up.

Charles's fascination with these warriors of the wood extended to the colorful nicknames many were given. These names served a practical purpose; if one of the party was captured and tortured, he couldn't be forced to betray the names of his comrades if he didn't know them.

Rake identified the members of the cast for Charles as they sat together on a log sipping coffee one night. "That black fella with the powerful arms is Cicero Steele. There's a man well named. The black beside him mending the saddle is Strawman; he favors straw hats, plays a beautiful harmonica, and patches us up when we're hit. That fearsome tatooed Indian is Montoga. Choctaw. He's vowed to find and kill a Tory swamper named Milhouse who killed his brother and stole his horse. Wouldn't recognize the man if he was in this camp right now. Figures he'll just kill all the Tories and Milhouse must have been among 'em.'"

Turning to the other side, Rake continued with a lean and solemn man dressed in stark black. "That's the Perfesser. Use to teach Latin and Greek literature. Over there you got the Spaniard Rojas."

Charles also came to know Whistler, Whittler, the fat van Gist known as Whale and his brother Minnow, and Maggot, who was aptly named.

Their reasons for being together in that pungent, malarial hideout were as different as their names and the colors of their skin. Strawman had escaped from a sadistic planter and dreamed of freeing his enslaved wife and two children. Boils, a fifteen year old shoeless farm boy, was seduced by the thrill of adventure. Cicero Steele didn't give a damn about any Revolution, he just liked killing whites. Good at it too.

One common thread among Marion's men was their hatred of Tories rather than the British. "Hell, any of you boys ever met an English man before this war started?" Whittler asked once while they were enroute to a storehouse raid. No one had. Their fight was with the despised Tories. The British just suffered by association.

Charles was in awe of the toughness and tenacity of the Swamp Fox and his band. He confided to Rake, "With a thousand fighting men like these the war could be won in a month — by either side."

Francis Marion, their leader, was an enigma. Every one of these fiercely independent warriors accepted the Colonel as their unchallenged leader. The man commanded respect without issuing a command. And when he did speak, every other tongue silenced.

Born at Goatfield Plantation in South Carolina, Marion was the sixth child of a wealthy family. He was so tiny at birth that the first clothing his grandmother sewed for him was an infant's shroud. But Francis fooled everyone and survived, though he was always an undersized and sickly child.

Despite his physical shortcomings, danger seemed to agree with him, and he had an unnatural attraction to the myriad swamps with their moss-hung cyprus trees. As a young man he took to sea, was shipwrecked, and returned to fight in the Cherokee War chapter of the French & Indian War. Afterward, he acquired Pond Bluff Plantation and settled into the tranquil life of a southern planter. But history wasn't through with him.

Marion was named a major in the Continental Army at the outset of the Revolution and served with distinction in the first successful defense of Charleston and at Fort Moultrie. Overcoming every adversity — battle wounds, snake bites, hunger, heat stroke, malaria — he personally led his loyal partisan soldiers for the duration of the war with an elusiveness that caused British Colonel Banastre Tarleton to lament, "The devil himself could not catch that man Marion."

While Marion was held in great esteem by the Patriots and earned the grudging respect of the British, the Tories hated him. He was a marked man. If taken alive there was no doubt that he would be executed as the leader of the rebels. Yet, if he were healthy, there was not a foray so dangerous that Marion would not take part in it. All of his men knew the special personal risk that Marion carried into every battle. Perhaps that is why they held their highest admiration for this slight, unimposing man who rarely spoke a word.

Rake and Charles knew that as officers or "ringleaders," they too would probably be shot if captured. To Rake's way of thinking, this just added to the fun. "That's war, Charles," he said, reveling in the danger. "If you didn't risk your life, what would be the purpose?" Charles just shook his head and thought, *If there is a Valhalla, then here's the man who'll preside at the head table.*

Marion's veteran Irregulars had a trick they'd use to flush out a suspected spy in their midst. One man under scrutiny was a new volunteer called Willow. Maggot took a seat close to the left side of the man, while the Perfesser sandwiched him in on his right.

"You say you served in Captain Brereton's South Carolina Volunteers, eh Willow?" asked Maggot in a friendly way.

"That's right," came the reply.

"Interesting soldier that Brereton," the Perfesser said. "Tell me, does that peg leg of his prevent him from riding at a gallop?"

"Yeah," Maggot added with interest, "Me and the boys was speculatin' on that very question ourselves." He and the Perfesser pressed tightly on Willow, who was slow to respond.

"I . . . I reckon he does the best he can."

"Reckon so," said Maggot, acting as if he were satisfied by Willow's response. "Now I hear tell that he didn't lose his right hand in battle at all; that it was bit off whole by a gator! Any truth to that?"

Again Willow seemed to choose his words cautiously. " . . . I guess so. What's it matter. Don't bother me!"

The Perfesser replied, "Oh, I'm afraid we will have to bother you, friend. You see, this gentleman here and I are well acquainted with your Captain Brereton — had drinks with him not four weeks back — and unless he's the first man in Creation to grow a second hand and leg, you're a damn liar!"

Realizing his cover was blown, Willow brushed aside his inquisitors and in a flash drew a knife from his boot and held it hard against the back of young Boils. "Stand back ya rebel trash, or the boy here gets it!"

"Easy men," said Rake with his hand out to steady any reckless notions.

155

"Let the boy be, friend. Take me in his place. I'd fetch a high price with British or Tory. Let him go and I promise you safe passage and myself as prisoner."

Willow considered this for a moment, then declined, snarling, "I'd say I have the upper hand here. You can go to hell, Rake Serling!" He started backing towards the horses, but as he drew close his foot slipped on some manure and Boils broke free and ran to safety. Willow jumped on the closest horse and lit off across the marsh.

The first man to get off a shot was the Perfesser, but Willow cut to the side and the ball ripped through some leaves over his shoulder. Whistler tossed a fowling piece to Boils for the honor, "Take'm boy!" Boils jerked his shot and it went high. By this time Willow was nearly out of range. The men instinctively turned to Rake, the best shot among them. Montoga tossed Rake his prized Ferguson rifle, but as Rake took aim, Whale interrupted.

"Let's make this more sportin'." Whale bent his rotund body to serve as a human step beside a large chestnut horse.

"No, no, no," Rake protested, but the boys would not let him shirk the challenge and ruin their fun. So Rake took several quick steps then jumped on Whale's back and up on the horse. Standing, steadying himself as best he could, Rake sighted down the long barrel, squeezed the trigger and the musket cracked fire. Spooked, the horse reared, sending Rake tumbling off its hindquarters and sprawling on the ground. No one took notice. They were all too busy watching the distant target and counting aloud, "one . . . two . . . three . . . FOUR!" With an audible whap to the back of the skull, Willow flipped out of his saddle and fell with a muddy thud among some cattails. One less spy to worry about. And for Rake, a ride worthy of any sports hero on the shoulders of the men.

Throughout October and into early November, Marion moved his small force to a series of camps along the Santee and Little Pee Dee Rivers, never spending two consecutive nights in the same location. The region was alive with Tory and British units trying to hunt down and crush the last pockets of American resistance. Partisan bands like Marion's had exacted a heavy toll on British and Loyalist forces and Cornwallis was in a rage, convincing himself that it was these despicable terrorist guerillas who were keeping the general populace from turning out in support of Mother England. It would be a feather in the cap of any officer who could stop these American rebels and many gladly took up the chase, including the most hated of them all, Lieutenant Colonel Banastre Tarleton, a fearless, merciless cavalry officer who led his green-clad Tory Legion on a take-no-prisoners killing frenzy that earned him the sobriquet: Bloody Tarleton.

Rarely could Marion match his enemies man-for-man, so he mastered a strategy of baiting his trap and snaring those he could. Intercepting word that Colonel Watts was marching 400 troops from Camden to Georgetown, Marion waited in thick woods along the route with all two hundred of his followers. Realizing that a pitched battle might prove disastrous, Marion shrewdly stationed several horsemen out in the open, with instructions to stand about nonchalantly. When Watts came into view, he thought he had caught a small detachment of the rebels by surprise, and immediately ordered his cavalry escort to hurry ahead and surround them.

As prearranged, Marion's men waited for the attackers to draw close, then feigning panic, they leaped up on their mounts and lashed them back towards the woods, where Marion's main body lay in hiding. The British cavalry came dashing in, only to be hit by a solid wall of musket fire. As men screamed and fell to the ground, the mauled remnants turned around and tried to escape, but the Swamp Fox's horsemen were on their heels. The chase continued clear back to the British position, where Colonel Watts's cannon opened up and halted the pursuit. The British suffered several men dead or wounded; the Americans, one man slightly injured. Thereafter, Marion harassed Watts whenever he saw an opportunity, contesting every bridge and swamp crossing, all the way to Georgetown.

Returning from one such foray, Rake decided to pass the time by reading aloud to the men another past letter he had received from Caitlin in which his much embarrassed brother-in-law Charles was prominently mentioned. Snacking on peanuts and shooing horse flies, the boys always enjoyed teasing their northern comrade-in-arms. And the more titilating the news, the better.

"Let's see now. Oh, you fellas are gonna *love* this part here!" Charles lunged for the letter, but Rake tugged his reins to the side.

"Damn it!" Charles cursed. "Nobody cares about your stupid letter!" Rake thought differently and put it to a vote. "All in favor of me handing this letter over to Charles, never to be seen again, say 'Aye!'" As he expected, not a peep. "All in favor of me reading it out loud for our mutual enjoyment, say 'Aye!'" "AYE!" came the overwhelming response. "It's unanimous then; with one abstention," Rake grinned at Charles. "I shall, therefore, continue."

"'These past few months at Oakmont have been heaven to me; the happiest times of my life. I particularly enjoy the *evenings*." Several men interrupted here with suggestive moaning noices followed by general hilarity. "'In the evenings my sweetheart and I like to stroll by the river's edge and watch the glorious sunset. Once we lay in the grass beneath a blanket of stars and fell asleep in each other's arms.' What's this!" Rake slapped Charles with the letter, "You're sleeping with my sister!" The boys cheered Charles lustily. Rake continued. "'But before your imaginative mind wanders into unseemly speculation, rest assured that Charles behaved, as always, like a perfect gentleman." This time there was a chorus of boos and catcalls and Rake smacked Charles once again with the letter, "Dammit boy, just when I was beginning to respect you!"

"Ain't no s'prise when you think about it," said Cicero Steele. "Godamighty! A female Rake Serling? Must be the most butt ugly woman in Mar'lan'!" Few men could make such a statement, even in jest, and not cause offense. But Cicero Steele was one.

"Thas only cause yo' sister don't live in Mar'lan'!" Whale added, but the laughs didn't follow, only a menacing glare from Cicero Steele that told Whale there was probably somewhere else, like at the rear of the column, where he should be right now.

Rake scanned the rest of the letter to locate the climactic passage. When he locked in on it, he gleefully threw up his hand. "Hold on boys! Hold on! This is the best part! 'I sense there is a question that my suitor longs to ask me, the ultimate question a man might ask a woman, but he is reluctant to do so. I offer every opportunity that a lady might to ease his shyness, but to no avail. I pray that my *lion on the battlefield is not a mouse when it comes to speaking from his heart.*'"

"DAMN YOUR SOUL!" Charles screamed out, lunging once more for the letter that Rake now held high above his head amid the uproarious laughter of the men. "I'm going to tell Caitlin you read her letter to everybody. Then, by God, you're a *dead man!*"

"Ha! If my sister wants to kill me, she'll have to wait in line — and it's a long one!"

"Oh she'll wait! Mark my words. You're history!"

As the journey quieted down and several languid miles passed by, Rake opened up a bit.

"I love my sister deeply, Charles. She's the dearest person to my heart. And I want you to know, and share with her one day if I don't make it back, how pleased and proud I am that she found a man of your quality to call husband. I wish I could have been there, at your wedding. What a time that would have been."

"That's exactly what Caitlin said; that her only unfilled wish was that you could have been there to share our happiness."

Rake nodded thoughtfully. "Well, I'm here now, and so are you. And I still haven't given you two a wedding gift. I'll have to think of something special. Something that no one else could give you."

Along with an intimate knowledge of the byways and paths that criss-crossed the South Carolina countryside, Marion's men knew the waterways. Rivers, streams, ponds and pools formed a perfect network for undetected transport of horses, men and material. Many a time the Santee, Pee Dee, Catawba, Congaree, their tributaries and the rain-swollen swamps that bordered them carried the Americans toward battle, or provided a means for escape. Floating in rafts and bateau lazily along with the gentle current provided a welcomed chance for these hardened, bare-knuckled brawlers to put aside any present miseries and idle away their time. Maybe get in a little fishing. It was common at these moments for men to recall past scrapes and to share stories with one another. Sometimes with a dash of embellishment.

"Rake," Boils said from his seat on the rail, "What was the wildest fightin' you ever got caught up in?"

"Well, son," Rake began while perched on a barrel in the center of the bateau, toking on his pipe, "I guess I've been in my share of tough situations, same as any man afloat here today, but there was *one* time that stands out from all the rest . . . No," he cut himself off.

"What's wrong?" Boils asked. A few of the others had also begun to take an interest.

"I'm not of a mind to tell you boys this story, you be'n a skeptical lot, always searchin' for the *scientific explanation* and all . . ."

His audience was being sucked in now. To a man they professed their utmost faith in Rake's tale, whatever it might be.

Reluctantly, Rake started in, "All right then, I'll take you at your word. Gather 'round and I'll tell you about a battle the likes of which no one has ever seen in this war, or in any other I'll wager." The crowd leaned in toward Rake as he took on a decidedly serious look.

"There I was, alone on a small patch of high ground hunched-up in the night. Tory dragoons from Tarleton's Legion — 50, maybe 60 of 'em milling around me, torches burning, trying to flush me out. But the footing was slippery and there were plenty of snakes about so they decided it was best to draw off for the night. What the hell. Figured they'd just walk in and snuff my candle in the mornin' — I wasn't goin' anywhere. And they were right as rain.

"I'll tell you true, boys, things were lookin' mighty bleak. Mighty bleak. I thought to myself, 'Rake ol' son, your number's about up. Best make your peace with your Maker.' But as it was only about six hours till sunup, I didn't see as if I'd have enough time.

"Just when I dropped to my knees like a proper Christian should, I

159

heard a rustlin' in the bushes behind me. I turned around and lo and behold, out strides the biggest, meanest ol' grizzly bear you ever did see, walkin' right towards me!

"Well I don't have so much as a pebble to defend myself with, so I'm thinkin' 'Mr. Bear, you're gonna do the job for those Tories, aren't you. By the time they get here in the mornin', you're gonna be pickin' your teeth with my bones.'

"Then I noticed there was somethin' *different* about this grizzly. He looked kind of . . . intelligent. And then it happened."

"What?" asked Boils.

"He *spoke* to me, that's what."

"Go on!" said Whittler.

"It's true. True as the tablets Moses carried down from the mountain. He says to me, 'Rake—'

"Wait a minute," Whale interrupted, "How'd he know your name?"

"Now there's a damn fool question. How should *I* know? Guess he was a smart ol' fella." Rake sensed his listeners slipping away. "Look, I was like you. I had a scoffin' attitude toward those who claimed forest critters could speak like people. Just nonsense to scare children. But Indians, they swear by the truth of it. Ain't that so, Montoga?"

"Animals speak all the time. Only special braves can understand 'em."

"There you go. Now this bear had a proposition for me. 'Rake,' he says, 'I admire you. You only kill animals for food and fur, never for pleasure. Those look to be Tarleton's men out there, judging by the green uniforms; the worst human varmints there is. If you'll allow me, I'd like to help you out of this bind.'"

Rake took a long, contemplative draw on his pipe. "I was a bit perplexed. What was the military propriety when it came to throwin' in with forest critters? But seein' as how dawn was comin', I decided to dispense with philosophy and accept that ol' bear's generous offer. We shook hand to paw on it and I asked, 'What can I do to help?' That bear just shot me a yellow, pointy tooth grin and says, 'Jest get a good night's sleep.'"

"And that's just what I did. Come first light, I awoke to woodpeckers beating a deep woods reveille — rat-a-tat-tat-tat rat-a-tat-tat — and all around me animals began to move into position.

"An eagle circled overhead once, twice, three times, then it dove straight down screaming into the Tory camp. That was the signal and all *hell* broke loose! A swarm of hornets attacked by air while crows kept up a steady bombardment from the sky. Squirrel mortars joined in with snake jaegers popping up all over the place, fangs flashing at Tory feet. Then the bear infantry charged in, supported by wolves on one flank and foxes on the other.

"Some of the Tories broke and ran for the creek, but the fish had towed all their boats over to the opposite shore during the night and a phalanx of angry beaver and squawking geese sealed off all the watery escape routes.

"Those who could jumped on their mounts to beat a hasty retreat, but the horses saw the lay of it, looked at one another, and began tossing those sorry villains flat on their backsides!

"Outnumbered and outwitted, the poor devils took to their feet in total flight, yelping and swatting at a red ant army that had infiltrated their pants. The animals chased them clear out of the county and, by all accounts, some of those Tories may be runnin' still!

"Boys, I mean to tell ya, Julius Caesar himself, with all the legions of Rome at his command, couldn't have directed a more brilliant attack — or had better soldiers to carry it out. Yessir, ol' General Grizzly sure knew his business . . . "

"What were you doin' durin' the battle, Rake?" asked Boils.

"Why I just sat peacefully on a stump smokin' my pipe, just like I am now. In fact, *this* is the very pipe."

"What happened then?"

"When it was all over, the critters decided to throw a right fine victory celebration; and that night I was their guest of honor! We feasted, drank and danced the Virginia Reel and jigs together until near dawn. Some of those fellas, particularly the foxes and deer, were mighty light on their feet."

Rake's eyes narrowed, "Now by the looks on some of your faces, I'd say that there are still a few Doubting Thomases among you. Well, consider this: have any of you *ever* seen me eat bear meat?" The men looked at one another, but none could answer. "No, and you never will either! Out of respect for that furry ol' gentleman of the woods who saved my skin."

Whale asked, "Why don't the animals talk when there's more than one fella about?"

Rake pondered. "Well, I reckon they're afraid we'll find out how smart they are, vote 'em all into Congress, and put all those dumb-ass sons-o'-bitches out of a job!" A most satisfactory answer everyone agreed.

Just then the bateau ran up on shore and the men began to disembark. As they were leaving, Boiles turned to Cicero Steele beside him. "Reckon he was yarnin' us, Cicero?"

". . . Could be true. Could be part true. Could be one powerful tall tale," Cicero offered. "No matter though. It's a good story, well told, and I 'spect it'll grow somemore with the next tellin'."

Chapter 22

December 15, 1780
Snow's Island, South Carolina

My Dearest Caitlin:

I pray you will forgive my lack of promptness in writing to you. So much has happened since my last letter that I hardly know where to begin.

Know, my love, that I am fit and well (I do believe this southern climate agrees with me). Also, that Rake and I are now comrades-in-arms! He is quite well too and sends his warmest regards to you and the Judge and asks to be remembered to his many friends in Maryland. So you see, my dear, you have nothing to worry about at all.

Undoubtedly you have heard about our misfortune at Camden under General Gates. Following the battle, I was taken prisoner for a brief period, but was rescued along with a large contingent of our troops by Colonel Francis Marion and your dear brother Rake and their stalwart band. Ours is an informal, yet highly effective strike force where social position and rank mean nothing. Under Marion's brave and clever leadership, we pick our opportunities to trouble the enemy and have enjoyed much success. I'm sure that Congress will send another army for the relief of the South. But until that day of liberation, the people of this region owe their freedom from tyranny to Colonel Marion and other indomitable leaders who refuse to surrender.

Rake and I have become fast-friends. His gallantry and deeds of valor are the talk of both armies. As for myself, I keep my head low as you made me promise at Oakmont.

You will be amused to learn that my skills as a camp

cook have not gone undetected. In fact, by general accla-
mation, I have been made head chef! I suppose we must
all serve in our own way.

The morale of the men here is high and there is much
good humor. I look forward to sharing with you stories of
these colorful lads as we stroll arm-in-arm at Oakmont by
the peaceful water's edge. How I long to hear your sweet
laughter and see the twinkle in your eyes once more. You
are ever in my thoughts.

Today, as you know, marks my 27th birthday. There is
word afoot that there is to be a "surprise" party for me
tonight at a road house some miles distant owned by a
woman named Fat Hat. Rake is to be master of ceremo-
nies (naturally) so it promises to be a lively affair.

I pray that all is well with you and my Oakmont fam-
ily. I know you have written to me, but no letter has reached
my hand since we departed Hillsborough last July. War is
cruelest to love.

Your Most Affectionate Husband,

Charles

P.S. I picked some lillies and wild flowers for you one
day while we rested our horses in a glade. The men taunted
me and think me quite mad in my feelings for you. They're
right. I am.

As he finished the letter, Charles tugged the bandage on his wounded left hand tighter, and spread soap on the nasty bug bite welts that ran up both arms. No reason to worry Caitlin over such minor discomforts. After sealing the letter with pine sap, he drew a gold locket from his pocket — a wedding gift from the Judge. He sat gazing at the miniature portrait of his wife for a long while, lost in private thoughts.

Charles had never been to the Jolly Horse Tavern, but knew it by repu-tation. Marion did not allow camp followers — due to his ever present fear of spies — but was liberal on leave so that his men could enjoy the comforts of the fairer sex. When they were in the area, the Jolly Horse was always their favorite house of debauchery.

The thin ploy the men used to lure Charles out of camp was that they wanted him to help them reconnoiter a forest road for a good hiding place to await a British pack train expected in a few days. Charles went along, pretending not to notice the jugs of hard cider and ribald joking that were never a part of regular scouting parties.

At a swollen ford the men climbed into canoes and paddled across, singing a raunchy soldier's song, with their horses on tethers swimming behind them. A mile on the other side, at a desolate crossroads, stood an oversized log cabin with a weathered wooden sign dangling at an angle from a single hook on its left side. Pictured was the head-on face of a wild-eyed horse with a silly, big-toothed grin. Above it was the word "Jolly," and below it, "Horse."

As the party rode up noisily and hitched their horses to the rail out front, several members slapped Charles on the back, laughing at how they tricked him. For his part, Charles appeared dutifully surprised.

Ready to greet them by the door stood the proprietress of the Jolly Horse, Hattie "Fat Hat" Wylie — 200 pounds of riotous good fun. And behind her wide frame, craning their necks for a better view, were her anxious serving maids. Hattie approached Marion's band with arms upraised.

"Gentlemen! Noble soldiers of the swamp! Heroes in the Glorious Cause of Freedom! Welcome to mah humble establishment." Spotting an old favorite, her entire face lit up. "Why Rake Serling! Lord a'mighty, sugah, you mean the Tories or the devil ain't caught up to you yet?"

Rake clasped both hands on Hat's fat ruddy cheeks and kissed her flush on the mouth. "Darlin', no Tory, no devil, no *angry husband* could ever keep me from your side. There's someone here I'd like you to meet . . . Hat, this handsome fella here is my brother-in-law Charles, married to my sainted sister Caitlin, and today marks the very day of his birth!"

"Well now!" said Hat, shaking Charles's hand, "I reckon we'll have to figure out a real special present for you then." She glanced over to her staff who started giggling.

"Not too special now Hat," Rake said with his arm around her shoulder. "Remember the part about him bein' married."

Hat gave Rake a sharp elbow to the ribs, "Why that nevah stopped you befo' sweetie."

"Don't listen to a word she says, Charles," Rake cautioned, with a wink to Hat.

"Well why ah we flappin' our jaws out heah when we could be coolin' our throats inside!" Hat called to the gathering, "Let's get down to some serious drinkin'!" With a cheer the men followed Hat and Rake, filing into the Jolly Horse.

Wood and pewter tankards flew off the shelves and every tap poured frothy ale and beer. In no time the men were singing and dancing to the foot-stomping music of fiddle, jugs, banjos, harmonicas and Jews harps. Those who were lucky found a barmaid to prance about with while others simply locked arms in a wild country jig. Over in a corner two wayward souls experimented with getting a cat drunk.

In the middle of it all, reigning supreme from the top of a table, stood Bacchus himself: Rake Serling, with a tankard in one hand and the prettiest, lustiest maid in the other.

More than anything, Charles wanted to buy a round for all his friends, but he was broke. Rake would not hear of it anyway. "Your money's no good here Charles!" And then turning to the others for a laugh added, "And if it's Continentals, it's not good anywhere!"

Every reason imaginable for a toast was called out, with the men repeating it and downing their liquor. "To my brother-in-law Charles!" Rake thundered. "To my brother-in-law Charles!" roared the chorus in reply. "He's not *your* brother-in-law," Rake informed them. "As long as the drinks are on you," Cicero Steele shot back, "We'll call him your goddam *mother-in-law!*" Rake resumed without missing a beat, "To my mother-in-law Charles!", followed by the unanimous response, "To my mother-in-law Charles!"

Fat Hat's place was a haven for Patriots. Her one rule: No British or Tory soldiers allowed. In this she was unique. It was unprofitable at best and life-threatening at worst to enforce such a policy, but enforce it she did.

Virtually all farmers, tradesmen, tavernkeepers, and merchants from the Canadian border to Florida conducted commerce openly with whichever force controlled their region at a given time.

In the capital of Philadelphia, the young society belles danced and flirted indiscriminately with British or American occupying officers.

For many noncombatants, doing business with the King's men was preferable — their money spent better and they were more generous with it. Armies from both sides sought to curry favor with the neutral sellers of supplies, and a clever, avaricious person could play one party against the other and profit handsomely. War meant good business.

Farmers, particularly, were concerned that their livestock and crops would simply be "appropriated" if they refused to deal. "Better to sell some, keep the rest, and pocket a tidy profit," went the common logic. Political opinion almost always took a back seat when money was on the line.

With his funds running low, Rake called Fat Hat aside and asked if he could trade his saddle for a couple more kegs of ale. Unleashing a squirt of tobacco juice in the general direction of a spittoon, Hat gave Rake's well-worn saddle a sharp-eyed once over, then agreed.

While the men drank their fill and then some, a huge pig turned slowly on a spit over an open fire out back. Periodically, one or two of the merrymakers would slip out to check on its progress, maybe pouring the dregs of his beer along the charred carcass, "for the flavorin', don't ya know."

A popular ceremony took place several times during the evening where the men would add their own special twist to the traditional first toast to His Majesty. Staggering outside they would line up facing east toward Mother England and drop their breeches. Then in unison they would hold their privates aloft crying out, "To the King!", and drain to the King's health.

The drinking and singing, dancing and gorging went on until the wee hours when Rake decided it was best to go. Men this drunk shouldn't travel by day. They might be intercepted, and no one was in shape for a fight. So one by one Rake hauled the revelers outside and helped them onto their mounts. Off to the side he saw Fat Hat herself saddling his horse.

"What are you doin', Hat? That saddle's yours now."

"Dahlin'," she replied, tugging on a leather strap, "If you don't have a saddle, how're you goin' to come a'ridin' back to me?"

Rake gave her a friendly bear hug which she returned in kind.

"If I was twenty yeahs younga, I jest maht be havin' your babies mahself," Hat said with an impish grin.

"Hat," Rake countered, "If you were a hundred pounds lighter we might be tryin' our luck right now!"

Hat gave him a playful slap, "Ahm too much woman for you, sugah."

"Too much for any man!" Rake laughed. "You best be wearin' your trousseau next time I return — I'm bound to make an honest woman of you."

"Look for the candle in mah window and the ladder in the bushes," Hat replied jovially. Then she gave Rake's rock hard stomach a pat. "Tho' ah gen'aly like mah husbands with a little mo' meat on their bones."

Rake climbed into his saddle, saluted his hostess with a flourishing wave of his hat, and called to the men to "Move out!"

On the leisurely ride back, Rake turned to his brother-in-law, "So Charles, did you enjoy our little surprise party?"

"Very much. I hope to return the favor one day."

"I'm sure you will," Rake nodded. "I don't suppose Caitlin would think much of all this though. She and I never did see eye-to-eye when it came to fun. Oh well. She's your problem now."

"Oh she's no problem at all, brother," Charles said smugly. "She *likes me.*"

Rake looked at Charles then threw his head back and laughed uproariously. He possessed that endearing quality of men who can laugh heartily at a good joke made at their expense.

That same evening, in another tavern some miles distant, sat a far less convivial group of wretched outliers. Human jackels who preyed on the weak and defenseless. Their large, brooding leader stared straight ahead through bloodshot eyes filled with raging madness. His name was Henry Fowler.

Life had taken a sour turn for the Serling's overseer since his violent departure from Oakmont. He drifted west, then south through the Blue Ridge Mountains. In the thinly settled frontier, with so many men off to war, he figured to find ready employment. But there was something demonic in his face and manner that people read intuitively. It said that here was someone to fear and avoid, so most did.

Fowler committed innumerable petty crimes, including stealing from the few planters who actually put him to work. At one point he signed on with a Tory regiment in North Carolina, but ran off after beating a man to death in a drunken brawl. Once in South Carolina, he latched on with various marauding bands of outliers and swampers. Even by their lowly standards, Fowler stood out as a merciless, cold-blooded snake. But all things considered, it was better to have him on your side than against you.

Charles had long since filled Rake in on the British patrol's visit to Oakmont and Fowler's betrayal. Rake had also received a letter from Caitlin detailing the matter. Shaking his head he told Charles, "I could tell you perverse stories from that man's youth that would make your hair stand on end. And as he grew older and took up drinkin', he became an even more evil creature. He's more like a vicious animal than a man in a fight. My best advice to you, Charles — avoid him."

Fowler rarely took part in the meaningless conversation going on around him; that is until a minor bit of information caught his ear like a clap of thunder. A scraggly outlier with a patch over one eye had heard some news. "There's a Continental major from Maryland ridin' with Marion. They say he's from way up in Massachusetts." Fowler knew immediately that this was his archenemy, Charles Royal, falling right into his murderous hands. He managed to contain his emotions.

"You know, that gives me an idea," he said to no one in particular. "Colonel Tarleton would pay right handsome for a Continental officer who could show him how to get his hands on Marion. May even be able to get a King's Pardon for the lot of us in the bargain."

His conspirators looked at one another. Their criminal exploits had made them hunted men with prices on their heads. They desperately needed a safe place where they could trade their booty, get drunk and do some whoring. Maybe Fowler was on to something.

"You supposin' we'll just march right into Marion's camp and haul this major out by the scruff of his neck?" asked a man named Tilly sarcastically.

"Don't be an ass," Fowler replied. "We'll lay low near their camp and pluck him out clean the first time he strays. Where are they now?"

"North along the Pee Dee somewhere," said the one-eyed man.

"Good. Get ahold of that half-breed tracker Felch. Tell him to meet us here tomorrow. In a few days we're gonna be as rich and free as a country squire!" The scoundrels raised their tankards and drank to seal the bargain.

Marion, as usual, had declined to join in his men's revelry at the Jolly Horse the night before. Someone had to keep a clear head. Now he needed a handful of volunteers to scout a reported supply route that the Tories would be using in a few days to transport fresh provisions to Georgetown. Marion's own larder was nearly empty and he knew the prospect of filling their bellies would appeal to his men. Problem was, most of them were hopelessly hungover.

"Major Royal."

"Sir."

"You appear to be one of the least inebriated of this sorry lot."

"Yessir, Colonel, I'm not much of a drinker anymore."

"Neither am I. I need you to do some reconnaissance. Choose the seven men you think best suited for the job and then see me in my tent."

There Charles received his general instructions — survey the road over a two mile stretch with careful attention to any possible ambush points by the enemy. Post a watch up the road to signal if the supply train should pass that way. An easy assignment Charles thought. He foresaw no problem.

Charles set out with his "volunteers" a little after noon. It was a breezy and bright December day with billowy white clouds moving slowly across the blue panoramic sky. A perfect day for a peaceful ride in the country.

Charles and his band of seven splashed across a small stream and rode out of the woods into an open hay field. As they plodded along there was little small talk and the only beverage being consumed was water. Colonel Marion's directions brought Charles and his group to their destination by mid-afternoon. At their first glimpse of the road they also spotted three men who appeared to be Tories lounging on the grass beside a train of about fifteen pack mules loaded with supplies.

"Hot damn!" said Whistler who turned to Charles. "Can we take 'em, Major?"

Charles's orders were to scout and report only. But here was an unguarded, tantalizing prize hanging right before his eyes. He looked to the others who appeared to share Whistler's enthusiasm for the chase. "Go on then," he chuckled like a mother to her children looking wild-eyed at their Christmas presents. Off they rode, whooping and waving their muskets, hoping to scare the Tories into a blood free surrender.

When they drew to about twenty-five yards of the supply train a voice from the wooded thicket just behind yelled "NOW!" and fire from twenty aimed rifles ripped through the late autumn leaves.

Whistler in front was struck several times. He was dead before he hit the ground. Three others were wounded and reeled in their saddles. Charles, who had been trailing his men, now galloped up shouting, "Pull back! Pull back before they reload!" But the stunned men just turned around on their horses in small confused circles until the second volley tore into them.

At the sound of a ghastly cry, Charles spun to his right in time to see the Perfesser clamp both hands over his face, blood spurting between every finger. His frightened horse bolted ahead while the Perfesser slowly tumbled off the back.

On Charles's left Boils had been stuck in the buttocks and was standing straight up in his stirrups, howling in pain. Charles slapped the boy's horse hard on its flank and sent it galloping away from the line of fire. "We have to get out of here *now!*" he yelled and the men responded as best they could. Before leaving, Charles glanced at the ground to where Whistler and the Perfesser lay. There was no movement. He spurred his mount onward.

Retreating quickly across the field, Charles directed his men through the stream and up the forest path they had come in on. Once they were safely out of sight in the foliage, Charles leaped off his horse and raced back to the edge of the woods. There he stood for several minutes, pistols in hand cocked and ready. But the Tories hadn't pursued them. Probably afraid of walking into a trap themselves.

Charles ordered the men to dismount and assessed the damage — two killed and five wounded. All had been hit except Charles himself. He helped them climb back onto their horses, which they did groaning. They had to reach Marion's camp by sundown or else spend the night bleeding through untended wounds. By the looks of two of the men, they would not live to see sunup.

Twilight cast an eerie orange and pink glow as Charles led his bloodied followers past the sentry and into Marion's camp. Men came running up shouting questions as they helped the wounded down. When Marion strode forward, the rest fell silent.

"Major Royal, what happened?"

"We fell into an ambush, sir. Along the road we were sent to reconnoiter. Our casualties are two men killed and five wounded."

Marion studied Charles's face and the anguish evident there. "You did well to bring the wounded back alive, Major . . . I assume you weren't followed."

"No sir."

Marion nodded slowly then walked off toward his tent. From being the center of frenzied attention just a few minutes before, Charles now found himself sitting atop his horse utterly alone. Sighing painfully, he slid to the ground. He reached for his reins, but they were already in Rake's big left hand. His right he placed tenderly on Charles's shoulder. Moments passed before he spoke.

"No need to punish yourself, Charles. You fight the best you can and sometimes the enemy is just going to get the better of you."

Charles, eyes downcast, said nothing.

Rake patted his shoulder lightly. "If you feel like talking later you know where to find me."

That night when he was all alone in his tent, Charles let loose his emotions, sobbing into his one threadbare blanket to muffle the sound. It was the first time he had cried since those dark days before Trenton. Now, as then, he held himself personally to blame for the death of the men in his care, and he punished himself through the bitter tears. It was not the military way to act. It was the human way.

For days thereafter, Charles kept mostly to himself. He checked on the wounded regularly and was heartened to see that all would apparently survive. Rake tried a feeble joke to lighten Charles's mood. "Young Boils now has precisely what he came here for — a battle wound and a story to tell the boys around the cracker barrel when he gets back home. Years from now he'll have everyone believin' he caught that shot while beatin' Tarleton's entire Legion single-handed."

There was a modest Christmas Eve celebration in which the men carefully divided and shared what luxuries they had — two oranges and a pear. Strawman played his harmonica and a few who knew the words sung Christmas carols. Those who weren't church folk sat listening in silent respect.

Christmas Day opened chilly under a gray-blue sky. Rake had come down with one of the ever present swamp fevers and lay in his sweat-soaked cot sipping a watery concoction of bitter herbs and generally feeling miserable. Charles gathered up the few articles of clothing he had plus Rake's things and wandered downstream aways to a small eddy where the men did their laundry. He thought he was alone.

Across the water with eyes like cheetahs hunched Fowler and his co-horts. It was the moment he had hungered for — the hated Charles Royal, the devil who had stolen his woman and ruined his life was now as helpless as a rabbit in his snare.

Suddenly they pounced. Charles looked up to see half a dozen crazed outliers splashing through the shallow water, fanning out in a human net he couldn't escape. Charles let out a cry for help just before the heavy butt of Fowler's pistol came crashing down on his head.

He lay dazed and bleeding on the muddy beach as one of the assailants spoke in haste, "Let's grab him and go! Someone might have heard the yell."

Fowler, though, was clearly savoring his moment of triumph. Slowly he drew his fearsome hunting knife and with a sardonic smile pulled Charles's head back rudely by his hair and laid the deadly blade across his throat.

"Do you know who I am *Charles Royal*," he hissed into Charles's ear. "I swore my vengeance on you at Oakmont and today is the day I collect my debt!"

"What're you doin', Fowler?" protested the one-eyed man. "You said we was goin' to trade 'm, not kill 'm."

"Shut your cursed mouth!" roared Fowler, whipping his knife about. "Unless you want some of this too!" The outliers slinked away in fear. With his head thrown back in a deep-throated laugh Fowler was about to finish the act when down the stream at a full gallop yelling like madmen with water flying higher than their horses rode Rake, Cicero Steele and Montoga with a knife clenched tightly between his teeth.

Before Fowler could react, Rake whipped his rifle from behind his saddle and in a one-handed swinging motion shot the knife clean out of Fowler's hand. He then leapt off his horse, tomahawk at the ready, and knocked Fowler tumbling back into the water. Cicero and Montoga went whooping after the panic-stricken outliers, riding and pounding them into oblivion.

Knee deep in the swirling water, Fowler and Rake locked horns like two bull moose. Charles, struggling to his feet, took two steps forward and collapsed to all fours, his head spinning.

Rake was slowly gaining the advantage when the last of the outliers came up behind him with a huge boulder and smashed it hard on Rake's shoulder, ripping a ten inch gash clear to the bone and sending him down into the water. Fowler shoved the man aside and took up the rock himself to finish the job when Rake swung his right foot about, catching Fowler behind his left knee. Down he went out of control with the rock crashing flat on his face, snapping off his nose at the bridge, blood spurting into his eyes.

The battered warriors staggered to their feet for the final climax. Simultaneously they spotted Rake's tomahawk beneath the water that separated them. Together they lunged for it, but Rake proved the swifter. He stood poised and rocking, tomahawk in hand, as Fowler timed his move. On he came grabbing Rake's wrist, but the blood in his eyes caused him to miss his grip. In a flash Rake broke free and with a deadly blow buried the blade of the tomahawk deep into Fowler's skull. His dying eyes gazed at Rake in shock, and then he fell lifeless into the water.

Rake turned slowly and sloshed his way to shore where Charles had laid watching helplessly. As he drew up to him, Rake stood wavering, and with a hint of that infectious smile said, "Never say I didn't give you a wedding present." He then slumped to his knees and passed out face down in the mud.

Cicero pulled the reins of his horse as he too left the eddy, while Montoga made certain that all of the outliers had been dispensed with. Standing on the narrow shore Cicero looked back on the carnage of bodies floating in the water with pools of blood spreading about them. "Damn!" he muttered. "I was goin' to do *my* laundry this afternoon."

Strawman made a poultice for Rake and Charles that was effective in fending off infection of their wounds; no small accomplishment in the bacterial swamps where even a tiny cut soon festered.

On December 31st the men in Marion's camp huddled around the campfire together to ward off the winter chill. There wasn't anything to eat and no liquor to celebrate the coming of the new year so the men passed the time sharing their plans for after the war.

"Movin' out of the South. Headin' up Philadelphia way," said Cicero Steele. "New capital and all. Should be plenty of work, even for a black man. Yep, set up a blacksmith shop and live high shoddin' the horses of those Congressmen."

"Just make sure you get paid up front," Rake cautioned. "And in hard currency." The others nodded in agreement.

"How 'bout you, Strawman. Care to join me?"

"Mebbe so, mebbe so. Got to collect my wife and young 'uns first. Then we'll be along directly."

"What about you, Rake?" Cicero asked.

"Well fellas, I have a mind to travel some. Head west beyond the Appalachians all the way to the grand Mississippi. Now there's a sight to see."

"Plannin' on doin' some trappin'?" asked Whale.

Rake shook his head. "Not my style. With all that free and open land, maybe I'll just set up my own country! Call it *Serling*. Then I'd make myself King Randolph the first."

"Who's Randolph?" asked Boils.

"Why that's my real name, boy," Rake said grinning. "But by God don't any of you try callin' me that!

"Yessir," he continued while relighting his pipe with a stick from the fire, "I'll probably marry myself a beautiful Indian princess to seal the deal, just like royalty does in Europe."

"That brings up an interesting question that's been weighing on my mind about you," said Charles. "With all the women you've known, why haven't any of them been able to nail your feet to the floor?"

Rake smiled sprightly, "I guess I just have dancing feet!"

"That's what the Injuns'll call you," Cicero added, "Dancin' Feet!"

With that Rake jumped up, ignoring his badly wounded shoulder, and led the men in a raucous jig around the campfire as they gave their best imitations of Indian war chants.

Colonel Marion stepped forward with news that brought an abrupt halt to the merriment. "We've got mail, gentlemen." He handed the packet to Charles who served as postmaster. To his personal surprise there was a letter for him with an official looking seal on it and two letters from Caitlin; one addressed to him and one to Rake. Charles opened the official letter first.

"Colonel?"

"Yes Major."

"I've received orders to join General Greene marching south from Charlotte."

"I'm aware General Greene is now in command of the Southern Army. Is he a good man?"

"I believe he is, sir."

"Better than Granny Gates I hope. Well, Major, we're going to miss you around here." Marion extended his hand. "You're a fine officer and a damn good cook."

"Amen," said Cicero Steele.

"Thank you, sir. I'll never forget my time here."

"Not as long as you have that brother-in-law to remind you," Marion replied. It was the first and only time that Charles had seen the man smile.

Charles handed Rake his letter. "It looks like Caitlin wrote to both of us."

"Let's open 'em together."

Both men read silently, not realizing that their letters were virtually identical.

173

. . . It is with unspeakable sadness that I inform you of the passing of the Judge. He had been out riding the north meadow with Junius when the weather turned quickly and the two were caught thinly clothed in a cold drenching rain. Shortly thereafter the Judge came down with pneumonia, protesting all the while that it was merely a common cold and refusing to take proper care or to send for me at the hospital. One night he developed a high fever and began drifting in and out of consciousness. By the next dawn, his noble heart was still.

I am heart-sick that I was not with him in his final hours, but Junius stayed by his side and held his hand through the ordeal of passing. I'm sure that was a comfort to the Judge . . .

The rest of the letter dealt with the funeral, the sympathies expressed by relatives and friends, and other mundane matters.

Charles looked at Rake, who sat impassively, his letter hanging loosely in his fingers. Without a word or a backwards glance he rose, folded the letter carefully, tucked it in his pocket, and walked off slowly towards the stream. Charles let him go. It was a time to be alone. If Rake wanted to talk later, they would. A rare glistening snow began to fall. Charles drew his blanket around him and stared reflectively into the glowing fire.

Chapter 23

After the debacle at Camden, Congress knew it needed to pick a new commander if there was to be any hope of resurrecting and reforming the Southern Army. It was also painfully aware that its track record in making such choices was dismal — Robert Howe who lost Savannah, Benjamin Lincoln who surrendered over 3,300 men plus all his stores after the fall of Charleston, and Horatio Gates of Camden infamy. Whether wise or chastened, Congress turned this time to George Washington to make the selection. His man: Nathanael Greene of Rhode Island.

The 38 year-old Greene, a former Quaker, was Washington's quartermaster general at the time of his appointment. A seasoned veteran of Bunker Hill and the New York and New Jersey campaigns, the bookish Greene had spent more than four years as a member of General Washington's senior staff, absorbing the strategic tactics of the master. He had learned his lessons well. By the winter of 1780-81, he was the right choice for this daunting independent command.

Greene realized from day one, as his predecessors had not, that his ultimate goal was to keep an army in existence; never to risk all in a single pitched battle. Washington had taught him that the longer the British were kept in the field; the more costly the war grew; the higher the list of fatalities mounted; the more pressure there would be on the King and Parliament to throw in the towel, and the more support the American Cause would receive from France and elsewhere.

As long as the American Army survived, the Revolution would go on.

"Major Charles Royal reporting for duty, sir."

"Royal! Welcome." General Greene rose from behind his writing desk, returning Charles's salute and offering his hand. "Have a seat. You must be weary after your ride. May I offer you some whiskey or brandy?"

"Brandy, please . . . thank you, sir."

"I've been asked by Congress to convene a courtmartial on the conduct of General Gates at Camden, but since you are the only officer hereabouts who was present, I believe I'll dispense with that little piece of politics without further ceremony." He crumbled up a letter and tossed it aside.

"I understand you've been serving with Colonel Marion's partisan army."

"Yessir."

"Savage fighting, I know. All the Carolinas are aflame. Marion, Sumter, Davidson and the rest; I hope to God I have the honor of shaking their hands one day. They've kept the Glorious Cause alive while inept politicians and selfish merchants would see us in ruins.

"I feel most fortunate to have you here, Major," Greene continued. "You're knowledge of the Continental Army and the partisan bands as well as your familiarity with the intricate waterways and roads throughout this country render you invaluable in the campaign to come."

"I am pleased to offer what meager abilities I have, sir."

"Your modesty is unnecessary, Major. Remember, we were comrades-in-arms at Trenton and Monmouth. You have long since earned your spurs in this man's army."

A piece of paper on the side of the desk he was leaning on caught Greene's eye and caused him to frown. "Damn that Jefferson," he cursed as he snatched it up. "All talk and no troops! Raw militia, half-naked and without weapons, that's what they send me. The dregs of three states. Like the locusts of Egypt they have eaten up everything green!

"Let me tell you our situation, Major. Our troops are inexperienced and ill-trained, though our Prussian friend General von Steuben is working night and day to whip them into a passable fighting force. We are short of everything that constitutes a modern army except malcontents — Smallwood has already left in a huff. Those officers and veterans who remain are still demoralized and smarting from their spanking at Charleston and Camden.

"There isn't enough food to feed the army for three days and every merchant from Philadelphia to Charlotte has refused to allow me to buy uniforms on credit. Major Davie protested when I named him head of our commissary that he knew nothing of money and accounts, but I reassured him — 'Major Davie, there is no money, and hence no accounts!'

"On the plus side, there are officers of considerable merit — von Steuben whom I've mentioned, Colonel William Washington and his cavalrymen, Colonel Edward Carrington of artillery, Otho Williams and John Eager Howard of the Maryland Line, Virginia's Colonel Harry Lee of the light horse, General Daniel Morgan whom I know you served under at Saratoga, and of course yourself. Together, with the assistance of the partisan forces, I believe we can make a fight of it.

"The main body is here at Cheraw where we can keep an eye on General Cornwallis, who intelligence tells us is now on the march from Camden. I've sent Morgan with a contingent of Virginia and Maryland militia and

Continentals with Washington's horsemen in support west to harass the British and Tory outposts beyond the Catawba. With any luck, Morgan will snatch-up Ninety-Six and force Cornwallis to split his force, giving us the opportunity to move down the coast and reclaim Charleston.

"Once you are rested, Major, I need you to ride hard to join Morgan. Tell him of Cornwallis's activity and to be at the ready. And provide him with your strategic knowledge of that country, particularly where the streams can be forded this time of year."

"I shall be ready to leave within the hour, sir."

Greene smiled. "It's good to have you back, Royal."

Charles saluted and turned to leave.

"Oh, one more thing. Gates's baggage that he left behind before marching on Camden has fallen into my possession. You're welcome to search though it. You may find some of your personal property there."

"Thank you, sir."

Charles did find his old trunk among the baggage. Inside, neatly folded, was the smart new uniform and overcoat that Caitlin had made for him. With schoolboy glee he tried them on. They hung on his frame as if they belonged to a big brother. He had to cut a new notch in the belt to keep his breeches from falling to his ankles. *Thank heaven Caitlin can't see the scarecrow she married,* he thought.

At the bottom of the chest Charles found his writing paper, quills and ink. Not knowing when he might have another opportunity to write and post a letter, he jotted a quick note to his wife.

Mrs. Caitlin Royal   *January 7, 1781*
Oakmont on the Potomac
Montgomery County
Maryland

My Dearest Caitlin:

Fortune has smiled on me in that I have recovered my trunk that I thought was forever lost after the army's defeat at Camden. All of my possessions were just as I left them, including my treasured (and only) dress uniform and great coat which you gave me.

I am wearing them at this very moment. Also recovered were my writing materials so I will attempt to be a better correspondent.

I am presently with General Greene's army in South

Carolina along the Pee Dee River at a place called Cheraw. I will be leaving within the hour to render what assistance I may to General Morgan's detachment operating to the west. It will be a pleasure to join the Old Wagoneer and renew acquaintances with my brother soldiers in the Maryland Line.

On New Year's Eve Rake and I received your letters bearing the sad news of the Judge's passing. My deepest and most heartfelt condolences, my love. The Judge was as good a man as I've ever known — like a second father to me. I wish I could be there now to comfort you.

Rake took the news particularly hard. While he is often reckless with his own person, he is most protective of those closest to him. And of these, you and the Judge were paramount. Rake remains with Marion's band, an assignment that fits his character like a glove, while I move on to a new calling.

The war has certainly made a traveling man of me. I've now visited every state except Georgia. Perhaps we can travel there together after the war. Until that happy day when we are once again united, I remain,

Your Most Devoted Husband,

Charles

P.S. We need no longer trouble ourselves on one matter; Fowler is dead.

Charles chose to journey alone so as to attract as little attention as possible from Tory sympathisers. He rode with a blanket drawn around his uniform as a disguise. Near dusk of the second day he located Morgan's encampment of about 600 at Burr's Mills on Thicketty Creek near the Broad River. Greene had described his own camp as "dismal." To Charles, Morgan's looked worse.

Before he could locate the old general, the old general located him.

"Damnation! If it ain't Lieutenant, excuse me, Major Charles Royal. It's amazin' the British, Tories, or Indians ain't lifted our scalps yet, eh boy!"

Charles, like most of the men in his command, took an instant liking to Daniel Morgan's rough-hewn backwoods way of talking. But Charles knew something the green militia didn't, that this buckskinned tobacco chawing down home mule skinner could win battles against the best the combined forces of Great Britain could hurl against him. Just don't invite him to a church social.

"Hungry Royal! Course y'are. C'mon. We'll take vittles in my tent." Morgan loped along in a painful gait on gout-swolled feet. He had been in well-earned retirement since 1779, but the call of a desperate nation and the chance to "crack my whip at the British Lion" brought him one last time to the field of honor.

"General Greene wishes me to inform you that General Cornwallis has marched out of Camden and to expect a visit at any time."

"Tell me somethin' I *don't* know, Royal," Morgan replied followed by a squirt of tobacco juice that hit the spitoon dead on. "Been doin' the dance of the loons with Tarleton's boys for nigh on a week. He ain't but five or six miles off to the south right now. Prob'ly sharpenin' his bayonets with a mean English grin plannin' to skewer my sorry ass in the mornin'!" Morgan cut loose a laugh that showed his lack of concern.

"Oh he'll get his chance. But not here. Tomorrow we're movin' twelve miles upstream to a clearing the locals call Hannah's Cowpens." Morgan pulled out a map a scout had drawn and spread it on the ground, placing rocks at the four corners.

"Here we are, scattered roughly over this area. I've sent word to Colonel Washington who's here at Wofford's Iron Works refittin' and to Colonel Andrew Pickens at Fairforest to bring up their forces without pausin' to button their pants. With Pickens' militia we'll number about 900. Not as many as Tarleton, and not as veteran, but enough to give him a fight. Not much choice anyway. The Broad's too high to ford and we ain't got enough boats. We either turn and bare our teeth or let Tarleton's dragoons slice us to pieces on the river's shore."

As he refolded the map, Morgan asked Charles, "Ever met Colonel Pickens, Major?"

"I only know of him, General. Among the partisans he's held in the highest esteem."

"And rightly so! One tough ass son-of-a-bitch. A man after my own heart. Says he'll fight his men without me if I chicken out. God bless his insolent heart! If his boys are half the soldiers that man is, then we just might pull this off. Fortune favors the bold, eh Royal?"

Hannah's Cowpens was indistinguishable from the hundreds of nameless pastures that dotted the Carolinas. Since the earliest arrival of the white man these public grazing lands were used to feed the herds of cattle that roamed the countryside. In this relatively level park-like setting, Morgan gathered his forces on January 16th and layed out his ingenious plan of battle.

Morgan knew that Ban Tarleton invariably charged his adversaries head on; firm in his arrogance that a massed onslaught of disciplined infantry and cavalry would put the rabblous militia to rout every time. Several successful skirmishes, including his butchering of Buford's militiamen along the Waxhaws, only hardened his conviction as to the invincibility of Tarleton's Legion.

Playing deftly the hand dealt him, Morgan threw conventional military strategy to the wind. He placed his raw Georgia and North Carolina militia at the front to serve as skirmishers behind several trees that dotted the battleground. About 150 yards back he positioned Pickens' force of about 300 militiamen in a long line. With his best troops — Maryland and Delaware Continentals (Charles among them) — he created a third line of defense, with Colonel Washington's cavalry out of sight behind one of two small hills in the rear.

The night before the battle, Morgan, Pickens and the other officers moved from campfire to campfire challenging the militia who would be in the first two lines to hold their positions and fire just two well-aimed rounds, then they could fall back in good order behind the American rear line where they would reform. The men took up the call to "hold the line." If they would, Morgan's trap just might work.

By 3 a.m. on the 17th, Tarleton's troops were up and moving into position on the southwestern end of Hannah's Cowpens. They consisted of two battalions of British Regulars — the 71st Foot and the 7th Royal Fusiliers — supported by three companies of light infantry, a troop of the 17th Light Dragoons, and a Royal Artillery unit boasting two light 3-pounder "galloper" guns. In all, Tarleton commanded some 1,100 men — the finest light troops in Cornwallis's army.

Pickens' scouts spotted the general movement of the British and rushed word ahead to the Old Wagoneer who personally hobbled from tent to tent shouting the alarm, "Boys! Get up! Banny is comin'!"

By dawn the Americans were deployed according to plan and awaiting the advancing Redcoats, who were in plain view just 300 yards off. Impetuously, Tarleton hurried his men forward while still not properly formed. His resplendent troops moved out with a united cheer. Upfield Morgan's rugged frontiersmen met the cheers with their best and most boisterous Indian war whoops. The battle was on.

Immediately when the British advance was within range, the American skirmishers opened fire, toppling a half-dozen of Tarleton's green-clad legionaires from their saddles and pouring hot lead into the infantry. Remembering their orders to "look for the epaulets," they began dropping every officer near the front. As the 7th Royal Fusiliers drew within a hundred yards, the advanced line of militia suddenly broke off and ran in the opposite direction towards Pickens' South Carolina boys.

Here was precisely what Tarleton had come to expect. Elated, he exhorted his troops to rush on, smack into Pickens' line of musketry which leveled an enfilading explosion of fire at fifty yards. A wave of British officers and men fell lifeless or in mortal agony into the high grass. Reforming as best they could amid the gathering smoke and constant popping of Pickens' guns, the British veterans valiantly pressed on.

Once again the Americans turned on their heels and appeared to be taking flight in panic. And once again the British infantry, now supported by Tarleton's dragoons, cried "Huzza!" and launched into what they believed would be a merry American bloodbath. Just as the Redcoat bayonets and sabres were about to plow into the Americans' backs, out from their right flashed Colonel Washington's white-coated horsemen, screaming, smashing and slashing their way through their ranks in a whirlwind of fury.

Washington's cavalry extorted a gruesome toll, but there were too few of them to halt the British drive, although most of their officers and sergeants were now out of action. Tarleton's men bravely followed the only order they ever received from their commander, to advance, which brought them staggering towards Morgan's third and final line of Continentals dug in on the highest hill.

Disorganized, but still in high spirits, the British infantry engaged the Delaware and Maryland veterans in bloody to-the-death combat with blades, fists and flayling rifles. Tarleton, looking on from the bottom of the hill, thought the day was now won and threw the 71st Foot into the fray. If these stubborn Continentals would only break, then he could call up his still fresh contingent of 200 dragoons to sweep by the small unit of Virginia militia guarding the American right and clear the field.

But the men in blue and homespun brown held firm, dealing death for every inch they gave up. Meanwhile Washington and Pickens had hastily reformed their troops — about 300 in all — who were now streaming through the swail between the hills in a hell-bent for glory countercharge. Morgan, who was all over the field directing the action, stood in the center of the Continental line when he received Washington's one line message: "They are coming on like a mob — face about and give them a fire and I will charge them!"

The Patriot line drifted back in an orderly fashion to a point marked by

Morgan for his final stand. At the instant Washington and Pickens' men launched their furious counterattack, the Continentals whirled about abruptly and sent a withering massed volley into the faces of the British troops. It was now the British line that cracked. On with the bayonet rushed Howard's Continentals while Pickens' men drove in the British left flank. Washington's dragoons rode right past the Marylanders, sabres flashing. Washington himself engaged Tarleton in a clashing mounted sword fight that ended in a draw when Washington's horse was wounded and Tarleton, his army in ruins, at last drew back.

All across the body-strewn field beaten British survivors grounded their arms and at last pleaded for quarter. Many in the militia shouted "Tarleton's Quarter" or "No Quarter," remembering how Tarleton had slaughtered Buford's militia after they had surrendered, but Colonel Pickens and other officers quickly stepped forward to quell any senseless killing. Less than two hours after it began, the Battle of Cowpens was over.

For the first time since their initial defense of Charleston in 1776, the Patriots could crow of a major victory over British Regulars in the South. Of the 1,100 British and Tory troops engaged at Cowpens, 110 were killed, 229 wounded, and nearly 600 taken prisoner. Tarleton's vaunted Legion, as he was to report shortly to a shocked Cornwallis, was no more. The American losses: 12 killed and 60 wounded.

Amid the cheering American troops, General Morgan kept a steady head. There was still Cornwallis to deal with and the Old Wagoneer had no idea where he was — fifty miles away or just over yonder rise bearing down on him.

"Be quick about it boys! Gather up the guns and supplies, don't forget the cannon, and let's be on our way!" By noon the Americans were indeed on their way with the wounded piled in wagons and only the dead to lay claim to the battleground. By the time the incensed Cornwallis had drawn his fractured army to the site six days after the battle, Morgan was resting with his victorious troops one hundred miles away to the northeast at the fords of the Catawba. Strike hard and vanish into the mists; the American Army of the South had at last learned the secret of the partisans.

"Major Royal."

"General."

"With your knowledge of this country, you're my man to ride like the wind and tell General Greene of our success."

"Yessir."

"Tell him I dare not venture east without knowledge of Cornwallis's whereabouts. If I know that gray haired wolf he's pokin' his sword behind every rock and tree along the Broad. I don't have the men or cavalry to take on his entire army, so I'll wait here for General Greene's orders."

"As soon as I find a swift horse I'll be off, General."

"One more thing, son," said the weary Morgan. "Have him choose my replacement. Father Time and these tired howlin' bones of mine are tellin' me it's the end of my fightin' days . . . Would you have a drink with me before we part company?"

"I would be honored, sir."

Morgan grunted as he reached for a hard cider jug on the table beside him, plucking the cork out with his teeth. "To your health and good fortune, Royal." After taking a deep drink he sighed contentedly. Wiping the neck with his sleeve he handed the jug to Charles.

Charles raised it to Morgan and then took it to his lips. When he pulled away, Charles coughed and nearly choked from the burning in his throat.

Morgan laughed. "An acquired taste I reckon!" Morgan motioned to some buckskinned men nearby who were also imbibing. "To fellas like us this nectar's as sweet and natural as mother's milk."

As Charles went off to find a horse, Daniel Morgan enjoyed one last round of backslapping and jawing with his beloved "backwoods rascals."

Cornwallis's angry pursuit of Morgan went ominously bad from the start — he set out on the wrong road and in the wrong direction.

Realizing that the usual hobblers of a march — heavily laden baggage wagons, officers' furniture, women and children — would slow his army to a crawl over the muddy furrowed roads, Cornwallis ordered that his troops cast aside everything that would impede their progress; even the tents were burned. They would live off the land like these jackrabbit Americans and run Morgan and his men into the earth.

When General Greene received the news of the smashing victory at Cowpens he was ecstatic. He also correctly sized up the British response — Cornwallis would tear off after Morgan with every man and horse under his command. And on the march he himself would be vulnerable to attack and destruction. Moving with speed to match Morgan and Cornwallis, Greene mustered his troops and supplies at Cheraw and took up the race to reach Morgan before Cornwallis did.

Greene had the advantage of knowing the terrain far better than Cornwallis. On February 4th he and Morgan, weaving their way north across countless overflowing waterways, met and merged their forces at Guilford Court House in North Carolina just above Greensboro. Greene surveyed the area personally, taking detailed notes and qualifying the site as a possible location for a future action.

Even with Henry Lee's well-drilled mounted legion and several local militia groups joining him, Greene knew that his patchwork army, hungry and ill-equiped, was no match for the 2,000 hardened veterans Cornwallis was driving relentlessly in his direction.

Throughout February Greene fled his pursuers, who were rarely more than a day's march behind. Both generals cracked their whips and their men responded. So difficult was the march that the trails of both armies were littered with the corpses of horses and men who had succumbed to cold, hunger, or sheer exhaustion. The goal was to be the first to reach the Dan River, across which lay Virginia and safety for Greene's army.

To divert Cornwallis so that the main body of his command could make good its escape, Greene detached Colonel Otho Holland Williams to the west with seven hundred mounted Continentals. Cornwallis took the bait and sent General O'Hara of the Guards and the vengeful Tarleton to cutoff the American flight and force a decisive battle. Brilliantly, Williams would scuffle with the hounds at his heels and then slip away, avoiding a major engagement while drawing the enemy further and further inland away from Greene's army.

By the time Cornwallis got wise to the deception, it was too late. Williams doubled back and arrived in time to assist Greene as he loaded up every craft on the southern side of the gray, frigid Dan and rowed and poled across. Lee's Legion protected the crossing in a sharp rear guard action with O'Hara and Tarleton's dragoons and then shoved off in the last boats to join the American army on the far shore. In what must have seemed like a cruel replay of events that took place on the ice-choked Delaware River four years earlier, Cornwallis looked out forlornly across the sleet-swept Dan at his American quarry, still within view just beyond his grasp.

Cornwallis could take solace as he rested his troops and sent out foraging parties from his new base at Hillsborough that, as he wrote in his upbeat report to his superiors, *There is not a single American soldier in arms against the Crown from Virginia down to Florida.* Of course this was overstating the truth — General Greene's army was alive and growing (thanks to Baron von Steuben's Continental recruitment efforts) just across the river in Virginia, while the partisan forces of Marion, Sumter and Pickens were still sharp thorns in the British Lion's paw in the Carolinas.

Cornwallis issued a florid proclamation inviting local Loyalists to turn out for the King and restoration of constitutional law. Those who responded would soon wish they hadn't. Kirkwood's Delaware men broke up Tory meetings while Colonel Pickens and Colonel Lee, borrowing a page from his friend Francis Marion's book, struck hard at newly forming Tory units, slashing and scattering them to the winter wind. The flood of volunteers Cornwallis had counted on quickly slowed to a trickle.

Meanwhile, General Greene across the Dan was feeling emboldened. Against the advice of all his senior officers and to the utter amazement of Cornwallis, he floated his army back across the Dan in early March with an eye toward forcing one more battle for the possession of the Carolinas. His chosen place for this decisive confrontation: Guilford Court House.

There was no doubt that Cornwallis would take up the gauntlet. Here was the opportunity that he and his chastened troops had lusted for since the debacle at Hannah's Cowpens. Correctly guaging his adversary's state of mind, Greene laid out a strategy designed to take advantage of his enemy's impetuosity and disdainful attitude towards American fighting prowess. Not surprisingly, he adopted a battle plan virtually identical to that used by Morgan at Cowpens. Greene was banking on the hope that the British had not yet learned their lesson.

You have a great number of militia, Morgan wrote to Greene just before the Battle of Guilford Court House. *If they fight, you beat Cornwallis; if not, he will beat you. Put the militia in the center with some picked troops in their rear to shoot down the first man that runs.*

Greene took Morgan's counsel to heart, placing a broad screen of militia across the flat wooded approaches with Colonel Washington's cavalry anchoring the far left of the line and Lee's Legion holding the far right. Behind this first defensive wall, sheltered by woods, were the two raw Virginia militia units of Stevens and Lawson, ready to move forward where needed. These volunteers had agreed to only six week enlistments and Greene rightly had no faith in them.

The cream of his troops — the Virginia, Maryland and Delaware Continentals — Greene held mainly in a third line on the slopes before Guilford Court House. Like Morgan at Cowpens, success depended on the first line riddling Cornwallis's advance, staggering the British juggernaught before it could reach the slopes. And to stiffen their patriotic resolve, Greene followed Morgan's sage advice and positioned steel-jawed riflemen behind the militia, guns pointed at their backs.

Coming up the Great Road from Salisbury marched General Cornwallis's column, unaware of the American deployment that lay in the valley of the tiny village ahead. His force on the right included a contingent of artillery, General Alexander Leslie's infantry regiment supported by the 71st, and the First Battalion of Guards. To the left of the road under Colonel James

Webster marched the 23rd and 33rd Regiments, along with grenadiers and the Second Battalion of Guards commanded by General O'Hara. Jaegers and light infantry brought up the rear while Lieutenant Colonel Tarleton's dragoons fanned out in the van, on the lookout for those elusive American wisps of the woods.

In all, Cornwallis marched approximately 2,000 troops toward Guilford Court House, where Greene awaited his arrival with over 4,200 men in line of battle.

> *Guilford Court House*   *March 14, 1781*
> *North Carolina*
>
> *My Dearest Caitlin:*
>
> *You will be pleased to learn that I am alive and wholly unharmed following the recent battle at Hannah's Cowpens. Forgive my tardiness in writing to you, but since that eventful day the army has been much on the move throughout the Carolinas, up into Virginia, and now back into North Carolina.*
>
> *I am presently with General Greene's main body, serving as second to Otho Williams in command of the Maryland Continental Line. It is General Greene's opinion that we should give battle to General Cornwallis's army, which our intelligence informs us is in our neighborhood and should be paying us a visit shortly.*
>
> *You should rest easily in the knowledge that I and my men are held in the third or final line of the expected enemy advance. Chances are that I will remain a mere spectator to the military pageantry (if any) unfolding down the hill before me. Perhaps I should prepare a picnic lunch!*
>
> *This evening as I write this I can see General Greene walking among the militia troops, offering good cheer and asking only that they greet the enemy with two or three well-aimed volleys before retiring in good order. This is precisely as I witnessed General Morgan do before Cowpens. Let us hope that the results are the same.*
>
> *I shall write you a longer letter when the demands on an officer of the Maryland Continentals are not so great. I don't wish to complain, but at times I feel more like a wet-nurse than a soldier! Perhaps the smell of gunpowder*

*in their nostrils will cause the sniveling around here to
cease for awhile.*

Your Most Loving Husband,

Charles

*P.S. The weather has been quite brisk of late and the
overcoat you made me has served me very well. Indeed, I
am the envy of every officer and trooper I meet as none
has one to rival it.*

Cornwallis's march had begun in darkness with hungry, grumbling men
whose store of flour had run out the day before and who had not tasted rum
in weeks.

About 10 a.m. on the 15th, Tarleton's horsemen and their counterparts
among Lee's Legion chanced upon one another in the dense woods, exchanging fire and clashing swords. Sensing that this might be more than a
typical minor skirmish, General Cornwallis brought his troops up fast toward the clearing that lay around the next bend in the road.

As the Redcoats pressed forward into the valley, Greene's two six-pounders positioned in the center of the first line of militia opened fire from about
six hundred yards away. Up came the British artillery to answer the challenge, providing cover for the British troops as they hastily moved into battle
formation.

When they were ready, Cornwallis ordered his men to a general advance
with pounding drums and blaring fifes. Behind a rail fence the main first
line of North Carolina militia watched with a mixture of awe and terror, like
a bird caught in the mesmerizing glare of a multi-colored snake.

Leslie's force on the British right took the lead. Cornwallis astutely
observed that the brush was less thick there and that if he could crush the
American left then it would flee into the denser undergrowth where it would
be at the mercy of British bayonets.

Cooly, calmly the North Carolinians held their fire until the Redcoats
had advanced to within 150 yards. Then, on order, they unleashed a roaring
fusilade that tore into the enemy line causing, as one British officer would
later report, "one-half of the Highlanders to drop on that spot." Only superior, well-disciplined troops could weather such a barrage and still advance
in good order. Leslie's courageous men were equal to the task. Ripping a
volley of their own, they went charging ahead yelling like banchees with

bayonets leveled.

Here was a terrifying sight that the untested militia couldn't handle. Off came their packs, down went their muskets, and away they flew, fearing the screaming demons in scarlet and white more than their own officers who threatened to shoot them down.

The American right stood its ground only slightly better. There, Lieutenant Colonel Webster's fusiliers absorbed a similar wave of fire at 150 yards and responded to their commander's order to charge before the rebels could reload. However, when they pulled to within forty yards they found themselves staring down the bores of steely muskets poised in line along the rail fence. Almost simultaneously both commanders shouted "FIRE!" and a massive explosion shook the earth. When the smoke cleared, it was the British who were moving ahead with the North Carolinians falling back in panic.

As the American center caved in the British advanced rapidly only to find themselves caught in an unplanned and galling crossfire from the unshakeable Lee with Campbell's Virginia Rifles on their left and the equally steadfast Washington, more Virginian riflemen, and Lynch's 110 diehard Delaware Continentals on their right. Off in the tangled woods, fighting favored the Virginia militia who fought in the only fashion they knew — hand-to-hand Indian style.

Trying desperately to press his initiative, Cornwallis brought up all his reserves into the fray — O'Hara's grenadiers and the Second Battalion of Guards. Cornwallis himself had a horse shot out from under him and was nearly killed or captured in the frenzied woods fighting.

It was the embattled Webster on the British left, wounded but still in command of the 33rd, who finally broke through to the American's third line, which he and his battle-weary men undoubtedly did not expect to see. Virginia Continentals and the 1st and 2nd Marylanders along with two six-pounders smashed into them before they could form with an enfilading fire followed by a headlong screaming bayonet charge down the hill. The Second Battalion of Guards rushed forward along with the fusiliers and the remaining Highlanders to shore up the British position and in a heartbeat savage to-the-death fighting engulfed the entire swirling, swarming battle scene — twisted lines of howling and swearing soldiers having been hopelessly enmeshed.

In the midst of the fiercest fighting, his father's sword in one hand and a cocked pistol in the other, Charles's eyes locked on those of General Cornwallis, not fifty yards away. Cornwallis looked confused for a moment as he searched his memory, then recalling their dinner together he touched his hat toward Charles. Charles bowed deeply in a show of respect for his

noble adversary who sat his horse bravely in the jaws of death right alongside his troops.

Seeing that his force was about to be overrun, Cornwallis took a cold,
calculated gamble. He ordered two three-pounders brought to a high point
on the Great Road beside the battlefield and instructed that they be loaded
with grapeshot. With the fallen O'Hara pleading at his feet not to do it,
Cornwallis had the cannons fire directly into the maelstrom of soldiers, metal
fragments ripping into the bodies of Englishmen and Americans
indiscriminantly. Shocked, the two forces drew apart. The better trained
British knew how to reform more quickly and as they did so Greene ordered
a general retreat, leaving his artillery and wounded behind. Always in the
back of Greene's mind was his ultimate goal of keeping his army intact to
fight another day.

When the final smoke cleared and the cries of the wounded men and
horses had stilled, Cornwallis could claim a paper victory at Guilford Court
House. Hollow indeed in light of the horrifying realization that he had lost
one-fourth of his army. As one cynical wag in Parliament assessed the
news, "With a few more such 'victories,' the war shall be lost."

Had Greene fully understood the precarious state of Cornwallis's army
following Guilford Court House, he undoubtedly would have taken up its
trail and stomped it into submission. Instead, Greene turned south with the
intent of merging with the forces under Marion, Pickens, and Sumter and
crushing the last significant British army in the Carolinas; Lord Rawdon's
detachment at Camden.

For his part, Cornwallis had had his fill of warring with Morgan and
Greene, and he certainly wanted no more torment from the pestilent partisans in South Carolina. As he wrote to his friend Major General Phillips in
Virginia, *I am getting quite tired of marching about the country in quest of
adventures.* Both he and his demoralized army craved new venues where
they might find the citizenry more friendly and the enemy less formidable.
So after a brief layover in Wilmington by the Cape Fear River, Cornwallis
marched his men north up the coast and out of North Carolina forever. He
envisioned better luck campaigning on the shores of the Chesapeake and
wrote to Sir Henry Clinton in New York about his plans. Clinton endorsed
Cornwallis's proposal and asked him to select an appropriate spot near the
water where he could be protected by British warships, rest and reinvigorate
his army, and await further orders. Cornwallis quickly settled upon what he
considered to be the ideal location: Yorktown, Virginia.

By mid-April the fortunes of war had propelled Cornwallis's and Greene's armies — figuratively and literally — in opposite directions.

Appropriately enough, it was on a small island in a dismal swamp that General Greene first laid eyes on the slight, wizened, unkempt fellow in a charred leather cap, a sword rusted inside its scabbard strapped to his side, sipping vinegar.

Charles made the introductions. "General Nathanael Greene, it is my pleasure to introduce to you Colonel Francis Marion."

The two war horses eyed one another for a moment, then grasped each other in a firm handshake.

"Colonel, your exploits in these parts have made you a legend in the North and to a grateful nation for whom you have fought so gallantly for so many years."

"Most kind, General," Marion replied. "I applaud your successes as well. And now it appears that the pendulum has finally swung to our side."

"Indeed, I pray it is so. There's still much work to be done. That's why I'm here, Colonel. To enlist your support, and that of Pickens, Sumter and the rest,"

"You can count on me and my boys, General."

Greene smiled. "I already have."

"Could I interest you gentlemen in some boiled potatoes? Know it's not much, but since Royal here left, the quality of our culinary cuisine has fallen off markedly."

"I had no idea you were a cook, Major."

"Best we ever had," Marion said matter-of-factly. "Several of my men gave me hell for sending him off to you before he gave us the recipe for his 'Gator au Boston'."

"Gator au what?"

"Never mind," Marion replied with a wave of his hand. "Probably couldn't make it as well as him anyway. Let's eat."

Over their humble meal Charles inquired about Rake's whereabouts.

"Gone."

"Gone, sir?"

"Gone home on leave."

Charles looked perplexed.

"Wasn't my idea. He just came up to me and said, 'Colonel, my father's died and I've decided to go home to Maryland for awhile to be with my sister'."

"You allow men to dictate the terms of their service?" Greene asked incredulously.

"This man, yes," Marion replied firmly. "Been with me in these putrid swamps fightin' Tories and Redcoats for six years without a day off or a day's pay. Reckon a little vacation was only fair. He'll be back by and by."

"How do you know?" Greene inquired.

"Cause he said so." Then turning to Charles, Marion winked knowingly. "When Rake Serling sets his mind to something, God pity the man foolish enough to stand in his way."

Over the next few days Charles enjoyed his reunion with the Irregulars of Marion's command. In his honor they staged a sprightly brawl pitting the camp's best eye-gouger against its keenest biter. Though the sharp-toothed gladiator succeeded in chewing-off the upper part of an ear, it was generally conceded that the eye-gouger had gotten the better of it. For once food was in good supply and Charles paid the men back for their hospitality by serving up several tasty meals. He also explained to Strawman his secret technique for preparing alligator.

But his stay proved to be short. General Greene had a job for him.

"Major Royal, I have prepared a letter for Congress and one for General Washington in the Jerseys, or perhaps New York; communications are so poor these days. Anyway, I've detailed our latest adventures and my current plans for harassing the enemy in South Carolina into submission. I want you to deliver them."

"Yessir."

"Don't look so downcast, Royal. You've served the Cause gallantly. It's time to let someone else hold aloft the standard for awhile."

"If you say so, sir."

"I do indeed!" Greene replied gruffly, masking his real intent. "Tell me . . . How long has it been since you've seen your wife, Major." Charles had to think. "Just about a year, sir."

"Don't you think it's time you went home for a spell then?"

Charles was speechless while Greene stood grinning ear-to-ear.

"After you've delivered the letters, take whatever time you wish to spend at home. Come back when you're rested and ready."

"Thank you sir!" Charles managed to say at length.

"I believe I'll learn much from our friend Colonel Marion, including how to take care of the people who take care of me. Bon voyage, Royal," Greene said, hand extended. Charles took it, then saluted and the two men parted company.

At dawn of the next day Charles was already mounted and traveling northwest along the shore of the Santee. He was anxious to make good time, but careful to avoid nests of Tory support. Should he write to Caitlin or just surprise her? It was a joyous thought as he rode along. The roads were muddy and miserable due to the almost constant rain. But nothing could diminish Charles's high spirits. For the moment the guns were silent, the flowers would soon bloom, and he was on the road home.

Chapter 24

Charles arrived in Philadelphia in late April and immediately found his way to Independence Hall where Congress was in session. He had spent the bitter winter with Washington's army at Valley Forge outside the city, but this was his first opportunity to clip-clop along Philadelphia's cobblestone streets and experience the city's vibrancy. On another occasion he might pause to see the sights, but now he was a man on a mission.

"Mr. Hancock."

John Hancock recognized his tavernmate in an instant. "Why Charles Royal! This is an unexpected pleasure indeed, lad. Look at you! A major in the army! You've come quite a ways since our days at Mr. Robinson's establishment."

"As have you, sir. President of Congress."

"Ah! An honorarium I would as soon dispense with as a painful corn on my big toe. All day long we debate words and ideas while brave souls like yourself do the *real* work of the Revolution. I would gladly trade a lifetime of 'President of Congress' for one moment's glory leading a cavalry charge."

Hancock happily parried the air with an imaginary sword. Charles, now the hardened veteran of the bloody real war, smiled respectfully.

"I have a letter for Congress, sir, from General Greene in the South."

"You were with him then, at Guilford Court House?"

"Yessir. And with General Morgan before that at Hannah's Cowpens."

"God! How I envy you!"

For the next two hours Hancock pumped Charles for every bit of information he possessed on the Southern Campaign — Gates's failure at Camden, the partisan warriors and their strategies, the battles of Cowpens and Guilford Court House, the present state of the army and Charles's impressions as to the spirit and morale of the troops, and the enemy's lingering strength in the South.

Charles seized the opportunity to voice the complaints of his men who hunger and go without even the basic necessities — from blankets, tents, and simple uniforms to shoes. "It is said with eminent truth that you can tell the American march from the British by the tracks of blood their soldiers' feet leave on the ground."

John Hancock appeared visibly moved and shook his head ruefully. "We in Congress know of your plight, Major. Believe me, we would gladly alleviate the needless suffering of the brave soldiers if it were within our power to do so. Truth is, we haven't a farthing. I met with Robert Morris who is in charge of our treasury yesterday afternoon. On this very table he opened and turned over a small money chest to demonstrate our fiscal state. It was empty. If not for the generosity of our French allies and our friends at European Courts we would all be as destitute as beggars in the street."

"What about the state governments?"

"Ha! They look to their own skins well enough when the war shifts to their locale. Otherwise, they turn a deaf ear to every appeal. Why, I have literally worn out quills in futile letters pleading for support. I'm afraid all rests on the strong shoulders of General Washington and the courage of men like you in the field. As for we bewigged members of Congress — we're just so many jabbering toothless pussycats!" Hancock pounded his fist on the table in anger and frustration.

That evening Charles dined with Hancock and other leading politicians at nearby City Tavern where Hancock would "have the pleasure of breaking bread with the young man who once baked it so well for me." The next morning Charles was on a fresh horse riding north to deliver Greene's letter to His Excellency, General Washington.

Charles had decided he would surprise Caitlin and not alert her to his leave from the army. So on a picturesque May morning with birds singing and the entrance flowers to Oakmont in regal radiance, Charles rode up to the door of the great mansion and dismounted. As a stableboy took the reins, Caitlin appeared at the entryway, wiping her hands on her apron. With a wide-eyed squeal of delight, she rushed from the porch and threw herself into her husband's waiting arms, kissing his face until Charles finally pried the two of them apart laughing.

"Charles! You're home!" she babbled. "How? . . . Why? . . . This is wonderful!" She hugged him tightly around the neck and pressed her body firmly to his.

"You know, this is exactly the reaction Colonel Marion had when I last visited him," Charles joked. "Of course, you kiss better."

"Come in the house. This is wonderful! Rake is upstairs. He'll be so happy to see you!"

As they walked out of the sunlight into the entry hall Charles looked up to see a powerful figure of a man paused halfway down the staircase. Dressed in the clothes of a wealthy country gentleman — forest green velvet jacket, cream colored breeches, white pleated linen shirt beneath a gold-checkered vest — Charles hardly recognized him.

"Rake?"

"Charles!"

Rake flew down the remaining steps two at a time and swooped Charles up in that manly bearhug that was one of his many trademarks. "Charles! It's great to see you! Home on leave like me, eh?"

"Yes I am."

"For how long?" Caitlin asked excitedly.

"Long enough to remember what a lucky man I am," Charles said, laying his fingers gently on Caitlin's soft cheek and gazing into her green eyes.

"What a grand day!" Rake announced to the walls. "Oakmont will roar with laughter and good times once more!" For the first time, in this setting, Charles saw some of the Judge's bouyant personality in his brother-in-law.

Caitlin locked arms with Charles and led him towards the dining room for refreshments. As they walked, Charles turned his head back and gave Rake's splendid attire a skeptical head to foot once over.

"One word to Marion and the boys," Rake cautioned, "And they'll be eatin' *Charles* au Boston."

The following day Charles, Rake, and Caitlin sat in the Judge's study when Junius strode in, hat in hand.

"Have a seat, Junius," Rake said, motioning to one of the red velvet upholstered chairs.

"Charles, Caitlin and I have been talkin' about Oakmont and how we're goin' to manage the place now that the Judge's gone.

"Junius, Caitlin and I would like you to go on runnin' Oakmont just as you've been doin'. You've done a great job. Place never looked more prosperous and that's a fact."

"Thank you, sir."

"For God's sake man, you don't have to call me 'sir.' We have the same father. You're like a brother to Caitlin and me. No one calls me sir anyway; 'specially not my men. From now on call me Rake, same as everybody else."

"Rake," Junius nodded.

"There ya go."

"Junius," Caitlin continued, "We want you to join us as equal partners at Oakmont. Any profit we make we'll split even-steven three ways. What do you say?"

Junius was dumbstruck. He spoke slowly, "You mean I get one-third of everythin'?"

"Not enough?" Rake asked innocently.

"Oh it's plenty fine, sir, ah Rake . . . But this is *your* plantation. I'm just a slave."

"Not anymore," Caitlin smiled. "In the Judge's heart you never were and Rake and I want to make it official. Henceforth you, your wife, and your children are free. Here are the legal papers, signed and dated." She handed them to Junius who caressed them in his hands as if they were the holy grail.

"Of course this means you're free to go anywhere you choose. We hope, though, that you'll consider our offer and stay at Oakmont and make it your home."

Junius was still in shock. "Can this all be true?"

"True as the gospel," said Rake. "Course bein' black you can't own property in your own right in Maryland. So we've drawn up a 'gentlemen's agreement.' Caitlin and I have already signed it and there's a place for your signature there. And with that, as far as we're concerned, the deal's done. You can read it if you like."

Junius looked into Caitlin's face and then into Rake's. Seeing the truth of it, he picked up the quill, dipped its pointed tip into the ink well, and carefully wrote *JUNIUS.*

"We're partners!" Rake bellowed, thrusting his hand toward Junius who took it with an incredulous chuckle. "Partners." His face grew into a wide grin as the words sank in. "Partners!" The three exchanged joyous hand-shakes as Charles looked on approvingly. These Serlings truly were a breed apart.

Rake suddenly remembered Charles's presence. "Oh, and if I'm killed in battle, I hereby will my stake to Major Charles Royal as a belated wed-ding gift."

"You already gave me a wedding gift," Charles reminded him softly. Caitlin pressed both of them to explain what the mysterious 'wedding gift' was all about, but neither man would tell her.

To mark the occasion, Rake offered Charles and Junius huge cigars from the Judge's humidor. As they lit up and leaned back with blue smoke curling through the room, Rake remarked contentedly, "The Judge would have loved this. . . "

Rake had decided before Charles's unexpected arrival that it was high time he returned to Marion's band. He missed the snakes, swamps, bugs, alligators, and Tories.

"Best to get back to the fun before it's all over. Now that Charles is here to keep my helpless little sister company," Rake teased, "I feel free to take my leave."

Caitlin knew her brother better than he thought. "Rake Serling, if my skirts were on fire and you heard the sound of a bugle and drums over the hill, why you'd leave me to toast!"

Rake laughed uproariously, pulling his sister to him and kissing her. "You're right Charles, she doesn't like me!"

"Oh she loves you. She also knows you very well."

Charles prepared pickled lamb chops with all the trimmings for Rake's farewell dinner. Afterwards, Charles, Rake, and Caitlin took a long lazy walk by the bank of the Potomac and sat sipping cool drinks on the great gazebo, laughing and teasing one another under a full silver moon until very late.

At sunup Rake, his horse saddled and pack mule loaded, stood before the manor house saying goodbye. "We'll all miss you in Marion's camp," he said to Charles. "I'm not lookin' forward to those goddam boiled potatoes!"

"Admit it, you only love me for my cooking."

"I'll admit that you're a man of many talents, Charles. Cookin's just one of 'em."

The two men embraced warmly.

"Give my regards to Fat Hat if you see her."

"Who's Fat Hat?" Caitlin asked.

"Later," Charles and Rake said simultaneously.

"Here, I've packed some linen shirts and underwear for you; and your favorite smoking jacket," Caitlin said, handing a bundle to Rake. "Thanks," he replied. Caitlin took him in her arms. "I love you! You take care of yourself. I can't imagine life without you in it." Rake nodded and they kissed each other on the cheek. After exchanging smiles, Caitlin turned and walked back into the house.

Once she was beyond view, Rake handed her bundle to Charles. "Ahhh," he began. Charles nodded, knowing the ribbing Rake would receive if such garments were discovered by Marion's men. "I'll take care of 'em."

With a last hardy handshake, Rake swung up onto his mount, straightened the long feather in his hat, and with a wave was happily on his way galloping toward the front gates of Oakmont and the war that lay beyond.

"Did Rake tell you about the papers he filed before he left?" Caitlin asked Charles.

"No."

"They were nomination papers, with signatures, for the special election they're holding for the Judge's seat on the General Assembly."

"Rake, a politician! Wonderful! He'll set those plump old squires right on their ears!"

"Charles, the name he placed in nomination was yours."

"Mine?"

"Uh-huh."

"How can I run for public office? I'm a soldier in the army. I've never been elected to anything in my life. Plus I'm not even a *resident* of this state."

"My darling," Caitlin smiled. She had prepared for his every protest. "Rake believes you'd be the perfect representative of the people. So do I."

"But what do I know about politics?"

"What does anyone know? Besides, you know more than you think. You met everyone who's anyone in Annapolis and the Judge told me they all loved you. And you sat at the very elbow of men like John and Sam Adams and John Hancock in Boston before the Revolution."

"That's another thing; I'm a Massachusetts man."

"You're an American first. You'll bring fresh ideas and a new vision to Maryland. You've spent all this time recruiting for the Maryland Continentals, training them, leading them into battle. Who would dare deny you the rights of a citizen?"

"I don't know how to campaign."

"We'll learn together."

"I'm too young. They'll want an older man with experience."

"Anyone with experience will have gotten it serving the Crown. There's a new age dawning, Charles, and you're exactly what's called for — a young intelligent war hero to help lead a new nation."

" . . . When's the election?"

"The fourth of July."

"Will I have an opponent?"

"Yes, and a formidable one I'm afraid. Dalton Seymour. Son of the richest man in Montgomery County. A man my father positively despised."

"I'll run on one condition," Charles finally said reluctantly.

"And what's that?"

"That you'll be my campaign manager and write all of my speeches."

"It's a deal!" Caitlin reached up and kissed Charles on the lips. "Now get dressed in your uniform. It's layed out on the bed. We have a tea scheduled this afternoon with a group of church deacons' wives."

"I thought women couldn't vote in Maryland."

"They can't, but they have absolute control over those who do."

"Oh I see, we've traded one form of tyranny for another."

Caitlin smiled sweetly. "You're learning, my love."

Throughout June Charles and Caitlin traversed the county meeting with the local powerbrokers and moneyed interests and shaking hands and kissing the babies of the common folk.

They made an attractive couple — Charles, wearing the uniform of a major with the celebrated Maryland Continentals who had brought honor and recognition to the state, and his beautiful wife Caitlin, daughter of the much admired Judge Serling and the administrator of the military hospital in Rockville that had provided excellent care for so many of the county's sick and wounded soldiers.

In marketplaces, before church congregations, at every sizeable public gathering they "pressed the flesh" and listened to the grievances large and small of the citizenry.

Their adversary, Dalton Seymour, took the more traditional, aristocratic approach to campaigning. His equally highborn representatives gave speeches stating Mr. Seymour's studied positions on various issues and attesting in the most glowing terms as to his character and fitness to govern. Seymour was unmarried, foppish, and somewhat effeminate. He was more comfortable in the drawing room or ballroom than on the campaign stump. His strategy rested on buying the support — through promises of patronage, or outright bribes — of the political hacks who controlled the county's voting blocks. He had the money and the connections and he didn't hesitate to use both.

As election day drew near, the citizens of Montgomery County reveled in what had become the first real political horse race in anyone's memory. All of Charles and Caitlin's hard personal campaigning had paid off. Starting with virtually no name recognition, Charles was now seen by many as a dynamic new leader who was willing to take on the old-line interests — and if there's one thing Americans always favor in a fight, it's the underdog.

It was not surprising then that a record turnout of nearly three thousand voters gathered at the Rockville Court House on July 1st for "Candidates Day," a special event at which both assembly candidates would be giving speeches from the same stage. Normally Seymour would have avoided such a direct confrontation with his opponent, but the race was too tight and to decline an opportunity to stand before so many people this late in the contest would undoubtedly tilt the scales in Charles's favor.

As was the custom, both candidates supplied great casks of liquid refreshment — ale, beer, short beer, and wine — for the electorate to enjoy. It was not at all uncommon for the quality of a candidate's spirits, rather than his civic spirit, to decide an election.

Under a merciless sun in a cloudless blue sky Dalton Seymour rose first to speak. He wore a freshly powdered wig and a burnt-orange colored coat with gold thread piping, a white ruffled shirt, and white breeches. Clearly here was a candidate with the aristocratic bearing and wealth that the people had come to expect in their elected officials.

"My dear citizens," Seymour began in a high clear voice, waving a white lace handkerchief in his hand which he occasionally used to mop his brow. "You see before you today two candidates vying for the honor of serving as your representative to the Maryland General Assembly.

"Your large numbers attest to your commendable attention to civic matters and suggest that you have not quite made up your minds as to which of us might best serve your interests in Annapolis.

"By no means have I come here today to denigrate my worthy opponent. If there were two vacant seats up for election I am sure that he would make an excellent choice for the second one. But as there is only one, you must select that candidate with the singular background and abilities that best qualify him for the post.

"Most of you knew me and my family's name long before this glorious summer's day. Since this land was first settled, Seymour's have stood beside you; clearing the land, fighting off the savages, and helping to make Montgomery County a haven on earth for every hardworking yeoman and his family. We have shared your triumphs, and felt your pain. We are one with you. For generations Seymours have held elective office and served you well. It is not for glory, or profit, or any thought of personal gain that we have sought positions in the public trust. Our only motivation has been to serve you the people.

"I stand before you as the latest in this long line of civic-minded men. My ancestors look down upon me at this moment, and upon you, crying from on high for us to support knowledgeable, experienced leadership against an outside usurper.

"My friends, Mr. Royal is not one of us. He does not speak like us. He does not think like us. When the war is over and his enlistment is up, why he may not even *live* with us!

"His connection to us is through his lovely wife, the former Caitlin Serling, daughter of our late beloved friend Judge Serling. Not only is she Mr. Royal's devoted wife, she is also his sole source of financial support, for the man is utterly destitute; poor as a church mouse!

"Now I ask you, as you consider on the fourth which candidate is best suited to represent you, do you choose a man from a family known to you who shares your problems as if they were his own? Or an outsider who seeks public office not out of a sense of noble purpose, but in the fervent hope of lining his empty pockets with gold from the public trough!" With a fist thrust in the air, Seymour punctuated his final remark. Loud, enthusiastic applause and voices shouting support rang throughout the large gathering, and he basked in it. Seymour's cronies had paid two dozen boys spread throughout the crowd a shilling each to pound on drums at the conclusion of Seymour's speech. Their clatter prolonged the generally favorable reception.

Charles applauded politely and waited until his opponent had taken his seat with a flourish before rising and stepping to the front of the stage. For a long moment he stood there, dressed in his major's uniform, smiling benignly and gazing out over the multitude.

At length he raised his arm, pointing to a farmer off to his right. "Hello Mr. Parsons! How goes it with your sick cow?"

The startled man called back, "Well enough, Major, thanks to the concoction your wife whipped up."

Charles nodded and turned to his left. "And good day to you, Mrs. D'Angelo. Have you heard anything from your husband and your brother in the Continentals?"

"Aye, Major. They're doin' fine, thank you."

"Good, good."

Then looking at someone in the middle of the crowd, Charles announced, "I see Reverend Stocker is with us today. The good Pastor and I have been discussing his hopes for having two acres of public land near his parsonage set aside for a new school and a play area for the children. Rest assured, sir, it will be among the first items I will support when I arrive in Annapolis."

"Bless you, Major."

"Friends, and I feel I am qualified to call you friends since my wife and I have had the pleasure of greeting so many of you during this campaign, I stand before you today accused of being an 'outsider.' Well, in a sense Mr. Seymour is absolutely correct! Yes, I am not an established political insider. I have never made a single backroom deal or sold out your interests to enrich myself, and I assure you that day shall never come!

"Mr. Seymour is correct on one other matter. I am not an aristocrat like he is. Oh I came from a prosperous family up north, but the Revolution, I'm afraid, has impoverished me as I know it has many of you.

"But when Mr. Seymour says that I am a stranger among you, there I draw the line. For when a man has demonstrated that he is willing to lay down his own life on your behalf, do you call him 'stranger' or do you call him friend?

"Service takes many forms, my friends. Like so many of you, and your husbands, brothers, sons, and cherished relations, I chose to serve in the Great Cause of American Freedom while others elected to stay home and profit from the heroes blood spent gallantly on the battlefields from Massachusetts to Georgia.

"It has been my honor in my service to my country to serve alongside the brave lads of the Maryland Continental Line, whose valor is well established and needs no further embellishment by me here today. I have commanded your soldiers in the field and been commanded by them. Together we've tasted the fiery smoke of battle and stood shoulder to shoulder against the sharpened bayonet charge of the cruel British enemy and his heinous Tory allies. As I endured every hardship imaginable alongside your brave men, I drew inspiration from their courage and devotion to duty.

"It is my fervent hope that I may be permitted to continue to serve those brave souls, and their loving families and friends gathered here today and throughout Montgomery County. In Annapolis, I will remember your voices well; your hopes for a better life for yourselves, your children, and your brethern fighting for all our liberties.

"I am not one of the old elite political aristocracy. I am a common man, one of you, who wishes nothing more than to see that your voices are heard loud and clear in the State House in Annapolis.

"My friends, we are on the threshhold of a bright new age; an American age. And I believe Maryland will lead the way just as it has led the army on the field of honor. So let us lock arms one with the other today, casting out tired old ideas, embracing the new, and march boldly into that bright new future together!"

For a moment there was absolute silence. For an instant Charles's heart dropped like a rock. Then, like a violent thunderstorm following a motionless calm, applause and cheering exploded into the summer's air.

Seymour and his startled cohorts cast their eyes about wildly at the overwhelming response. Clearly this man Royal had latched onto an emotional impulse in the people that they had not anticipated. These *were* revolutionary times in more ways than one, and the voters were anxious to change the established order of things. It truly was a new age.

On the day of the election Charles and Caitlin rode in their carriage to the polling place early. Charles cast his vote and after shaking hands with a few well-wishers they returned home. It was not until the afternoon of the following day that the votes were tallied and the results known. Caitlin and Charles were sitting quietly on the front porch after dinner sipping coffee when a mounted messenger approached. Without ceremony he handed down an official sealed envelope. Charles held it in his hands. He looked over at Caitlin who was doing everything in her power to hide her anxiety. With a deep sigh, Charles slid his finger under the seal and burst the letter open.

THE MONTGOMERY COUNTY BOARD OF VOTERS
DOES HEREWITH DULY ATTEST AND SWEAR
TO THE FOLLOWING VOTE COUNT
FOR THE OFFICE OF STATE ASSEMBLYMAN
FOR SAID MONTGOMERY COUNTY

CHARLES ROYAL   2,722
DALTON SEYMOUR   1,894

Dated July 5, 1781

Charles walked heavily, solemnly back up the stairs. Standing before Caitlin, he betrayed the results with a wink.

"You won?"

When Charles nodded, Caitlin lunged for the letter. As she read it her face lit up.

"Oh Charles, this is wonderful! I'm so proud of you!" She stood and hugged her husband and kissed him warmly. "It looks like we're going to Annapolis!"

"Appears so."

Returning to her chair Caitlin savored the lopsided returns. "Ooh! This is pretty decisive. Must have been my cure for Mr. Parson's cow that turned the tide."

"Undoubtedly."

After the fatigues and uncertainties of the campaign, Charles and Caitlin drank in the news of victory in subdued contentment. There would be no boisterous celebration. No ball or banquet to mark the occasion. Just the quiet realization that a new chapter had opened in their lives. As they sat together peacefully watching the reddish glow of a summer sunset across the fields, all thoughts were turned to the future — to a new life filled with promise. The war had no place in this hopeful world. But its dark clouds lingered and rumbled beyond the golden crops, beyond the white fences of Oakmont, somewhere just beyond the setting sun.

Over the weeks that followed, Charles busied himself with preparations for his and Caitlin's trip to Annapolis for the swearing in and his first session as a delegate to the General Assembly.

His constituency kept up a steady stream of petitions and requests for political favors. Charles received all who visited him with warmth, or at least civility. Some of the requests were ridiculous, such as the digging of a new five mile canal for the sole benefit of an upriver planter. These Charles dispensed with on the spot. Others, he agreed to support or study further. He was new to this game and wisely didn't overcommit himself. "In public life you never want to promise what you can't deliver," the Judge had advised him during their ride home from Annapolis. Charles made it his motto.

As was the custom, Charles was offered all types of "gratuities" from the grateful citizenry for advancing their interests at the state level. Sometimes it was a lamb or a chicken. Or perhaps a couple bushels of corn. Once he was presented with a fine yolk of oxen. Each of these he turned down, just as the Judge had before him. "It's the right of the people to express their needs and concerns to the government," Charles told Caitlin. "There is no fee for it."

He did have to admit to her, however, that "It's nice after all these years in the army to at last be doing a job where I have the prospect of being paid something." Charles and Caitlin laughed at their own ignorance when they realized that neither one knew how much an assemblyman gets paid.

Of all the gifts Charles was offered and declined, there was one he couldn't turn away — a bright bouquet of flowers from a little brown-eyed girl with freckles and a pigtail (she had probably picked them in Oakmont's front yard). These Charles and Caitlin graciously accepted.

August's sultry days found Charles finishing his last minute correspondence while Caitlin met with Junius on plantation matters. Annapolis awaited. On the evening before their scheduled departure, though, fate paid them an unexpected call in the form of a military courier who galloped up the road to Oakmont with a dispatch that would shatter their carefully-laid plans.

August 17, 1781

Major Charles Royal
Oakmont on the Potomac
Montgomery County, Maryland

Dear Major Royal:

I'm afraid your leave has just ended. You are to muster all area Continental troops and any militia units you can and march them without delay to join forces with the army under the command of General Lafayette, presently encamped in or near Williamsburg, Virginia. You will receive further orders upon your arrival. Speak to no one of your destination until you are well underway. Godspeed.

- Greene

Charles had no idea what prompted this terse, emphatic letter. There had been a lull in the fighting everywhere except in South Carolina. So why was he being rushed to Virginia where Lafayette commanded little more than a reconnaissance-in-force to keep tabs on the crippled, but still potentially dangerous force under Cornwallis?

How would Caitlin take the news? Her heart was set on Annapolis. Once again the war had forced its heartless way between them. Caitlin came out on the porch just as the rider was passing out of view.

"That was a military courier, wasn't it?"

"Yes."

Her face tightened. "What did he want?"

"Here," Charles handed her his orders.

After she read the message she closed her eyes and sighed deeply. "Well, it appears Annapolis will have to wait."

"I'm so sorry."

Caitlin shrugged, then hit upon an idea. "You know, my bags are all packed and everything here and at the hospital has been put in order; how about I travel with you to Williamsburg?"

The novel notion caught Charles off guard. Before he could voice his usual stream of reservations, Caitlin sprang to the occasion.

"I've never been there you know, and I'd love to see it; the capital of Virginia and all. I promise I wouldn't be in the way — why I could even help you should any of the men get sick or injured on the road. Please Charles, *please*. Say I can come." Her warm expressive eyes were overflowing with childlike yearning. Given time Charles could easily come up with a dozen reasons why it was a bad idea. But those eyes melted him like butter in the hot sun.

"Alright."

"Wonderful! You'll see. You'll be happy I came. It'll be an adventure for both of us!"

Somewhere inside, Charles sensed the truth in that.

Chapter 25

With nearly 300 troops, seven supply wagons, thirty pack mules and one wife, Charles led the way down the long dusty familiar road south into Virginia.

Rumors were flying among the soldiers that they were on their way to a major engagement. Cornwallis had gained reinforcements by merging with the Loyalists and British Regulars formerly under the command of Major General William Phillips, and there was talk that a Royal Armada had set sail from New York City bound for the Chesapeake.

Charles chose not to engage in the excited speculations. While he was fairly certain that hostilities would escalate — governments hated to foot the bill for dormant armies — it seemed more likely that the theatre of action would be in New York or New Jersey where Washington and the leader of the French forces in America, General Rochambeau, had been sparring with Sir Henry Clinton's main army of Redcoats and Hessians for more than a year. New York City, Boston, Philadelphia, Charleston; these were prize pieces easily recognizable to European powers with their chess-like approach to war. What in the marshy, sparsely populated Virginia Tidewater could hold any comparable attraction?

Almost from the outset, Caitlin's prophecy as to her value on the journey proved to be true. The men seized upon the flimsiest excuse of an ailment to visit with her, and her good cheer added immensely to the soldiers' morale. In fact, they virtually ignored the regimental surgeon, but that was fine by him. He was able to spend more time swigging whiskey and playing whist.

Charles had first met Marie Joseph Paul Yves Roch Gilbert Motier de La Fayette during the devastating winter at Valley Forge. There they developed an amiable relationship — it was hard not to take a liking to the gracious, lively, personable French boy-general; especially when the story of his prelude to America became known.

Born in 1757 to a very wealthy aristocratic family with a noble tradition of military service, the infant Gilbert inherited the title Marquis before his second birthday when his father, a 27 year-old colonel in the French Army, was struck and killed by a British cannon ball at Minton. The young Marquis also inherited an insatiable, lifelong fascination with the glory and pageantry of war.

At age sixteen Lafayette was betrothed in an arranged marriage to fourteen year-old Adrienne d'Ayen, the daughter of another French family of immense wealth. Named a captain in the army of Louis XVI, Gilbert and Adrienne seemed destined for a fairy tale life of glittering balls at the Palace of Versailles and, when the need arose, duty as a gentleman-soldier.

But young Lafayette was impatient for action. The succession of wars with England that had stretched back for a century had been followed by more than a decade of peace. France had entered a period where it was trying to rebuild its commerce and extend its influence through diplomacy. War was the last thing on anyone's mind. Anyone except Lafayette.

Benjamin Franklin and Silas Deane were America's official representatives to France at this time. By day they met with the King's Minister, the Comte de Vergennes, and other high placed officials to whom they pleaded for money, munitions, and badly needed supplies — most of which the officially neutral French government denied them. Covertly, they sought to entice French privateers and experienced soldiers to cast their lot with the American Cause. They promised rich inducements to the sea captains and inflated rank for the military men — neither of which they had any authority to make good on. In time, Congress grew weary of the endless stream of European adventurers who came striding into their meetings in Philadelphia making outlandish demands and brandishing grandiose military appointments signed by Dr. Franklin.

A few of these were legitimate, capable officers who proved to be of immeasurable service to the amateurish American Army — von Steuben, Thaddeus Kosciuszko, Baron de Kalb, Casimir Pulaski — and of these the one who would most distinguish himself was the youngest and least experienced; the Marquis de La Fayette.

Franklin met with the rich, energetic French nobleman in Paris and listened to his dreams of fighting for the great cause of liberty in America — a land he had yet to visit. Franklin saw something in the youth and drafted letters of introduction to Congress for him and the sixteen soldiers-of-fortune who were to accompany him.

King Louis XVI received information from a spy about Lafayette's plans and ordered the Marquis to remain on French soil. Lafayette appeared to accept the edict of his monarch while he secretly bought and had fitted-out a ship, *La Victorie*, for the voyage — a secret he kept even from Adrienne. When preparations were ready, Lafayette slipped away and set sail with his men from Le Havre, just as His Majesty's guards appeared on the dock to haul the headstrong Marquis back to Versailles. As they cleared the harbor under a strong tailwind, Lafayette turned to his little group, "I am an outlaw. I prefer to fight for the liberty of America rather than lose my own liberty and languish in a French prison." The first of many adventures in this remarkable life had begun.

After a storm-tossed 59-day Atlantic crossing, *La Victorie* ran aground off the South Carolina coast. Lafayette and his men rowed ashore, but before they had even splashed their way to the beach they were met by a hail of musket fire. Colonel Huger's South Carolina militia had mistaken them for a rogue band of Hessians who were terrorizing the area. Following a fine meal at Huger's home, Lafayette and his followers mounted horses and began the long ride to Philadelphia where Congress was in session.

Listening attentively, the Congressmen were impressed with this gallant French nobleman who had risked a vast fortune and the wrath of his king to serve in the American fight for freedom.

A solemn Lafayette concluded his case before them by saying, "After the sacrifices I have made I have the right to exact two favors. One is to serve at my own expense. The other is to serve at first as a volunteer in the ranks."

His modesty and passionate devotion moved the Congressmen to confirm his commission without delay and to accept the officers who accompanied him as well into the Continental Army.

The nineteen year-old major general and his followers were then pointed in the direction of General Washington's encampment.

The name of the Marguis was already familiar to the Commander-in-Chief. Franklin had written him directly from Paris urging Washington to "protect that amiable young nobleman from his extreme generosity."

Washington and Lafayette took an immediate liking to each other that quickly blossomed into a more familial bond. To the elder man, Lafayette was like the son he never had. And to Lafayette, who had never known his own father, Washington became his mentor and hero. As he later wrote to Adrienne, "(Washington's) name will be revered throughout the centuries by all who love liberty and humanity."

Washington honored his young charge by inviting him to become a member of his senior military staff or "family." At Valley Forge the two were virtually inseparable. Lafayette ingratiated himself with the other officers in Washington's command when he deferred in giving advice, stating, "I am here to learn, not to preach or teach."

Lafayette also became close with Washington's brilliant aide-de-camp, Colonel Alexander Hamilton, and the corpulent General of Artillery, Henry

Knox, with whom he shared a love of military literature. The tall, hand-some, rail-thin Lafayette and the short, roundish Knox were also devout epicures who enjoyed discussing gourmet meals and wines. As they noted with good humor amid the meager circumstances at Valley Forge, at least they could still *talk* about dining well.

Lafayette earned his baptism by fire at Brandywine where he fought bravely and took a bullet in the leg. He also distinguished himself at Monmouth and Barren Hill.

Charles welcomed the opportunity to serve under this man whom he knew and admired. Having Caitlin along might prove beneficial in a way that had not previously occurred to him — she spoke French fluently.

The march reached the outskirts of Williamsburg on September 8th and entered the city once scouts determined that the Americans were in control. After securing quarters for Caitlin, Charles went immediately to Lafayette's command post in the former royal governor's mansion.

"General Lafayette, Major Charles Royal of the Maryland Continentals reporting for duty."

"Welcome Charles!" replied Lafayette after returning Charles's salute. With a smile he embraced his familiar comrade-in-arms and kissed him on both cheeks. Charles, in the American fashion, extended his hand.

"It's good to see you once more, sir."

"And you, my friend. It has been, what, three years since we last parted?"

"About that, General."

"Please, 'Gilbert.' Let's not stand on formalities unless the occasion calls for it."

Charles nodded. "I understand General Cornwallis is in the neighbor-hood."

"If you had stood on that very spot two weeks ago you might have been addressing him instead of me."

"Then he remains within your grasp?"

"Yes, if only my hands were a bit larger. He is ensconced with 7,500 men or so in Yorktown; a deep water port on the York River about twelve miles away. It's uncertain but likely that he intends for General Clinton in New York to send transports to whisk him to safety."

"Is our role then to wave goodbye from the docks?"

The Marquis began to speak, but decided it would be wise to clear the room first. "Leave us. Everyone." When the last guard had closed the door behind him, Lafayette excitedly told Charles of the new strategic develop-ments.

"Their Excellencies General Washington and General Rochambeau are under forced march from New York as we speak. Their van should arrive here within a week. Admiral de Grasse's immense fleet is positioned at the mouth of the Chesapeake to wall-out any attempts at a breakout by sea. If de Grasse is successful, and we can detain the Redcoats until the main body of the army arrives, then I believe the game will be up for Lord Cornwallis's army. In short, he is ours!"

Charles, like Lafayette, grasped the enormity of that exquisite prospect. If Cornwallis's force could be destroyed or captured, the British would have clear control of only New York City in the north and Charleston in the south; mere toeholds on the vast continent. London would be forced to either commit all of its remaining resources to the struggle in a last desperate effort to save the jewel of its empire, or give up the ghost forever. Never in the six bloody years of conflict had the possibility of an American victory looked brighter.

"How many troops have you brought with you, Charles?"

"Three hundred."

"Continentals?"

"About two-thirds."

"Good. My adjutant, Captain Broyles, will see to their bivouac. And as for yourself, may I offer you lodgings in this handsome mansion?"

"Thank you, sir, but I have the pleasure of my wife's company for a brief while."

"Charles! You've married! Excellent! I must meet this lovely lady. We shall have a dinner in her honor!"

"Please don't trouble yourself."

"Nonsense! It will be my pleasure. A welcome divertisement from the drudgery of this infernal cat-and-mouse game I've been playing with Lord Cornwallis since June. We'll make it a ball! Invite the ladies of Williamsburg. Show them that American gentlemen can dance as well as any Englishman. You do dance don't you Charles?"

"Not very well I'm afraid, though my wife is excellent."

"Splendid! I shall look forward to her company all the more. Friday evening. Dinner promptly at seven." Lafayette led Charles to the door. "There is excitement in the air, mon ami. Can you feel it?" He flung the door open, "Captain Broyles, you will accompany Major Royal and see to the needs of his men. Sergeant! Locate my chef and steward and have them join me immediately!"

Walking arm-in-arm window shopping along Duke of Gloucester street the next morning, Caitlin and Charles were approached by a scruffy old private in a tattered uniform. His few remaining teeth were yellow and he obviously hadn't met with a shaving razor in awhile. At his side was an equally unkempt teenage drummer.

"Mrs. Royal, is it not?"

Caitlin's look said that she could not place this fellow.

"It's *me* ma'am. Isaac Cooley! Me and my boy Hebron was under yo' kindly care up at the Rockville hospital 'bout a year ago. Don't ya recollect?"

Caitlin shook her head pleasantly. "I'm sorry, Mr. Cooley. So many soldiers passed through."

"It's alright, ma'am. Here! This might kindle yo' mem'ry." He pulled up his shirt right there in the street to reveal a nasty, snaking six inch scar on his upper left side. "Goddam Tory! Two fingers this way and I'd be a moulderin' in my grave! Course, two fingers t'other and the son-of-a-bitch would've missed entirely."

Caitlin and Charles listened patiently, fearful of bursting into laughter if they looked at each other.

"Also took a ball in mah rump!" Cooley reported, appearing ready to drop his drawers. "We believe you!" Charles quickly interceded, "That won't be necessary."

Cooley shrugged. "Hebron had the fever real bad. But Mrs. Royal, why she sat right alongside him the whole time; coolin' his burnin' head like she was his right ol' maw. Say thanky to Mrs. Royal, Hebron!"

"Thanky, ma'am," Hebron replied with a nervous grin.

"You're welcome, Hebron."

"You must be the husband, Major."

"Yes I am."

"A lucky man you are, sir. Many a fella owes his beatin' heart to yo' lady here. When me and the boy arrived at the hospital, word we got on the sly was, 'Get Mrs. Royal to care for ya. Them damn surgeons'll kill ya deader'n Caesar's Ghost. Mrs. Royal, she'll see ya through, or if ya dies anyway, ya dies a happier man!"

"I'm glad the two of you are feeling better," Caitlin said, concealing her mirth.

"Thanky ma'am. We best be goin'. Move along boy! If y'all is ever in need of anythin', jes ask for Isaac Cooley of Westminster County. Ma'am. Major."

As the Cooleys moved beyond earshot, Charles leaned toward Caitlin and said tongue-in-cheek, "We *must* remember to look them up after the war." Caitlin smirked and gave him a playful slap on the chest. Ahead the man turned about and waved. Smiling broadly, Caitlin and Charles waived back.

Caitlin stood erect before the full length mirror. With a critical eye she looked herself over from top to bottom. She had her hair done up under an evening bonnet that complimented the sky blue billowing gown she wore. On her feet were polished lavender slippers.

"And you thought I was foolish for packing something formal," she teased her husband who sat on the bed secretly admiring his wife's beauty.

"What do I know?"

Caitlin pinched her cheeks to add color. "A banquet followed by an evening of dancing — I could certainly learn to enjoy the Marquis' idea of conducting a war."

"Something tells me that by the end of this evening you will be the conqueror and he the vanquished."

"Ready?"

"You look . . . magnificent!" Charles just had to say.

Caitlin looked back toward the mirror unsure. She was always modest when it came to her looks. After a deep breath she smiled at Charles and curtsied. "Sir, your date is ready."

"My 'date' will be the belle of the ball." Charles took Caitlin's shawl and draped it around her shoulders. "I'll try not to step on your feet tonight."

Caitlin bussed his cheek. "I'm sure you'll do just fine."

Every lamp, candle, chandelier and fire pot was aglow as Caitlin and Charles passed by the liveried servants and into the courtyard of the governor's mansion. Many of the guests had already arrived, including virtually all of the leading local gentlemen and ladies, dressed in their finest evening wear. The senior officers looked smart in crisply pressed uniforms and white gloves with bright polished ceremonial swords hanging by their sides.

Champagne in tapered crystal glasses was served from a silver tray before the front door. Once inside, Caitlin and Charles moved along the official greeting line, at the head of which, in a powdered wig, stood their gracious host, the resplendent Marquis de Lafayette.

"Well! Our guest of honor has arrived!" he enthused as Caitlin approached. Charles made the introductions.

"Monsieur le Marquis de Lafayette, may I present to you my wife, Mrs. Caitlin Royal."

With a deep bow the Marquis took Caitlin's hand and kissed it. "Mrs. Royal, this is a singular pleasure! Your husband and I are old comrades-in-arms, but never did he tell me that he possessed the heart of so beautiful a lady."

"Thank you, Monsieur. And I would be honored if you would feel comfortable in addressing me as Caitlin."

"Of course, if you will know me as Gilbert."

Caitlin curtsied slightly. The Marquis took Caitlin's arm in a gentlemanly fashion and escorted her to the banquet table where the first course was about to be served. Lafayette's place was at the head of the table and he seated Caitlin to his right, with Charles beside her. The remaining guests looked for their elegantly scripted place cards and sat down.

The Marquis was pleasantly surprised when Caitlin spoke to him in his native tongue as the meal was being placed before them. "Gilbert, I don't know if Charles informed you, but I am fluent in French if you would prefer to carry on any discussions in that fashion."

Lafayette's face lit up in astonishment. "Charles, is there no end to your wife's gifts?" Then turning to Caitlin, "For the benefit of my other guests who do not speak French, I think it best that we converse in English."

"Of course, you're absolutely right."

"But I must compliment you, Madam. Your French is as pure as if it were your first language."

"Merci, Monsieur. I was fortunate to have spent two and a half years as a student at l'Ecole Durand in Paris."

"L'Ecole Durand! My wife Adrienne studied there as well."

"Your wife Adrienne?"

"Yes!"

"Adrienne d'Ayen?"

"Yes!"

"Adrienne d'Ayen is your *wife?*"

"YES!"

Caitlin and the Marquis clasped both hands together and burst out laughing. From that point on they chattered away as if they themselves had been long lost school chums. So engulfed were they in conversation that two of the courses came and went untouched. Charles noticed that several of the ladies who had looked forward to exchanging playful banter with the dashing young French nobleman were casting evil eyes at his wife — jealous of her magical hold on their famous host.

Charles was outside their conversation too, except for one point when Lafayette called over in surprise, "Charles, I was not aware that you're an accomplished cook!" Charles shot an icy glare at Caitlin who slumped into her chair cringing, offering only a sheepish "sorry."

Following a dessert of fruit pies and creamy pastries, the dining table was removed from the room, the chairs placed against the walls, and the musicians changed the tempo of their pieces to more lively dancing tunes.

Lafayette danced the first dance with Caitlin. Then, as protocol required, each lady had a turn on the dance floor with the Marquis.

Charles danced with his wife, but she knew that her husband would rather be with the other officers in an adjoining room sipping French brandy, smoking cigars, and discussing the issues of the day.

"It's alright dearest," she said after their third straight reel. "You've fulfilled every obligation and more. Go, enjoy your cigar with my blessing."

Charles smiled at her clairvoyance and kissed her on the cheek. When he hesitated, Caitlin had the last word. "Go! Go! I'll be fine. Run along."

Charles enjoyed a convivial smoker as much as any man. In the large wood-inlaid study where portraits of past royal governors still glowered down form the walls, he and other Continental and French officers mingled freely with the politically appointed militia leaders and well-heeled local citizens. Conversation naturally focused on the prospects of a major engagement taking place in the vicinity.

"I should think Lord Cornwallis would skeedaddle before our forces are strong enough to drown him in the river," said a rotund importer wearing a comically ill-fitted wig.

"Perhaps so," Charles replied.

"Have you heard the rumors about General Washington's whole army marching on Williamsburg, Major?" asked a spindly faced deacon of Bruton Parish.

"I am not at liberty to discuss such matters, gentlemen. My years in the military have taught me that a hundred rumors rarely add up to one fact."

"Aye sir," the importer persisted, "But if it's true and Cornwallis is not able to make good his escape by sea or land, then doesn't it portend a lengthy siege that would cripple commerce for this region?"

Charles bristled at the implication that the economic impact of the war was of more concern to these people than the patriotic issues at stake. Nonetheless, he controlled his temper.

"Gentlemen, I'm not a merchant. I'm a soldier. My interests lie more with the young lads who may be asked to give their life's blood for the cause of liberty than with those whose sole concern is whether there is a profit to be made or not."

The locals appeared to take offense, but before they could speak Charles said, "Excuse me," and left them for the better company of some familiar men in blue uniforms across the room.

In the ballroom, Caitlin sat exchanging pleasant small talk with an elderly matron, while on the dance floor the Marquis held the rapt attention of half a dozen enchanted damsels who pressed about him. Out of the corner of his eye he could not help gazing at Caitlin, who rarely returned his glances.

Around midnight the party began to wind down. Young ladies might dance till dawn and blissfully sleep away the following day, but Lafayette and his officers had to be up with the rooster's crow, sharp and able to put in a fatiguing day's work. Paying their respects to their host before departing, Caitlin wished to offer a special invitation.

"Merci, Monsieur, for a wonderful evening," Caitlin said as the Marquis took and kissed her hand.

"Please, it is I who must give thanks. This has been the most enjoyable evening I've spent since I first landed on your shores. And I have you to thank for it, dear lady."

"You are most gracious, sir. On behalf of my husband and myself I would like to invite you to visit us at our home in Maryland for as long as you wish just as soon as your duties permit — perhaps over the coming Christmas holidays."

"I would be delighted, Madame," Lafayette replied with honest enthusiasm. "What fun the three of us will have! But there is one condition — if I come for Christmas, Chef Charles must agree to prepare the holiday feast!"

Charles glanced at Caitlin and shook his head. "As you wish."

"Excellent!" the Marquis smiled, and then turning to Caitlin he said, "I shall write to Adrienne about this special night before my head touches the pillow."

"And I shall write to her upon my return to Oakmont next week."

"Caitlin," Lafayette kissed her hand once more.

"Good night, Gilbert."

Chapter 26

On September 25, 1781, the final detachments of the allied American-Franco Army arrived and were combined with Lafayette's holding force in Williamsburg. On the 28th, under overall command of General Washington, they moved out in two columns to launch the siege on Yorktown.

For once the numbers overwhelmingly favored the Patriots — 5,700 Continentals, 3,100 militia, and 7,800 French troops in dazzling white uniforms to face the 7,500 British Regulars and a few hundred Loyalists waiting nervously down the road with General Cornwallis. A two-to-one advantage in men plus abundant supplies and equipment, including a complete siege train. Washington had never known such a decisive advantage.

As he rode proudly with his French counterpart, the Comte de Rochambeau, at the front of this formidable procession, Washington might have reflected on the timely series of fortuitous events that brought him to the verge of his greatest triumph.

After conferring and considering their various options, Washington, Rochambeau, and Admiral Comte de Grasse, commander of the French fleet operating in West Indian waters, agreed on a coordinated land and sea campaign on the Chesapeake. The grand prize: General Cornwallis's army and the prospect of destroying British dominance in the South.

Deception on a large scale was one of Washington's greatest gifts, and he used it in masterly fashion to cloak his intentions from General Clinton who was holed up in New York City with over 20,000 veteran troops and a fleet of warships.

For more than a year Washington's army had hovered outside the city, jousting with Clinton's Regulars and Tories, contesting isolated outposts, but lacking the strength to do anything more. Sir Henry was well aware of Rochambeau's arrival with 3,000 crack French troops to augment Washington's army, and of the small but dangerous French flotilla under Admiral de Barras anchored at Newport, Rhode Island. Anxiously he sought intelligence on where the combined forces of his enemies intended to strike.

Washington played his cards perfectly. He wrote official letters about his plans to launch an all out assault on New York City. Then he saw to it that these letters *accidentally* fell into the hands of General Clinton's spies.

Clinton was overjoyed at his good fortune. So certain was he of Washington's strategy that he actually ordered Cornwallis to send 3,000 reinforcements to New York.

On August 19th, under the strictest secrecy, Washington and Rochambeau stole their army out of camp under the cover of darkness bound for Virginia. To complete the deception, Washington mapped out a theatrical plan whereby all tents were left intact and a skeletal force was ordered to walk about between the campfires and the British lookouts to give the impression of a full and bustling encampment.

The ploy worked to perfection. By the time Clinton realized he'd been fooled, Washington's army was crossing the Delaware, leaving Clinton too far behind to attempt a march to overtake him. A humiliated Clinton's only hope now was that the combined fleet of Admiral Graves and Sir Samuel Hood could race to the mouth of the Chesapeake, sail up the York River, and pluck the trapped Redcoats off their precarious ledge before the American eagle could swoop in and devour them.

Here again fortune favored the allies. Admiral de Grasse with twenty-six ships-of-the-line had kept his end of the bargain, arriving off the Virginia Capes on August 30th, six days before the British Navy appeared on the horizon. De Grasse immediately set up an arching blockade in anticipation of his enemy's arrival. If the French could hold their position during the impending sea battle, Cornwallis's army was all but doomed. If they were defeated, then Yorktown would be evacuated and Washington and Rochambeau's long forced march would be for nothing — and the end of the Revolution would be nowhere in sight.

On the bright, balmy morning of September 5th, the lead ships in Graves's fleet caught sight of the French Armada guarding the mouth of the bay. Both admirals, their vessels, and every crewman sprang to action. Frantic maneuvering of the enormous ships into line of battle consumed the next several hours. Testing the mettle of their captains, the great white sailed crafts cut and weaved as nimbly as they could through the choppy seas.

Admiral Francois Joseph Paul, Comte de Grasse was a giant of a man who possessed energy, courage, and a rare competence in guiding a large fleet in battle. Not only didn't he fear the mighty British Navy, he relished the chance to engage it on the high seas and send it to the depths of a watery grave.

At 4:15 on the afternoon of the 5th the stage was set for the epic sea battle of the war. Both lines of warships unleashed fearsome broadsides and sought to close on each other. Almost immediately, several vessels were engaged in smoke-choked combat at point blank range with seamen pouring galling cannon fire across the water; ripping through sails, toppling masts, opening gaping holes in wooden hulls, and tearing into men's bodies with unspeakable horror. Blood rolled across the heaving decks making safe footing impossible, while the screams of the wounded, particularly those who couldn't move out of the terrifying path of the fires that seemed to appear everywhere, were as deafening as the cannons' roar.

Suddenly at sunset, with no clear victor established, the British fleet inexplicably broke off the fight and drifted out of range. The fiercest naval engagement of the Revolution was abruptly over in a little more than two hours.

Like bruised and weary heavyweights, the two fleets bodded and weaved in line of battle but threw no punches over the next few days. De Grasse, with superiority in number of ships and positioning of his fleet, was still snarling for a fight. Graves, assessing the mauling he had taken, decided he was not. On September 9th the Royal Navy put about and set sail for New York, leaving Lord Cornwallis's forlorn army to its fate.

While de Grasse (assisted by the arrival of the smaller fleet of de Barras) stood watch at the mouth of the bay, the allied land forces moved on Yorktown. Following a carefully laid out siege strategy, the French troops took up their positions on the left, while the Americans put their sappers to work digging trenches on the right; surrounding the town on all but the river side.

Washington was laboring under one disadvantage that Cornwallis was not aware of — time. De Grasse could be persuaded to remain in the waters off the Virginia Capes only until the end of October; he had to make his base in the West Indies before the stormy season struck. It was not uncommon for sieges to drag on for months. To be successful, this one would have to be over in days.

Digging went on around the clock and by early October the first parallel was completed. Fifty-two mammoth siege guns were hauled into position and on October 9th Washington himself touched off the first round, launching an unremitting 24 hour a day bombardment of the formerly drowsy tobacco port.

Charles looked on with admiration when Governor Thomas Nelson personally took aim at his own magnificent residence on a distant hill, the finest home in all of Yorktown, and sent a cannon ball smashing into its side.

While the constant explosion of shells kept British heads low behind their meager fortifications, sweaty shirtless men with picks and shovels labored by torch light to advance the allied lines.

Cornwallis didn't have enough men to dig and defend extended trenches of his own, so to repulse his tormentors he established a string of ten redoubts (small detached earthen forts) around Yorktown. These redoubts had to hold. If they were breached, the French and American sappers could zig-zag their siege lines ahead unimpeded and the terrifying heavy guns could be brought forward to a point where they could pulverize every building and hiding place in the town.

From its outset, the siege of Yorktown was conducted in the formal European style that went back centuries. Every step and rule in this deadly vice-tightening was common knowledge to generals on both sides. Accordingly, a besieged garrison was obliged to defend its position until the enemy's artillery had opened a substantial breach in its works. At that point the commander under attack was expected to send out a small fighting sortie in a manly show of defiance. Following this the officer in charge was allowed to surrender his force with dignity and be accorded "the full honors of war."

It was considered bad form for the commander to hold out for long after the breach was clearly established. The attacking force might then be compelled to launch a final massive assault resulting in considerable and needless loss of life for both sides. Looting, pillaging, and angry retaliation were often the upshots of such breaches in established military etiquette.

On the night of October 11 the allies attempted to turn their vice a full twist by beginning a second seige line that would bring them to within three hundred yards of the British inner defenses. Once completed, infantry would pour in, the heavy artillery would be brought into play to provide covering support, and if necessary the allied army would storm out and by sheer weight of numbers overrun the remaining overmatched British defenders.

This second line was established on the far right of the American position, and to complete it, Redoubts 9 and 10 which guarded the British left down to the river's bank would have to be put out of action.

Lafayette was given the honor of securing these vital posts. His plan called for a daring simultaneous night attack with the bayonet by two assault teams comprised of 400 hand picked men, each chosen from the best units in the army. Redoubt 9 was to be taken by the French contingent commanded by Colonel Guillame des Deux-Ponts. The attack on Redoubt 10 was to be carried out by Colonel Alexander Hamilton, with his second-in-command Major Charles Royal of the Maryland Continentals.

"Gentlemen," Lafayette spoke above the barrage of booming cannon and the crackling of musket fire on the evening of October 14th, "Our strategy is the model of simplicity." He held up a small hand drawn map. "You will lead your soldiers with stealth into positions in the trenches here and here closest to Redoubts 9 and 10. Muskets are to remain unloaded with bayonets fixed. Artillery fire directed at the enemy within these fortifications has softened them and sharpshooters will keep their lookouts from detecting your advance until you are upon them. Move in quickly with the blade and finish your task. Each squadron will have a color bearer who will run up our standards so we will know when the works have fallen. Bon chance, mes amis. Now, to your posts!"

To sweeten the adventure Lafayette offered a prize in gold from his own pocket to the trooper in each French and American contingent who was first to scale the enemy's walls and haul down his flag. To soldiers whose pay was sporatic at best, this provided a real incentive.

Hunched and scurrying along the interior line in single file, skin blackened by soot, the crack strike forces moved into position. Tension showed on every hardened, silent face as the men pressed against the dirt walls, waiting. Then, at eight o'clock precisely, six cannon fired in rapid succession, the signal for the attack to commence. Hamilton looked to Charles on the far side of the American line and with a nod and a wave of his sword led the Continentals over the top. In a wave they rushed forward without a word over no-man's land, bayonets pointed at the ready. Quickly they brushed past the sharp British abatis that protruded from the earthen walls and swarmed over the mounds and into the redoubt on three sides as the surprised British and Hessians yelled and lashed out with whatever they had to stop them.

Desperately, brave men of both sides tore into one another in a swirling mass of confused fighting where the clash of sharp metal and the dull thud of lethal hand held weapons filled the air along with battle cries, curses, and the agony filled screams of the wounded.

Charles stood on the highest parapet, his father's sword in hand, directing the turning of an enemy cannon when the British commanding officer suddenly sprang up beside him with saber drawn. In a flurry they clashed swords, thrusting and parrying in a deadly unorchestrated dance in full view of the American soldiers watching from the nearby trenches. Back and forth they went, straddling fallen bodies and debris that covered the uneven ground. Then with a mighty swing of two right arms the swords crashed into each other and the inconceivable happened — both blades snapped off clean just above the hilt!

Shocked and confused, both officers looked at their now useless weapons and then at each other, not knowing what to do next. Shaken free from his personal battle, the British officer looked around at the carnage taking place below. Realizing immediately that the game was up, he began frantically waving his arms overhead and yelling to get Hamilton's attention, "Quarter! Quarter!" Charles seized the situation and hollered above the battle's noise, "Alex!" When Hamilton turned around and looked up, Charles pointed to the British officer attempting to surrender.

"Hold off, men! Stand fast!" Hamilton cried out and the officers of both armies took up the call. Redoubt 10 had fallen and the American flag was quickly run-up the pole amid the huzzas of the victors and their cheering, hat waving comrades in the trenches nearby. Redoubt 9 was soon claimed by the French and for the soldiers in the assault the night's grisly work was complete. As they moved the wounded and the prisoners out, the men with the shovels moved in. By dawn of the following day the second parallel was virtually complete. And the thundering cannonade continued pounding all along the line.

Charles, weary but unhurt, stood in the trench eyeing his stub of a sword, oblivious to the jubilant young French general who approached.

"Charles! Magnificent!" Lafayette said with a hearty slap to Charles's shoulder. "We are victorious!"

"Yes, sir, the redoubts are ours."

"Charles, your sword," Lafayette said with feeling. "It was a gift, was it not?"

"From my father. I've carried it throughout the war. Almost lost it several times. But somehow it always stayed by me and never let me down. Now it's lost." Charles let the useless hilt fall to the ground.

Lafayette smiled sympathetically, "Come, we must report this night's events to Their Excellencies. They will want to thank you and the other brave men personally."

Charles nodded and with a gentle prompt from the Marquis they walked off in the direction of headquarters.

From their newly established close-in vantage point in the second parallel, American and French artillerists poured hard shot, cannister, and hot shot (inflamatory projectiles) into the heart of the tottering Yorktown defenses. Buildings caved in under the bombardment and men, horses, every living thing scrambled for cover to escape the ghastly conflagration. Even General Cornwallis and his senior officers were forced to take refuge, huddling in a dank storage cave near the beach.

British return fire by fewer and smaller cannon was ineffective. Many were destroyed by allied shells and ammunition was running perilously low. Cornwallis cast about in desperation for an escape route as the wall of destruction closed in around him.

On the dark night of the 16th, with only sixteen small boats at his disposal, Cornwallis latched on to a plan he had rejected a few days earlier — a breakout across the York River and through the weaker French and American lines surrounding Gloucester on the far bank. Ironically, he seized on the same last hope gamble as Washington when his army was trapped on Long Island. Fog had been the Americans vital ally that night. A far worse turn from Mother Nature greeted the British trapped in Yorktown. Before the second loading of the escape crafts, as Cornwallis would later report to his superiors in London, "A most violent storm of wind and rain . . . drove all of the boats, some of which had troops on board, down the river."

Despondent, knowing that Washington had him in his talons and that to continue to struggle would be futile, Cornwallis gravely resigned himself to the unthinkable. In the name of humanity, he would have to surrender his army. Having done everything that Sir Henry in New York and Lord North in Parliament could rightly expect of him, and having conducted his actions in a manner consistent with the accepted procedures of siege warfare, Lord Cornwallis had high expectations that he would be permitted to capitulate with all the honors of war.

At 10 a.m. of the morning following the ill-fated crossing attempt, a single brave drummer boy climbed the British hornwork and beat the time that signaled a parley. French cannoneers finally noticed him and called out a general cease fire. A British officer appeared waving a white flag. Across the now eerily silent field jogged a Continental lieutenant who blindfolded the officer and led him behind the allied lines.

During the negotiations that followed, Cornwallis asked that his soldiers be permitted to surrender their arms with colors unfurled, after which they would be allowed to return to their homelands in Great Britain or Germany, having given their oath that they would not participate further in this war. He asked Washington for a twenty-four hour reprieve in the bombardment as the request was considered.

Washington, mindful of the harsh terms forced on General Benjamin Lincoln following the fall of Charleston, was not in a generous mood. The soldiers must march out with their standards cased to the designated field of capitulation and relinquish their arms. Remaining British warships must surrender to the French Navy as well. Thereafter, the troops would become prisoners of war and be assigned to detention areas in Virginia, Maryland and Pennsylvania for the duration of the Revolution or until formally exchanged. Only high ranking officers (who were permitted to keep their sidearms and personal property) were to be paroled. Washington expected a reply within two hours or else the ceasefire would be lifted, the bombardment continued, and, in all likelihood, the British defenses would be taken by storm.

On the 19th, facing no choice except the annihilation of his stalwart men, Cornwallis bitterly agreed to Washington's terms. That afternoon, with heads downcast and tears streaming down many a cheek, the valiant, colorful remnant of the British Army marched out of its battered fortifications in loose formation toward the grassy field on which they were to lay down their arms. Burgoyne's surrender at Saratoga had been a major disaster. This, every private in scarlet and white knew, was an infinitely more crushing blow.

Mrs. Caitlin Royal   *October 19, 1781*
Oakmont on the Potomac
Montgomery County
Maryland

My Dearest Caitlin:

It is the evening of one of the most spectacular and eventful days of my life and I wish to capture a description of it on paper for you while it is still fresh in my memory. A second letter on these proceedings will go to Rake.

Today it was my immense good fortune to have a front row seat to one of the landmark historical events of the Revolutionary War — the surrender of the British Army at Yorktown to the combined French and American Army under the command of General Washington and the French leader, the Comte de Rochambeau.

The siege of the small port of York went remarkably well and with great alacrity. Begun in the first week of October, we find ourselves victorious in scarcely two weeks time, which might establish a new record for the speed with which such a military excursion has been brought to a happy conclusion.

Terms agreed to by the commanders of the opposing forces called for a full capitulation with only a very limited exercise of the honors generally accorded in such ceremonies. It is believed that His Excellency General Washington offered terms consistent with those granted General Lincoln by Lord Cornwallis at Charleston — a position which the officers and men of this army, many of whom personally suffered with shame at that surrender, wholeheartedly concurred with (not that their counsel was sought).

The major body of troops in York was ordered to march out this afternoon with their colors cased to a place we dubbed appropriately enough "Surrender Field," there to lay down their weapons and surrender themselves to our charge. Along both sides of the processional road officers and men were aligned meticulously by units — French soldiers to stand to the enemy's right, Americans to the left.

By prearrangement, officers were assigned their vantage points. To my great satisfaction I was placed in the front row, standing right next to His Excellency's senior grade officers, all of whom were mounted. General Washington was in plain view to me sitting high and proud upon his great bay steed with the stars and stripes of our infant country dancing merrily in the breeze above his head. Directly across the narrow road positioned in similar fashion beneath their own impressive fleur-de-lis were our courageous and generous allies the French, looking grand in their finest uniforms.

Many of the local gentry from Williamsburg and Hampton Roads turned out as well (now that the shooting had ceased and there was no apparent threat to their personage).

Elegant, polished carriages and simpler carts filled the open pastures behind us. On the wagons stood civilians of every social class, many holding small children aloft, hoping to view the historic event and the famous leaders who shaped it.

Muffled conversations ceased entirely when the musical strains of trumpets, drums, and fife signaled the approach of the vanquished foe. Every neck (including mine) craned in their direction, straining to catch a glimpse of his lordship riding in their van. But to our great disappointment, General Cornwallis was nowhere in sight — a fact realized immediately by myself and other officers familiar with his visage and quickly conveyed to the troops on both sides of the road.

It was left to his second-in-command, General Charles O'Hara of the Guard, to comply with this most distasteful duty. Later it was learned that General Cornwallis had taken sick. But many a skeptic believed a different story — that the gallant soldier who took his place at the front of his troops on parades of victory didn't have the stomach to lead his followers when vanquished.

On a lighter note, I must mention before it slips my

mind that the British marched to that delightful children's tune "The World Turned Upside Down." Under the circumstances, how very appropriate!

Strict orders had been issued to the rank and file of both the American and French forces that there was to be no taunting or ridiculing, much less violence, leveled at the conquered. I was as proud as I've ever been to witness this order being carried out without any notable exception. Indeed, if there was any poor sportsmanship on exhibit it was by the British, many of whom cursed their lot openly and loudly and hurled their weapons down violently in rattling heaps; an obvious attempt to render them useless for any future purpose.

The formal surrender, which took place not twenty paces from where I stood, provided its own portion of drama. General O'Hara approached, dismounted, and offered his sword to General Rochambeau, an afrontery that may or may not have been intentional. That thoughtful gentleman, with a silent gesture, deferred the honor across the way to its rightful recipient, General Washington.

Since O'Hara was not the commanding, but a subordinate officer, His Excellency directed that the sword be given to one of his own subordinates. He made the perfect choice in Benjamin Lincoln whose heart must have soared, having been beaten and humiliated at Charleston the year before and now accepting the sword of surrender from that very same army. The capriciousness of war was never more in evidence than here. Indeed, many a shirt button popped in pride this glorious day.

I dined this evening at a banquet hosted by His Excellency General Washington at which General O'Hara shared the head table. The two appeared to engage in enjoyable conversation.

Tomorrow begins the mundane task of organizing the prisoners now in Yorktown for their places of detention; a process that may take as long as the actual siege.

I will end now with what I hope is not a necessary reminder of my deepest affections. I do not know at this early juncture where my next duty assignment (if any) will be. Of course, you will be informed immediately when I hear something.

Your Most Devoted Husband,

Charles

Lord Cornwallis's letters detailing the events of Yorktown to Sir Henry Clinton in New York and Lord North in London were not nearly so well received. As it turned out, Washington was wise to have pressed the siege unremittingly to its conclusion. When Clinton received the news of the surrender of Yorktown's garrison, he already had eight thousand troops in transports on the high seas sailing to their relief.

Across the Atlantic, Lord North took the news as he would "a ball to the chest," rushing about like a man who'd lost his wits repeating again and again, "Oh God, it's all over!" Shortly thereafter he would resign as Prime Minister and a pro-American administration would sweep into power. In nearby Westminster Abbey, King George III, the last King of America, sat alone drafting a letter for his abdication of the Crown.

When Charles handed the letter he had written to Caitlin to the dispatch officer for posting, he was surprised to receive something in return — a formal invitation from the Marquis de Lafayette to a banquet in honor of his officers to be held the following Saturday evening at a tavern in Williamsburg. Charles hastily indicated in the place designated on the invitation that he would be pleased to attend and returned it to the dispatcher.

How odd, he thought, that this year that had begun with him starving, shivering, and hopelessly depressed in a malarial swamp in South Carolina, now found him an officer in the victorious Continental Army, invited to lavish banquets in his honor. And that he would be an elected representative to the Maryland General Assembly to boot! Charles laughed aloud at the capriciousness of his own fortunes. Then he left to find a laundress to clean and press his uniform for Saturday night.

Chapter 27

As Charles and his fellow officers stood about making small talk and awaiting their host, few could keep themselves from casting a side glance at the long linen-draped buffet tables heaped to overflowing with all manner of delicacies.

Three succulent roasts dominated the display. Between these were platters of sliced duck with cherry sauce, glazed hams, and several varieties of steaming soup. Vegetables were piled two feet high in decorative arrangements flanked by wicker baskets filled with savory fresh baked breads whose delicious aroma set every palate to watering. Frosted cakes and French pasteries were also well represented. Anchoring the end of each table were huge decanters of red and white wine with long stemmed glistening glasses stacked behind them.

When it came to throwing a banquet, the Marquis de Lafayette was without peer.

Against the back wall waiters stood poised and silent wearing red vests and white gloves. A few of the men in uniform admired the feast up close, but by some unspoken agreement no one dared defile it until the young general arrived.

From an adjoining room at the stroke of seven Lafayette made his entrance, his arms upraised in Gallic greeting. He wore an impeccable white uniform with a blue coat trimmed in buff. By his side hung a magnificent dress sword in a cream colored sheath.

"Gentlemen! Brother officers in the Great Cause of American Liberty! I bid you welcome! Thank you all for accepting my invitation on such short notice. As you know, many of us will be departing soon to serve on other fronts far away and I could never forgive myself if I did not bring us all together one last time to 'eat, drink, and make merry' as the Roman Legionnaires put it so long ago.

"This is an informal occasion, my friends, so please help yourselves to the buffet and take a place anywhere you like. The serving attendants will see to your every need . . . Players!" Violins and flutes caressed the air with gentle chamber music as the officers filled their delftware plates and took their seats along the wooden benches. The vast cornucopia of foods was then transferred to their tables and every glass filled.

Lafayette was the first to stand with his glass raised high. The other officers rose for the toast. "To our glorious victory at Yortown, and in special remembrance of our fallen brothers and the ultimate sacrifice they made." Glasses clinked around the room and the men drank deeply. Toasts then followed in honor of His Excellency General Washington, His Excellency General Rochambeau, the Noble Comte de Grasse, the Gracious King of France, Louis XVI, the Glorious Cause of Liberty, and, finally, to the benefactor of this opulent feast, General le Marquis de Lafayette (who also received three boisterous cheers from the wine-loosened tongues).

Just before eleven the Marquis raised his hand to silence the well fed and jovial crowd that was now milling about the room smoking cigars and drinking whiskey and brandy.

"Friends! May I have your attention!" When he had it Lafayette announced, "As a commemorative to our victory and the conviviality of this evening I've had made for each of you a silver tankard with your name and rank inscribed upon it. Sergeant Rousilliere is passing among you know with them." A rumbling of pleasant surprise swept through the room as the men received and admired this unexpected gift.

"And as a special token of my gratitude and admiration for those brave officers who led the critical assaults on Redoubts 9 and 10, I have an additional remembrance."

A corporal stepped from Lafayette's side and placed a narrow wooden box on the table before them. Cutting the twine with his knife he removed the lid. Those closest peered inside and oohed at the treasures that lay within — six exquisite dress swords, each inlaid with silver and gold and bearing the family crest of the Lafayettes on the base of the blades and the top of the sheaths.

"Colonel Alexander Hamilton!" the Marquis called out proudly. Hamilton pressed through the assembly and received his coveted trophy.

"Colonel Guillame des Deux-Ponts!" In addition to his sword and sheath, Deux-Ponts exchanged three kisses on the cheek with the Marquis.

The second to the last sword went to Captain Daniel Shays of Massachusetts who, unlike the others, eyed it in a way that suggested he was assessing its resale value.

And finally, "Major Charles Royal!"

Charles stepped forward and with both hands extended received his prize. He noticed that his victory sword was different from the rest. Extracting it a few inches told the tale — the new blade had been fused onto the old hilt from his father's sword. The Marquis must have retrieved it later from the ground where Charles had discarded it. His sword that had been lost was whole once more; and better than ever. Charles looked up at his friend, unable to find words to express his feelings. Lafayette smiled knowingly and nodded.

In a final toast, the Marquis had every glass refilled, then stood for a moment in silence.

"Brother officers. I said in my first toast that many of us would be leaving soon for places far away. I must share with you now that I am among these." A rumbled reaction swept across the room. "In my opinion, the play is over. The duty that called me to your shores, to make your fight my own, has been accomplished. His Excellency General Washington has granted me permission to return to my King and country. I don't know what course our future lives will follow, if we will ever embrace once more or stand side by side again on the glorious field of battle, so I wish to take this opportunity to say to each one of you, adieu, bon chance, and may prosperity and happiness be your rewards for the sacrifice and valor you've displayed throughout the Revolution."

Silence filled the room until it was replaced by a smattering of applause that quickly swelled into a thunderous ovation. The young Marquis bowed several times, tears of emotion spilling down his cheeks. Hands were thrust at him from every direction and he happily shook them all. The teenage nobleman who had disobeyed his King and risked his family's position and vast fortune on a wild military adventure was now returning home not an outlaw, but a national hero.

Mrs. Caitlin Royal   *November 10, 1781*
Oakmont on the Potomac
Montgomery County
Maryland

My Dearest Caitlin:

Wonderful news! I have just received word from my commanding officer that I am to be furloughed from the army effective January 1st. My status will be "on extended leave until such time as military exigencies necessitate reactivization into service." Fancy language that simply means I am free from any obligation unless major hostilities reconvene, which at the present seems highly unlikely. It's the next closest thing to a discharge.

Hundreds, perhaps thousands of soldiers have been

assigned similar status. With the victory at Yorktown ending the reign of Lord Cornwallis, and the lengthy inactivity of General Clinton in New York, it must appear to the
great minds in Congress that we soldiers are no longer
necessary, and therefore to be dispensed with!

My last official duty is to march a detachment of British and Hessian prisoners to the new detention center in
Frederick, Maryland. This should be accomplished by
early next month. Then it's home to Oakmont and Christmas together. And there's more good news! Our friend
the Marquis will be accompanying me and will spend the
holidays as our guest.

Let me know if you have heard from Rake. The only
active field of conflict is in South Carolina where General
Greene and the partisan forces (including Marion's) are
clashing swords with Lord Rawdon's Regulars and Tories
holding Charleston. With Rawdon's defeat or departure,
only Sir Henry in New York will remain to represent the
King in force. Our combined armies are already on the
road north to see that he doesn't stir from his comfortable
bed to make mischief.

While preparations are underway for our march to
Frederick, the Marquis has invited me to accompany him
on a journey to visit and pay our respects to Mrs. Martha
Washington at Mount Vernon Plantation. The two have
been faithful correspondents since the Marquis joined
General Washington's family at Valley Forge. Mrs. Washington expressed her disappointment that they could not
meet when the Marquis passed by with the army earlier
this year. Now he intends to make amends (the Marquis
could never endure the thought of a lady upset with him!).

We'll ride out tomorrow, just the two of us. The weather
is fine and I'm looking forward to seeing the famous man's
home and greeting his first lady. I shall give you a full
accounting when we are together again.

Until that most happy reunion, I am

Your Most Admiring Husband,

Charles

No artist's canvas could capture the sweeping autumnal splendor of the Virginia countryside, alive with the vibrance of turning leaves cascading down in a heavenly rainbow of colors; the crisp air whispering of winter's bracing advance.

Now apart from the dust-clouded rumbling and clanking of an army on the move, Lafayette could breathe in the invigorating nature, watch the great flocks of birds winging their way south in v-formations, and let his imagination wander to thoughts unmilitary.

"You know Charles, I've read that the Hindus of India believe that our spirits will one day return to the earth in the body of an animal."

"Certain Indian tribes here share that belief."

"Given the choice, what animal would you like to be?"

Charles thought for a moment. "Maybe an eagle . . . You fly high in the heavens and all creatures admire your bravery and beauty. An eagle has strength, elegance, and a look of wisdom about him."

"Hmm," Lafayette grunted approvingly. "I don't think I'd like to be a bird though. A bird can have its wings clipped or, worse, be caged. Could you imagine anything more terrible than the anguish of a creature born to soar above the clouds being confined to a small prison. How a bird can sing so sweetly when locked in a cage is a mystery I may never know.

"For my choice, I'd select a bumblebee."

Charles laughed, "A bumblebee?"

"Certainment! Consider if you will — a bumblebee's very sound strikes terror into creatures a thousand times its size, and why? Because it is utterly *fearless*. It will give its life in an instant just to inflict a pang of pain to its enemies. And because it is fearless, all others must fear it. Even the mighty jungle lion will cease its roar and run like a scared jackrabbit at the buzzing of the bumblebee. Yes, Charles, the indominable bumblebee — the true King of Beasts!"

Martha Washington was seated outside by the backdoor when the Marquis and Charles rode up the long entryway flanked by towering trees that General Washington himself had planted years before. Somehow, even at a distance, she recognized her young visitor. She placed her knitting in a basket and stood smiling, her hands clasped before her.

Lafayette vaulted down from his mount and offered an aristocratic bow. For a second the two stood silently admiring each other. For Lafayette it was a cherished moment; like a family reunion with the wife and intimate confidant of the man he venerated like a father. Martha's eyes and countenance bespoke her satisfaction and pleasure at receiving the handsome young gentleman-soldier who was now like an adopted son.

"Monsieur, welcome at last to Mount Vernon."

"Madame Washington, tell me how you have managed to grow younger since we last parted."

Martha pursed her lips, "You need not waste your charms on me, Gilbert. Remember, we are family." She took Lafayette's hand in hers and they both laughed nervously. "It is *so* good to see you," Martha said with heartfelt sincerity.

Lafayette turned to his traveling companion. "Madame Washington, may I present Major Charles Royal of the Maryland Continentals."

Charles stepped forward and took Martha's hand. "It is a pleasure to meet you, Mrs. Washington."

"The pleasure is mine, sir. The sterling record of the Maryland Continentals would make you an honored guest in any patriotic home."

"Thank you."

"Gentlemen please, let's step inside for some refreshment." The Marquis and Mrs. Washington locked arms and walked together through the entrance of the great white manor house with Charles behind.

In the cozy blue dining room the three enjoyed coffee, sweet rolls, and animated conversation between Mrs. Washington and the Marquis. Like old friends they exchanged interesting and amusing stories and anecdotes about General Washington, punctuated with bursts of laughter. It was as if each had pieces to the same puzzle, and as they shared them, the man they both loved became fuller and richer and more fascinating than ever before.

Martha asked about certain sensitive issues involving the plight of the army and the back-breaking difficulties that her husband had stoically endured throughout the years. Lafayette knew that his commander had not wanted his wife to worry and so had withheld the worst of it. Rather than talk in specifics, he shared his intimate knowledge of the General's steadfast course in the face of adversity that would crush a lesser man, and of Washington's boundless courage which never failed to inspire his men. Martha nodded and seemed pleased.

The Marquis listened with unmasked delight to tales of Washington's pre-Revolution adventures as a youthful militia colonel with Braddock and his work as a frontier surveyor for the Fairfaxs. He revelled in the image of young George canoeing with Indians and backwoods scouts through the vast uncharted wilderness. "Had I known him then," he told Martha, "We would have been as brothers."

After an hour and a half of rapt conversation, the Marquis suddenly remembered the other member of the party. "Charles! We've been so engulfed in our stories that we've neglected you entirely!"

"No problem at all," Charles said reassuringly. "I'm enjoying this immensely."

". . . Charles Royal," Martha said with a quizzical look. "I *know* that name is familiar to me."

"I hardly think—," Charles began, but Martha was now even more convinced.

"Yes, yes. It was from my husband. In one of his letters. He mentioned you, I'm sure of it. Excuse me for a moment."

Martha abruptly left the room and was gone upstairs for several minutes. When she returned she was holding a tall stack of old letters tied with a lavender ribbon. Fingering through them she opened and scanned several quickly.

"No . . . No . . . No . . . Ah! Here it is! I knew it! It's a letter George wrote to me describing the engagement at Monmouth Court House. Please, may I read it to you Major?"

Charles shrugged good naturedly, "Sure."

"Here, 'While the great victory that was meant to be ours quickly turned against us, and all was in chaos and disarray, one junior officer, Charles Royal of Massachusetts, stood fast on the line of battle exchanging hot lead and steel with the enemy and protecting our retreat — as well as our honor.

"'While I and my subordinate officers labored to rekindle the patriotism of our men and fashion a counterattack, young Lieutenant Royal, though greatly outnumbered, held the foe in check.

"'When at last we were able to come to his aid, I found him standing bravely and calmly among his troops (which numbered scarcely thirty by this time), sword drawn and facing down a line of British Regulars perhaps six times his number. Though he was in our view, our presence to his rear was surely unknown to him amid the roar of battle. Death was pressing fast upon him and his men, yet not a step did they yield; nay, not an inch!

"'I have seen fit to promote Lieutenant Royal two grades to Major and recommend his gallantry and that of his men to Congress by dispatch. It is upon the shoulders of such men as these that our new nation shall rise and take its rightful place among the most honored of societies.'"

Charles was stunned. The Marquis elated. "Charles! You're a hero!"

Charles shook his head. "I was just a soldier doing his duty."

"Well you're *both* heroes to me," Martha said. "Now if you will excuse me, I'll see to our dinner and have the servants prepare your rooms for tonight. Please, don't get up"

When she left, the Marquis reached over and slapped Charles jubilantly on the shoulder. "Charles! A hero!" Charles just sat there, thunderstruck, shaking his head.

After a day spent touring Mount Vernon, Lafayette and Charles took their leave of Mrs. Washington and rode south to rejoin the last of the evacuating army at Yorktown. Charles's ensuing march to Frederick was slowed by chilly rains, mud-clogged roads, and the natural inertia of the prisoners who were in no hurry to enter the waiting stockade. Having been in their shoes after Camden, Charles could sympathize. He was also on his guard against possible breakouts, sending mounted troopers ahead to investigate any hiding places for a Marion-style ambush.

On December 15th Charles signed over his prisoners to the military warden at Frederick. Pausing just long enough to feed and water his horse, he began the short ride to the southeast across the barren fields of Maryland to where he would pick up the Potomac River Road that led to Oakmont. He had awoken that morning with the sniffles and these had now grown into a full-fledged cold.

Charles arrived home to find that Caitlin was not about the manor house. Probably off seeing to the needs of the new patients from Yorktown who were carted to the Rockville hospital. Wet and weary, Charles welcomed a steaming bath and then slipped into bed where he remained until the next morning. During the night a fever joined with his cold to escalate his misery and render him as weak as a dishrag. He thought of sending for Caitlin, but didn't wish to deprive the sick and wounded soldiers who needed her care more.

He lay shaking between the sweat-dampened sheets when Caitlin arrived home just before nightfall. There was a murmuring of voices in the front hall followed by a rush of footsteps up the stairs. Caitlin stood silhouetted in the open doorway, still wearing her coat, peering into the semi-darkness.

"Charles," she said softly.

Charles managed a low garbled response. She moved to the bedside and pulled up a chair, placing a cool hand on his flushed, clammy forehead.

"You have a fever. I'll fix you something for that. How long have you been ill?"

Charles's eyes cracked open for an instant. "Two days, maybe three."

"Well you're home now and I'm going to take care of you." She left the bedroom and went downstairs, returning fifteen minutes later with two drinks on a tray. The first was a lime flavored concoction with a white powder swirling in it.

"Drink this down, all of it." She tilted Charles's head forward from the pillow as he emptied the glass. She propped his pillows up behind him for support.

"This is a special blend of herbal tea. Finish it and lie back down. I'll be back to check on you in an hour."

Charles felt better almost immediately. Whether it was because of the liquid medicine or the sound of Caitlin's confident, soothing voice he didn't know — or care to know. So this was the medical attention that Private Cooley and all the other veterans were so fond of. Now Charles had joined their ranks of admirers. And he received a small special bonus that none of the others had. In the doorway Caitlin stopped, haloed by the light in the hallway, and turned her head.

"I love you."

The Marquis de Lafayette arrived at Oakmont on December 23rd. Caitlin was there to meet and welcome him at the door.

"Gilbert! You've come! Welcome to Oakmont Plantation." The two embraced.

"My dear Caitlin, nothing short of an enemy battalion could have kept me from your doorstep."

"How *good* it is to see you, Gilbert," Caitlin said as she took his cloak and handed it to a servant.

"And you . . . Where is my dear friend Charles?"

"Resting. I'm afraid he's come down with a nasty strain of fever, but I think he's over the worst of it."

Charles overheard the conversation and threw off the woolen blanket draped over his lap as Caitlin and the Marquis approached the study where he sat by the fire. When they entered the room Charles immediately arose with a smile to greet his comrade-in-arms.

"Gilbert! Now our Christmas is complete! Did you have any trouble finding your way?"

"None whatsoever. You should have been a cartographer, mon ami."

"Maybe in my next life. Please, have a seat."

"I'm sure we could all do with a hot drink. I'll see to it," Caitlin said.

"Please, don't trouble yourself."

Caitlin merely waived off the Marquis' comment. Both men stood as she left for the kitchen.

"Cigar?" Charles offered.

"Perhaps later," the Marquis replied, leaning towards the fire and rubbing his reddened hands.

"So Yorktown es finis?" Charles asked.

"Yes. Six months from now passing farmers will point and say, 'Was there really a battle fought in these fields?'"

"It's a pity men don't heal as easily as the earth," Charles commented. The Marquis nodded.

"What are your plans now, Gilbert?"

"Well, this is the last stop on my long American journey, Charles. From here I'll make my way to the nearest port and sail for France. Hopefully the seas won't be too unkind for this time of year."

"Surely you've already planned for a triumphal return visit."

"Oh I expect to return one day. But there's much to attend to in my homeland. A wife and family I've neglected. Property and fortune that is in God knows what state." Then the Marquis added with a grin, "Perhaps I will have to retire on a state's pension before I'm yet thirty."

"You. Retire? That's something I can't even begin to imagine."

"Nevertheless, a new age begins for all of us now that the Revolution is winding down."

"So you believe it's over?"

"Pretty much. If the London gazettes can be believed, there's little stomach left in Parliament to prolong the fight. Legislation has been introduced making it a treasonable act to support even the *continuance* of the war. Quite a turn, eh? Those British politicians are a boundless source of amusement."

"And what of the separate war with France and Spain?"

"All will be resolved together. The British Lion roared at the world, and the world roundly slapped it on the snout. England needs time to bind its wounds just as America does."

"If we are to be a free nation, then we will require a new government. Republic or monarchy do you think?"

Lafayette pondered into the flames. "A democratic republic. Only George Washington could be made king — the people would accept no other — and I have it personally from His Excellency on numerous occasions that he finds the concept of an American monarchy utterly abhorrent."

"Still, when a crown is actually placed over a man's head, who among us could cast it away?"

Lafayette fixed Charles with a hard look. "Washington could, and would."

Both men stood and smiled as Caitlin rejoined them.

"Coffee is served, gentlemen." she announced, carrying a silver tray that also held a basket of bread with butter and fruit preserves. "Don't let me interrupt your conversation."

"Not at all," Lafayette said accepting his cup. "We were just speculating on the political future."

"Gilbert believes that America is through with kings for the moment."

"I agree," Caitlin said as she poured the coffee. "Soldiers didn't march off to war; fight, suffer, risk death, just to exchange one form of absolute tyranny for another."

"But how can we be governed without a strong central leader?" Charles asked. "Will every important decision be made by cursing, torch-bearing mobs in the streets?"

"We're soldiers, Charles, you and I. But our day has passed in this land. It's now up to the elected representatives of the states to determine, with the consent of the people, the form of government that will best ensure their happiness."

"Oh wonderful," Caitlin said facetiously. "The same Continental Congress that labored for years to lose the war is now entrusted with saving the peace! God help us all!"

Charles smiled. "Welcome to democracy."

Caitlin turned her attention to the Marquis. "Were you aware, Gilbert, that Charles has been elected a member of our Maryland General Assembly?"

"Charles! You said nothing of this. So now you're a soldier-politician."

"Soldier-politician-cartographer," Charles replied.

"Soldier-politician-cartographer-*chef*," Lafayette and Caitlin responded in unison as all three laughed.

"My husband will be governor one day," Caitlin said proudly.

"Now that would be a novel turn," Charles grinned. "We'll have gone from a Royal Governor to a Governor Royal!"

On Christmas morning the three exchanged gifts. Charles and Caitlin gave the Marquis a magnificent brace of pistols in a handsome polished mahogany case. The Serling family crest, granted by King Charles I, was etched onto the case and the hammer of each gun. The family heirloom had been a prized possession of the Judge.

The Marquis presented Caitlin with a gold and pearl necklace. Charles received four bottles of excellent French champagne and a humidor filled with West Indian cigars.

For the promised yuletide feast, Charles prepared duck l'orange with an almond stuffing served with sweet potatoes, sauteed carrots, pickled beets, and steamed greens. He received rave comments for his dessert: an apricot flambé.

Throughout the day, friends, acquaintances, and crass political opportunists dropped by. The presence of the famous French general was a decided treat to all; unintentionally adding to Charles and Caitlin's stature in the community.

Late in the afternoon Caitlin, Charles, Gilbert and Junius made the traditional rounds to the slave quarters where they doled-out gifts and good cheer. The mansion itself was adorned in evergreen and festive streamers. In the evening, Caitlin played the piano while Charles, Gilbert, Junius and the house servants sang holiday songs and enjoyed eggnog and roasted chestnuts. Not since her childhood could Caitlin recall a more pleasing Christmas.

For Charles, thoughts returned to the dismal Christmases spent at Valley Forge and Snow Island — with ragged, starving soldiers huddling together to stay warm around flickering fires.

On the day following Christmas, Charles's fever returned. Caitlin sent him straight off to bed. As he lay there he could hear Caitlin and Gilbert downstairs gibbering away in French. Charles was glad she had a healthy companion with whom to pass away the time. It made his personal miseries more bearable.

With Caitlin all to himself, though, Gilbert soon fell hopelessly under her spell. Perhaps it was the way she voiced her perfect French. Or the way her face lit up and her green eyes twinkled when she smiled. Maybe it was the importance she seemed to place in everything he said. Or perhaps it was just the primitive physical attraction any healthy young man would feel in the presence of this beautiful, lusty woman.

Did she feel something too? He had to find out. Seated together on the great gazebo with the wind blowing gently through the leafless trees, the Marquis made his move.

"Oakmont is so beautiful. It's like heaven on earth," he began.

"Yes. It's been my home my whole life. I can't imagine a more perfect place to live. My father told me once that when he first brought my mother here she said to him, 'I'm on the watch for the serpent and the apple, for this is surely Eden'."

"How many children did your mother have?"

"Five."

"How many reached adulthood?"

"Just two — my brother Rake and myself."

"Ah . . . how precarious life can be."

Caitlin smiled gently and looked off across the river, the wind lightly lifting her soft dark hair.

"Caitlin, you are familiar with the Latin phrase 'carpe diem'?"

"Of course, 'sieze the day'."

"Precisely. Life is short and precious opportunities should not be allowed to slip by."

Caitlin's furrowed look said she was unclear of his meaning. Lafayette reached for her hand.

"When two people come together — in Eden — is it not preordained that their feelings for one another, their passions, are pure?"

Caitlin now saw the direction of this conversation. She abruptly took her hand back and said in a firm steady voice, "Your attentions border on the unwelcome, sir."

The Marquis was instantly crushed. Embarrassed. Like a slap to the face, Caitlin's words had dashed his amorous advance and sent his emotions reeling. He looked away, unable to speak.

Sensing that she had derailed Lafayette from his unwelcomed track, Caitlin reached out to put his feelings on a better footing.

"Gilbert, I know there's someone you long for. A voice, a touch that your whole person cries out for. But that someone's not me. It's a lady who is far, far away. And she yearns for you every bit as much as you do for her. It's Adrienne."

". . . You're right," Lafayette replied, looking down at his hands. "Of course, you're right."

"And when she takes you in her arms and your bodies are pressed warmly together, you'll realize the absolute truth of it."

Upon reflection, the Marquis nodded.

". . . Are you angry with me, Caitlin? I could not bear it if you were."

"A handsome young man who longs for the love of his wife; where's the offense in that?"

Caitlin smiled at Gilbert. And when the first hint of a smile appeared on his face she leaned over and gave him a reassuring hug.

The Marquis, wisely, decided to change the subject.

"Your brother is called Rake? An uncommon name, no?"

"His real name is Randolph . . . He joined the Maryland Continentals as an officer when the war broke out, but he's spent most of the past six years fighting with Francis Marion's Irregulars in South Carolina."

"Ah! The famous Swamp Fox — now there's a man I'd like to meet one day. Your brother serves under him?"

"He's Marion's second-in-command, though from what little he's told me, the soldiers of the swamp take their orders from no man simply because of rank.

"Serving with those gladiators suits Rake, though. He thrives on the thrill of hit and run warfare. Taking orders is something he could never do."

"He's a brave man, your brother?"

"Recklessly so. He'd rather die gallantly charging the enemy through a hail of bullets than live a hundred years in peace at Oakmont."

"A man after my own heart."

"Oh you'd love him alright. Real fighting men always do." Then she added with a sly smile and a roll of her eyes, "And so do the ladies."

The sun was setting in a brilliant orange glow directly upriver, causing a broad shimmering reflection of dancing silver on the water that Caitlin and Gilbert admired in reverential silence.

"It's getting chilly," Caitlin said at length. "It's best we went inside."

Walking back to the mansion arm-in-arm, Lafayette felt compelled to offer an invitation. "I will be leaving in a few days to return to France. May I carry back to Adrienne your pledge that you and Charles will visit us in Paris one day soon?"

"Of course, Gilbert. I know I speak for Charles when I say we would be delighted."

"Good! The four of us will have the grandest time. Perhaps we will tour all of Europe together!"

"That would be grand. But I must tell you there are unresolved matters here that must be attended to first. The Revolution has scattered Charles's family to the wind. He must find them and see to their well-being. And his family's property in Boston was very extensive; he must recover what he can. And, of course, there are his duties now that he's an elected official."

"I understand, Caitlin. I seek nothing more than your promise that you and Charles will come one day. Having received it, I'm entirely pleased. There is no timeframe — the invitation will stand as long as I do.

"Now we must also agree to correspond; the four of us."

"Of course."

"All is well then. We live at Chateau de la Grange outside the city. When you arrive in Paris, merely call out, 'Where is the house of Lafayette?' Everyone will know."

The Marquis paused on the porch. He looked back over the rolling land, past the stately trees, past the gazebo, to the river beyond. "I do love Oakmont. I could be happy settled here."

"I believe you're destined for many more adventures before you're ready to settle anywhere, Gilbert."

The Marquis smiled, and then they went inside.

Charles suggested to Gilbert that he accompany he and Caitlin to Annapolis to Charles's swearing in and to sail out of that port. Lafayette agreed and on a frigid but clear January 7th they set out. Caitlin had made arrangements in advance for a one-night stopover in Baltimore. Somehow word reached the mayor that the illustrious Marquis de Lafayette would be paying a visit and the whole town turned out, waving French and American flags while a military band played popular French tunes.

Lafayette was partly honored, partly surprised, and mostly amused. When it came to digging trenches, fording rivers, hand-to-hand combat, and organizing impromptu parades, these Americans were without peer.

The corpulent mayor stood on the bunting-draped stage burbling praise on the Marquis that was so gandiose it would have made an emperor blush.

Lafayette gamely endured nearly two hours of handshakes, backslaps, baby kissing, and tedious conversations with the local leading citizens. All of this followed by a lavish banquet and reception in his honor at the mayor's house that evening.

Lafayette insisted to Charles and Caitlin that they be off early the next morning before the good citizens of Baltimore could engulf him in any more "ceremonies designed for the public viewing of the bizarre Frenchman."

Annapolis, however, had also gotten wind of his approach. A 16-man mounted honor guard bearing the flags of France and the United States met him on the road to escort him into the city. With many of the state's leading military and political figures on hand — including the governor — the rounds of speeches, toasts, dinners, and receptions approached the proportions of a royal visit. The Marquis' charm and natural good humor were wearing thin. He was no more comfortable being the center of adulation in Annapolis than he had been as a nobleman at the Court of Versailles.

The Marquis stayed just long enough to witness Charles take his oath of office and assume his seat in the General Assembly. The merchantman *Alliance* was bound for Brest on the afternoon tide and he booked passage on it.

On the dock Charles, Caitlin, and Gilbert said their farewells.

"It will be good to escape those praise-filled speeches," the Marquis said jovially. "A few more days of that and my swelled-head might capsize the ship!"

"You've done America a great service, Gilbert," Charles said. "You won't be forgotten."

"I'll return one day to see how everything turns out. Hopefully one Revolution will be sufficient."

"Goodbye, Gilbert. Safe voyage," Caitlin said with a hug and a kiss to his cheek.

The Marquis kissed her hand. "I shall miss you both very much."

Charles and Gilbert shook hands, which grew into an embrace. Then the Marquis turned and jogged up the gangplank. When he was on board, the sailors castoff the lines and made sail. Slowly the massive craft circled away from the dock. Lafayette stood by the railing cupping his hands to his mouth.

"We'll meet again, in Paris!" he shouted.

They were the last words Charles and Caitlin heard from their friend. All that was left were waves across the spreading water until the figures on the ship disappeared; and the ship itself became a tiny aberration on the distant line where sky meets sea.

When the General Assembly adjourned in early April, Charles and Caitlin returned to Oakmont to get their affairs in order before their extended journey north.

During the legislative session, Charles had proven to be a staunch advocate of the soldier in the field, introducing bills for military pensions for those who had served for at least nine months and requiring the state to make good within a year on the soldiers' back pay. He championed the rights of widows and orphans to receive compensation in cash and land for their losses, and for the debts of the men who fell in battle to be forgiven.

He also voted in favor of a proposal that confiscated Tory property should be used to pay off the state's war debts. And he spoke out strongly on the need for better kept public roads — a sore subject for him and every other trooper.

While Charles was busy at the state house, Caitlin wrote a stream of letters on his behalf to anyone in Boston — relatives, friends, public officials — who might have any information on the whereabouts of Charles's family. No one had a clue.

"At least we have a place to sleep," Caitlin told Charles over dinner one evening. "Your Aunt Ophelia has invited us to stay with her while we're in Boston. In fact she was quite insistant."

"That's Aunt Ophie."

"When will we be leaving?"

Charles sighed. "I've circled the 31st of May on the calendar."

"You seem a bit apprehensive."

". . . It's been so long. So many years. If anyone was still alive wouldn't I have heard by now?"

"Maybe not. How would they know where to reach you?"

Charles nodded.

"Whatever the outcome," Caitlin continued, "We'll just have to face it. At least we'll know once and for all."

"Yes we will," Charles replied. His eyes wandered to the misty window and to the gentle rain falling outside. ". . . The final chapter in every war is a personal one."

Chapter 28

The May flowers were in glorious bloom and the first crops, already waving in the gentle breeze that swept the rolling fields, held the promise of a bountiful harvest. Oakmont was alive and in all its splendor as the pilgrims met with Junius one last time. The great adventure north would begin the next morning. It was a time for final details and farewells.

"When you reckon you'll be back?" Junius asked Caitlin as the three strolled aimlessly up the lane by the blacksmith's forge.

"I don't know exactly. We'll be gone several months. Perhaps as long as a year."

"Any word from Master Rake?"

"It's just Rake now, Junius. You're a free man, remember? And an equal partner here."

Junius nodded. "I know. I just slip back from time to time."

"Rake is . . . God knows where. My last three letters have gone unanswered. While we're gone, you should open any mail that comes in and forward anything important to me. Here." Caitlin handed Junius a piece of paper. "That's Charles's aunt's address in Boston. Ophelia Royal. We'll be staying there. Or she'll know how to reach us."

"You'll be in complete charge here at Oakmont. I've spoken with the constable and written letters to all our customers and suppliers telling them to deal with you directly. I've explained to them that you're a free man and our overseer now. You have the authority to make any decisions that need to be made."

"Yes, ma'am."

"Caitlin, please."

". . . Caitlin."

"The stongbox is under the Judge's bed like always. Here's the key. You've got the books already . . . I guess that's about it."

"You want to keep the big house closed?"

"It's better that way. If you moved in, the neighborhood gossips would have a field day. No use inviting trouble."

Junius nodded.

"If you keep a low profile, everything should be fine. Contact Reverend

Stocker if there are any problems or if you need advice. He can be trusted."

Caitlin, Junius, and Charles paused by a fenced-in corral and watched a muscular young horse being broken.

"I'll do the best job I can," Junius said softly, reflectively.

Caitlin turned her gentle eyes to his. "I know you will. I think the Judge always knew you'd be running this place one day."

Junius grinned and modestly shook his head. "The place ain't been the same since he's been gone. Lord, how I miss that man."

"We all do. He'd be proud of you, Junius. Proud of the way you've kept Oakmont up and running."

"You know what I miss most? The way the Judge *loved* the sportin' life. Why he'd take that big black stallion there to the county fair next month, sure as shootin'. Haggle with the gentlemen on the odds. Then watch with eyes as big as saucers as I'd ride him to victory."

"Sounds like the Judge isn't the only one who loved the sportin' live," Charles said.

"Yessir," Junius chuckled, "But now I'm a man with responsibilities."

". . . Don't those responsibilities include checking on the livestock at the county fair?" Caitlin offered innocently enough. "Looking for animals that could improve our bloodlines?"

"I reckon it does."

"And while you're there anyway, it would be downright unneighborly not to admire the horses that the other planters are so proud of."

"True enough."

"And if one of them suggests that he breeds a better and faster horse than we do at Oakmont, well you just can't agree with that."

"No, I don't s'pose that would be right."

"So if a contest were arranged — let's say a *horse race* — well then, that would fit in perfectly with your responsibilities, don't you think?" Caitlin's conspiratorial smile brought a similar response from Junius.

"Can't have no one insultin' the honor of Oakmont can we?"

"I should say not!"

Junius looked admiringly at the powerful jet black beast strutting proudly around the corral, its first rider holding its great mane with both hands. "He's a fine animal. Fast too . . ." His thoughts were precisely where the Judge's would be if he were here — fixed on the hoof-pounding approach to the finish line, a roaring crowd cheering home their favorite, and this ebony beauty two lengths up on all comers, and pulling away.

Caitlin looked at Junius and smiled; partly because of a first-time revelation. My God, how much Junius looked like their father. More than she or Rake, who favored their mother.

It was a good and right time to part.

Caitlin gave Junius a hug and kissed his cheek. Charles shook his hand.

"I'll be over to see you off in the mornin'."

"It's not necessary," Caitlin said with a smile and a shake of her head. "You have other responsibilities."

Caitlin and Charles had decided to take the large carriage. It required two horses. The ride would be long, arduous and bumpy and the big carriage offered greater comfort, plus ample space for the three trunks, several smaller bags, and the two riding saddles. A necessary accompaniment were the two muskets and two pistols along with flints, gunpowder and cartridges that Charles stowed under the front seat. A war, though dormant now, was still officially in progress, and highwaymen would be a constant danger along isolated stretches of even the main post road. A man and woman riding alone in an elegant carriage made for a tempting prize.

Caitlin had decided that this was to be her belated wedding trip and together she and Charles had poured over maps, circling places they wanted to visit. Philadelphia certainly, but also many of the locations where Charles had been during the war (particularly battlesites), and points of interest they had read about. One place they would not be visiting was New York City. The British Army and Royal Navy under the command of Sir Henry Clinton still occupied this last major toehold and forlorn hope for reclaiming the Crown's lost colonies.

Caitlin was also insistant that they steer clear of General Washington's army keeping watch outside the city. She allowed Charles to pack his uniform just in case, but was not about to let her husband wander too close to the snare of the Continental Army, which could still reactivate him if it chose to.

The morning Caitlin and Charles rolled through the front gates of Oakmont and out onto the open road was bright and sunny, with billowing white clouds on a vast blue mural that stretched beyond the farthest horizon. An aria of birds entertained them and seemed to fly ahead, leading the way. All appeared perfect. Then Caitlin, in a nonchalant way, dropped a bombshell.

"When we return, I'm going to free all our people."

"All the slaves!" Charles said in amazement.

"Yes," came the calm reply.

"But there must be 150 of them."

"One hundred and seventy-three to be precise."

"Good God. Who'll work the place?"

"They will if they wish. Everyone who wants a job for wages will be welcome. Their families too. But if they choose to leave, they'll be free to do so."

"Does Rake now about your plan?"

"I don't know. I've written to him, but he hasn't gotten back to me yet. But I *know* he'd approve. So would the Judge if he were alive."

"How do you know?"

"He told me so. Before you and I met. He was waiting for Rake and I to reach maturity so it would be our choice too. All were to be freed by the provisions of his will. Only he never got around to revising the will he wrote twenty years ago."

"And he was a judge."

Caitlin shrugged.

"Did you mention this to Junius?"

"No. Perhaps I should have. But I think Rake and I should be there when the announcement is made. There'll be many details to iron out."

"Will you keep Oakmont?"

Caitlin thought hard before answering, then she spoke quietly, almost inaudibly.

"No."

"Are you certain?"

". . . Yes."

"What about Rake?"

"And Junius."

"Yes Junius. They have a stake there too."

"Rake doesn't want to be anchored to a huge plantation. When this war's over he'll be riding off to the frontier or wherever the pounding drums promise new adventure. I'm not sure all of America can hold him in.

"As for Junius, he loves the land like the Judge did. Rake and I love it, but not in the same way. I'd sell my interests to Junius, and I'm sure Rake would too, but the deed would never be legal."

"Why not?"

"No black man would be allowed to own that much land in the state of Maryland."

"That's not right."

"No, it's not."

"So what's the solution?"

Again Caitlin paused. "Oakmont will be broken up into smaller parcels. Junius will have his choice. The others we'll sell piecemeal and divide the proceeds three ways."

"Then what?"

Caitlin's face was placid, without apprehension or concern. Charles was the worrier; Caitlin the optimist.

"I'll live happily ever after and grow old with my husband."

"But what about Oakmont? Your family's past is there."

"Yes, but my present is here. And my future lies with my husband somewhere up this road. All the rest is just scenery."

Charles's expression showed that he was not yet comfortable with all this. But it was Caitlin's choice, and she was at peace.

Valley Forge. Charles's home four years before. The home of the Continental Army under George Washington for six grueling months. The wounded, freezing breast where beat the faint and failing heart of the American Revolution. Could this lush green meadowland; this warm flowered paradise possibly be that place?

"See the cabins there and there!" Charles stood upright in the carriage, pointing to the ghost encampment on the distant slope. "That's where we were. And see that cabin on the far right and up a bit, that's where I was quartered! Hyah!" Charles gave the reins a quick snap. He could hardly wait to get a closer view.

"It looks like everything's fallen into disrepair," Caitlin said as she glanced about.

"No. This is as good as Valley Forge ever looked."

The place that had housed several thousand soldiers and a variety of camp followers was utterly deserted this day. Only the occasional bird song and the sound of the breeze ruffling the verdant leaves disturbed the cathedral-like setting. Far off to the southwest a farmer could be seen tending his grazing cows. Obviously the events that had transformed Valley Forge from an insignificant dot on the map to a stirring symbol of patriotic stoicism had already begun to recede into time. The pastoral tranquility that had existed long before the arrival of the ragged horde in continental blue had returned to reclaim the land. Yet there still remained a few edifices of man to stamp and verify this particular valley as an historical weigh station.

The door that had protected Charles and his comrades against the bitter winter winds lay ignobly on the ground in front of his cabin, its leather hinges rotted away. Charles, with Caitlin behind him, peered into the dark, stark, one-room hut.

"That was my bunk," Charles said, pointing to a lower right bed in the corner by the chimney. "We slept as many as ten officers in here. Can you believe it?"

The cabin, like all the buildings still standing, had been pilfered by locals and souvenir hunters. Just some papers and trash remained, mingled with leaves on the floor. Charles sat on the rough wooden slats that had been his bunk. They creaked, buckled and nearly collapsed under his weight. Charles wanted a remembrance too. With his pocket knife he pryed a small mica encrusted stone from the chimney bed and put it in his pocket.

Caitlin stood in the doorway trying to imagine her husband and the other poor souls cramped into this windowless cell. She couldn't. Charles's infrequent letters had left out many of the harsher details of his time here. Now she understood why.

Unharnessing the horses so that they could rest and forage, Charles took Caitlin's hand and together they walked the hallowed grounds, speaking only in reverential tones.

"Here's where the artillery park was set-up. It commanded a one mile approach from Philadelphia. We didn't think the British would send more than a scouting party to harass us, but we had to remain alert.

"And over there was the parade ground where Baron von Steuben put us through our paces. General Washington watched us from that knoll."

A chill shivered through Charles as he approached and identified a stately old elm tree by a pond. "That's the tree I froze solid against," he said evenly. "Had it not been for Rainbow Samuels, that's the spot where I would have died."

Caitlin took Charles by the hand and led him to the tree. "Let me have your knife."

Leaning into her task, she chipped away the bark until she had cleaned a clear space on the trunk of about a foot square. Then, as Charles watched, she chiseled an inscription:

Charles Royal
Lieutenant in the 21st Mass.
Frozen here February, 1778
Lived to fight another day.

The two-story stone house along the Schuylkill River that served as General Washington's headquarters beckoned to them. It was the only building waiting for the troops when they trudged into Valley Forge that December, and it remained the dominant structure.

There was no response to their knock on the door, so Charles and Caitlin let themselves in. Scavengers had picked the place clean. Even the nails that had held the pictures on the walls were gone. Charles and Caitlin investigated the small upstairs bedroom that had served as Washington's office. It was the first time Charles had been to this inner sanctum, yet he could vividly feel the great man's presence. The look of concern, the furrowed brow as report after report told the Commander-in-Chief of the terrible suffering of his men.

Outside again, Charles wandered off across a meadow, a strand of straw between his teeth, searching his memory and the undulating terrain for clues to the secrets of Valley Forge. Meanwhile, Caitlin took a break to wash out some things in the river. Charles returned to find his wife relaxing on the bank, her bare feet dangling in the cooling waters. He was carrying a long, charred piece of metal and grinning.

"Know what this is?"

She smiled and shook her head.

"It's a bayonet! Or it was. We used them to cook meat over the campfires."

"Did you do much cooking while you were here?"

"Not really. Wasn't much to cook. Once, though, I had to prepare a meal that no one savored; including me."

Caitlin's curiosity was aroused.

"Sure you want to hear this?"

"Yes, I do."

"Well," Charles said, settling down on the grass beside her, "There was a long, bitterly cold stretch in January when food was virtually nonexistent. Men ate the frozen bark off the trees. Boiled shoe leather. Anything to fill their aching bellies. Some went mad with hunger. Ran off howling into the woods, never to be seen again." Charles closed his eyes and shook his head at the painful memory. Then he continued.

"There was a small dog. Scrawny. Playful. Licked everyone's face. *God,* how the men loved it. It belonged to a lieutenant in my cabin. As hungry as we were, no one wanted to touch that dog. But that lieutenant, I think his name was Devon, he volunteered to make the sacrifice. His voice cracked. Tears rolled down his cheeks. He handed the dog to a Captain Meade who received it solemnly and took it around back . . . and slaughtered it.

"I was chosen for the thankless task of preparing the meal. I'll tell you, my hands shook and it wasn't from the cold. I used a bayonet, just like this one. One vile officer made light of it — called it 'spot on a spit' — no one thought he was funny. You have to understand, we were starving men who did what we had to to stay alive . . . Those were hard, hard times."

". . . What about the lieutenant. Devon. Did he . . . partake?"

"No. He just sat on his bunk, crying. Two days later he wandered off alone into a thicket and —" Charles pulled an imaginary trigger beside his temple.

The amber sun was setting to the west as Charles hitched the team of horses. It was a lovely, warm evening, but Charles and Caitlin decided to return to the inn rather than pass the night at Valley Forge. Too many troubling memories. Too many ghosts still walked this land. Charles took one last look back. There were no campfires burning; no bustling camp movements. No snow. No shivering soldiers. No suffering.

All, at last, rested in peace.

Boston had been ravaged. New York and New London set aflame. But Philadelphia, the erstwhile home of the Continental Congress; the birthplace of the Declaration of Independence; bore no ill effects from its British occupation. Indeed, from a social perspective, the billeting of the Howe brothers' army and naval forces in the City of Brotherly Love marked the unquestioned high-point of the Revolution.

Rich Tory merchants and city officials opened their arms and offered the company of their lovely daughters to the King's military emissaries who reciprocated by spending George III's gold lavishly on balls and banquets that made the local provincial officers look like poor country bumpkins.

As a result, Philadelphia at war's end was the most prosperous city on the eastern seaboard. Its shops were bursting with all manner of luxuries — furs, jewelry, the latest European fashions; treasures that were simply unavailable elsewhere.

Caitlin surveyed the abundance of wares like a child turned loose in a candy shop. Deprived like everyone else of such upscale staples as current books, imported satins and lace, and fine English china, she quickly set aside any lingering animosity she held for the British and went on a buying binge. Within three days she filled four large crates and made arrangements for them to be shipped back to Oakmont. All that remained was to purchase gifts for the people she intended to meet up north.

"What size dresses do your sisters wear?" she asked Charles on their last day in Philadelphia.

"Let me think. Sarah is about your height, but not nearly so . . ." Charles motioned clumsily with his hands to indicate breast size.

"I see. And Sally?"

Charles shook his head. "The last time I saw her she was only fourteen."

With so little information to go on, Caitlin elected to buy Sarah and Sally matching gold earrings. For Charles's mother she selected a jeweled broach. And for Joseph, a handsome pair of kid leather riding gloves. She would decide what to give Aunt Ophelia when she met her and determined her tastes.

"Do you think this is right — buying gifts for people when we don't even know if they're alive?" Charles asked.

"Charles!" Caitlin scolded, "They *are* alive! Alive until we have proof otherwise. I'll have no more such talk!" Caitlin's tone was adamant and left no room for further discussion.

Following brief visits to the battle sites at Brandywine Creek and Germantown, the pilgrims' next stop would be Trenton. The weather was hot, but not unseasonably so for June. Charles and Caitlin kept to the main highway as much as possible. It provided the most safety, was the one road in relatively good repair, and offered clean, comfortable, affordable lodging in the country inns situated about every twenty miles.

Here they could expect to find a private bedroom and the enjoyable company of fellow travelers. News from the Canadian border to Florida passed through these wayside stopovers. Conversation around the long, clattering public dining tables rarely involved politics or the war, though. There were still too many open, emotional wounds. The delightful stranger sitting by your side might suddenly turn ugly if it were discovered that you supported opposing sides in the conflict. Better to pass a peaceful, pleasant evening and part friends in the morning.

"Where you folks bound for?" an elderly gentleman asked Charles over dinner one evening.

"Boston."

"You from those parts?"

"I am, yes. My wife's from Maryland."

"Ah! The missus and I are Marylanders ourselves. Headin' home to Baltimore we are."

Charles risked being indiscreet. "Are you a veteran, sir?"

"Aye, lad. Served under Otho Williams with the Maryland Continentals early in the war.

"Really!" Charles beamed. "I was with Colonel Williams myself later on; in the Southern Campaign."

"Nasty business I hear'd. Angry fightin' in the Carolinas, eh?"

Caitlin overheard and leaned over Charles. "My brother's still there, fighting with Colonel Francis Marion's Irregulars."

Directly across from Caitlin a large, red-faced man grumbled loudly at this revelation and stood up from his bench. He hurled his knife on his plate in obvious displeasure and strode out of the room in a huff.

Once he was gone, the elderly man turned to Charles. "Even when this cursed war is over, there'll still be bad blood in this country to last a life-time."

Charles inquired about the man's trade.

"I be a shipbuilder, lad. Forty years at my craft — from boy apprentice to master shipwright. Later in the war my brothers and me received Letters of Marque and took to privateering. Right profitable business that. Took nigh on fifty prizes before we was sunk off the Eastern Shore in the fall of '81. Biggest goddam fleet of Royal Navy I ever seed."

"My family had a merchant fleet in Boston before the war," Charles said. "Thirty to forty seagoing vessels in all, counting fishing boats."

"Impressive. And now?"

Charles shook his head and shrugged. "Won't know until we get there."

"If you're ever down Baltimore way, look me up. Waverly's the name; Sam Waverly. Just ask by the wharves. They'll point ya to me yard." The two men shook hands.

"And if your travels take you to Annapolis, drop by and say hello. I'm Charles Royal and I'm the delegate to the General Assembly from Montgomery County."

"Sweet Jesus, Mary! Did ya hear that? We've got ourselves a reg'lar politician at our table. Be on your guard folks! If ya feel a strange pair of hands in your pockets, they're probably his!"

Everyone within earshot laughed, including Charles.

A light summer rain was falling on the day Charles and Caitlin slogged into Trenton. Little had changed in the five and a half years since Charles's life-altering day there; except, of course, it was considerably warmer. While Caitlin rested upstairs, Charles ordered a mug of rum in the tavern where they had secured a room.

"Let me guess: you'd be a Continental soldier back to relive his glory," the barman said without looking up from the glass he was drying.

"How did you know?"

"You ain't the first one. Hell, you ain't even the first one this week."

"There doesn't appear to be much to see."

"Sure there is, if you know where to look." The barman called over to a gray-haired gentleman near the chimney, "Mr. O'Neil! Fella here's interested in the world famous Battle of Trenton."

"That so? Well now, were you a participant?"

"Yes sir, with Colonel Glover's Massachusetts regiment under General Sullivan."

"Glover you say? First into town they were. Up King Street to Colonel

Rall's headquarters right there across the street." O'Neil pointed through the window to a large brick building.

"That's right," Charles concurred.

"Then they moved south of town and sealed off the enemy's retreat over the Asunpink bridge. That was Cadwalader's job, but his militia never made it across the Delaware that day."

"Right again."

"Of *course* I'm right! I saw the whole thing. Spoke to soldiers after the fight. Even done a map. Want to see it?"

Charles brought his drink over to the table as the old man pulled several similar printed sheets from his inside coat pocket. On the parchment was a sketched layout of the town with dozens of markings indicating the regiments involved in the battle and their movements. On the back of the sheet was a full page narrative written in a flowery, amateurish style that nevertheless accurately depicted the events of December 26, 1776, the follow-up engagement on January 2nd, and their significance. Charles was impressed.

"You did this yourself?"

"Yessir. Had it printed up at the College of New Jersey nice 'n neat. Sell 'em for fifteen cent each . . . ah, ten cents for real-life veterans such as yerself."

Charles purchased a copy. Outside the rain had worsened and there was the rumbling of thunder. Charles's countenance was as gloomy as the weather.

"I was hoping to walk the grounds once more, but we're only here for the day."

"Well, lad, at least you have a little momento."

"I've always wondered, what became of the prisoners taken here?"

"Shipped west into Pennnsylvania. Sat out the war there. Not bad duty I imagine."

"No, I suppose not."

"As for the wounded left behind, well some of them didn't travel nearly so far."

"What do you mean?"

"Say hello to Private Hans Haupt of von Knyphausen's Fusiliers!"

A large sandy-haired young man sitting quietly at the table until now smiled broadly and extended his hand.

"Hello, sir. I am the enemy."

Charles's jaw fell slack as the old man laughed and slapped his knee.

"Never fails, eh Hans! Mister, you look like you seen a ghost!"

"I'm sorry," Charles said, accepting the young stranger's hand. "I've never actually *met* a Hessian before."

"To be correct, you still haven't, sir," the young man replied in clear if accented English. "I come from a tiny village in Brunswick, a small principality which you are probably not familiar with."

"You were wounded here at Trenton?"

"Yessir. A bullet in my left leg below the knee and a severe blow to the head."

The old man interjected, "And when His Excellency General Washington moved out on the double, he wasn't about to let no enemy wounded slow him down, so he left them to the kind attention of the good folks of Trenton. We turned the church into a makeshift hospital. Course it didn't do Colonel Rall much good, seein' as how he was dead."

Charles was still stunned. Here he was sharing a drink in a tavern with the most hated and feared of all America's wartime enemies — the coldblooded, mercenary Hessians. And stranger still, he liked this man.

"You never returned to your regiment, Private Haupt?"

"No, sir. None of us did."

"Why not?"

Hans paused, collecting his thoughts. "You, sir, and your fellow soldiers fought for your homes, for your families, for your freedom. All good reasons. We fought for none of these. Ours was a very poor land. We were young men, boys really, of humble origin from Brunswick, Waldeck, Anhalt-Zerbst, Hesse-Hanau, and nearby regions. We joined the armies of our nobles so that we could *eat*.

"We were shipped off to your land where we were slaughtered like cattle, just to make our lords rich. We fought for ourselves and our brethern. We fought bravely and with pride. But when we are wounded or captured, we are of no value anymore. So we were forgotten. Our sacrifices in blood, forgotten. Would you wish to return to such an army, sir?"

Charles looked at Hans, but didn't speak. This was all a revelation to him.

"In your country, every man can own land if he's willing to work hard with these," Hans held up his large calloused hands. "This Trenton town, these people, they helped me to heal. Then they gave me work to do. I work hard in the fields. And then they *paid* me. My brother soldiers and I spoke. We all decided the same. It is here we will stay. And, by God, if the war comes again, we fight with the Americans!"

Charles felt shivers run through him. He had come expecting to relive his own Trenton experience. Instead, he discovered an aftermath to the battle that he could not have possibly imagined.

This time it was Charles who extended his hand, "Welcome to America, Hans."

It was still raining — more drizzle than rain — as Charles and Caitlin set out the next morning. Princeton lay a distance of eleven miles away over the mud-clogged highway. By mid-morning the dark spell had broken, giving way to a drying sun and the happy chirping of birds.

Upon entering the town, Charles turned the carriage off the Princeton Road and onto the Saw Mill Road that he had marched in on with General Sullivan's column on the day of the battle.

At Frog Hollow Ravine he stopped the carriage, climbed down, and in his mind's eye relived with satisfaction Mawhood's routed 40th and 55th infantry regiments. He could see them throwing down their weapons and streaming back toward the safety of the buildings on the college campus, with the tired but game Patriots whooping at their heels in hot pursuit.

With Caitlin as a one-person audience, Charles related the events of that January day. He pointed out the placements of the American and British forces, and gave a running narrative on how they advanced, clashed, and retreated and reformed. Caitlin listened patiently, mildly amused at how animated Charles became at times.

Inside the stone dormitory known as Nassau Hall, Charles was pleased and surprised to discover that a defining artifact of the battle remained intact.

"I can't believe it's still here! Just as we left it!"

"What, that picture with the hole in it?"

"That was a portrait of King George. The last of the Redcoat resistance was holed-up in this building. We thought it was going to be the devil flushing them out." Charles took Caitlin's arm and led her hurriedly to the front window with a view of the broad green college yard.

"Just beyond that white fence there, Captain Alexander Hamilton rolled up a cannon and sent a single, perfectly placed shot through this window, decapitating the King!"

"Oh, c'mon!" Caitlin said with a turn of her head. "You can't expect me to believe *that* story."

"It's true! I was there! The British inside were so terrified that they immediately tossed their weapons out the windows and pleaded for quarter."

"I shouldn't wonder," Caitlin said facetiously, "What with the William Tell of cannoneers right outside their door!"

"You don't believe me?"

"I don't believe you."

Charles's continued pleadings couldn't dent Caitlin's armored resolve. She wasn't about to believe this particular cockamamy story.

The last battlesite that the wayfarers planned to visit in New Jersey lay to the east at Monmouth Court House. For both Charles and Caitlin, this rural speck on the map held a special bonding significance. It was here that Charles received the severe wounds that disabled him for a time from active service — and led him to the only place where he knew he would be welcome — to Oakmont Plantation and Miss Caitlin Serling.

Ironically, Charles and Caitlin arrived at Monmouth four years to the day since the celebrated battle. Little remained from that fateful, brutally hot June 28th beyond the eternal contours of the land and the forests to suggest to even a seasoned observer like Charles that two massive armies totalling over 23,000 men had met, clashed, bled, and died here; and then passed over these fields like some violent, man-made summer storm. Just some unkempt graves, a few broken wagon wheels, and, if the visitor was willing to bend and carefully comb through the knee-deep grass, a rusting metal fragment or crackled strip of leather.

Stopping the carriage alongside Cranberry Road, Charles strode purposely about 200 yards across the field with Caitlin trying to keep up.

"Here's the spot where I was struck by the bullet in the shoulder!" Charles revealed to Caitlin, passing his hands slowly over the unmarked patch of ground that held intense personal meaning to him. The log rail fence that he and his men had leaped behind, frantically firing and swinging their flintlocks at the unstoppable tidal wave of Redcoats about to overwhelm them, was broken down in several places, exactly as it must have been left by the British as they burst through and stormed past.

"We held here for as long as we could, then fell back and reformed on that knoll up the hill. God it was a hellish day. Hellishly hot from the sun and the incessant fire from cannons and muskets. I'll bet as many men died from the heat as from the enemy's flint and steel that day . . ."

As Charles turned to get his bearings, hand on his brow to ward off the sun's glare, Caitlin knelt down and gathered a handful of the dark warm earth. She wrapped it in a small handkerchief and put it in her bag — a treasured souvenir that she would one day share with her husband at some far away place, or perhaps present to their children as a hallowed family heirloom from their father's war years.

With difficulty, Charles located the spot near the West Ravine where he believed he stood when he was wounded the second time.

"The enemy was advancing from that direction. Only determined pockets of resistance kept them from overrunning and slaughtering the whole damned terror-stricken militia and the rest of Lee's command that was in full retreat. Of course, Lee was God knows where.

"I was certain my fate and that of my heroic comrades was sealed when, suddenly, General Washington rode-up, in full view of the British sharp-shooters. Fearless he was. Inspiring. I've never seen a more resplendent sight than the Great Washington astride his powerful charger that day. I wish I had the skill with words to describe it to you — the bravery; the majesty of it.

"Wayne's regiment dug in here. Greene's and Stirling's took up positions on that ridge. And then General Knox's heavy guns unleashed a blessed infilading fire that stopped Cornwallis and Clinton in their tracks . . ."

Charles's voice trailed off. Caitlin watched him turn inside himself. She could almost feel him reviewing all the events that had been carefully catalogued and stored in his memory for years. Now, on the very ground where it had taken place, he could at last bring to life and reflect on the Battle of Monmouth Court House.

When he returned from his self-induced trance, Charles looked about on the ground for a log or shard of wood that might have been the very one that struck him down after the explosion that ended the battle for him. He found nothing.

"What happened after you were hit in the knee?" Caitlin asked.

Charles shook his head slowly. "I don't remember anything from that point until I awoke in the field hospital with bandages all over. I do recall my first thought — had I lost the leg? Then, fearing the worst, I tried wiggling my toes. They worked! I guess I was one of the lucky ones."

"At Lee's courtmartial, did you testify that you actually witnessed him fleeing the field?"

"No. He was on the far side of the battle from me. Well out of view. I was called in as one of the few surviving officers of the first assault. I provided an accurate account of the battle from where I witnessed it, giving special commendation to my soldiers and those of other companies who stood fast. By God, it was a proud day for the Massachusetts Continentals under Enoch Poor and John Glover. And for the 1st and 2nd Maryland. A *proud* day."

"And for Lieutenant Charles Royal," Caitlin added softly.

Charles smiled slightly, "I'm sure all this talk of battle bores you."

Caitlin shook her head. "I love the way it fascinates you."

"It does! It's as if I'm watching a grand play. Only I'm also one of the players. Oh, in a small, insignificant role, but right up there on the stage with the rest. It's fascinating. Horrible, ghastly, heart-wrenching . . . but in the end, fascinating.

"You know, I never cared much for any of my studies in school. But this Revolution, it's a subject I never weary of. And the more I learn of it, the greater my enthusiasm to learn more."

"I'm pleased about one thing."

"What's that?"

"That the war is an academic subject for you now. That you're an interested student rather than an active participant."

"True. Unless something unforeseen happens, my days as a Continental soldier are behind me."

"Hallelujah!"

Charles laughed. "I doubt if the wives of *all* returning veterans have that same reaction."

"It's lunchtime. Let's set the basket under that stand of birches. And you can regale me with more tales of your legendary heroism."

"Only if you agree to accept my version of the cannon ball decapitating the portrait of King George back in Princeton."

Caitlin replied sweetly, "Not a chance."

Now began the long, arcing trek to Saratoga, with a brief side visit to Morristown where the Continental Army had endured another miserable winter encampment.

So far the weather had been cooperative and there were no serious incidents of the kind that often beset wayward travelers, particularly in wartime. But from here on the route taken must be chosen with great care to avoid the still vibrant pockets of Loyalist support. Hatred and vengeance are at their worst as a war nears its end. Scores must be settled before peace revokes the license for crime-free killing.

Charles plotted a course on his maps through central New Jersey to Morristown, and then northeast into New York, crossing the Hudson above Peekskill. The countryside was largely rural and it would leave he and Caitlin more vulnerable to marauding bands of robbers, but they would avoid any conflicts still simmering along the coast. It seemed the better road to travel.

Occasionally they would be joined by the carriages of other travelers for a few miles. This offered conversation, news updates, and an added measure of security. They also shared the rutted road with many a farmer's wagon; hauling crops to market, wheat to the local mill, or supplies from town back home.

The Royals stayed in rustic country inns when available, or slept out under the stars. The rolling pastoral hills of New Jersey — some cultivated, others as virgin as the days before any Europeans visited these shores — offered a soothing tranquility that suggested nothing of the searing battles or , the armed battalions that crisscrossed this land for more than five years.

One evening after tending to the horses and enjoying a delightful supper of Charles's Road House Rabbit Stew, Caitlin and Charles relaxed contentedly by their small campfire. In the ebony sky above a full moon dominated the night, with a twinkling blanket of stars too numerous to count spreading to the edge of every distant horizon. Wisps of clouds would pass before the moon like the sheerest of white linens, and then draw away. The croaking of toads and the infrequent hoot of an owl were the only suggestions to Charles and Caitlin that they didn't possess this dark-hewn paradise all to themselves.

"We seem to be making good time," Caitlin said, her arms wrapped around her drawn-up legs.

"Yes," Charles replied as he absentmindedly tossed small sticks into the dancing flames. "We're a couple of days ahead of schedule."

"Hmmm. So we'll reach Saratoga by early next month?"

"If the carriage and horses hold up."

Caitlin slid close beside her husband. "I'm enjoying our little honeymoon."

"Me too."

"One day, when we have children, maybe we'll take them on this same trip. Show them where their father was during the war."

Charles warmed to the thought. "How many children shall we have?"

"Oh, a dozen perhaps." Caitlin's look told Charles that she was pulling his leg. "Four or five would be a nice number I think."

"Girls or boys?"

"An even mix. I like the thought of a large family, don't you?"

"Yes. Provided it's different from *my* family."

"How do you mean?"

Charles looked off to the distance. "My father and I were very close. My sisters too. And Joseph; sweet, kind, innocent Joseph. But Robert and I never got along. Not until that last moment together at Saratoga. And Mother — well, of all the children, she favored me least."

"Sure you aren't imagining a little?"

"It was as if she barely tolerated my presence. Like a mother bird that instinctively knows there is something wrong or different about one of her hatchlings and pushes it out of the nest. My mother was the coldest woman I've ever known."

"And are you afraid that's the sort of mother I'll be?"

"No! No! It's just that the thought of bringing a new child into that sort of environment worries me."

"Put your fears to rest, my pet. I asssure you, ours will be the *happiest* of homes. Ringing with the laughter and mischief of *all* our children."

"You make it all sound so pleasant."

"It will be," Caitlin cooed as she drew her lips close to Charles. "And I think the pleasantness should begin . . . here."

In the soft allure of her enchanting green eyes, Charles saw her meaning. And shared her desire for passion. Together they slipped beneath their thin blanket. And passed the warm night underneath the moon's silvery glow in a loving embrace.

Charles and Caitlin had planned a lengthy stayover in Saratoga, perhaps a week or more. There was much to see and relive, plus it was well placed geographically for a period of recuperation after the long bumpy ride from Maryland before pushing on to Boston.

They arrived in town on the evening of August 1st. Charles asked about for a local guide familiar with the battlefields and everyone he spoke to suggested the same person: Old Angus McBride.

McBride's Revolutionary War pedigree, it turned out, was impeccable. Connecticut born and raised, he was a founding member of the New Haven Sons of Liberty. He joined the Governor's Footguards (whose captain was an ambitious and volatile zealot named Benedict Arnold) and marched off to Cambridge when news came of the Patriot's stunning showing at Bunker Hill. Arriving too late for the glory of battle, the unit was soon merged into the nascent Continental Army.

During the fighting in and around New York City during the fall of 1776, McBride, now a master sergeant, distinguished himself for bravery, particularly during Colonel Knowlton's heroic stand at Harlem Heights. Suffering bayonet wounds in the head and neck that no one thought he would survive, Sergeant McBride was heaped on a hospital carnage wagon bound for the military hospital in Danbury — or more likely to his grave.

But the tough old trooper pulled through and rejoined the army in early September of 1777, just prior to the decisive fight along the Hudson.

At Bemis Heights he had himself reinstated to active duty and volunteered to serve wherever needed. He was assigned to help steady the Connecticut militia positioned on the American left. As fate would have it, the commanding officer was Major General Benedict Arnold.

McBride was in the heart of the most furious fighting at both battles at Freeman's Farm. He even participated in the storming and capture of the key Breymann Redoubt that sealed the victory for the Americans and marked a turning point in the war.

His valor in the face of the unremitting British and Hessian fire eventually cost McBride his left leg, which was mangled by a cannon ball and had to be amputated above the knee. His days as a soldier abruptly over, the crippled McBride decided to stay on in Saratoga where he scratched out a meager existence as a battlefield guide and part-time tinsmith.

While Caitlin caught up on her correspondence and saw to the replacement of an axle on the carriage, Charles and Angus McBride took the horses and rode off the next morning at dawn to tour the countryside. No one knew the battlefields, the strategies, the generals, and the high drama of it all better than Sergeant McBride. With the encyclopedic knowledge of a hidebound historian and the gift of the natural storyteller to bring it all back bigger than life, he held Charles spellbound all day as he shared his tales of events at every vantage point.

"Gentleman Johnny was a born gambler, but his luck finally ran out after the second fight at Freeman's Farm on October 7th," McBride related as they sat their mounts overlooking the river as the sun began to set. "He was whittled down to six, maybe seven thousand men by then. Beaten, demoralized, some even mutinous. We, on the other hand, had over 20,000 troops itchin' to finish the fight, includin' Stark's New Hampshires and those tough ol' boys from the Hampshire Grants, still aglow from their spanking of the Hessians at Bennington.

"Burgoyne played his last card, but it proved to be a mocking joker. He tried to steal a night march on October 8th, hoping to cover the eight miles to Saratoga where he might load his remaining army on boats and escape upriver to Canada. But torrential rains doused his plan. The militia and Stark's men cut off his retreat, and the game was up."

To Charles, McBride appeared to be lost to the present, standing once more on two good legs, embracing the glorious news spreading through the ranks like straw in the wind that the unimaginable had happened — the British and their Hessian allies had surrendered. And America had claimed its greatest victory in the Revolution prior to Yorktown.

In Angus McBride, Charles had found a kindred spirit.

"Thank you for this day, Sergeant McBride," Charles said as they turned their horses about for the trip back to town. "Your narrative was stirring."

Brought back to the present, the humble old trooper deferred any credit. "It's the courage of the brave soldiers of both armies who fought and died here that's stirring, Major. I'm just the poor chronicler of their immortal deeds."

"You should write it all down. Share your insights with the new nation," Charles implored.

"A worthy idea, sir. There's just one problem — I can neither read nor write."

Charles was momentarily stunned by this confession. "I'm truly sorry to hear that. Your eloquence suggested otherwise. I meant no offense."

"None taken sir. None at all."

As they rode back through the growing darkness to Charles's lodging, he couldn't resist sharing a thought that troubled him. "It's a pity that your vast knowledge about the monumental events that took place here will die with you."

"Aye, sir. But in my heart I'm certain that the story of Saratoga won't die with me. It has a permanent place of honor in American history."

Charles knew this to be true. But he also knew the tragedy caused by the cruel fate that left this wise, devoted old soldier an illiterate. *So much to share with generations as yet unborn,* Charles thought. *So much lost.*

Over dinner that evening in the tavern, Caitlin brought up an idea she had been mulling over.

"Charles, I'd like to place a special marker here. A remembrance to my cousin Nigel."

"That's a wonderful thought. Only you're not certain he's . . . gone."

"I know. If one day by some miracle I find out he's still alive, well then we can all have a rich laugh about it at my expense. But if he is truly lost, I'd never forgive myself for not leaving some sort of memorial here. He saved my life."

Charles nodded. "You're absolutely right. Have you decided what might be appropriate?"

"Yes. A nice headstone. We'll place it out on the field. On an unmarked grave. We'll make it his."

"Tomorrow morning we'll find a stonecutter."

"And Charles."

"Yes."

" . . . Would you like to leave something in honor of Robert?"

Charles thought for a moment. "Thank you. Yes, I would." Caitlin smiled and reached across the table and squeezed her husband's hand gently.

At the stonemason's the following day they selected two almost identical granite slabs. They decided to inscribe them simply: *Robert Royal* and *Nigel Serling.*

After paying the artisan they made arrangements with him to have the stones delivered the next day to a location on the battlefield near Middle Ravine. Sergeant McBride had helped Charles locate it during their tour. It was the place, as clearly as Charles could remember, where he had seen Robert struck down. That would do.

In the afternoon, Charles took Caitlin riding along the old River Road. At the familiar path by the Great Ravine he turned left and found his way to the remnants of the abandoned flour mill.

"Where exactly are you taking me?" Caitlin asked.

"You'll see," is all Charles would say.

Beyond the mill Charles picked-up the cart path that led them through the deep woods to their destination. There in a small clearing it stood. The woodman's cabin where Caitlin had been held prisoner on that fateful night.

She gasped the moment she saw it, "Oh my God!"

For a long while they remained in their saddles silently viewing this personal landmark. It was in this sorry little cabin that their lives had been altered forever, and where Sub Altern Nigel Serling of His Majesty's 53rd Regiment had met his fate.

Slowly, solemnly they approached the cabin and dismounted. It was obviously abandoned, with high grass growing unmolested on what had been the front path. It was Caitlin who pushed in the broken door. Standing just inside, they scanned the bare walls for any clue to their past. None remained, except the rough-hewn bed frame where Caitlin sat when Charles entered through the back door to free her.

A minute or two passed. Then Caitlin smiled softly at Charles. She took her husband's hand and led him outside. Without speaking they mounted their horses. Each took a final glance back at the cabin, fixing its image for all time in their minds. Then, instinctively, they turned to one another.

Charles said simply, "Let's go." They nudged their horses and headed for home.

Caitlin and Charles arrived early the next morning at the memorial site. Caitlin approved of Charles's choice. She selected a shady spot near a group of maple trees richly arrayed in bright green leaves and Charles set to work digging two shallow holes, side by side.

It wasn't long before the stonemason and his assistant arrived. They lowered the blocks into position, packed the dirt firmly against them, and with a tip of their hats departed.

Caitlin and Charles sat alone together beneath the trees. It was a lovely day with the sun shining brightly and a cool wind blowing in off the river. There were other markers scattered about — a few bent crosses made of sticks, a small unkept flower bed — but the headstones inscribed *Nigel Serling* and *Robert Royal* clearly dominated this gravesite now.

"Should we say something?" Charles wondered aloud.

"You mean like a prayer?"

"Sure. Wouldn't that be appropriate?"

Caitlin shrugged. "I'm sure the Good Lord knows all of the heroes lying beneath these fields far better than we. I can't think of anything I might add that would further recommend their spirits beyond what He already knows."

"I guess you're right . . . It certainly is a lovely spot don't you think?"

"Mmmm," Caitlin purred. She was adrift for awhile in her own thoughts before speaking.

"Nigel was a very special young man, Charles."

"I'm sure he was. But I never really got to know him."

Caitlin shook her head slowly as a smile lightened her face. "He was everyone's favorite. Dear, sweet cousin Nigel. My Aunt Rebecca cried like a baby the day he announced he was using his inheritance to purchase a commission in the Royal Army.

"He was a gifted painter, did you know that?"

Charles indicated that he hadn't.

"Studied with some of the finest portraitists in London. He even traveled to Venice and Milan to view the works of the Masters. He had such a promising future . . .

"And he was in love! Hopelessly, wonderfully in love. She was a beautiful girl, every bit as sweet as he was. They had played together as children. And then they fell in love.

"I can see them walking in the public gardens at Wembly, hand-in-hand. People, total strangers, would just stop and smile as they passed.

"Just before the first battle here, Nigel told me a secret. He had proposed to his love by letter, and by the return post she accepted! They were to announce their engagement together on his first leave home. But he was just bursting with excitement — like a little boy at his first fair — and he had to tell his joyous news to someone; so he shared it with his cousin Caitlin."

The pleasant look drifted away from Caitlin's face. "I wrote to his fiancé, her name is Patricia, right after I returned to Oakmont. But I doubt if the letter ever got through. How could it. I want to write to her again when we reach Boston. She should know the true story of Nigel's courage. And she should hear it from me."

"Do you really think it would help her after all this time?"

"If it were me, I'd want to know. And the valor of his final act would be a comfort."

"It's so strange when I think about it," Charles said. "The more I learn about these men who I called my enemies, the more I admire them. I guess it's well that we never meet one another before the battles. I could never bring myself to shoot at a friend."

Caitlin stood up and brushed the twigs from her skirt. Charles joined her. Caitlin placed her hand on Nigel's headstone. "He sacrificed his life for mine. His happiness for ours . . . I was wondering Charles, what would you think, if one day we had a baby boy—"

"*Nigel Royal,*" Charles said, in complete harmony with her thoughts. "It would be a fine name."

There are few places on earth as charming and, at times, breathtaking as the great rolling hills of the Berkshires. In mid-August the landscape of forests and fields, streams and mirrored lakes is alive with all manner of life. Charles and Caitlin rolled along the road, thoroughly enjoying the panoramic scene. One moment they were beneath a cathedral-like canope of towering trees; the next, out in the open under the bluest of skies with staggered rows of majestic, hazy-topped hills beckoning them onward to the east.

Their destination this day was the historic village of Deerfield on the farside of the mountains. And once their, to locate Charles's old comrade-in-arms, Rainbow Samuels.

"Do you think we'll find him?" Caitlin asked.

Charles wasn't very encouraging. "The last I saw of him was in May of '78, when we were moving out at Valley Forge. We fought in different units at Monmouth. Afterwards, I went south and we lost touch. If he survived the war, he would have probably returned to Deerfield, if only for a short while."

Rainbow Samuels — wildman, scoundrel, bigamist, and free spirit — had been one of Charles's few close friends during the war. Indeed, one of the best and most trusted friends he had known in his life. To virtually all who knew him, Rainbow Samuels was an unforgettable character whose larger virtues — courage, loyalty, boundless good cheer — overshadowed his minor vices.

"I'm looking for a Continental veteran, a man by the name of Rainbow Samuels," Charles said to the grizzled proprietor of the Dancing Bear Tavern in Deerfield. "Do you know him?"

The man stroked the stubble on his chin as he considered his reply. "Mebbe yes, mebbe no. And who might *you* be?"

"My name's Charles Royal. This is my wife Caitlin. You have no need to be concerned. We're old friends of his."

The barkeep was not convinced. "You ain't no *constable* are you?"

"No. Like I said, a friend."

Casting a jaundiced eye up and down Charles, the man finally said, "You got five dollars?"

Charles handed him the money.

"Where you stayin'? Over at Mrs. Whitney's boardin' house?"

"Yes."

"Hmmph. I'll see what I can do. Ain't promisin' *nothin'* though. So don't expect your money back."

"I understand." And with that, Charles and Caitlin left.

"Friendly sort," Caitlin said sarcastically as they crossed the main street outside.

"We'll never find Rainbow by making inquiries with the clergy in town. I've got a feeling that man knows where to find him."

Sure enough, that evening while Caitlin and Charles were dining along with the other guests at Mrs. Whitney's table a bellowing, all so familiar voice called out from the front porch.

"By thunder! Is it the devil's lie or has my old friend and former cook Charles Royal come to pay his respects!"

Charles shot Caitlin a look of excitement and sprang from the dining room table. As soon as the soldiers' eyes met on the porch, Samuels stepped forward and lifted Charles clear off the ground in a friendly bearhug like he was a rag doll.

"Ha ha!," Samuels roared. "You're the happiest sight these eyes have seen in many a moon! And who's this? Not the woman spy from Saratoga?"

"Yes it is!" Caitlin replied beaming. "And now Mrs. Charles Royal!"

"Well I'll be damned!" Rainbow shouted, hoisting a surprised Caitlin into the air, just as he had Charles. "Sounds like a fairy tale! Boy rescues damsel in distress. Then they up and get married. And to think, I had a part in it. Ah, it does my romantic heart a world of good."

"I want to thank you, Mr. Samuels, for assisting in my rescue that evening."

"My pleasure ma'am. Or should I say *his!*" Rainbow cocked his head in Charles's direction. He checked Caitlin out admiringly. "You were right as rain, Charles. She's a real looker! Didn't get much of a view that night, what with all the commotion. But now I see plain — here's a woman worth riskin' your life for."

Caitlin blushed. "Thank you sir. Charles was right about you too."

"How's that ma'am?"

"He said you had the gifted tongue that could charm a nun from her habit."

Rainbow roared approvingly, "Now there's one conquest that's alluded me. But then, I ain't dead yet!"

The night was cool and clear and the three sat down on the porch chairs to catch up. Rainbow, as usual, was arrayed in his favored frontiersman's clothes — a fringed and beaded Indian hunting frock and buckskin pants with deerskin moccasins. His hair and beard were as long as ever, but were now more silvery gray than Charles recalled. His ruddy complexion and red nose gave notice that he has not parted company with his old nemesis — the bottle.

"It's Providence's own hand that we reunited on this day. Tomorrow me and my wife Singeewah, we're headin' west, maybe all the way to the Ohio."

"Had enough of civilization have you?" Charles asked in a jocular way, but for once, Rainbow was deadly serious.

"I don't belong here anymore, Charles. Me and the other boys, we fought in the Massachusetts Line — Bunker Hill, Bennington, Saratoga, Monmouth, Germantown — hell, the whole damn turkey shoot. Fought hard, fought brave. Some died. Most of us who survived are carryin' a souvenir or two." Samuels lifted his frock to reveal an ugly scar running down his right side.

"But them damn *politicians* and *merchants* in Boston," he practically spit the words, "Now that the war's won and their precious homes and hides have been spared, they turn on those who saved them!"

"You mean back pay?" Charles interjected. "That's been a thorn in every veteran's side."

"Sure back pay. But there's more. Men who marched off to fight for the Cause, they come back years later to find their property taken; their farms foreclosed; their wives and young'uns beggin' in the streets while the rich got richer!" Samuels seethed with anger. "It just ain't right, Charles. Somethin's *got* to be done. Or else, by Jehovah, there'll be a *second* Revolution!"

Charles had never seen Rainbow so inflamed.

"Congress and the state governments haven't done right by the soldiers," Charles agreed. "We all know that. But civil war can't be the answer. Did we fight to free ourselves from tyranny only to tear at each other's throats like mad dogs? It will take time—"

"Ha!" Samuels broke in, "Time's the ally of politicians. Time for people to forget. Time to organize and crush any uprising. No Charles. The only time we need is time to *act!* The widows and orphans and the poor returning veterans, their time is *now.*"

There was a lull while the passionate exchange cooled down. This was not the happy reunion that Charles had anticipated. It was left to Caitlin to try and bridge the schism.

"Your wife, Singeewah, she's not with you?"

"No," Samuels replied, as glad as anyone to change the subject. "She's off with her people, saying her goodbyes."

"Which tribe is she from?"

"Mohawk — one of the Iroquois tribes."

"And you'll be living with her people . . . out west?"

"I reckon we'll trap beaver and hunt furs in the old Six Nations country. Trade with the French maybe. I have a hankerin' to see those Great Lakes you've heard tell of. Maybe even float down the Mississip all the way to Spanish New Orleans. Now there's a *real* adventure.

"Farmin' never appealed to my wanderin' nature. So I figure one day I'll set up a tradin' post somewhere along the Ohio on some nice. unspoiled land. Then when the American settlers show up — and God knows they will — well I'll be right there ready to sell 'em whiskey and dry goods. Man's got to look to his future, eh Charles?"

"That's what we're doing. And the first step is to settle my affairs once and for all in Boston."

"A step back before a step forward."

"Something like that."

Samuels looked up to the dark sky. "Well, I best be on my way. Want to get a good early start in the mornin'"

Charles and Caitlin nodded.

Rainbow thought for a moment and then removed a necklace that held a small pouch and placed it around Caitlin's neck.

"This isn't necessary," she said. But Rainbow Samuels was a man whose gifts were hard to refuse.

"That's a secret medicine bag. Indians believe it'll ward off evil spirits. It's also suppose to contain magic that can make a woman fertile." Rainbow grinned at Charles. "Just in case the war took a little more out of your stallion here than he'd care to admit."

Charles took the ribbing good-naturedly.

"Ma'am," Rainbow tipped the brim of his hat to Caitlin. Charles and Rainbow then locked eyes. They shook hands. Then they clasped their left hands over their handshake and held fast. Then, slowly, with no words spoken, they loosened their grip. Rainbow Samuels turned and trudged off down the road, headed west. In the morning Charles and Caitlin hitched up their carriage for the final leg of their journey, and headed east.

Chapter 29

Following the familiar Lexington Road, Charles and Caitlin jostled their way toward Boston. This was the same route that the British had marched out on so boldly to confiscate the military stores at the armory in Concord back in April of 1775, and then staggered back along bloodied and beaten later that same day.

"Once we get settled in we'll take a ride out here if you like," Charles suggested. "We can visit the green in Lexington and the old Concord Bridge where it all began."

"Sounds exciting," Caitlin replied. "You never told me where you were during Lexington and Concord."

"Serving drinks at Mr. Robinson's Tavern as I recall. I looked out the window and saw the Redcoats marching in columns. I guess you could say I saw history pass me by."

"You caught up to it later, dear. Where's Bunker Hill?"

"On a neck of land in Charlestown, south of Cambridge. It's an easy ride out of Boston."

"Good."

"I'll show you the very spot where I threw off my haversack and ran."

"Shall we place a marker there?" Caitlin asked with an amused look.

Charles pretended to consider it. "I don't think so."

"How much further do we have to go until we reach your aunt's house?"

"At this rate, about two or three hours."

"Any guess as to how far we've traveled?"

Charles looked back over his shoulder. "I'd say about a lifetime."

"Make that two."

Many of the landmarks of his youth remained to remind Charles that he was nearing home. They passed Harvard, where Charles had spent one inglorious year, and took the ferry across the Charles River. Following Beacon Street to Tremont, they pulled the carriage up in front of a modest two story brick home.

"Whoa!" Charles called with a tug on the reins. Caitlin looked at him and he nodded. "We're here."

Before their feet had touched down on the well-worn cobblestones a stately, gray-haired matron was out the front door and walking briskly their way. Her exuberant smile said she was family.

"Welcome home Charles! And this must be your precious bride Caitlin." Without waiting for a reply, Aunt Ophie marched right up and embraced Caitlin warmly and kissed her on the forehead.

"It's a pleasure to meet you . . ." Caitlin's voice trailed off, not knowing the proper address.

"Aunt Ophie. Call me Aunt Ophie. Half the people in town call me that, whether they're related to me or not. And the other half, well I won't *tell* you what they call me.

"Charles!" She embraced him as well.

"How are you Aunt Ophie?"

"I can't complain. But then I didn't just take a buggy trip all the way from Maryland. How was your journey?"

Aunt Ophie locked arms with Caitlin and led her inside, leaving Charles to tend to the baggage and team.

"You must be tired, dear. Would you like to rest for awhile?"

"I'm fine, really," Caitlin replied. "You have a lovely home."

"Yes, well, it's plenty big enough for an old spinster like me. It'll be a joy to have people around."

"You're very kind to take us in."

"Nonsense! Your family. I'm the fortunate one."

Charles staggered in under the weight of a heavy suitcase in one hand and Caitlin's trunk buckling his back.

"And how is my favorite nephew?" Aunt Ophie asked cheerily.

"I don't know. Which one do you mean?"

Aunt Ophie gave him a playful slap. "Always the jester this one. My God, what's it been? Six years?"

Charles counted to himself. "I believe so." He carried the wearying load up the narrow stairway. "Which room is ours?"

"The large bedroom at the end of the hall. It's all made up."

"I hope we're not putting you out," Caitlin said. Aunt Ophie brushed away her concern.

"Come into the dining room. I have hot coffee and some fresh baked rolls. Or would you prefer a cool drink?"

Later in the day after they'd settled in, Charles and Caitlin joined Aunt Ophie in the front parlor. With the pleasantries aside it was time time to get down to business.

"Have you received any word from them at all?" Aunt Ophie inquired.

"Nothing," Charles replied solemnly. "I wrote to you that I was with Robert at Saratoga. At the end."

Aunt Ophie closed her eyes and nodded. "I received the letter."

"Robert told me that Mother, Sarah and Sally were evacuated to Nova Scotia when the British abandoned Boston. And that Joseph was to follow by land. He knew no more."

"That's as much as I know, too," Aunt Ophie said. "I've tried every way I know to contact them, but never a word. The Revolution shut down all but military correspondence. I pray to God that they are alive and well, but I fear the worst."

"The Royal Governor of Nova Scotia wasn't helpful?"

"Hardly. He lost his only son at Bunker Hill, and supposedly hates all Americans. I have many political friends. Unfortunately for us, they're all on the Patriot side. I'm sorry, Charles. I've failed completely."

"You did all you could. No one could suggest otherwise. But the issue remains, what do we do now?"

The three thought to themselves. It was Charles who broke the silence. "I see no alternative; I'm going to Nova Scotia and making inquiries directly."

"There's still a war on, Charles, and you're still an enemy officer," Aunt Ophie reminded him. "If you arrive in uniform, you'll be arrested. If you travel in civilian clothes and are detected, you could be tried as a spy — and hung."

Charles hadn't traveled this far to be turned back empty handed. "I've already considered the risks, and I'm going."

"*We're* going," Caitlin corrected him.

Charles was about to protest, the danger in such a journey was very real, but one look at his wife's determined face and he knew he could save his breath. She was going.

"Before taking such a drastic step, let's make a last attempt to reach them through the mail," Aunt Ophie suggested. ""If we receive no response, then you can go. All we'll have lost is a little time."

Charles looked at Caitlin. After all these years, a delay of perhaps two or three months did not seem unreasonable. Perhaps by then the treaty would be signed ending the hostilities and making travel safe once more. And in the meantime, there was other family business to attend to.

"Fine," Charles said at length. "I'll draft a new round of letters tomorrow."

"And I'll call on Dorothy Hancock and Abigail Adams," Aunt Ophie added. "They're close friends of mine. Perhaps they can pull a string or two."

"What's become of the house on Joy Street?" Charles asked, abruptly changing the subject. "And all the business interests?"

"The house has been divided into private apartments and rented-out by your brother's old manager, Maxwell Chessman. He's pretty much taken over all of the family's business affairs."

"What! Just like that! Walks in and claims all of our holdings?"

"First of all, the family's businesses were in a shambles after the British left and the mobs in the street had their fun burning, stealing, or destroying everything that had belonged to the Loyalists. Second, with Robert off to war, someone had to run things here. Mr. Chessman was Robert's hand-picked choice. And third, Mr. Chessman didn't just move in, he *bought* the family's interests."

"Bought them! From whom?"

"From the Commonwealth of Massachusetts."

Charles was totally confused.

"By the provisions of the Confiscation Act," Aunt Ophie continued. "All property belonging to known Tories, whether present or absent, was taken by the state. It was then sold off to the highest bidder, with the revenue used to finance the state's war debt — and to line the pockets of a few Boston politicians I don't doubt."

"Wait a minute. I'm not a Tory. I served for the duration of the Revolution with the Patriots. How can they sell-off my property while I'm away fighting for the Cause? This is a hellish nightmare!"

"Yes. But all quite legal I'm afraid."

"Well we'll see about that! Tomorrow I'll pay a visit to Mr. Maxwell Chessman. He'll not steal from *my* family and get away with it!"

"No violence Charles. I want you to promise me; just talk." Caitlin's voice was stern but laced with an edge of fear.

Charles, red-faced with rage, replied in measured words. "We'll talk for now. But by God, no *shirker* is going to to take what rightfully belongs to the Royals."

Without realizing it, Charles had assumed the same attitude of righteous indignation as Rainbow Samuels. Whether the veterans were returning to a pathetic, rock-strewn farm or vast family holdings made no difference — loss of property and forced impoverishment were a bitter reward for years of selfless service to their country. If Samuels were there at that moment to call for a Second American Revolution, he would have had his first recruit.

"What about you, Aunt Ophie?" Charles inquired. "Without your income from the family businesses how have you been able to survive?"

"If I tell you, you won't get angry will you?"

"No."

"Mr. Chessman has continued the payments of his own volition. The rents from the Joy Street house, they come to me each month. He's not an evil man, Charles. He's a businessman who seized an opportunity."

This was all too much for Charles to absorb. His head was swimming. "I'll visit him tomorrow . . . Perhaps he'll prove to be fair-minded . . . Maybe we can work something out . . ."

"The war has proved to be an upheaval for everyone, hasn't it," Caitlin mused aloud.

"Yes it has, dear," Aunt Ophie agreed. "But now that the two of you are here, perhaps we can start putting the world right again."

Suddenly Aunt Ophie remembered something important. She arose quickly and went to a tray on a side table.

"You've received some mail already." She leafed through several letters and extracted two. "Both for Caitlin. From Maryland." She handed them to her.

Caitlin eyed the addresses, which were written in Junius's hand. One appeared to be a letter from Rake that Junius had apparently forwarded unopened. She slid her finger under the sealing wax and popped it open. Her face grew into a peaceful smile as she read its contents.

"It's a letter from Rake. Rake's my brother. He's fighting with the partisans under Colonel Marion in South Carolina," Caitlin informed Aunt Ophie. "Listen to what he writes:

> *"We learned through reliable informants that the British are about to evacuate Charleston and Savannah. General Carleton has ordered the entire army to be placed on transports and put to sea by the end of the month. When the last of them passes over the horizon, the South will be free at last! A glorious day! A glorious, hard-fought victory! All that will remain is to subdue a few remaining nests of Tories. Once that chore is done, the Revolution in the South will have come to a happy conclusion."*

Caitlin turned to Charles, "Can it be true?"

"I would think so. Rake would not have reported a rumor. With the evacuation of Charleston, that would leave only New York City in British hands. This is one more major step toward the successful climax of the Revolution."

"Oh my!" Aunt Ophie exclaimed. "I have a friend who's the publisher of the *Boston Gazette*. Would it be alright if I share the information in your brother's letter with him?"

"Certainly. Everyone should know such joyous news."

"What else does he write?" Charles asked.

Caitlin scanned ahead. "Now that the hostilities have about ended, Rake has received permission from Colonel Marion to take his leave. He mentions an upcoming going-away party that the men will be throwing for him at a place called 'Fat Hat's'. What's that?"

Charles could scarcely conceal his grin. "I'll tell you later."

"You always say that but you never do," Caitlin mumbled as she continued to read. Her eyes widened happily when she got to a passage near the end.

"He'll be returning ro Oakmont. In fact, by the date of this letter he may be on the road home now. Oh this is *wonderful*. I'll tell you truthfully, I never thought my brother would survive this war. With every delivery of mail I half expected to receive a letter of condolence from Colonel Marion. But the shooting has stopped and he's still standing!"

After Rake's signature there was a postscript.

"He received my letter about my desire to free all our people upon my return. Here's what he writes:

"Never have we been in closer accord. Having fought,
lived, and suffered together these long years with so many
men of color, it is unthinkable to me that they should be
held in bondage. With your indulgence, I will discuss the
matter in private with Junius if I arrive home before you.
When you and Charles return to Oakmont, we will call all
of our people together and make our announcement."

After finishing, Caitlin handed the letter to Aunt Ophie to deliver to her newspaper contact.

"I'll be back in plenty of time to prepare dinner," Aunt Ophie announced as she tied on her sunbonnet and slipped out the door.

The smile of satisfaction on Caitlin's face seemed etched there as she opened the second letter.

"Who is that one from," Charles asked.

"Junius . . . It appears we'll have a record crop this year . . . He won the stakes race at the county fair . . ." Caitlin's face lost its glow as she read further. "There's a problem. The old constable's moved on and the new one refuses to honor Junius's letter of authority . . . A few of the local roughnecks have stolen some of our cattle and are harassing our people . . . Junius is going to speak to Reverend Stocker . . ."

"What can we do?" Charles asked.

"Nothing from here. Thank God Rake's on his way. He'll know what to do."

Early the next morning Charles arose and dressed as quietly as he could so as not to awaken his wife. After a quick cup of coffee in the kitchen he saddled up one of the horses and rode off in the direction of the North End wharves where he expected to find Maxwell Chessman.

At the end of Battery Street, near the harbor where the Royal's various warehousing and shipping enterprises were centered, the scene was both familiar and entirely new. Charles spun about in his saddle as he looked with amazement at the beehive of activity. Merchant ships were tethered to every mooring while several others lay just off shore, awaiting their turn at an open berth. A small army of workers was in constant motion — loading, unloading, setting jibs and hoists, moving wagons and draft animals into position. Orders were shouted by foremen on every dock and on the shore, filling the air and giving direction to the flow.

Just off the beach two monstrous new storehouses were well underway, the new blond lumber rising plank by plank as the carpenters' hammers toiled incessantly.

Charles had never witnessed such vigorous mercantile activity. Amid all the clamor he felt strange, somehow alone, certainly out of place. Workers were bustling all about him, but no one took notice of his presence, so he called over to a blacksmith in a leather apron.

"Excuse me, sir. Can you tell me where I might find Mr. Maxwell Chessman?"

The smithy wiped his brow with a soiled sleeve. "Follow the boardwalk till you come to a gray brick building. You can't miss it. Mr. Chessman's office is on the second floor."

Charles thanked the man and rode off. He knew the building quite well. It had been his brother Robert's headquarters, and their father's before him. Now, like everything else, it appeared to belong to the usurper Chessman.

"Who should I say is calling, sir?" asked the clerk from behind his tall counting desk.

"Charles Royal."

The clerk looked nervous. "Just a moment sir, if you please. I'll find out if Mr. Chessman can see you." He disappeared down a corridor, then returned a minute later with a look of relief. "Mr. Chessman will be pleased to see you, sir. Straight ahead to the end of the hall."

"Yes," Charles replied. "I know."

Charles walked through the open door of the large, well-appointed office that was a familiar fixture from his youth. Behind an artistically carved mahogany desk sat Maxwell Chessman — a little grayer, balder, and plumper than when Charles had last set eyes on him.

Chessman rose immediately. "Charles Royal! Welcome home from the war." Chessman waived out two assistants who cradled their papers in their arms as they left, closing the door behind them.

"I had no idea you were returning to Boston."

"My wife and I just arrived yesterday."

"Your *wife*. Well congratulations. I'm afraid I haven't been as fortunate in affairs of the heart. The demands of running a large business have proven to be a jealous mistress. May I offer you a drink?"

"No. Thank you."

"Please, have a seat."

Chessman resumed his chair. Charles, reluctantly, sat down in the chair across from the desk.

"Well Charles, what can I do for you this fine day."

"You can return my family's business, which you stole."

Chessman's face dropped. "Would you mind repeating that."

"What part didn't you hear?"

"Are you calling me a *thief?*"

"Yes."

Chessman jumped to his feet, pounding the desk with his fist, "Sir! You have thrown down the gauntlet! As a gentleman I *demand satisfaction!*"

Charles stood glaring. "Choose your place and weapons."

It was Chessman who blinked first. "There must be some misunderstanding," he said with palms upraised.

"You've taken possession of everything my family owned. Even our personal residence. And you haven't paid a *penny* for them. That brands you as a thief — there is no *misunderstanding*. Your place and weapons."

Chessman searched Charles's face where he met only steely resolve. He had stared down many an adversary in a tough business negotiation, but he knew better than to meet this combat-hardened soldier in a contest of arms that he would surely lose.

"Charles," he pleaded, "You are misinformed. I *bought* your family's interests."

"Not from any family member."

"No, that part's entirely correct. I made a contract of purchase with the Commonwealth after the property was seized under the Confiscation Act of 1778."

"Like a *serpent* you slithered in and made your pact with the State House devils!"

"Charles. It was *they* who approached *me*. The businesses were in ruin. Bankrupt. They needed someone to take over who could bring them back to life. Put the people back to work. Even then I turned them down; out of loyalty to your brother and your late father whom I loved. That's when they confirmed to me that Robert had been killed at Saratoga. Only then Charles; *only then* did I agree to terms."

Charles was somewhat mollified. Chessman's explanation jived with Aunt Ophie's. But even if he wasn't a thief, Chessman had claimed the Royal's inheritance as his own, and that could never be brushed away by a signature on a contract. Family honor, at the very least, demanded satisfaction.

"You're back now, Charles. And I'm pleased to see you survived the war. Really. What do you want of me? How can we make this right?"

"I want my family's fortune restored."

"Charles. You don't understand. The family fortune was all lost. Fate laid claim to it the day Robert sided with the Loyalists. When the siege of Boston was finally over, the rabble of the streets stole or burned everything the British hadn't carried off. Finally the state stepped in and gathered up the broken pieces of that once great empire that had been the Royal's and turned to me. I swear to God, that's the truth of it.

"I want to do right by you and your family, Charles. Would you accept a position with my company? I'm sure we could create something that would be worthy of your standing in the community. You have done yourself proud in the Revolution Charles. You would be an asset to me."

"Sir! You are *despicable!* You disgust me! For some meaningless job and a few pieces of silver you expect me to sell my birthright? If I did I wouldn't be worthy of it!"

"Charles, please, let me finish—"

"I assure you, the affable, misdirected boy you once knew is gone forever."

"I realize that—"

"I could force you to meet me on the field of honor, where you would most certainly die. But I prefer to ruin you, like you tried to ruin me and my family.

"The next time we meet, Mr. Chessman, will be in *court!* " With that Charles turned abruptly and marched out the door.

"Charles, please, be reasonable!" Chessman called after him, but to no avail.

Out in the hall Charles's glowering demeanor sent the eavesdropping clerks scattering in all directions, like rats when a bright light suddenly enters a room.

Without breaking stride Charles hurried down the stairway and out to the street. He unhitched his horse from the rail, mounted, and trotted off. His business for this day accomplished.

Back at Aunt Ophie's, Caitlin had already made a list of officials to whom they would write. They would try the Royal Governor again, the Mayor of Halifax, the city constabulary, even the coroner. She came up with the idea of placing an advertisement in the Halifax newspapers offering a reward for information leading to the whereabouts of the missing Royals.

Charles had just returned home and was placing his hat on the peg in the front hall when Caitlin called to him from the parlor. "Charles? Is that you?"

"Yes." He joined his wife who was seated at Aunt Ophie's writing desk.

"Did you speak with Mr. Chessman?"

Charles nodded with a sigh.

"How did it go?"

"Not very well. Oh he gave me a song and dance about his innocence of any wrongdoing. Even offered me a *job*. Can you imagine that?"

"What happens now?"

"Looks like we'll have to take him to court."

Caitlin appeared visibly relieved. "I was afraid you'd challenge him to a duel."

"What are you doing?"

"Oh, I'm composing the letters for Nova Scotia."

"Good. You're a much better writer than I am. What are you saying?"

"Just that we're seeking four lost family members who supposedly arrived in Halifax following the evacuation of the Boston Loyalists in March of '76. I give their names and ages and then I list our address at the bottom of the page."

"Sounds about right."

"I'm also creating an advertisement for the newspapers offering a reward to anyone who provides us with information that helps us locate them."

"Caitlin, I don't have any money to pay a reward."

"Hush! *We* do." She returned to her correspondence.

"Is Aunt Ophie home?"

Without looking up from her paper Caitlin replied, "She left already — something about a women's suffrage meeting."

"Then we have the house all to ourselves."

"Mmmm."

"Caitlin. We have the house *all to ourselves.*"

Now Caitlin looked up from the desk. Charles's sly grin confirmed his meaning. *Well,* Caitlin thought to herself, *I suppose these can wait.*

Charles had never hired a lawyer before, but it was clear he needed one now. In Boston he knew of three. There was John Wayland, the most prominent and respected attorney in town. Talk was that he might even run for mayor in the next election. There was one problem though — Wayland had been the Royal's lawyer for twenty years and would undoubtedly be under retainer to Maxwell Chessman now.

Then there was John Adams. An excellent choice except that he was otherwise occupied with the American Delegation at the Paris peace talks.

Finally, Charles had known a lawyer by the name of Thaddeus Mantooth from his Sons of Liberty days. Mantooth was a celebrated debater with a lucid mind and a razor-sharp wit who had built a thriving practice. On the downside, he had a flair for the flamboyant that sometimes got him into trouble, and he was fighting a running battle with the bottle. One afternoon, Charles paid him a call.

"Charles Royal! Mars is in his heaven! The hero returns home at last!"

"It's good to see you again, Thaddeus."

"Please. Sit. I followed your progress during the war, Charles. Yours and all of our comrades in the Sons. It became a kind of hobby to me.

"We have our share of distinguished veterans I'm proud to say. But you, you top the list!"

"You flatter me."

"You even served at Yorktown didn't you. You were there at the surrender. Oh please, tell me all about it."

Charles willingly shared with Mantooth a twenty minute narrative of the siege and final capitulation ceremonies at Yorktown. Mantooth sat entranced, interrupting only rarely with a declarative "My God." When Charles had finished, Mantooth pushed back from his desk with his hands clasped behind his head.

"Charles, I would give my right arm to have experienced *one tenth* of the adventures you've known." A riding accident as a child had left Mantooth a cripple who had to rely on a cane to get around.

"I can assure you, there were far more disasters and difficulties than glorious victories."

"All adventures to me. You entered the war as a raw private and by your skill and daring rose to be a major, standing alongside the Great Washington himself on the final field of valor," Mantooth said, shaking his head in admiration.

"You make it sound far more grand than it was, Thaddeus. I was little more than a spectator in uniform at Yorktown. And as for Bunker Hill, about the only memorable thing I did there was pee down my leg at the first approach of the enemy."

Mantooth laughed. "Charles, your modesty only adds to your legend in my mind. So, is this just a social visit, or do you come on business?"

"Business I'm afraid. Do you know a man by the name of Maxwell Chessman?"

"Of course. He's the most prosperous businessman in town. Employs half the city."

"And do you know the source of his wealth?"

"Not really."

"He stole all the mercantile holdings that belonged to my family before the war."

Mantooth rose, turned and stood looking through the pains of his window, his back to Charles. "That's quite a charge. Go on."

"He was my father's general manager when he was alive; then my brother Robert's. When Robert took a commission with the Loyalist forces and went away to fight he left Chessman in charge. Robert was killed at Saratoga as you might know. The rest of my family sailed off to Nova Scotia with General Gage. Apparently the family's interests suffered. In 1778, based on the Confiscation Act, Chessman swooped in and bought what remained, probably at a pittance. I've been down to the wharves. I've seen the great prosperity all about. But it was all built on an act so foul that it would do credit to Macbeth.

"I spoke to Chessman. He claims he's lily clean. It's clear that if my family's honor and fortune are to be restored, it must be through the courts."

Mantooth had remained silent and impassive during Charles's recitation. The look on his face was more troubling than hopeful.

"Would you agree to a settlement of some sort?"

"I want justice."

"*Justice?* You'll have to define that term for me. The longer I've practiced law, the less clear the concept of justice has become. Mr. Chessman has taken possession of Tory property by payment to the government under the provisions of the Confiscation Act of 1778. Am I correct on this?"

Charles grudgingly indicated that he was.

"Then you have no case."

Charles did not take the verdict well. " . . . There are other lawyers in town."

"Yes there are. Perhaps you should avail yourself of their services."

With a deep breath, Charles regained his composure. "Thaddeus, hear me out.

"I'm just one of the thousands of civilians who took up arms during the Revolution. We weren't professional soldiers. But we believed in the ideal of liberty, and we were willing to fight for our rights and for those we left

281

behind.

"For seven long years we suffered — wounds, sickness, hardships of every type. We watched as our friends fell lifeless beneath the enemy's onslaught. Yet, in the end, against all odds, we prevailed.

"Now the veterans return home. And what do we find? A hero's welcome from a grateful nation? No. Farms that are lost to back taxes. Small businesses swallowed-up by those who stayed far away from the cannon's roar. A government that afflicts the soldiers who fought its war with greater miseries than anything inflicted by the enemy.

"Is this the just reward for a Patriot's love of country — a victory laurel made of thorns?

"And here's a final thought to consider: If we don't address this gross unfairness, then who will be willing to fight in the future if, God forbid, there is a threat to our nation's new freedom? Young men will look about them, see old soldiers in rags, ruined by the last war, their families reduced to poverty. And these young men will say, 'These were the *victors?*'

"We've won the war, Thaddeus. Will we lose the peace?"

Charles's speech from the heart touched Mantooth deeply. This was more than one individual's plea for justice. It was a battle for all the disenfranchised veterans. A battle that this crippled member of the Sons of Liberty, who was denied the chance to actively serve in the Revolution, seized as his own.

". . . I'll need the names and last known addresses for all your former commanding officers. I'll use them as character witnesses. Have them to me by next Tuesday. We'll spend the day together. I'll have many questions to ask you."

"Does this mean you'll represent me?"

"You fought your war," Mantooth replied. "Maybe this one's mine."

Caitlin had mailed the sheaf of letters of inquiry to Nova Scotia. Now they would have to wait in hope for some reply.

With the balmy autumn weather, Charles suggested to Caitlin that they take a ride out to visit Lexington and Concord. And so, with a picnic lunch all packed, they set out.

In Lexington they met a wizened farmer who claimed to be a member of Captain Parker's militia company on the fateful morning of April 19, 1775.

"Ask around and you'll find nearly every fella from 8 to 80 claimin' to have been mustered on the Green that day. Truth be told, there was only a handful of us. We knew right off we weren't no match for Major Pitcairn's column of Regulars.

"We decided among ourselves not to fire unless the Redcoats should insult or molest us. Hell, we were farmers and shopkeepers, not soldiers. Twenty minutes before the Brits arrived me and some of the boys were sittin' over yonder at Buckman's Tavern wettin' our whistles for godsake.

"Major Pitcairn rode onto the Green as his infantry advanced at a trot and yelled 'Disperse you rebels!'. Captain Parker, he ordered us to do just that. But some of us, we'd sworn an oath never to run before British troops, so we held our ground and leveled our muskets, come what may."

"So who fired the first shot?" Charles asked anxiously.

The farmer searched his memory, then shook his head slowly. "Cain't rightly say. I just remember a couple of cracks, then all hell broke loose. 'Fire, damn you, Fire!' the British officers cried. And fire they did! First volley went high. But the second . . . well that's when we started fallin'. The Regulars turned into wild animals, firin' at any man in view who held a rifle. In a matter of minutes the Green was cleared."

"What were your losses?"

"Eight killed, nine wounded. The rest of us scattered back along the road to Concord. To spread the news and to get ready for the rest of the day's fightin'. They beat us at the first, that's for sure, but when the last smoke cleared, it was *them* what was bleedin' their way back to Boston!"

Charles and Caitlin treated the farmer to an ale at Buckman's and then returned to their carriage for the seven mile journey along Great Road to Concord. On the way they passed the Bedford crossroad where a rock marker was inscribed with the words Meriam's Corner, a site where some of the fiercest fighting took place.

Nearby they met twin brothers who were veterans of the fray. In an ironic twist, both men had been shot in the left arm and both were amputated, which maintained their perfect symmetry.

Climbing into the carriage behind Caitlin and Charles, the brothers directed them to the armory that had been the Redcoats objective that day, and then through the marketplace where stores had been looted and put to the torch by the invaders. Finally, they reached North Bridge over the Concord River where the local militias drew-up under Colonel Barrett and fired the salvo that began the British retreat back down the sniper-infested road toward Cambridge.

Charles enjoyed the vivid account thoroughly. At various junctures he stopped the carriage and walked ahead with the twins, recreating in his imagination the ebb and flow of events that day.

The afternoon was winding down. A decision had to be made. Caitlin suggested that they find accommodations for the night rather than try to navigate the roads back to Aunt Ophie's in the darkness. Charles agreed and the brothers directed them to the Wayside Inn.

The next morning the singing of birds awakened them early. It was another crisp, delightful day.

"We indulged your pleasures yesterday, my dear," Caitlin said to her husband. "So today it's my turn."

"What would you like to do — anything at all."

"Well, I noticed that they rent rowboats on the Concord River. Charles, you've never taken me rowing . . ."

"Then today's the day!"

It turned out to be a splendid idea. The smooth clear water and the tapestry of turning autumn foliage overhead murmured of peace and tranquility. Charles did the rowing while Caitlin sat in the back beneath her white sunbonnet, smiling contentedly.

They rowed across Walden Pond where Caitlin was struck by the dense forests with their timeless beauty. "Wouldn't it be wonderful, Charles, to build a small cabin near the water's edge where we could just sit and mark the passing of the seasons?"

"You're a thorough dreamer."

They arrived back home just before sunset to find that Aunt Ophie was away at one of her meetings again. Charles spotted a note with just his name on it sitting on the side table. It was sealed. While Caitlin left to freshen up, Charles opened it.

> *Dear Charles:*
>
> *I learned today that you have returned to Boston. What wonderful news! You have no idea how much I've thought of you since we last parted.*
>
> *It is imperative that I speak with you. Please meet me at the Tea Room on Wednesday at 4:00. Unless I hear from you otherwise, I will be waiting for you there.*
>
> *With Heartfelt Affection,*
>
> *Celeste*
>
> *P.S. Please destroy this note immediately and tell no one of its contents.*

Caitlin returned shortly, a towel in her hands. "What's that?"

" . . . A letter for me."

"Who is it from?"

"Celeste."

Caitlin froze for a moment. Charles had told her all about Celeste one night long ago. How she had broken his heart. Caitlin had never imagined that this lost love might ever reappear. A dozen emotions now vied for control of her, but she surrendered to none of them.

"What does she say?"

"Here," Charles replied without hesitation, handing his wife the note. "See for yourself."

Caitlin read the brief, mysterious message to herself.

"I think you should go see her."

"What! Why?'

"Why not?"

"I have nothing to say to her. It's been years. I'm a happily married man now."

"Perhaps you should tell her that instead of me."

This was not the first time Charles had been stopped in his tracks by Caitlin's crystal-clear logic.

"Most wives wouldn't want their husband to sip tea with a former girl-friend," he replied.

"Most husbands wouldn't have shown their wife this letter."

"Have it your way then. I'll meet with Celeste. But under one condition."

"Which is?"

"That you tell me the *real* reason you want me to go."

Caitlin looked deeply into her husband's eyes. "I love you Charles. You mean the world to me. And I know if I say 'Don't go' you won't."

"That's right."

"And then what? You'll always wonder in the back of your mind why she had to see you. What was so —" Caitlin looked at the note to find the exact word, "So '*imperative*'. No Charles. See her. Hear what she has to say. If not for her sake or your own, do it for me."

" . . . Would you like to come?"

"Thank you. No."

"I promise you, it will just be tea."

Caitlin smiled as if she didn't need this reassurance. "I know."

"Now that I think about it," Charles said brightening, "Maybe we'll get a good laugh out of this."

At the Tea Room, Celeste was seated at the very same table where she had broken off her relationship with Charles. She was even facing the same direction. She smiled radiantly at Charles as he approached. *The years have been kind to her,* Charles thought. She was still a stunning, if fragile, beauty who would be a welcome adornment on almost any man's arm.

"It's been a long time, Celeste."

She patted the seat of the chair beside her and Charles sat down.

"Oh Charles. My knight in shining armor! How good of you to come."

The term 'knight in shining armor' struck Charles as odd, but he let it pass without comment. He noticed a wedding band on Celeste's finger. He also noticed how quickly she covered it with her other hand.

"This place never changes does it Charles. I love it here. Always so bright and pleasant. People always seem happier when they're out in public, don't you think?"

Celeste prattled on for some time — about the weather, the latest fashions from Europe, a recent banquet she attended for the new President of Harvard (including who sat next to whom at dinner). *Same old Celeste,* Charles decided. As a love-struck youth he would sit enraptured, happy that she would even speak to him at all. Now, he was just bored, and growing a bit testy.

"Listen, Celeste," he finally said, cutting her off in mid-sentence. "What was so imperative that I had to meet you here?"

She stared at him blank-faced.

"Celeste? Your note?"

The lightness seemed to draw away from her face, revealing for the first time etched lines around her eyes and brow. Her gaze was downcast for so long that Charles began to wonder if she would ever speak.

"I have suffered greatly these past few years, Charles."

"Are you ill?" Charles asked in a considerate way.

" . . . Not in the medical sense. I am ill at heart."

She waited for Charles to question her further. When he didn't, she just went on.

"I'm married. To your old friend Phillip. Phillip Overton. You remember him."

Charles did, but not fondly.

"He's a doctor now. In practice in Cambridge with his father. We have a grand house there. You should see it. The largest on the block. With servants."

"So, what's the problem?"

Tears suddenly welled in Celeste's eyes. "I'm just so *miserable*. He's such a hurtful man, Charles. Phillip that is. He ignores me whenever we're at a social gathering, or rudely insults me in front of his friends, just so they can all *laugh* at me. He's mean and I *hate* him."

Charles didn't know what to say. "Why are you telling me all this?"

"Take me away Charles! Please! Out west. To the territories. Anywhere."

"You can't be serious."

"You've been everywhere during the war, haven't you? You must know somewhere I could escape to. Where I'd be happy."

"Celeste, have you lost your mind?"

"Oh Charles, I should never have sent you away. But we're here now. Together again. Just like before. Only better. I've learned alot of things, Charles. I know how to . . . please a man."

Charles was incredulous. "You want to leave your husband, just like that, and run off with me?"

"Yes! Today! I have my chests packed already."

"I'll bet you have children, too."

" . . . Yes."

"How many?"

" . . . Three."

"And what about them?"

"I don't care!" Celeste sobbed. "Don't you understand, I have to get away!"

"Celeste, did it ever occur to you that *I* might be married? I am you know. *Happily* married."

"I could make you happier, Charles. I *know* I could. Let me prove it to you."

"Celeste, this conversation is crazy. It's also over. You are never, *ever* to contact me again." Charles arose but Celeste lunged after him, clutching him with both hands as she nearly fell to her knees.

"Please, Charles, *please!* If you don't take me away I don't know *what* I'll do. I'll, I'll kill him in his sleep! I will! I *swear* I will! And his blood will be on *your* hands Charles. Not mine, *yours!*"

Charles knocked her hands away so violently that Celeste fell to the floor.

"You obviously have a serious problem, Mrs. Overton. But I'm not the solution."

Charles arrived home to find Caitlin in the parlor reading a book. She was engrossed in it; or pretended to be.

"How did it go?" she asked without raising her eyes from the page.

"You wouldn't have believed it. I told her never to contact me again."

287

"Mmmm," Caitlin replied as if only mildly interested. And there the matter was left, and was never discussed again.

Charles decided he wanted to show Caitlin the landmarks from his boyhood. To try and share with her those precious times he had spent strolling these streets and walking by the shore with his father; asking questions, listening to stories, dreaming dreams.

For her part, Caitlin relished the opportunity to learn more about Charles as a child. So they set out together walking along Tremont and Boylston Streets, past the farmers' and the fishermen's markets, down Atlantic Avenue to the ocean, then along the beach.

They paused to watch the small sailboats and ketchs gliding effortlessly out over the gently rolling sea, wisps of white foam surging upward at the touch of their bows. Overhead, white gulls circled, searching the blue-gray waters for their next meal.

"My father loved the sea," Charles said, casting his eyes to the distant horizon. "It was a love I never shared, but I could appreciate it in him. He'd tell me tales of the dastardly pirates he'd met and of the faraway places he'd seen in his youth — the ports of Western Europe of course, but also those of the Mediterranean. He made the beautiful señoritas of Spain and the camel-riding Moslems of the Great Sahara come alive for me. Once," Charles revealed in a hushed tone, "He even visited Jerusalem in the Holy Land."

Caitlin wasn't sure if all this were true, or just the exaggerated tales that a father might tell to entertain his wide-eyed little boy. No matter. After all these years Charles still accepted them as gospel.

"See that lighthouse up ahead. Whichever direction we began our walk in, we always seemed to end up here. Wave!"

Charles started waving vigorously up at the lighthouse for no apparent reason. Perplexed but game, Caitlin did likewise.

"Father always said to wave at the lighthouse when you pass by. And smile. Because the person at the top of the lighthouse was your very special friend."

"Did you ever get to meet the person in the lighthouse?"

Charles thought for a moment. "No, actually I never did."

Charles had planned their tour so that it would bring them to a particular place that Caitlin had heard him speak of often. "Guess what's just around this corner," he asked grinning.

"Don't tell me . . . Tell me."

"I'd rather show you." Taking his wife's hand, Charles quickened his pace. And as they came around the bend of shops, there it was, the old familiar sign — Robinson's Tavern.

Inside the doorway Charles paused and scanned the room. "My God! Nothing's changed at all! Not a thing. See those two sots seated at the end of the bar — they were our most reliable regulars. And I guess they still are!"

Being mid-afternoon, the tavern was less than half full. Charles and Caitlin seated themselves at a table by the window. A middle-aged man wearing an apron approached.

"What can I get you folks?"

Charles gave Caitlin a knowing smile then turned to the man. "I'd like a word with the proprietor, Mr. Robinson, or his wife, Mrs. Robinson. Are they about?" Charles stretched to see around the man.

"I'm sorry, sir, they aren't. Mr. Robinson's retired. I'm the proprietor now. Name's Tilley. As for Mrs. Robinson, well sir, she's gone to her glory."

Charles's whole countenance dropped. For a minute he couldn't speak. Finally he mumbled, "A beer and . . ." He looked at Caitlin.

"Two beers would be fine," she said to Tilley. He nodded and left to fetch the drinks.

"I'm so sorry, Charles. I know how fond you were of the Robinsons."

Charles sighed deeply. "Well, it has been a long time. Can't expect the whole world to stand still for me."

"I'm sure Mr. Tilley wouldn't mind if you wanted to look around the place a bit. Maybe see your old quarters behind the kitchen?"

Charles smiled weakly. "No. It was the people I was hoping to see."

When the drinks arrived, Charles and Caitlin sipped them and looked out the window at the passerbys outside in the street. They made small talk until Caitlin remembered something that might perk-up Charles's spirits.

"Did Aunt Ophie mention to you that we've been invited to dine with Governor and Mrs. Hancock?"

"No," Charles replied. His mood did seem to improve with the news.

"Remember Aunt Ophie said she was going to pay a visit to Dorothy Hancock, hoping she might be able to assist us in our search? Well John Hancock was home at the time, and when Aunt Ophie spoke your name, she said the Governor visibly brightened and began to ask a stream of questions about you. You never told me you were so familiar with the Governor of Massachusetts."

"I first met him here at Robinson's. In the months before Bunker Hill I served him as a coach driver on occasion."

"Well, according to Aunt Ophie, the Governor *insisted* that we be his and Mrs. Hancock's guests for dinner. Aunt Ophie will be attending too."

"When is this glorious gala to take place?"

"A week from this Saturday."

"Is there room on our social calendar?"

Caitlin pulled out an imaginary book and pretended to flip through its pages. "Let's see. Saturday, Saturday. Ah! Here it is. Now let me look . . ." She closed the invisible book and smiled. "As chance would have it, that's an open night for us."

Pondering this unexpected development, Charles just had to chuckle. "I use to stare at his horse's butt. And now I will be his guest for dinner at the Governor's Mansion. I wonder which will prove to be the more enjoyable experience."

On their trek back to Aunt Ophie's, Charles and Caitlin ducked into the Globe Bookstore to browse a bit. Caitlin quickly found her way to the section containing novels, and in short order she selected a half-dozen which she placed on the counter. She rejoined her husband who was immersed in a thick volume on the military history of Ancient Rome.

"Is it interesting?" she inquired.

" . . . Yes. I wonder how much it costs?"

"Charles! How often do we get to visit a bookstore? We'll take it. Now look around and see if you find anything else you like."

After awhile Charles decided to get just the one text. He brought it to the counter and placed it on Caitlin's stack of books, which had now grown to more than a dozen.

The elderly lady behind the counter smiled as she read the title on Charles's book. "This is one of my former employer's favorite works. Were you in the Continental Army by any chance, sir?"

"Why yes."

"Then perhaps you know him — General Henry Knox?"

"Of course!" Charles exclaimed. "I know him very well. A gentleman of great virtue and a military genius in the art of deploying artillery."

"You probably also know then that General Knox was a bookseller here in Boston before the Revolution. He and his beloved wife Lucy. Such a delightful couple."

"Has he returned yet? From the war? I would dearly love to see him again."

"Not as far as I know. And I would. Old Henry Knox could no more stay away from a bookstore than a bear from a honey tree. And we have the widest selection in all of Boston."

Charles scribbled a quick note. "If he should appear one day, would you please give him this."

"Certainly, sir. I'll be sure to add it to the rest."

As the clerk tallied the purchases she said to Charles, "You're a student of military history then, just like old Henry?"

"More and more as time passes. Perhaps one day I'll write my own account of the Revolution," he said in jest.

Looking up from her tally the lady offered words of encouragement. "I hope you do, sir. And when it arrives, I promise we'll display it right there in the front window for all the world to see."

The Royal's carriage (with Aunt Ophie in back) arrived at the Governor's Mansion right on time. Two liveried stablemen took the reins as Charles stepped down and assisted his wife and aunt who were both dressed in formal evening gowns. For a moment, before ascending the wide marble steps, they paused to gaze up at the imposing residence.

"Shall we?" Charles said, offering his arm to Caitlin. The other he extended to Aunt Ophie, and together they walked ahead.

It was to be an intimate dinner party with only sixteen invited guests. There was no formal greeting line, just John and Dorothy Hancock to welcome everyone as they arrived.

"Charles Royal!" said the Governor, clasping both hands on the sides of Charles's shoulders. "Welcome home! And this must be your lovely wife, Caitlin. Delighted." Hancock took Caitlin's hand and gave it a gentlemanly kiss. "And hello to you, Aunt Ophie."

"John."

Mrs. Hancock also greeted her guests and, taking Caitlin by the arm, guided her around the elegantly appointed reception room, introducing her to the other arrivals. Aunt Ophie needed no such introductions. She just launched into conversation with a couple of her old friends. Governor Hancock led Charles into his study where formally dressed men of prominence stood sipping champagne.

"Have you returned to Boston for good, Charles, now that the war's winding down?"

"I don't know, sir. My immediate concerns are to locate my scattered family and to reconcile the Royal mercantile interests."

"Ah yes. I understand that you intend to take Mr. Chessman to court to press your claims."

Charles was not surprised to learn that the Governor had heard of his confrontation with Chessman. It was a small town with many ears and wagging tongues. What he didn't know, and what he had to find out in a discreet way, was whether this most powerful man had any more than a dispassionate interest in the matter.

"It wasn't my first choice, Governor. But family honor required me to take action."

"Of course. But you may be facing a more formidable opposition than you realize. Mr. Chessman has made a great success of his business. He provides gainful employment to hundreds of our citizens. In fact, it wouldn't surprise me if he was the single largest private sector employer in Massachusetts."

"But at what cost to me and my family? Are those who fought in the Revolution to be summarily relieved of their civilian possessions by those who did not?"

"Of course not. I'm not taking sides here, Charles. Just playing devil's advocate. In my official capacity I must remain impartial in judicial matters. Surely you understand that."

"Certainly." Charles was relieved. If the weight of the Governor's office and the state were on the side of his adversary from the outset, then there would be little practical reason to continue the fight.

"On your other pressing concern, how goes your search for your family?"

"Not well I'm afraid. We've posted more letters to Nova Scotia — their last known location — but as yet have not received a single response."

"Hmm. If the Revolution were not still officially at issue I would be pleased to address the Royal Governor there on your behalf. But as it is, we are still enemies, and any intervention by me might do you more harm than good."

"I understand, sir. And I thank you for your concern."

"I can tell you this, Charles. It does not go well with the British sympathizers who fled Boston. Sea traders tell ghastly tales of distinguished, honorable citizens of our former days who have been brought so low as to be common beggars in the streets of Halifax. I pray with all my heart that this has not been the fate of your family."

Charles nodded stiff-lipped. Rumors held that immigrants with high tastes and few marketable skills were dealt with harshly, even brutally, by the Nova Scotians, despite their personal sacrifices and avowed allegiance to Mother England. In a cold, barren land where men earned a hazardous living off the cod in the North Atlantic, there was no place for aristocratic idlers who expected to be waited upon hand and foot. When the money and treasures they had brought with them ran out, many had indeed fallen into a societal abyss.

An impeccably attired butler in powdered wig entered the room and rigidly announced, "Ladies and gentlemen, dinner is served!"

Place cards stood on each plate around the dining table. The Governor, of course, sat at the head of the table. Charles had been given the place of honor to his right. Caitlin, following the latest fashion, was not seated beside her husband, but at the far end of the table.

Governor Hancock fancied himself a military man, although serving as a militia captain on Boston Common prior to the Revolution had been the extent of his active service. He enjoyed dining with actual veterans, gleaning from them the particulars of various battles without ever having to submit his own person to the potentially debilitating effects of enemy cannon fire.

On this night though, the dinner conversation shifted in a decidedly different direction.

The only man at the table in uniform sat directly across from Charles, at the Governor's left. He did not recognize Charles before they were introduced, but Charles knew him — he was the celebrated general from New Hampshire, John Stark, the hero of the Battle of Bennington.

"General Stark has made a most eloquent appeal before the representatives at the state house on behalf of the valiant Massachusetts men who served under his command during the war," Governor Hancock informed Charles.

"Eloquence has rarely been a term used to describe my way of speaking, sir," came Stark's gruff response to Hancock, "So let me ask you plainly: when will the soldiers of Massachusetts be receiving their back pay? And when will their widows and children receive their pensions?"

Hancock made no attempt to avoid the question. "I don't know, General. At the present time there is not money sufficient to the task."

"Damn," Stark said with unmasked contempt.

"This time last year the Commonwealth was *bankrupt*," Hancock continued. "Our coffers were bare. Even now we are just beginning to struggle out from under the staggering debt of the Revolution."

"And do you expect the plight of the poor government to console the weary soldiers who must watch their families in hunger and want over the coming winter, Governor?"

"No, sir, I do not!" Hancock replied testily. "But it is senseless to point the finger at the state government or at Congress and cry 'There is the source of all our misery'. Sir, I wish there *were* some great money bin under my office. Then when worthy veterans called on me for their pay I would say, 'Here, good soldier, take this shovel and bucket down those stairs and claim as much gold as you deserve'. But I'm sorry to report, sir, that this delightful fantasy is just that.

"But I promise you this; as long as I am governor, as long as I draw breath into my body, I will strive unceasingly to redress the grievances of the courageous men who served the Cause. Of all the duties of my office, I place that first."

While this was not the answer General Stark had wanted to hear, it was one he could grudgingly accept.

"Is the situation much different in Maryland, Charles?" Hancock asked, shifting to his right.

Charles looked at Stark, then back at the Governor. "No, sir. The Pennsylvania Line under General Wayne mutinied at one point and very nearly marched in open rebellion against Congress. The New Jersey and Connecticut forces too were up in arms. I have sat in the Maryland General Assembly and I know the frustrations from both sides. They say patience is a virtue. If that is so, then it is a most unpopular one."

Over the following weeks, Caitlin and Charles's patience in regards to their family search ran out. Dozens of letters written. Not a single reply.

"What are we going to do?" Caitlin asked in frustration as she sat at Aunt Ophie's writing desk. Aunt Ophie on the sofa and Charles standing by the window shared her discouragement.

Charles breathed deeply. "There's no alternative." He looked at Caitlin. "We're sailing for Nova Scotia as soon as possible."

Caitlin's smile spoke of a certain optimism. Charles had concerns. He knew they would have to proceed with great caution. The land they would be traveling to was not only a British colony, it was teeming with displaced American Tories. What sort of reception would Charles and Caitlin receive if word leaked out that an officer with the American Continentals was passing among them without an armed escort? For safety's sake they would stick to their business. Make the necessary inquiries. Reveal as little about themselves as possible. And leave just as quickly as they could.

That very morning Caitlin wrote a letter to the Imperial Hotel in Halifax to make reservations. Meanwhile, Charles rode down to the waterfront and left word that he was seeking a captain who could transport he and his wife to Nova Scotia. The waiting time was over. Everything was now in motion.

Charles had met several times with Thaddeus Mantooth since their first encounter in his law office. So he was not at all suspicious when he received a note from Mantooth suggesting that they get together once more before the Nova Scotia voyage, even though the attorney proposed that they meet in the evening, and at Robinson's Tavern, rather than in his office.

As Charles dismounted and hitched his horse to the rail in front of

Robinson's he noticed the inordinately large number of horses tethered about him. *Must be a busy night,* he thought.

Once inside he caught sight of Thaddeus waving to him from a table by the chimney. They shook hands and Charles sat down as Mantooth loosened the ties on his ever present leather portfolio crammed with papers.

"Barkeep! What would you like, Charles?"

"Whatever you're drinking is fine."

"Two more rums if you please."

Mantooth fiddled through his notes. "You were able to book passage then?"

"Yes. We sail Saturday on the morning tide."

"Saturday. Well then, it's good we were able to get together beforehand. I've been able to get us a court date."

"When?"

"In early February."

Charles looked disappointed. "Is that the earliest date they could give us?"

"Charles, we're talking about the court system of Massachusetts. Be glad that we were given a date during our lifetimes."

"Do you need any further information from me?"

"I'm set for the time being. Naturally, we'll meet when the court date draws near to discuss our strategy. But as for now, I'm feeling confident about our chances. How about you?"

Charles shrugged and smiled weakly.

"Always the cautious one, eh Charles? Maybe *you* should have been a lawyer."

Charles laughed. "No, Thaddeus, I willingly defer all legal considerations to you."

Mantooth secretly glanced over Charles's shoulder to a man on the staircase. The man nodded once, then disappeared up the steps.

"You know, Charles, this place hasn't changed much at all since our old Sons of Liberty days."

Charles looked about. "No it hasn't. Except, of course, that the Robinsons are no longer here."

"That much is true. Hey, why don't we finish these drinks upstairs in our old secret meeting place. What do you say — for old-times sake?"

"Why not," Charles agreed with a smile. Maybe the ghosts of the old conspirators still haunted the room. When they reached the bottom of the stairs, Thaddeus motioned for Charles to go first. Charles opened the door on the upper landing to a darkened room. Two steps inside he walked into a heavy canvas hanging from the ceiling.

"What the—"

"SURPRISE!!" roared a chorus of voices in unison as the barrier fell to the floor and behind it stood not a ghost or two, but the living, breathing Sons of Liberty! Laughing and rushing forward to clasp hands with the thunderstruck Charles Royal.

"Charles is here, we're complete once more!" cried Sam Adams above the merriment.

"Here, take a seat, Charles," said another old familiar face. "For years in this room and on battlefields across the land you've served us. Now it is our honor to serve you!" The speaker was Paul Revere.

Cigars and strong drink quickly became the order of the evening as the celebrants toasted the Noble Sons of Liberty, the Glorious Cause, Charles's return and so forth. And when they couldn't think of anything else to toast, they simply went back to the beginning and started over. One toast from the earlier days was not offered on this night though — no one raised his tankard with the familiar refrain, "To the King!"

When he got over his initial shock, Charles was nearly in tears with joy. To think that these famous Patriots, men he once served drinks to and watched with silent awe, would gather together to celebrate his return to their midst was an honor greater than any knighthood ever bestowed.

At ten o'clock there was some commotion near the door. Charles started to turn around, but Mantooth quickly covered his eyes. Charles was wild with anticipation. "What mischief am I in for now!" he shouted.

Then, without comment, Thaddeus removed his hands and Charles looked upon the kind and benevolent face of his dear old friend, Mr. Robinson, leaning on a cane.

Charles gasped and leapt to his feet. "Mr. Robinson! God bless you, sir! Please, take my seat."

Mr. Robinson placed his hand on Charles's cheek. "It's good to see you, son. Back here among your friends."

"Get Mr. Robinson a drink! Drinks all around!" someone called out.

Charles crouched down beside his old employer so that they could hear each other through the festivity. Mr. Robinson was bent and frail now and had suffered a stroke that left him partially paralyzed. But the twinkle still glistened in his merry eyes and the rosy red cheeks were there to tell the world that here was a man who loved life.

"Look, Charles, I brought you a gift."

Before Charles could say a word, Mr. Robinson produced an old, handbound notebook.

"In here is where my Maude kept all her recipes." Mr. Robinson presented the volume to Charles as if it were the holy grail. "She would've wanted you to have it."

Charles accepted the gift with respect. "I shall treasure it."

Mr. Tilley came over to shake Mr. Robinson's hand. "It's good to see you back where you belong, sir."

"Business is good I trust."

"Can't complain. At least if business falls off and I need a drink, I'm already here!"

Mr. Robinson laughed. "I see you haven't gotten around to changing the name of the place."

"No, sir, and I don't intend to. Everyone knows this is Robinson's Tavern. I'd sooner change my own name than the one that hangs over the door."

"Have you met my friend Charles? Best barman I ever had."

Tilley offered his hand. "A pleasure. If you ever want your old job back, just let me know," he added with a grin.

"Charles is coming back? Wonderful news!" said Mr. Robinson, a bit confused, as those within earshot burst out laughing.

"No, no Mr. Robinson . . ." Tilley said, patting the old man's shoulder. Then turning to Charles, "You explain it to him."

Jokes, singing and general hilarity marked the evening, replacing the serious political discussions and occasional heated arguments that filled this room in bygone days. One of the best stories came from Mr. Robinson himself.

"Charles took to cooking more than bartending you know. It became a source of pride to him, so me and the missus kept mum. Except for once when she says to me on the sly, 'Pious folks usually say Grace *before* the meal. But when Charles does the cookin', they pray *after* it!'"

Laughter roared through the room as Charles protested in vain. Mr. Robinson milked the story for all its worth, holding his stomach in mock pain and rocking back and forth moaning "Oh God! Oh God! Oh God!"

It was after 2 a.m. when Charles finally returned home. He was feeling the effects of the hard liquor, but was still careful not to wake anyone. He took his boots off in the front hall and tiptoed up the stairs. In his bedroom he slipped gently under the covers. Just when he thought he had gone undetected, Caitlin spoke in a groggy voice, "Did you have a good time?"

"Yes. Sorry I'm so late."

She merely patted his chest and went back to sleep. The next day she wasn't angry at all. She had been in on the plot all along.

Chapter 30

Fortune favored Caitlin and Charles on their journey north. Even hugging the coast offered scant protection this time of year. The frigid Atlantic in November could turn ugly in a heartbeat and send the helpless bobbing ships that dared trespass upon her to a watery grave with a single angry blow of her northeast wind.

Once in Halifax, the Royals checked in at the Imperial Hotel and immediately went about their task. Caitlin had a Boston printer create flyers offering a $500 reward in gold for anyone who could lead them to their missing relatives. She and Charles posted these at every public place around the town.

Together they visited the constable and made the tedious rounds of government officials. They were excited to discover the existence of a Department for Loyalist Affairs. Then frustrated when that source proved as useless as the rest. Too many years had passed, they were told. Many of the former Boston refugees had died under the harsh conditions. Others had moved, and moved again. Some to England. Some back to America. There was not even a cold trail for Charles and Caitlin to pursue.

At each stop, Caitlin would do the talking. She spoke with an indistinguishable accent, which was preferable to Charles's Massachusetts twang. And on a practical level, a woman searching for her lost relations was far less likely to be questioned about her political leanings than a man.

It was predictable that Caitlin and Charles would be accosted by a small army of avaricious locals, hungry for the hefty reward which represented more than a year's wages to them.

Not knowing what else to do, Charles and Caitlin checked out every plausible lead. All proved to be blind alleys. And as the number of these mounted, so did their frustration.

Weeks passed. They had been reduced to riding out alone into the snowy countryside, asking at every small village the same tiresome questions, and receiving the same headshaking responses. Charles was first to face the seeming reality that they had failed.

"Winter will soon be here in full force," he said to Caitlin late one dark afternoon, staring at the steam rising from his coffee cup. "We've already been here longer than we planned."

Caitlin was slow to respond. "What are you suggesting, Charles? That we give up and go home?"

". . . What else can we do?"

"Continue to search! We've barely scratched the surface. With all the flyers we've handed out and the people we've spoken to, why word may have already reached them and they're heading this way to meet us right now."

". . . You don't really believe that."

Caitlin sighed deeply. "Look, Charles. If we leave now, that's it. The end. And I don't want it to end this way, do you?

"Let's leave no stone unturned. Otherwise, years from now we may be asking ourselves, 'Why didn't we do this or that? Why did we give up so easily?'"

Charles snapped, "Caitlin! How much is enough!" She backed off in shock. It was the first time he had ever raised his voice to her. Charles was almost instantly contrite.

"Oh God! I'm so sorry. Forgive me, please. It's just that I'm so *tired*."

Caitlin nodded. She was in a forgiving mood. Also, though she would never admit it, deep down she was beginning to share Charles's feelings of lost hope.

"I'll tell you what," Caitlin said. "Let's give it one more week. If we uncover no evidence in that time, we'll sail back to Boston. Deal?"

". . . Deal."

With one week to go, Charles and Caitlin redoubled their efforts. They revisited government officials to see if any news had turned up, and they broadened their search further and further up and down the coast. It was on the evening of the very last day that they had allowed themselves that they received word from an itinerant peddler that there were two young American women, who may or may not have been from Boston, who were serving as housemaids for the wife of a ship's captain in a home about thirty miles up the coast at Owl's Head, above Clam Bay. The man knew no more and refused to leave his name and address for any potential reward, feeling it was his Christian duty to pass along the information.

This lead was sketchy at best. Caitlin and Charles had pursued dozens of others with more credibility and come up with nothing. But it was their last day, their last possibility, remote as it might be. And as Caitlin had said, *Let's leave no stone unturned.* They decided that Charles would check it out on his own, while Caitlin remained behind to pack their belongings for the voyage back.

They arose the next morning before dawn and dressed by candlelight.

Caitlin handed Charles a single piece of luggage just as he was leaving.

"Here, I want you to take this with you."

"What's inside?"

"Clothes. Nice things for your mother and sisters. If you find them there, then they may be living in destitute conditions."

Charles was still puzzled.

"They might be embarrassed to meet your wife wearing rags," Caitlin explained. "Just use your best judgment."

"I do love you," Charles smiled. "But the chances of finding them there—"

"Go! And be careful."

Charles was mounted, with the bag strapped behind his saddle, and making his way up the coastal highway just as the sun broke over the horizon ahead. It was a bitterly cold morning and the treacherous ice under the horse's hooves made for slow progress. Still, Charles pushed on, and by noon as he passed Clam Bay the temperature had climbed above freezing and the sky was a dazzling bright blue.

"Excuse me, gentlemen. Is that village up the road Owl's Head?" Charles asked a group of fishermen spreading their nets on the beach.

"You American?" one snarled.

"Yes I am."

"Goddamn all Yankees!" spat another. "Why the hell don't ya go back to yer own goddamn country where you belong!"

Charles was on a mission, so he let the insult pass. "I'm looking for two American women. They'd be in their twenties. They are my sisters. I was told they might be in Owl's Head."

"If you find 'em will you and them get the hell out of our country?"

"Just as quickly as we can."

"Good! That's Owl's Head. Now get yer ass outta here so we can get back to work!" Charles spurred his horse up the road.

The tiny village was situated on a large bluff with a panoramic view of the ocean. Charles rode up to the largest house; a two-story white building with porches on both floors that looked out over the sea. He knocked on the door.

"Yes?" said a young maid.

"Who is it, Hannah!" barked the voice of an old woman from another room. "I'm not paying you to talk with strangers!"

"State your business, please," the woman said curtly.

"My name is Charles Royal. I'm searching for my family who were evacuated here from Boston in '76. There's my mother whose name is Morgana, my brother Joseph, and my sisters Sarah and Sally."

At the mention of the last two names the maid's eyes grew wide. "Sarah and Sally?"

"Who is it girl?" shouted the old crone inside.

"Just a minute, Madam!" The young woman pushed Charles back and stepped outside herself, closing the door behind her.

"I don't know about the other two, but Sarah and Sally work here like me, for that witch in there."

"Then you know where they are?"

"Hannah!" Heavy footsteps could be heard moving quickly toward the door.

"Around the back. Last shack on the left." The maid turned about and disappeared inside the house before Charles could even thank her.

Standing alone on the porch, the news he had just heard struck Charles like a lightening bolt. *My God, they're here!*

Leaving his horse where it was, he jogged around the house through the knee deep snow. Beside a path running directly back from the house stood six rickety shacks, three on each side. A trickle of smoke was visible coming from the third one on the left. When he came up to it, Charles cupped his hands and tried to peer inside. But there was only a single window and it was so cloudy that Charles couldn't see in. He knocked on the rough planked door three times. A moment later it swung open and Charles stood staring at a young woman wearing a plain, well-worn gray dress with a knitted shawl around her shoulders. The woman's sunken eyes did not appear to recognize him.

". . . Sarah?"

Suddenly the woman's mouth fell open in astonishment. "Charles? Charles!" She threw her arms around his neck with such force that they stumbled backwards, falling together in the snow.

Inside another voice cried out with excitement, "Charles!" Out rushed a second, younger woman. She too threw herself on the pair in the snow. Crying, laughing, the three tumbled over one another like bear cubs at play.

"God in heaven, Charles! How on earth did you ever find us?" Sarah marveled.

"Who cares," Sally said, smiling ear-to-ear. "He did!"

"Why don't we go inside," Charles suggested.

By any standard, the shack was a pathetic hovel. A single room with a filthy old blanket nailed to the ceiling affording the only privacy. The chimney sent as much smoke into the room as escaped out its top. There was a small table with only two chairs. Charles could see the shame on his sisters' faces at their pitiful circumstances. But of course he said nothing. He turned a large log upright and used it as a stool.

"I had all but given up hope. We were set to sail back to Boston tomorrow."

"We?"

"My wife, Caitlin. She's with me here."

"Your wife!" Sarah exclaimed. Both she and Sally pulled together the tops of their humble dresses. "She's here?"

"Well, she's waiting for us back at the Imperial Hotel in Halifax. *God,* she'll be ecstatic to see you!"

"Oh, Charles, you must tell us all about her," Sally pleaded.

"Of course, but first, where are Mother and Joseph?"

Sarah looked at Sally, then spoke for the two of them.

"Mother died of pneumonia our first winter here. Her spirit was broken and death came as a blessing to her. As for Joseph . . ." her voice trailed off. The sisters looked at one another, tears welling up in their eyes.

"Joseph was killed last spring when he interfered with some low-life rabble who were clubbing seals to death on the beach. You know Joseph and his big heart. He could never stand idly by and witness such cruelty. Yet he had no means to prevent it. Except by sacrificing his own life."

Charles could feel the anger burning inside him. "What happened to the villains? I pray they were hung."

"Nothing. They were never even brought to trial."

"What! What kind of barbarians live in this land?" Charles was beside himself.

"We have no rights here, Charles. They can do anything they want to us and get away with it. And they do. There is no court to take our grievances to. Officially we are refugees. In truth, we are despised outsiders.

"But I have faith, Charles. Those murderers did not escape the justice of the Almighty. And when their Day of Judgment comes, they'll suffer a thousand times more than they would have in this world.

"As for Joseph, God knew him far better than we. He gave him a simple mind, but a beautiful soul. I imagine him now in some heavenly garden, tending to his flowers as lovingly as ever. And we'll all be united there again one day, Charles. And we'll be happy once more."

"Your faith has grown," Charles said.

"Without it, how could we have possibly survived these past years?"

"You must be hungry, Charles," Sally said. "But we have nothing to offer you except water and some turnips. I'm so ashamed."

Charles shook away her sadness. "Seeing the two of you here, alive, is as much refreshment as I can stand."

"We really have nothing now," Sally lamented. "Just the three of us, together once more."

"Yes," Charles replied. "Well I say *Hallelujah anyway!* The war did its worst, yet the Royal family survived! We will never be poor again. We have each other."

Charles's sisters began bombarding him with excited questions about Caitlin: How did they meet? Where was she from? Were there children yet? Where did they live?

Charles suddenly remembered something. "Wait here, I'll be right back!" He dashed out the door before Sarah or Sally could stop him. In a couple of minutes he returned, carrying the bag Caitlin had packed.

"Here! A gift from your sister-in-law."

Both Sarah and Sally gasped at the contents inside. What was a simple present from Caitlin was like a pirate's treasure chest to them.

"Oh Charles!" Sarah exclaimed, holding up one of the dresses. "Do you have any idea how long it's been since we've had something new to wear?"

Giggling like schoolgirls for the first time in ages, Sarah and Sally quickly ducked behind the hanging blanket to change. When they emerged, Charles couldn't help but notice how Caitlin's dresses hung on their emaciated frames.

"You both look breathtaking!" he lied. "Like two fairy tale princesses ready for the ball!" The expressions on Sarah and Sally's faces showed considerably less confidence.

"She's a dear to think of us like this," Sarah said. "You've married well, Charles."

"Better than I deserve. And you'll learn the truth of that soon enough for yourselves. Come on. It's time to say goodbye to this sad place."

The sisters looked about their decrepit lodgings for the last time. They would be taking no happy memories with them. Their meager personal possessions fit easily into two sailor's duffle bags, and then they left, not even bothering to close the door behind them.

At the blacksmith's shop in the village, Charles rented two horses. The warming sun had made the footing much better than on Charles's ride in and they made good time back to Halifax, arriving at the Imperial Hotel as the sun was setting.

Charles decided it would be fun to surprise Caitlin. He led the way through the high-ceilinged public room to the large and elegant dining room, keeping a sharp lookout for his wife. But Caitlin was nowhere to be seen.

"She must be in the room," Charles said with growing excitement as he made his way to the broad stairway. Charles didn't notice the self-conscious looks on Sarah and Sally's faces. It had been so long since prosperity had left them that they felt out-of-place in such rich surroundings, as if every eye in the place was upon them and judging them unworthy.

Charles could barely contain his glee as they reached the door to his room. "Shhh," he whispered conspiratorially to his sisters. He knocked twice. "Caitlin. Sweetheart. It's me." They could hear movement inside the room. Charles quickly stepped behind his sisters so he could take in Caitlin's first expression.

When the door was unlatched and swung open, a grinning Charles made the introductions.

"Caitlin Royal, it is my pleasure to introduce Sarah and Sally Royal."

For a moment Caitlin just stood there in shock, her hands to her mouth and her eyes as wide as spoons. Then she flung her arms wide crying-out in joy, "I have sisters!"

She rushed to embrace them and the three hugged and rocked and laughed in the hallway, tears streaming down every face, including Charles's. Over dinner in the hotel that evening the women became fast friends. Chattering like monkeys, they all but ignored Charles, who nevertheless enjoyed the scene as much as any he had ever witnessed. Here was a whole new family again, and it was wonderful to see.

The next day before they sailed, Caitlin improved the economic well-being of many of Halifax's finest shopkeepers by taking her new best friends on a buying spree. Charles figured that he was permitted to tag along to carry the bundles.

At a little after two in the afternoon, their ship set sail out of Halifax Harbour bound for Boston. Charles could already see the spirits of his sisters rising like the tide on a sea of good fortune. And Caitlin — he had never seen her more happy. So happy in fact that she and his sisters had completely forgotten that today was December 15th; Charles's birthday.

With all the animated talk of the past twenty-four hours, the subject of the Royal's family fortune back in Boston had never come up. Charles knew that storm clouds were gathering ahead, just over the horizon, but he had no intention of disturbing the perfect bliss of this day. He thought to himself as he gazed out to sea, *There'll be time enough for tomorrow's problems tomorrow.*

A little boy came up behind Sarah and tugged at the bottom of her skirt. "Where are we sailing to, lady?" he asked.

Sarah stroked his hair and smiled sweetly. "To a new world."

Chapter 31

"Aunt Ophie!" Sarah called out, her head thrust just inside her aunt's front door. There was no answer.

Turning to Charles Caitlin kidded, "I hope we don't give her a heart attack."

"Aunt Ophie!" Sarah repeated.

"Aunt Ophie!" Sally called too. "We're home!"

Suddenly Aunt Ophie's voice could be heard from the back of the house. "Sweet Jesus!" And out she rushed, embracing her long-lost nieces in a familial scene like those with Charles and Caitlin in Nova Scotia.

"I had all but given up hope of seeing you two children again! Let me look at you — why you're both beautiful grown women now!

"Where's your mother and your brother Joseph?"

It would take days to catch-up on all the past events, all the lost time. But over lunch in Aunt Ophie's kitchen that afternoon, talk shifted for the first time to the family's fortune.

"I'm afraid the news there is not good," Charles replied to Sarah in answer to her inquiry. "Bleak, in fact. Do you remember Robert's manager, Maxwell Chessman?"

"Yes."

"It seems Robert left him in charge when he went off to war. After he was killed at Saratoga, the state took control of our various businesses and properties under something called the Confiscation Act of 1778."

Aunt Ophie broke in, placing her hand on Sarah's arm. "You did know about Robert, didn't you, dear?"

Sarah nodded. "The Department for Loyalist Affairs sent us a note."

"Did you know Charles was with him at the end?"

"No. I want to hear all about it, Charles. Every detail. But first, finish what you were saying."

"Yes, well, this Confiscation Act allows the government to appropriate Tory property and sell it to help finance the war. Our various enterprises had apparently fallen into a sorry state and Mr. Chessman was approached about purchasing them lock, stock and barrel. A bargain was struck and he took possession of everything, even our house on Joy Street."

"So we're broke! Paupers!" cried Sally. "How are we to live?"

"Easy! Simmer down," Charles soothed. "We're not dead yet. I've hired a lawyer and we're pressing our claims in court."

"But our chances aren't very good, are they?" Sarah asked, sensing the answer already.

"I won't deceive you. The law is on his side. But I promise you this: if we go down, we'll go down *fighting*. Chessman may have his claws into our worldly possessions, but he will *never* take away the Royal's family honor."

As the court date drew near, Charles received a message from Thaddeus Mantooth calling for a meeting in his office to discuss strategy.

"Charles, virtually all of the practical, substantive legalities in this case favor your opponent. So our best tactic will be an emotional appeal. We'll tout you as a genuine war hero who returned home only to find that every comfort left behind had been spirited away by a military shirker — the same argument you used to convince me that first day to take up your case. Do you remember?"

"Yes."

"On the other side of the coin, we must discredit the character of one Maxwell Chessman. His lawyer will try to portray him as an honest, innocent businessman. My job will be to show him as an unscrupulous profiteer."

"I must tell you, Thaddeus, I'm uncomfortable with all this."

"Look Charles, law, at its best, is a dirty business. The only question you must ask yourself is do you want to win? If not, or if you're in doubt, we can call this whole thing off. Well?"

Charles considered the matter. He was not the only one involved. Sarah and Sally had a vested interest in the outcome. And then there was Caitlin — always giving, always supportive. No, he decided, there would be no surrender without a battle. "I'm ready to proceed, Thaddeus. As you've said. Come what may."

"Good. Now I must ask you a very sensitive question: Was there anything in your conduct during your term of service, anything at all, that Mr. Wayland might use to impune *your* character?"

"I retreated at Bunker Hill with the others."

"No problem. It was your first action under fire. A green soldier. You stood your position as well as most. No one could fault you there. Anything else?"

"Yes," Charles sighed. "During the disastrous New York Campaign of

'76. We were beaten time and time again. Sometimes after making a staunch defense, but usually we just broke and fled in panic. I was among those who ran from the battlefield, Thaddeus."

"On more than one occasion?"

"Yes. Several times."

Now it was Mantooth's turn to sigh deeply. "That could be a real problem for us, Charles. Let us pray that Mr. Wayland's investigation does not reveal it."

Mantooth pulled a stack of letters tied with twine from a drawer in his desk. He told Charles with a look of satisafaction, "These I received following the inquiries I made to the list of your commanding officers that you gave me. To a man they speak of you in glowing terms. Greene, Marion, Wayne, Morgan, von Steuben — these names will ring like a chorus of angels in court, and they will all be singing your praise!

"There's one more item I need from you, Charles. The dates of Robert's, Joseph's, and your mother's deaths, just as closely as you can."

Charles appeared confused. "What possible purpose would that serve?"

"Maybe none at all. It's a long shot. Just trust me on this."

Robert died at Saratoga in October of '77. I'm certain of it because I was at his deathbed. Mother perished, according to my sisters, sometime during the winter of '76-'77. As for Joseph, he died a year ago; in the spring of '82."

"Damn!" Mantooth muttered.

"What is it?"

"Nothing."

Mantooth had one last point to cover. "I'll need to put Sarah on the stand. To testify about the events on the evening that Robert sent you packing. Mr. Wayland will, of course, cross-examine. I don't expect he'll be kind. It might be rough on her."

"I'll discuss it with my sister, Thaddeus. But I wouldn't concern yourself with her performance. She has endured pure hell these past few years. If they couldn't break her spirits in Nova Scotia, then there's nothing on a witness stand in Boston that she couldn't handle."

"She's pretty tough, your sister?" Mantooth asked, smiling.

"Tougher than me," Charles replied. "I seem to surround myself with strong women."

With all of Mantooth's questions laid to rest, Charles had one of his own. "Has it been determined who will preside?"

Mantooth answered like a bailiff announcing the magistrate's entry into court. "The Honorable Judge Ben Bates!"

"Is he a good choice for us?"

"That's hard to say. He's an honest and impartial man. Wholly uncorruptible. And he can't be intimidated — which is to our advantage if Hancock or any of the fops from the state house try to meddle.

"On the other hand, he's no Blackstone lawyer. He favors his own independent judgment over court precedent, so he's hard to predict. Sort of like a Biblical king or a Caesar, meting out justice swiftly from the throne."

The interview concluded, Charles stood up, extending his hand across the desk. "Then we are prepared for battle?"

Mantooth smiled confidently with a glint in his eye. "And damned be he who cries nay, enough."

Charles arrived back at Aunt Ophie's to an empty house. He recalled Caitlin mentioning a meeting she might attend with Aunt Ophie. Apparently they had all gone.

It wasn't long before he heard the clattering of footsteps coming up the front steps.

"Charles!"

"In here!"

Caitlin and the other women joined Charles in the parlor, shaking to warm themselves up.

"How did the meeting with Mr. Mantooth go?" Caitlin asked.

"Well enough. We discussed our strategy. What to anticipate from the opposition. I believe we're well prepared going in."

"Well that's good to hear."

"Oh, Sarah," Charles called to his sister who was hanging up her scarf. "Thaddeus is going to call you as a witness."

"To what?"

"That night on my birthday, when Robert sent me away. He needs someone who was there who can substantiate the details."

"My, that was so long ago. Well, I'll do my best."

"So, where were you ladies on this cold, gray day?"

"Attending to the needs of people who are in far greater want than we are," Aunt Ophie replied firmly, warming herself by the hearth.

Caitlin sat down beside her husband. He took her raw, red hands between his and rubbed them for warmth. "Oh Charles, you wouldn't believe the number of poor widows and orphans created by the Revolution. Just to have a warm fire and a roof over their heads is beyond the means of so many. They live in the streets, Charles. Without shelter, even in winter! They fight the wild dogs and pigs in the gutters for sustenance. When I think of all we have and how destitute they are . . . it's just so overwhelming."

"Your wife has a good heart, Charles," Aunt Ophie smiled approvingly. "As do your sisters. With time they may become the new champions of the 'wretched displaced.'"

"But what about you, Aunt Ophie?" Charles teased. "I can't imagine the charitable legion of Boston marching forth without Ophelia Royal leading the way."

"Perhaps it's time for this old soldier to step aside. For all I've tried to do in my life, there appears to be ten times the work now. Wars don't end when the shooting stops. For people like me, that's just the beginning."

On the day before the trial was to begin, Aunt Ophie took Caitlin on a ride to visit the Massachusetts Veterans' Hospital in Waltham. Sarah and Sally chose to remain behind, providing them with an opportunity alone with Charles to discuss a sensitive matter that was troubling them.

As usual, elder sister Sarah broached the subject for the pair. She sat across from her brother, appearing nervous. "Charles, Sally and I have been talking, about Caitlin."

Her tone gave Charles concern. "Yes? What about her?"

Sarah glanced at Sally for support. "It's her *generosity*. She buys us *everything* we want, and dozens of other items that we never even ask for . . ."

"Go on."

"We *love* her, Charles. But we feel like such poor relatives in her presence. How can we get her to stop lavishing us with gifts without hurting her feelings?"

"Yes!" Sally added, concurring with her sister.

Charles paced slowly as he considered his response. He walked over to the window and looked out. "That's a tough question. The truth is, I don't think you can."

Sarah and Sally appeared crest-fallen, but Charles continued.

"Caitlin just gives and gives to those she cares about without ever keeping an account. To say to her 'Don't be so generous' would be the same as saying, 'Don't be Caitlin.' The gifts she gives to you come straight from her heart, and if you shunned them, you'd break it."

Charles turned to face his sisters and offered a confession that he had never shared with anyone before. "If anyone should feel uncomfortable, ashamed, it's *me*. I was poor on the day I met her and I've been poor every day since. She provides for *everything*. The clothes I wear, like the clothes you wear; that carriage and the horses that brought us here from Maryland;

the entire cost of the trip; the trip to Nova Scotia; the reward for your safe return; the list goes on forever.

"One of the few things she didn't buy was the wedding ring on her finger. Her *father* gave me the money for that. Judge Serling — one of the finest men I've ever met. I wish you could have known him."

Charles half sat on the window sill. "When I proposed to Caitlin I immediately told her why she *shouldn't* marry me! 'I'm poor, not a penny to my name,' I protested. Know what she said to me?"

Sarah and Sally, hanging on his every word, shook their heads.

"'Kiss me this instant or I'll die in your arms.'" Both sisters clasped their hand to their heart.

"That's the woman who, for reasons known only to herself and God, consented to be my wife. I haven't been able to provide for her one day since. Not one.

"You've seen us together for two months now. So I'll ask you: Does she despise me, as any woman would have the right to, for being a wholly dependent husband?"

Sally answered gently, "She loves you."

Charles nodded. "And she loves you too. And that's why you must not hurt her."

There was a silence in the parlor as Sarah and Sally absorbed all that Charles had said.

"Perhaps one day we can pay her back," Sarah offered.

But Charles smiled, "You cannot pay back a gift."

In the two weeks preceeding the trial word had spread throughout the city — fueled by a feature article on the front page of the *Boston Gazette* — and interest had grown to a crescendo, people speaking of little else.

Here was an issue that touched virtually everyone. And everyone seemed to have an opinion and was anxious to voice it. Indeed, the case of Royal versus Chessman prompted more tavern brawls and catfights than any topic since the early days of the Revolution.

At stake were the rights of returning veterans on one side, and on the other, the more pedestrian concerns of the working class people of Boston who were starting to prosper by the grace of Mr. Chessman's budding mercantile empire. Virtue versus prosperity — a case worthy of everyone's attention. And without the prospect of a hanging offense anywhere else on the docket, it promised to be the most intensely watched adjudication of the session.

Normally, seats on the courtroom benches were barren except for the occasional student of law, the family members of the soul on trial, or, in the farthest reaches, a few drunks sleeping it off.

But for this case the courtroom was packed to overflowing, with people lining the walls right up to the railing. And a series of criers by the door stood ready to spread any developments to the crowd gathered in the street outside. The prospect of witnessing two of the city's most talented lawyers having at it in verbal combat only added to the entertainment. Here was high theatre. And best of all, everyone agreed, it was free!

"All RISE!" The bailiff pounded the butt of his staff on the floor three times to signal the start of the afternoon session. Judge Bates entered through a door to the right of his bench. He wore a traditional black robe, but eschewed the white powdered wig that was standard headwear for British jurists.

"The First District Court for the Commonwealth of Massachusetts is now in session!" the bailiff intoned. "The Honorable Judge Ben Bates presiding. All petitioners having business before said court shall step forward now and be recognized!"

Thaddeus Mantooth rose to formally begin the proceedings. "Your Honor, if it pleases the court, I wish to submit the petition of my client, Major Charles Royal, against Mr. Maxwell Chessman of Boston, charging Mr. Chessman with unlawfully confiscating various goods and properties belonging to the Royal family, the sum of which are contained in papers previously submitted to this court."

Judge Bates shifted his gaze to the adjacent table. "Sir, you are Mr. Maxwell Chessman, the defendant charged in this petition?"

"I am, Your Honor."

"And Mr. Wayland has been selected by you to represent you in these proceedings?"

"Yes, sir."

"So noted." Judge Bates wrote briefly on a sheet before him, then put his quill down. "I have reviewed the materials submitted and accede to your joint request that I rule on this matter without benefit of jury. Since this is a civil matter, and by our excellent turnout today one of concern to many, I am predisposed to allow a certain informality. But please be advised and respectful that this remains a court of law. If the members of the gallery wish to remain, they will maintain their silence at all times. Failing to do so, I will have the court officers clear the room of all but directly involved persons.

"Mr. Mantooth, you will call your first witness."

"The prosecution calls as its first witness — Major Charles Royal!"

An audible gasp laced with murmurs flooded the courtroom, forcing Judge Bates to reach for his gavel. "Order! Order in the court!" he thundered, striking his gavel on the wooden disk before him.

Charles was sworn in and stood in the witness stand. As Mantooth had instructed him, Charles appeared this day in uniform.

"Your name and rank, sir," Mantooth began.

"Charles Royal, major in the American Continental Army."

"And what is your term of service in this army, Major?"

"I enlisted in a local Patriot militia company in January of 1775. Following the Battle of Bunker Hill in that year, my militia unit was joined with others to form the American Continental Army surrounding Boston. I have remained in service to this day."

"And what is your current status?"

"Following the Siege of Yorktown I was placed on extended furlough."

"Subject to recall at any time should hostilities recommence?"

"That is correct."

"Now, you did not embark upon your military career as a major, did you, sir?"

"No. I enlisted as a private."

"A private! Well, that's a most impressive rise through the ranks. Did you have a patron or sponsor who promoted your interests?"

"No, sir."

"Did you purchase your commission, as is the custom in the British Army?"

"No, sir."

"Did any politician intercede on your behalf? Or any family member? Or anyone else *living or dead* to advance your military standing?"

"No, sir."

"Well then, sir. It seems that your meteoric rise can be attributed to only one thing — personal merit."

"I . . . suppose that could be suggested . . ."

"Please, Major Royal. Your modesty, I'm sure, would prevent you from sounding your own trumpet. So allow me to be immodest for you. You stood your place as a raw recruit, a lowly private, in the lines on Breed's Hill. A piece of ground now hallowed for bravery in the hearts of all who hold dear the Noble Cause of Freedom!

"And from there, with selfless devotion to duty, you reenlisted for the duration of the Revolution, willingly subjecting yourself to all manner of harm, deprivation, disease, illness, and even torturous death. And each of these demons visits its worst on you and your courageous brothers-in-arms in the dark years that follow.

"Many deserted — 'Sunshine Patriots' the gifted quill of Thomas Paine has called them — but you Charles Royal, you were one of those who stood the test by fire and the sword. And it is to men like you that we must now give thanks for the rich blessings of freedom that we *all* now enjoy.

"And through this time of great trial you were judged worthy by your superiors, who promoted you to greater service. First elected corporal by your brother soldiers in the militia. Then to lieutenant by General Henry Knox with the approval of His Excellency himself, *General George Washington.* And finally, as a reward for your heroism in the face of the enemy onslaught at the Battle of Monmouth Court House, General Anthony Wayne, again with the approval of His Excellency General Washington, promoted you to your present rank of major.

"Have I captured the jist of it, sir?"

"Your facts are essentially correct."

"Well, sir, for such extraordinary devotion for, what, seven long years, you must have emerged from the war a wealthy man."

"Sir?"

"You were one of the *victors,* Major. The spoils of war? Tell us about them."

Charles stood silently for a moment. "I don't know of any 'spoils,' sir."

"What? Come now. Are we to believe that 'To the victor goes the spoils' did not pertain to you?"

"I received no 'spoils,' sir. Nor did any of the officers or men of my acquaintance."

"Nothing? Nothing at all?"

"No, sir."

"Just the uniform on your back, eh Major?"

"No, sir. My wife made this for me." Charles pointed to Caitlin, who smiled sweetly back at him. A small ripple of laughter passed throught the gallery, just as Mantooth anticipated.

"You fought, endured every imaginable hardship, even laid your very life on the line for your country — and it was not even willing to *clothe* you!"

"I object!" Wayland said, leaping to his feet. "Counselor would have us believe that our soldiers were sent naked into battle. Absurd!"

"Sustained."

"You, as a soldier, were of course paid, Major. Surely that much is true."

"Well, sir, like all soldiers I was *entitled* to pay. But like so many others, I rarely received any."

"Why not?"

"When money was available, it was an unspoken rule that the men were paid first, then the officers. But more often than not the money ran out before the men did, so there was nothing left for us."

"So you went without."

"Yes, sir."

"In your seven years in uniform, have you estimated the total sum of military pay you received?"

"Yes, sir."

"And how much would that be?"

"About thirty-five dollars."

There was an audible gasp, which prompted Judge Bates to pound his gavel.

"*Thirty-five dollars.* Why, that's five dollars a year! About what an enterprising beggar can make in a fortnight. And you, sir, an officer! How did you survive?"

"As best I could, sir. Many were in the same boat. Often, when a man was sent home wounded or on leave, we would pool what resources we had and give it to him. So that he might buy himself something to eat on his journey. But usually there was nothing to give."

"And so the poor soul left the army flat broke and hungry."

"Yes, sir."

Mantooth stepped closer to Charles. ". . . And there was occasion when *you* were that poor soldier, isn't that true, Major?"

Charles looked at Caitlin as he answered quietly, "Yes, sir."

Mantooth artfully paused for a moment, pretending to review some papers on his desk while the sympathetic impact of his last point was given time to take root.

"Major Royal, it would be miraculous indeed if you had fought gallantly from Boston to South Carolina and back again and personally escaped the ravages of war. But that was not the case was it."

"No, sir."

"You suffered camp fever and very nearly froze to death at Valley Forge, did you not? And at Monmouth Court House you received not one but two battlefield wounds."

"Yes, sir."

"And following the Battle of Camden in the Carolinas you were taken prisoner by the enemy."

"Yes, sir."

"And when you escaped, rather than march home to a veteran's retirement that no one could justly deny you, you chose instead to serve your country further, volunteering to serve again *without pay* with Colonel Francis Marion's celebrated freedom fighters in the dismal swamps of South Carolina; enduring every imaginable — and unimaginable — hardship."

"And when, after fighting bravely in the glorious victories at Cowpens and Guilford Court House, you subsequently returned to your lovely wife Caitlin, to her home in the state of Maryland, did you *finally* say 'I have done my duty for the Cause' and retire to a richly deserved life of domestic bliss? No! You rushed to the clarion sound of the bugle and drum one last time! To Yorktown. Where the fate of our struggling nation and all future generations swung in the balance."

Mantooth turned his back on Charles and addressed the gallery. "We, who stayed safely behind in Boston, read about that great confrontation. We all know that pivotal to the victory was the successful storming of Redoubts Nine and Ten. You did not stand idly by, as we did, and expect others to carry the American flag over the earthen battlements into the bayonets of the bloodthirsty foe. What role *did* you play in this action, Major?"

"I was second-in-command to Colonel Alexander Hamilton in the assault on Redoubt Ten."

"And you attacked with muskets blazing?"

"No, sir. Silently with unloaded muskets. Relying solely on the bayonet."

Again Mantooth played to the gallery. "Charging headlong into an entrenched enemy position with *unloaded muskets*. Where else in the annals of recorded history is there courage to rival this!

"And in the end, Major, against all odds, you were successful?"

"We carried Redoubt Ten."

"And what happened within forty-eight hours?"

"General Cornwallis asked for terms of surrender."

"And surrender he did! The whole British Army under his command. In what will undoubtedly prove to be the final decisive battle of the Revolutionary War. The battle that sealed American independence! You, Major Charles Royal, you are an American hero!"

From his seat, John Wayland clapped — loudly, slowly, rhythmically — in a show of derision for Mantooth's theatrics. But before he had clapped four times, others throughout the audience took up the response and suddenly the courtroom exploded into a thunderous ovation.

Down came Judge Bates's gavel again and again. "Order! Order!" he cried, but to no avail. Finally, exasperated, he stood waving his gavel at the gallery. "By thunder! I will have order in my court this instant or I will have you all thrown out!" It was only after this threat that the crowd quieted down.

Triumphantly, Thaddeus Mantooth continued. "After Yorktown, now on extended furlough, you at last decided to look to your personal interests. And with your bride you returned to the city of your birth and youth, where you first embarked on your glorious military journey. You expected to find your family's wealth, your considerable commercial holdings, your family's *own home* happily awaiting your return.

"But what a terrible surprise greeted you! *All was lost!* Oh, it was still there. Just as you left it. But you were told, 'Sorry, it doesn't belong to *you* any longer. While you were away, fighting for our freedom, all of your worldly possessions were sold, and you are not entitled to one penny of the proceeds.'

"You left as the son of one of the wealthiest and most respected families in this city. You return . . . to utter poverty. If there is fairness in this, it wholly escapes me. If all the veteran fights for is lost even if he *wins*, then all is lost indeed! Shall this be the legacy we leave to future generations — our brave soldiers marched off to war and defeated our enemies, only to return home to face an even more heartless foe: impoverishment. Is this to be the reward for a Patriot's love of country!

"Your witness," Mantooth announced, resuming his seat with an air of satisfaction.

Wayland began slowly. "Major Royal, your war record is distinguished and you are to be applauded, as you have already been in this courtroom, with I myself leading the way. But the issue we are here to determine, sir, is whether or not you and your family were unlawfully deprived of your possessions.

"You were but a youth of twenty-one years at the outset of the war, but even so, prior to that time you were employed on three separate occasions in the Royal shipping business; once by your late father, and twice by your elder brother Robert, who is now deceased. Is this true?"

"Yes, sir."

"And in each instance, what was the result of your employment?"

"It didn't work out."

"You were *discharged,* sir. Fired as it were by your own family members for failure to perform your duties in a conscientious and responsible manner. True?"

". . . As you say, I was very young."

"Furthermore, you showed a far greater interest in engaging in scandalous Bacchanalian drinking bouts and debaucheries in many of the taverns and brothels around the city."

"I made many mistakes for which I am today ashamed."

"Would these include having been expelled from Harvard College?"

"Yes."

"You have never demonstrated any interest whatsoever in your family's enterprises, Major. Your only claim to them is by birthright."

Skillfully shifting gears, Wayland asked, "You enlisted in the Massachusetts militia, correct?"

"Yes, sir."

"Yet now you appear to serve with the *Maryland* Continentals. Are you a turncoat, sir? A Benedict Arnold?"

"Objection!" Mantooth cried out. "Major Royal has *never* betrayed his country! *Never!* And the insinuation is intolerable!"

"Sustained."

Wayland continued, subtle damage having been done despite Mantooth's protests. "You are a citizen of which state now, sir, Maryland or Massachusetts?"

Charles hesitated, then answered, "I am an American."

"Perhaps if I rephrase the question. At the conclusion of this trial, will you and your wife remain in Massachusetts, or return to Maryland?"

". . . Return to Maryland," Charles replied, eliciting murmurs throughout the courtroom.

"And so, sir, you have returned, briefly, to this city for what purpose? Not to rebuild the Royal shipping interests — as Mr. Chessman has done. Not to offer gainful employment to hundreds of our hardworking citizens — as Mr. Chessman has done. Not to pay thousands of dollars in badly needed taxes to the Commonwealth each year — as Mr. Chessman has done, but to *ravage* what remains, take your tidy profits, and runoff with them to Maryland — leaving the people of Massachusetts to poverty!"

"I object!" Mantooth was near bursting in anger. But the mood in the courtroom was shifting rapidly and he knew it. Was this man, this Maryland man, attempting to line his own pockets while depriving the good citizens of Boston of their livelihoods? And then planning to slip out of town, leaving them to unemployment and misery?

"Sustained! Counselors, I warn you both, I have had just about enough of your soapbox speeches."

"Yes, Your Honor," Wayland replied, unrepentantly.

"Major Royal, when your father passed away, the management of the family businesses fell to your eldest brother Robert, correct?"

"Yes."

"And who was your brother's trusted general manager; his second-in-command to borrow one of your military terms."

"Maxwell Chessman."

"Maxwell Chessman? Not Charles Royal — his own brother? Why would he not choose you?"

"My brother had little confidence in my abilities."

"And rightly so, based on your own admissions in this court under oath.

317

He passed over his own brother and chose an outsider. A man with years of experience in your father's employ — Maxwell Chessman.

"In your opinion, Major Royal, was Mr. Chessman the best choice for the position?"

"Objection, Your Honor. What Mr. Wayland is asking for is pure conjecture on the part of the witness."

"Overruled. The witness's opinion on this issue is of interest to these proceedings. You will answer the question, Major Royal."

"I was not consulted on the decision," Charles replied.

"That was not the question, Major. Was Mr. Chessman the best choice to run the businesses in your brother's absence?"

". . . He was an *appropriate* choice."

"Have you been to the waterfront since your return to the city, sir?"

"Yes."

"You have seen then, with your own eyes, the bustling activity of workers gainfully employed. The rise of new buildings, the construction of new ships that will sail one day soon from this port to trade around the world."

"I have seen."

"This is all due to the skill and tireless efforts of one man, and his name is *not* Charles Royal. It is *Maxwell Chessman*. Appropriate indeed!

"I have no more questions of this witness at this time, Your Honor."

"The witness will stand down."

Thaddeus Mantooth reached inside his portfolio and withdrew the packet of letters. He gave Charles a wink as he untied them. He had a surprise here, even for Charles. A letter arrived that morning; the most glowing tribute of all. The letter was sent from Paris, France and bore the seal of the Marquis de Lafayette.

"If it pleases the court, I would like to introduce at this time a number of letters sent to me by the former commanding officers of Major Royal. The first is from General Henry Knox, who speaks glowingly of Major Royal's ingenuity in transporting the cannons from Ticonderoga to Dorchester Heights during the winter of '76."

Mantooth was drawing his first breath to begin reading when Judge Bates cut him off.

"Mr. Mantooth, am I to assume that all of those letters are laudatory as to the personal and military character of your client?"

"They are, Your Honor."

"Fine. Hand them to the clerk and they will be so noted in the record."

"But Your Honor—"

"Counselor, we are *not* here to adjudicate the military competence of Major Royal, or to sit in judgment as to the character of either of the contestants in these proceedings. The jurisdiction for that lies in a higher court. We will restrict ourselves *solely* to the legalities involved. Is that understood?"

". . . Yes, Your Honor." Mantooth dejectedly handed his letters, his most powerful artillery, over to the court clerk unread. Moving back toward his desk he glanced over at Wayland, who had to struggle to control his glee. Both attorneys knew that a serious blow had been struck — and to whom.

"Call your next witness, Mr. Mantooth."

"The prosecution calls to the stand — Miss Sarah Royal."

Mantooth kept his questions to Sarah brief and to the point. He hoped to lull Wayland into doing the same.

"Miss Royal, you were, of course, present on the evening of December 15, 1774 at the birthday celebration in your home for your brother Charles?"

"Yes, I was there."

"Was your brother Robert also in attendance?"

"Yes, we all were. Except for Aunt Ophie. She was out of town."

"I see. Now, at the outset, was your brother Robert disturbed about something?"

"Yes."

"And what do you suppose was troubling him?"

"Well, he snapped at Charles for being late, but it was more than that."

"Really?"

"Yes, he arrived home that afternoon in a very foul mood."

"Do you know why?"

"No."

"Well perhaps I can enlighten you here and now." Holding aloft a multi-page document, Mantooth turned to Judge Bates and spoke in a large voice that filled the courtroom. "Your Honor, I have in my hand a written financial account for the Royal Shipping Company dated December 15, 1774. In it you will find that during each of the previous six months the company showed a loss. The losses growing each month, with the last one reported — November — being the most distressing of all. The report was prepared for Mr. Robert Royal by his 'second-in-command,' his trusted general manager — *Maxwell Chessman.*

"Your Honor, I would like to submit this document as evidence of the poor manner in which Mr. Chessman managed the business while it belonged to the Royals, which is in sharp contrast, as defense counsel has noted, to the exemplary way he is managing it now that it is in *his* possession."

Judge Bates nodded his consent. "Hand the document to the clerk who will enter it as evidence."

"Now Miss Royal, during the birthday dinner that followed that evening, an argument occurred?"

"Yes."

"Involving, principally, your brothers Robert and Charles?"

"Yes."

"And during this heated exchange, Charles expressed that his heartfelt sympathies lay with the Patriot Cause."

"Yes."

"And this further exacerbated Robert's already foul mood. After all, as Charles well knew, Robert was a devout Tory."

"Yes."

"Did Charles back off in the face of stern confrontation? Did he retract his commitment to the Cause?"

"No, he did not."

"He stood his ground then, come what may, willing to sacrifice all the comforts of a wealthy young man if need be."

"Yes."

"It has been said, Your Honor, that 'In the boy lies the shadow of the man.' I would suggest that herein we see the nascent Charles Royal, American hero. And he paid dearly for his convictions, did he not Miss Royal? What was the result of the argument?"

"In a rage, Robert ordered Charles out of the house. Out of our lives, forever."

"And facing such a devastating sentence, Charles must surely have relented."

"No, sir. He put on his cloak and hat and left with nothing more."

"No money?"

"None but what he had in his pockets upon his arrival."

"So poor Charles was cast out into the cold, cold winter's night because of his simple, unflagging devotion to the Cause of Freedom. Did Robert have a change of heart the following day, or in the days that followed?"

"No, sir. To the best of my knowledge my brothers did not speak again. Not until Robert lay on his deathbed at Saratoga. Charles visited him there."

"And did they then, finally, make their peace?"

"Objection, Your Honor. The witness does not claim to have been present at that time. Any testimony she might give, therefore, is mere conjecture."

"Sustained."

"I have no further questions, Your Honor."

"Mr. Wayland, your witness."

"Miss Royal, on that fateful night of December 15, 1774, did Robert say to Charles, 'Leave this house, but still retain all the benefits of your position within this family, including your inheritance.' Or did he say, 'Go now, with only what you wear. You are disowned?'"

Sarah thought, then answered, "I'm not certain what, precisely, was said."

"A fair answer, Miss. Memories can be faulty, particularly after the passage of so much time. That is why we lawyers prefer to have things in *writing!*" As he spoke that last word, Wayland held high a paper of his own.

"If it pleases the court, I should like to submit into evidence this legal decree prepared, signed, and notarized on the date of December 18, 1774. The signature is that of Robert Royal and the document reads in part: 'I hereby declare that Charles Royal is disowned and is no longer entitled to the benefits attendant to his former station as a member of the Royal household. Furthermore, any debts or obligations of any sort entered into by Charles Royal are henceforth his and his alone.' The document goes on, Your Honor; mostly standard legal parlance which I won't waste the court's time with by reading aloud."

"Submit the document to the clerk and it will be so entered as evidence."

At his seat beside Thaddeus Mantooth, Charles appeared stunned. Robert had seen fit to ostracize him formally; legally. They had had their differences, but this was the harshest blow of all.

"By your own testimony, Miss Royal, Robert did not recant his decision that Charles was to be cast out of the family dwelling place, disowned, disinherited. As the eldest male heir, he was head of the household when your father passed away, isn't that true?"

"I guess so," Sarah mumbled.

"Come now, Miss Royal, speak up!"

"Yes."

"And as head of the household he was fully empowered under the laws of the Commonwealth of Massachusetts to make decisions regarding the family's assets, properties, and businesses. And his decision, which he put in *writing,* was that Charles Royal was no longer entitled to *anything* belonging to the Royal family! Charles Royal has returned to Boston to lay claim to property that was legally denied him three-and-one-half years *before* the Confiscation Act ever went into effect! And so we are left to ponder one simple, solitary question: Why are we here?

"No further questions, Your Honor."

"The witness will stand down. Court is adjourned until 10 a.m. tomorrow." Judge Bates's gavel sounded the end of the first day of testimony in Royal versus Chessman. From the looks on the faces of the opposing sides, there could be no doubt as to who had gotten the better of it.

Caitlin leaned over the rail, speaking to her husband, "You'll probably want to meet with Mr. Mantooth for awhile. We'll go back to Aunt Ophie's and start dinner." Charles nodded.

As she passed by, a shaken Sarah touched Charles's arm. "I'm so sorry, Charles."

"You did nothing wrong," Charles replied with a feeble smile.

With all that had happened, Charles wasn't sure how badly the day had gone. He was no legal expert. Maybe the contest was closer than it seemed. But back at Mantooth's office his flickering hopes were quickly extinguished.

Mantooth sat behind his desk, rubbing his face with his hands. Before Charles even asked, Mantooth volunteered the answer. "Yes, we were routed in there today."

"Now what?" Charles asked. His tone was level, not judgmental.

"We must now fight a defensive battle. We don't have sufficient arguments left on our side to take the offensive.

"I've heard it said that on the battlefield, one side may think it has gained a seemingly insurmountable advantage — and it is at that moment that it is most vulnerable to a counterattack."

"I'd say there is plenty of precedent for that."

"Good. Then that's what we must wait for. So far, I must concede, Mr. Wayland has had the better of me. But he may be overconfident now and slip up. And if he does, I must be ready to pounce."

"I have confidence in you, Thaddeus."

Mantooth was surprised by Charles's simple statement of support. After today's performance he would have expected a tongue lashing.

"Thank you, Charles," he replied. "The first battle may have been lost, but it's the last one that counts. And there's still plenty of fight left in me, by God! Tomorrow, you'll see, we'll rise again!"

Late that night, sitting alone in his office by candlelight, Thaddeus Mantooth decided on a bold, unorthodox strategy. One that, if it worked, would throw Mr. Wayland off his carefully crafted plan and, hopefully, cause him to falter.

"The First District Court for the Commonwealth of Massachusetts is now in session!"

Judge Bates was just settling into his seat when he said, "Mr. Mantooth, you may call your next witness."

"Your Honor, I have no more witnesses."

No one in the courtroom was taken more off guard by this statement than lawyer Wayland.

"Very well then. Mr. Wayland, you may call your first witness."

Mantooth was gambling that Wayland would not expect to begin his defense so early in the trial, and would therefore not be fully prepared. Sure enough, Wayland whispered some hasty instructions to his assistant, who immediately scurried out of the courtroom.

"The defense calls as its first witness — Mrs. Caitlin Royal."

Caitlin and Charles exchanged astonished looks. What could possibly be the reason for calling her to the stand?

"Mrs. Royal, when you first met your future husband he was a lieutenant in the army at Saratoga, isn't that correct?"

"Yes, sir."

"And you were . . ."

"I was serving as a nurse volunteer."

"With the Continental Army?"

". . . No, sir."

"Then with whom?"

". . . With the British Army."

The courtroom erupted as a hundred voices shared this startling revelation.

"Order! Order in the court!" Judge Bates called out, rapping his gavel several times until the crowd quieted down.

"You were employed as an aide to the *British* Army?"

"That was a disguise, sir. My true reason for being within British lines was that I was a spy for the Americans."

Once again the gallery came alive and Judge Bates had to redouble his efforts to silence them.

"My, my, you *were* a busy girl weren't you! So how, pray tell, did you make the acquaintance of Lieutenant Royal?"

"After the second Battle of Freeman's Farm, Charles requested and received permission to cross the lines to visit his brother in the British field hospital. He had seen Robert wounded during the battle."

"And let me guess — you were Robert's attending nurse?"

"Yes."

"Then you were present when Charles and Robert met for the last time, at Robert's passing?"

"I was in the hospital the entire time Charles was there, but I was away caring for other patients."

"During the period when you were in the presence of Robert and Charles did you hear Robert say that he retracted his earlier decree that Charles was disinherited?"

". . . No, but it could have happened while I was away."

"But you did not hear it yourself."

"No."

"Even on his deathbed, Robert maintained his unequivocal course."

"Charles and Robert parted as brothers and friends."

"Oh did they, Mrs. Royal? Did they really? Are we to believe the word of a devious spy on this matter? Or are you now merely a devoted wife defending her husband?"

"I object most strenuously, Your Honor! Counsel is badgering this witness!"

"Sustained."

"I do apologize, Mrs. Royal, if I have caused you any distress. I want you and this court to know that I hold you in the highest respect and admiration.

"When you first met your husband, he was a soldier without material means. Would you grant that as a fair statement?"

". . . I would."

"And during the period of your courtship, he inherited no money to your knowledge; received no substantial back pay; laid claim to no 'spoils of war?'"

"No, he did not."

"And after your marriage, and in the time that followed, to this present day, he has also not substantially improved his personal monetary worth, has he?"

". . . No."

"Then you must enlighten me; how has he been able to provide for his good wife?"

Caitlin looked askance upon Judge Bates.

"You will answer the question please, Mrs. Royal."

"I am blessed to have been born into a family of comfortable means."

"And so it is *you* who must support *him?*"

Caitlin stood hurt and silent.

"You needn't answer that, my dear. Your pain, your shame—"

"I am *not* ashamed of my husband, sir!" Caitlin shot back with eyes burning.

"Oh course not! Certainly not!" Wayland said retreating. "He was a brave soldier, defending his country, and you were justifiably proud of him.

"Still, it is fortunate indeed that at least *one* of you had the good sense not to have been thrown out by your wealthy family."

Caitlin was about to explode in righteous indignation, but the artful Wayland struck first. "No more questions, Your Honor." He turned abruptly and returned to his seat.

"Your witness, Mr. Mantooth."

Mantooth appeared to be deep in thought before starting in with Caitlin. Actually, he was giving her time to cool down.

"Mrs. Royal, your family, the socially prominent Serlings of Montgomery County, Maryland, have been described by you as of 'comfortable means.' Your family owns the largest plantation in the county I believe. Approximately how many acres is it?"

"Seven thousand."

Murmurs of astonishment flooded the courtroom.

"My goodness, Mrs. Royal! If seven thousand acres of prize farm land constitutes merely 'comfortable means' in Maryland, I say we adjourn these proceedings at once and all of us move to Maryland immediately!"

Laughter rippled through the court. Even lawyer Wayland and Judge Bates chuckled.

"As Mr. Wayland has shown, you, Mrs. Royal, have proven more than willing to share your wealth with your husband. With you by his side he is once again a man of considerable riches, living on a beautiful, peaceful plantation by the banks of a gently flowing river. What bliss. What comfort. What security in which to live out one's life. An honored war hero. An elected delegate to the Maryland Legislature. A life brimming once more with promise.

"Yet your husband did not choose to retire to the comforts of Oakmont Plantation, did he Mrs. Royal. Instead, he brought you and he on a hazardous journey north, to Boston, to the scene of so much unpleasantness in his life. Why?"

Though they hadn't discussed her testimony beforehand, Caitlin caught the jist of Mantooth's direction and followed the course.

"Not for himself, sir. For as you suggest he had little to gain and much to lose.

"But Charles could never rest until he knew what had become of his family in Boston, scattered as he had been by the war. Secondly, there was the question of what became of his family's personal property. This was and is a matter of deep personal honor to him — to uphold his family's legacy. And thirdly, there dwells within him the remembrance of the hundreds of other Revolutionary War veterans he has known who, like himself, served valiantly to secure all of our freedoms only to return home to find that battlefield victories have led to civilian defeat."

"The pattern with Charles Royal is constant!" Mantooth announced. "He is still fighting for what's right, no matter the personal cost. And, of course, he must look to the welfare of his beloved younger sisters, Sarah and Sally, who were also impoverished by the war."

"Yes."

"Thank you, Mrs. Royal. I have no further questions, Your Honor." Mantooth smiled contentedly as he stepped away from the stand.

Before Judge Bates could dismiss her, Caitlin asked, "May I say something else, Your Honor?"

"Yes, of course, Mrs. Royal."

"Your Honor, I have seen the legions of widows and orphans who are the saddest victims of this long war. Their men are silent now. So who speaks for them, Your Honor? Who remains to champion their claims against the villainous usurpers?" Caitlin looked directly at Maxwell Chessman, who turned away. "A few men like my husband, sir. In the Maryland General Assembly he leads the fight for the widowed wife and the fatherless children. And when we return, whatever the outcome of these proceedings, he will do so again.

"Some people devote their lives to personal gain, Your Honor. Charles Royal has followed a different path. And I believe the still soldiers salute him."

For the first time since the trial began, Judge Bates appeared visibly moved. "You may stand down, Mrs. Royal.

"Mr. Wayland, call your next witness."

"The defense calls to the stand — Dr. Phillip Overton."

As Overton was being sworn in, he cast a sardonic smile at Charles, who didn't blink.

"Dr. Overton, as a young man before the war you were familiar with Charles Royal?"

"Yes. We traveled in the same social circles."

"I see. You were friends then?"

". . . I'm not sure I would go that far."

"But you were in his presence during that period; at taverns, dances, other social events."

"Yes."

"By the standards of your group, would Major Royal be considered a reveler? A man with a marked taste for wine, women, and song?"

"Oh yes."

"Have you ever seen Charles Royal drunk?"

"Yes, many times."

"In the company of scarlet women?"

"Many times."

"Objection, Your Honor. What possible bearing can a few youthful indiscretions have on these proceedings?"

"If it pleases the court, Mr. Mantooth has labored tirelessly and with flourishing dramatics to present before us Saint Charles Royal. I am merely trying to establish that he is considerably less than that."

"Overruled. But now that you've made your point, Mr. Wayland, let's move on."

"Certainly, Your Honor. No further questions."

"Your witness."

"Dr. Overton, your generally amiable relationship with my client soured at some point; why was that? Wasn't it because he was forced to seek employment as a bar attendant at Robinson's Tavern and you and your rich, boorish friends took pleasure in taunting him?"

"No sir! You are misinformed. It was because I won over the affections of the woman he loved, Miss Celeste Bradford. Now *Mrs. Phillip Overton.*"

"He was jealous, then?"

"Yes, everyone knew it."

"And the two of you came to blows, isn't that correct?"

"Indeed so! He assaulted me, without provocation, at Robinson's Tavern."

"And by accounts he dealt you a sound thrashing."

"Once again sir you are misinformed. Many of my friends in attendance confirmed my belief that *I* had the best of it."

"Oh really! Shall I produce a half dozen eye witnesses in this courtroom who will swear under oath that you *begged for mercy* from Charles Royal on your cowardly knees? Or perhaps that is your definition of having had the best of it!"

Scattered laughter prompted Judge Bates to rap his gavel.

"Your Honor, I ask that this witness's evaluation of Charles Royal's character be stricken from the record, since he is clearly hostile and biased."

"So moved. This witness's testimony shall have no bearing in this case. You may step down, sir."

Chagrined, Overton was passing through the rail gate on his way out of court when he spotted his former love interest, Sarah Royal. He cocked his head in her direction, but Sarah's icy glare sent him on his way.

"Call your next witness, Mr. Wayland."

Wayland pretended to be reviewing the papers on his desk, buying time.

"Mr. Wayland?"

"Your Honor, I . . . did not expect to call my next witness so soon . . . He's not here right—"

Suddenly the doors of the courtroom flew open and in rushed Wayland's assistant, grinning broadly. With him was a distinguished looking gray-haired man who possessed a military bearing.

Visibly relieved, Wayland virtually shouted out the name of his surprise witness. "The defense calls to the stand — Colonel Temple McVee!"

Of all the people in the packed courtroom this day, only Charles knew who this mystery witness was and his significance. Charles and John Wayland — who could scarcely wait for Colonel McVee to be sworn in.

"Your rank, sir, is Lieutenant Colonel in the Continental Army?"

"Yes, sir."

"And prior to the Revolution you were a clergyman, were you not?"

"I was a minister of the Congregational Church assigned to a parish in Amherst."

"Excellent. Now sir, would you tell this court about your military background and the context in which you came to know the plaintiff, Charles Royal."

"In additional to my pastoral duties, I helped to form a militia company in Amherst, which I subsequently commanded. We were among those who answered the call to arms prior to Bunker Hill."

"Then you took part in that battle?"

"I did."

"And after that . . ."

"I was given command of the 21st Massachusetts Regiment and promoted to my present rank. In the months that followed — throughout 1775 and '76 — I served with the Continental Army encamped around Boston, and then in the New York and New Jersey campaigns. In December of 1776 I developed a debilitating camp fever and was evacuated to a hospital in Danbury, Connecticut. There I recovered, but with lung damage that prevented my return to active duty. Since then I have served as a recruitment and training officer.

"Charles Royal was a lieutenant with the Massachusetts Line. He served under me at various times during the series of battles in New York and New Jersey."

"At various times? Could you explain that term?"

"So many were killed or wounded, or simply ran away, that companies had to be continually reformed from the shattered remnants. Command responsibility shifted constantly as a result."

"I would like you to share with this court your honest assessment of Charles Royal as a junior officer under your command."

Colonel McVee looked directly at Charles as he spoke. "Lieutenant Royal . . . did not distinguish himself at that time, either as a soldier or as an officer of troops."

"Please be more specific, Colonel. Are you saying that Lieutenant Royal shirked his responsibilities?"

". . . He did not exercise them in the manner prescribed."

Let me be more blunt, sir: Did Charles Royal run off in the face of the enemy?"

". . . Yes."

Murmuring spread once more through the court. Wayland could smell blood.

"He turned on his heels, threw down his weapons, abandoned the brave men entrusted to his care, and ran for the hills!"

"That's not exactly accurate; his men ran off with him."

"Oh, thank you, Colonel! I stand corrected! Lieutenant Royal *led* his men in panicked flight!"

The noise level in the courtroom increased, forcing Judge Bates to pound his gavel and call for order. The tide was rolling in Wayland's direction.

"As commanding officer, well aware of the disgraceful conduct of your subordinate, you would, of course, take action in this matter. What did you do?"

"I summoned Lieutenant Royal to my tent."

"And there —"

"I told him of my disappointment in him."

"A harsh rebuke! Entirely warranted. But surely, sir, such cowardice called for sterner measures. Did you, at any time, remembering that you are under oath, suggest or state that Lieutenant Royal should be *courtmartialed!*"

". . . Yes."

With that the courtroom erupted, people leaping to their feet with fists thrust in the air and shouting curses. It took a full minute of gavel pounding for an exasperated Judge Bates to finally regain control.

Wayland, the seeming conqueror, smiled up at the magistrate, "No further questions, Your Honor."

"Your witness, Mr. Mantooth."

"Colonel McVee, your revelation about my client's conduct at that time certainly elicited a strong reaction of shock in this courtroom. But wasn't it the case that any number of men retreated — sometimes orderly, sometimes in a rush — during the campaigns you mentioned?"

"Yes, sir."

"In fact, any man who did *not* step lively to the rear would, at some point, have been killed or captured."

". . . I hadn't thought of it that way. But I guess you're right."

"Well simply put, sir, at the beginning of the campaign the Patriot Army was entrenched on Long Island, below Manhattan, and five months later, after numerous confrontations with the enemy, that same army had been driven out of New York City, up the Hudson River, across into New Jersey, and then pushed out of *that* state.

329

"In order for the army to get from Brooklyn Heights, New York to Newtown, Pennsylvania, every single soldier in that army; including Lieutenant Royal, including *you* sir, including His Excellency General Washington *himself,* had to retreat approximately *two hundred miles.*

"If the army had *not,* sir; if it had instead stood toe-to-toe with the British Lion at any point along the way, then it would have been *annihilated,* and the Revolution lost."

Where Wayland's tactics had brought the gallery to a fevered pitch, Mantooth's left them breathlessly hushed.

"Colonel McVee, you intended to level a courtmatial against Lieutenant Royal, yet you never did. Why not?"

"Many men performed poorly at that time. They were untrained civilians for the most part, confronting the most powerful military force on earth. It was, as Mr. Paine has written, 'The times that try men's souls.'

"Over the days that followed my tongue lashing of Lieutenant Royal in my tent, I surreptitiously watched for his reaction."

"Weren't you afraid that he might desert the army one night, as so many others had done?"

"Yes. But there was something about Lieutenant Royal . . . something that I can't put into words . . . I felt he deserved a final chance.

"But before the final verdict was in I took sick and was sent away."

"Was that the end of the matter then?"

"No, sir."

". . . Please continue."

"I was still concerned that Lieutenant Royal had not learned his lesson. Too many fine young boys had already died because of incompetent officers of all ranks. So I kept touch on his progress through correspondence with his commanding officers."

"And what was the final verdict?"

Once more Colonel McVee cast his eyes directly at Charles. "I am exceedingly proud to report that Lieutenant Royal emerged as an *exemplary* officer. The inexperienced, ineffective young man I knew died at Newtown, and in his place arose a man who would serve with valor and distinction; a credit to his country as a soldier, an officer, and as a Patriot."

". . . No further questions, Your Honor."

"The witness may stand down."

As Colonel McVee passed by the place where Charles sat, he paused, reached into his inside coat pocket, and handed Charles a well-creased, yellowed piece of writing paper. Charles didn't have to open it to know what it was. The two veterans' eyes met for a telling moment. Charles fingered the piece of paper, then placed it in his own pocket, still folded.

330

On impulse, Charles turned in his chair as Colonel McVee reached the courtroom door. The old commander turned too, and gave Charles an informal salute. A wholly private scene played out in this public forum. And then he was gone.

Before Judge Bates could ask for the next witness to be called, a disruptive commotion flooded into the courtroom from the street outside.

The judge instructed the bailiff to "See what all that ruckus is about."

The bailiff dutifully went and opened the window and called down, "You there! Constable! Why the activity? Court is in session up here."

"Glorious news! The captain of a merchantman has just arrived with a dispatch from London — George III has issued a proclamation calling for the cessation of all hostilities! *THE REVOLUTION IS OVER!*"

The bailiff immediately spun about, shouting for joy, "Word has arrived from England! King George has surrendered! *THE WAR IS WON!*"

Cheers and wild celebration exploded in the overcrowded courtroom. People hugged, hats flew into the air, and on the bench, Judge Bates threw his arms high in exultation. "Court is adjourned for three days of celebration! God Bless the United States of America!"

There was a mad rush for the doors. The booming cannon from the Charlestown battery already signaled the spreading of the glorious news, and the party that was instantly in progress, complete with a fireworks display that would soon light up the city.

Inside the courtroom, the Royals hugged one another, tears streaming down many a cheek. Thaddeus Mantooth and Charles embraced.

"I'll call all the Sons together at Robinson's tonight, Charles. We'll celebrate like never before! You'll be there of course."

"I wouldn't miss it for the world," Charles grinned.

"Excellent! Until then — Ladies!" Mantooth waved his hasty farewell. There were people to see, songs to sing, and tankards to drain.

Charles and Caitlin left the courtroom arm-in-arm. Out in the street pandemonium had broken out everywhere. Fortunately, it was only a few blocks to Aunt Ophie's house. In Aunt Ophie's parlor, the Royals opened their finest bottle of port and filled their glasses. They turned to Charles to offer the toast. Following his lead, all glasses were raised.

"We have, all of us, served and suffered in this long war for American independence. And so it is entirely fitting that we should all drink now to our glorious victory. God Bless the United States of America!"

"God Bless the United States of America!" they all repeated in patriotic harmony.

Later, in their bedroom, Caitlin held Charles's well-worn major's uniform lovingly before her.

"I'll let you in on a little secret. When I was sewing this for you, to give you as a present on our first Christmas together, I said a prayer each day. I prayed that no enemy bullet or bayonet, no knife or shell fragment or any other instrument of war would ever pierce its fabric and harm the one I love. And look! Not a hole to be seen! Just this rent in the seat of the pants."

Charles grinned, "That's more the result of the soft life with you at Oakmont, I suspect."

Caitlin's green eyes twinkled as she patted her husband's belly. "I shall make a properly plump country squire of you yet."

As she turned away, caressing the uniform one last time before folding and storing it away in the bottom of their trunk, Charles bent and gave her a gentle kiss on the cheek. "Thank you."

Chapter 32

The trial was winding down now and to most observers, John Wayland held a commanding lead — the opposition's case was weak, based on an emotional appeal that Judge Bates had all but unilaterally rejected. Wayland could have quit while he was ahead and probably walked out of court a decisive winner, but he didn't.

"The defense calls to the stand — Mr. Maxwell Chessman."

During the preceding two days of testimony, Maxwell Chessman had been a virtual nonentity. Like a member of the gallery he sat and listened and kept his own counsel. Now, on the final day, he was thrust onto center stage.

Wayland began slowly, calmly, confidently. "Mr. Chessman, when Robert Royal spoke with you, just before his departure with his majesty's troops for the New York campaign, what were his instructions?"

"He told me that I was to take full charge of all business activities and to use my best judgment in the management thereof, being mindful at all times of how he might act under prevailing circumstances."

"Much like the parable in the Bible of the Master who entrusts his three servants with equal portions of his estate before journeying to a far-off land. Interesting. Only in your case, the Master was fated never to return. Pity. Now we'll never know how he would have judged you — good servant or bad. How would you assess your performance, Mr. Chessman?"

"I did the best I could, sir."

"The good and faithful servant then?"

"I pray so, sir."

"In his last instructions, what did Robert say to you in regards to his younger brother, Charles?"

". . . Nothing, sir."

"Nothing? No word at all? Not even a mention of his brother?"

"No, sir."

"Why do you suppose that was the case?"

"Charles was never very active in the business. And by this point he had been disowned by the Royal family." The audience chuckled at this unintentional play on words.

"Prince Charles the Departed, eh?" Mantooth added to sustain the jest.

"Going back for a moment, you must have had some very trying times during the British occupation of the city. How were you able to hold the businesses together during that turbulent period?"

Chessman smiled at his own ingenuity. "I ordered every ship we had afloat to be put out to sea, to reside in safe harbor at our base in the West Indies, or at our fishing docks near the Great Banks until the closed port of Boston was reopened and it was alright to return."

"And in so doing, you kept the Royal's vast merchant fleet from being confiscated as war booty — by either side."

"Exactly so."

"Well done, good servant! Roughly speaking, how many ships were you able to save for your employer in this manner?"

Chessman tallied in his head. "I'd venture to say — three packets, a half-dozen brigantines, an equal number of fishing sloops and trawlers, and perhaps fifteen to twenty smaller coastal vessels which were used primarily for cod fishing."

"The cod trade was an important activity for the Royals?"

"Oh yes."

"Good, good . . . Now Mr. Chessman, after the British departed, you were able to bring your craft home. But all was not well in the city, was it?"

"No, sir. The war had decimated the city and impoverished the citizens. The provincial government was bankrupt. Men were off fighting for one side or the other. And money was very scarce."

"Yet you carried on, despite all adversities, to justify the faith placed in you by your employer.

"That is until the state stepped in. Tell us about that."

"When the Confiscation Act of 1778 was enacted into law, among the first properties siezed were those that had belonged to the Royals. One of my assistants suggested to me bitterly that it appeared the act had been created solely for that purpose. For a period of three months thereafter, all who had been employed by the business, including myself, were thrown out of work."

"How many employees are we talking about?"

"Approximately seventy to eighty at that time, many of whom were elderly folks who had devoted more than half their lives to the enterprise. The day I called everyone together to make the announcement — well, it nearly broke my heart."

"All seemed lost. But you, alone, kept up the fight. What happened next?"

"I had received rumors of Robert Royal's fall at Saratoga the previous autumn. There was no one left in the family I could turn to."

"What about Charles Royal?"

"No, sir. Charles was off fighting too, with the Patriots. Or dead for all I knew. And as I and others have stated, he was never a factor where the family's businesses were concerned."

Wayland seized this last statement to reinforce a key point. "During the entire Revolution, did you *ever* receive a single communication, any letter at all from Charles Royal asking about the state of his family's enterprises?"

"No, sir."

"Did any member of your staff, to your knowledge?"

"No, sir."

"Please, go on."

"With a skeleton crew I attempted to conduct business with what few assets had not been confiscated. Then one day I was visited by a member of the Confiscation Act's Commission for Disbursement. He proposed that I purchase the operations myself, in my own name."

"Did you know this person prior to his visit to your office?"

"No, sir."

"Why do you suppose he approached you instead of someone else?"

"Perhaps because of my former management experience. I received the impression that he and the political powers at the state house were concerned about the high unemployment in the city, and that civil unrest might follow if the people couldn't soon find work."

"What happened then?"

"We met a few more times, including that instance in your offices, Mr. Wayland. And then we finally struck a bargain over drunks one evening soon after."

"And what was the price agreed upon?"

"Twenty thousand dollars."

"Did the Commonwealth of Massachusetts exhibit good judgment in releasing the businesses to your care, Mr. Chessman? Did you indeed put Boston back to work?"

"Yes, sir. It was slow going at first, but over the past three years I am pleased to report that business has increased several fold."

"Magnificent! The good servant has become the good master!"

"By year's end we expect to have two more six hundred ton cargo ships in service to ply the reopening European trade, and by early next year we shall have built the largest warehouse ever seen in Boston."

"You, sir, have taken the broken pieces of a shattered shipping company and built of them an even greater enterprise than had existed before! Through your leadership, Boston may well emerge one day soon as America's major commercial seaport — rivaling or surpassing New York City itself! And with this phenomenal growth you have provided gainful employment for . . ."

"About eight hundred people."

"Eight hundred!"

"With the anticipation of adding around fifty more next year when the new warehouse opens."

"Eight hundred and fifty Massachusetts citizens put back to work," Wayland mused aloud. "Providing for their families, paying taxes to the Commonwealth, rebuilding their lives. You, sir, are to be congratulated and thanked by *all* the good citizens of this city. As well as Cambridge, Salem, Gloucester, Plymouth, and other surrounding communities.

"Without you we might well be standing in a Boston rife with all the scourges of the despondent unemployed — drunkeness, thievery, brawling, murder. But *with* you we enjoy prosperity for ourselves and our children. God bless you, sir. Your witness."

With his emotional appeal to the high ground, Wayland had stolen a ploy from Thaddeus Mantooth's book. Now it was Mantooth's turn to climb down into the trenches.

"You have testified here that you paid the state twenty thousand dollars for the Royal's property."

"The former Royal's property, yes, sir."

"Was that a fair bargain?"

"I believe so."

"Not fairer for you than for the state?"

"No, sir."

"While Mr. Wayland was introducing us to Saint Maxwell the Benefi-cent, I had plenty of time to add up the items listed on the Decree of Dis-bursement that you signed with the state. It includes several of the ships you mentioned, plus ten buildings in and around Boston, personal property that belonged to the Royal's household, including the family's stately residence on Joy Street, and land holdings in this state, the West Indies, and some two thousand acres of land in Western Pennsylvania that the late Colonel Royal purchased following his service in the French and Indian War.

"Conservatively, I place the value of your acquisition at well over $250,000! Or more than *twelve times the amount you paid.* We should *all* have the opportunity to make such a 'fair bargain.'" A smattering of laugh-ter spread through the court.

"Sir, I did not even have to pay *that* much," Chessman blurted out. "I probably could have closed the deal by agreeing to pick up the bar tab that night. The government never complained about the price I offered."

"How could they! There is space provided on the Decree for the submission of three bids. Entirely appropriate since provision five, right here, states that three authorized bids by qualified persons *must* be submitted before any disbursement may be allowed. Yet I see here only one name, and one bid, Mr. Chessman — not three as the act requires; just one — yours.

"It appears we have a problem."

"I bought the business fairly and legally," Chessman growled.

"So you say, sir. But the document, well, that says otherwise. And as Mr. Wayland adroitly pointed out early in these proceedings, *that's* why we lawyers like to have things in *writing!*"

Mantooth had scored a decisive blow. He shifted tack to keep the momentum rolling.

"It appears, Mr. Chessman, that nearly everyone went off to fight in the Glorious Revolution — everyone but you. Why not?"

"I had duties and responsibilities."

"As did we all, sir. Robert Royal left far greater responsibilities than you had when he marched off with his Loyalist brigade. And Robert, the Loyalist, left you, his trusted 'good servant' behind to watch the shop. By all common logic, sir, that would brand you a Tory!"

"I object!" Wayland cried.

"Why, pray tell! Would Robert, being of sound mind, have left a *Patriot* in charge? Never! Remember, Robert turned out and legally disowned the avowed Patriot in his own family. And he chose instead to entrust his vast fortune to his close friend and confidant, Maxwell Chessman, a man who shared his views in all things."

"I am a Patriot, sir! A loyal Patriot!" Chessman protested. "I stood the lines as much as Charles Royal at Bunker Hill!"

Now it was Mantooth who smelled blood. "Under whom did you serve?"

"Sir?"

"Who was your commanding officer, and remember, you're under oath."

"General Ward was in command."

"That's common knowledge. Who was your *immediate superior?*"

Chessman did not reply.

"What was your rank?"

". . . Lieutenant."

"Who was your captain?"

Again Chessman failed to answer.

"What was your company? Your regiment?"

Mantooth stood glaring. Chessman looked like a helpless rabbit trapped in a snare.

". . . I was prepared to do my duty, but I took sick," he finally sniveled.

"I see," Mantooth said with mock sympathy. "Probably the same malady that afflicted Lord Cornwallis at the surrender of Yorktown — a severe lack of intestinal fortitude."

"I am no coward, sir!"

"Oh no? Then have your pick of the list: shirker, profiteer, Tory sympathiser, traitor."

"Your Honor, I must protest!" Wayland called out to Judge Bates, whose gavel fell time and again. But Mantooth was sallying forth with guns blazing and only by physically restraining him could he be silenced.

"You say you thought Charles Royal might be dead somewhere. Are you sure you didn't mean *hoped!* With Robert *and* Charles gone, who would be left to foil your evil plans. And if you succeed in your villiany, then one day the epitaph on your headstone will read: 'Here Lies Maxwell Chessman, *To the Wicked Go the Spoils!*'"

Chessman shook his fist in Mantooth's face. "Sir! You have dealt me irreparable harm! I will have satisfaction!"

"A duel? You wish to challenge me to a duel?"

"Yes!"

"Oh, very well, Mr. Chessman. And what shall it be?" Mantooth affected a classic fencing pose. "How about cods at sunrise!" Peels of laughter crashed through the courtroom. Mantooth pretended to draw a fish from an imaginary sheath. He wiggled it and then hurled it in Chessman's direction. The gallery loved the pantomine, though Judge Bates was beside himself, pounding his gavel with both hands.

The contest that had begun the day squarely in favor of the defense now appeared to be a real horse race. With the heightening drama, not a single person had left the courtroom, for any reason.

Against his better judgment, John Wayland chose to call one last witness.

"The defense recalls to the stand — Charles Royal."

"Major Royal, or perhaps I should address you as the Honorable Mr. Royal since you are an elected representative of the Maryland Legislature."

"Whichever you prefer."

"In your capacity as a servant of the good people of Maryland, you must deal with many of the same problems our politicians face here in Massachusetts. For example, how to pay off the state's staggering war debt."

"That is true."

"As we are all now well aware of, Massachusetts fell upon the clever scheme of confiscating the property formerly held by our enemies — namely the Tories — and selling it to meet our war obligations. Was this a tactic that the Sate of Maryland also considered?"

"Yes."

"And debated. In its House?"

"Yes."

"And were you present at any of these debates?"

"Yes."

"Your Honor, what Major Royal says is all true. It can be verified through the Maryland Public Voting Record, a copy of which I now hold. In the vote on Maryland's version of the Confiscation Act, Charles Royal voted — 'Aye.'

"You were in favor of the measure then, sir.?"

"Yes."

"Then why is it that what was right in Maryland is so wrong in Massachusetts? I thought we were now the *United* States."

"I am not a Tory, sir. My property should never have been confiscated."

"*Your* property? Mr. Royal, have you forgotten? You were disinherited."

Mantooth interrupted. "By a *Tory* because of his *Patriot* convictions. Thus it was all null and void."

"Mr. Mantooth!" Judge Bates scolded. "You know better than to make such an outburst!"

"I apologize, Your Honor."

"You may continue, Mr. Wayland."

"Is it true, as Mr. Chessman has testified, that you never wrote to him or any of his associates about your family's business?"

"That is true."

"Why the lack of concern?"

"I was otherwise occupied with more vital matters, such as staying alive."

"Still, it is more than a little curious that you should appear now, in this court, pressing your claims to a business that was *ruined* while under your family's care, and then miraculously resurrected under Mr. Chessman's.

"Is it your belief, sir, that you could now run the business as well or better than Mr. Chessman?"

Charles had to think for a moment. The notion of him actually operating the business had never occured to him. "No, sir."

"Then from a purely practical point of view, the business is now in the better man's hands?"

". . . I would have to agree with that."

"Good. You are an honest man, sir. No further questions, Your Honor."

"Your witness, Mr. Mantooth."

"Major Royal, if you had returned home to Boston *after* the Battle of Saratoga in October of 1777 and *before* the enactment of the Confiscation

Act of 1778, then surely we would not be here today. You would have easily assumed your rightful position as the male heir to the Royal estate, perhaps retaining the services of manager Maxwell Chessman, making him *your* 'good and faithful servant.' But alas, you chose a different course. You remained in the army, in the service of your country — fighting its battles, enduring its hardships — while far away from the flashing steel and the cannon's roar that filled your ears, back here in Boston, insidious events which you could not possibly be aware of were at work that would deprive you and your family of your inheritance.

"That is the crux of this case, Your Honor. For three days we have danced like so many wood nymphs around the one burning issue — is it right that a soldier's wordly possessions can be snatched away and sold while he is off defending his country."

"I object, Your Honor. Counsel is not questioning this witness, he's just wasting all our time with political rambling."

"Sustained."

"Major Royal, your brother was killed at Saratoga in October of 1777 and your mother died during the winter of 1776-77, correct?"

"Yes, sir."

"Then, Your Honor, *prior* to the Confiscation Act, the rightful heir to the Royal family estate was Charles Royal, a *Patriot*. Therefore, the state was not empowered to confiscate any property, and everything must revert to the rightful owners, the Royals."

"Objection, Your Honor! There was another brother. Older than Charles. Ask him when Joseph Royal died."

Judge Bates turned to Charles. "Did you have an older brother named Joseph, Major?"

"Yes, Your Honor."

"And when did he die?"

"Last spring."

"Then he was the eldest living Royal family member at the time the Confiscation Act was passed into law?"

"Yes, Your Honor."

"Was he a Tory or a Patriot?"

Here was the pivotal question of the trial. Every body shifted forward to hear Charles's reply. Charles looked at Thaddeus Mantooth, whose eyes pleaded with him to speak the one word that could win this case.

"My brother Joseph . . . was the most gentle and peaceful creature that God ever placed on this earth. He was my better in more ways than I can count. Including politics. Joseph's beautiful nature placed him above choosing any political persuasion."

"Then he was neither Tory nor Patriot?"

"Yes, Your Honor." Charles looked at Mantooth. He could see the disappointment in his face. But also the understanding.

On the opposing side, Wayland had the look of relief that a man might have who just dodged a bullet.

Mantooth didn't know what else to say. He was spent. One last shot, he thought, one last shot.

"If Joseph was neutral, Your Honor, then my point is entirely valid. The Confiscation Act specifies the appropriation of *Tory* property only."

"Oh give it up, Thaddeus," Wayland said, fatigue causing him to inadvertently voice his thoughts aloud.

"What's that you say, Wayland? Do you think I would take the advice of a Tory sympathiser?"

"Order in the court!" Judge Bates bellowed.

"Who are you calling a Tory sympathiser, you decrepit cripple! I sent three sons to the Massachusetts Line, by God!"

"While you stayed safely behind!"

Wayland rushed out from behind his table. "Watch your tongue, old fool, or I'll kick your safe behind!"

Judge Bates was livid as he smashed his gavel down. "Order! Resume your seats immediately!" The crowd was now pressing forward excitedly as the action intensified.

"Tory sympathiser!" Mantooth taunted. "If the Redcoats had won, you'd be sitting on that bench right now, wearing a stupid wig and spouting the King's Law!"

"Damn your soul!" Wayland fired back. "Damn *all* the Sons of Liberty!"

With that something inside Mantooth just snapped. "AHHH!" he cried, swinging his cane down toward Wayland's head. Wayland caught it in midflight and lunged for Mantooth's throat. The two old barristers locked arms and tumbled to the floor, fists and curses flying.

The gallery sprang to its feet, cheering on the combatants and hastily placing bets on the outcome. Judge Bates smashed his gavel so hard that the wood splintered in two. He hurled the broken handle at the brawlers then hurried down to help the bailiff and court clerk pry them apart. In an instant all five of them were rolling on the floor. Charles and Chessman looked on with astonishment, but most of the audience was ecstatic to be witnessing this most unexpected development. A fist fight! By two lawyers! Right here in court! It would take a mass hanging to top this.

Finally, Mantooth and Wayland were pulled up off the floor. The only damage came to Judge Bates. "Damn *both* your souls! I think you broke my *goddam thumb!*"

Judge Bates returned to his bench to attempt to regain order in his court. With his gavel shot, he removed his shoe and pounded the heel on his desk.

"Order! Damn you, order! Court is now in recess until three o'clock this afternoon at which time I will render my verdict. Court's adjourned!" The judge rapped his shoe down one last time. "Bailiff, find my physician and tell him I need to see him in my chambers *now!*"

When court reconvened promptly at three, order had returned. About the only thing in evidence to remind everyone of the excitement that had taken place that morning was the splint strapped to Judge Bates's hand.

"Major Royal and Mr. Chessman, I would ask you gentlemen to stand as I intend to address both of you. As for Mr. Mantooth and Mr. Wayland, the two of you are to *sit* there and *don't move,* or by God I'll have the *both* of you thrown out!"

Judge Bates began with Charles. "Major, you have distinguished yourself as a brave and selfless defender of America's freedom. And a country that did not thank you and the other veterans for your invaluable service would not be worthy of any blessings from the Great Provider above. Furthermore, only those without heart or mind would fail to understand your cries for justice in the face of events that appear to have deprived you of your worldly possessions while you were away on the battlefield.

"Still, there are other realities to consider. You, sir, did not arrive when the Royal businesses were a wreck, or in receivership by the state, but after they had attained their zenith. Mr. Chessman made what he had every reason to believe was a fair and legal purchase, and then transformed a money losing operation into a large and prospering enterprise — a major employer that is a source of pride and accomplishment for hundreds of good, hardworking people in this community.

"You have proven yourself to be an officer of character and rare achievement. These laurels are yours for life, sir, and you may bear them with honor back to your new life in Maryland. But you, by all the testimony given in this courtroom, including your own, have no head or inclination for business.

"During these past few days as I sat here listening to the witnesses, a scene kept playing in my mind. It was the Biblical trial where King Solomon was asked to judge between two women who claimed to be the mother of a single infant. As all Christians know, the wise King Solomon ordered that the child be cleaved in half, so that each mother might claim her share. King Solomon knew that the true mother would cry out that the babe be spared and given to the other woman.

"I am left with the conviction that it is Mr. Chessman who would cry out at the thought of harming this business. It is he who built it, nurtured it, saw it through the difficult times. And, of the two of you, it is clear that only in his hands will it thrive in the future.

"Major Royal, your future lies elsewhere. But we poor souls in Boston must look to our own well-being and that of our neighbors. I'm certain you wouldn't want your military honors to be tainted by innuendoes that you exploited them for your personal gain, while impoverishing other worthy veterans. No sir, I do not see such base motives in your character at all.

"And as for you, Mr. Chessman. I would be less than candid if I didn't admit that you have the *look* of an opportunist. Some might even say a war profiteer. While across the way stands a veteran, some would argue a hero, of the Glorious Revolution. To rule in your favor would certainly not make you a popular figure around Boston, sir. I'm sure many of your current employees are veterans. And their exertions would undoubtedly diminish, even sink to the activities of saboteurs, if word spread that you built your fortune by assuming the property of another veteran while he was off fighting on your behalf.

"And then there is the matter of payment, sir. Even in their depleted condition, the Royal family holdings were formidable. As has been pointed out, the Confiscation Act requires competitive bids, and this was apparently not the case in your acquisition.

"You, sir, paid a very low price and were the sole bidder. This might lead some to suggest shady dealings, sir. Not I. Not this court. But the stigma would remain nevertheless, to sully your fine reputation which, as every gentleman of virtue knows, is your most treasured asset."

Judge Bates lifted a single sheet of paper from his desk. "Therefore, gentlemen, with profound respect for your honorable qualitites and reputations, and considering the best interests of fairness to which you both subscribe, I issue the following ruling:

> *It is hereby decreed that Maxwell Chessman shall be entitled to retain all of the properties purchased by him from the Commonwealth of Massachusetts under the Provisions of the Confiscation Act of 1778, and to receive all benefits to be derived therefrom, provided the following stipulations are met:*
>
> *1) Maxwell Chessman shall pay to the Royal family a sum equal to the amount paid to the Commonwealth of Massachusetts for the former Royal properties — twenty*

thousand dollars — that sum to be distributed in equal portions to the three surviving adult descendants of the Royal family: Charles Royal, Sarah Royal, and Sally Royal.

2) Ownership of the 2,000 acre tract of land in western Pennsylvania shall be ceded to Charles Royal as the eldest heir of the family.

3) Ownership of the Royal's former residence on Joy Street in Boston will revert back to the family.

In exchange for these concessions, Charles, Sarah, and Sally Royal, and all of their descendants, hereby relinquish forever any claims they have to the aforementioned properties acquired by Maxwell Chessman, or to any action against the Commonwealth of Massachusetts in this matter.

When he finished reading the document, Judge Bates placed it on his desk. "I suggest that you accept the judgment of this court as fair and equitable, gentlemen. Let the healing process begin here."

It is a hard compromise for all involved, but each, in turn, does accept it. For the first time since the trial began, Charles and Maxwell Chessman's eyes met. Slowly they closed the distance that separated them. And they shook hands.

The gallery cheered and applauded, and even Judge Bates smiled, forgetting for the moment the pain from his throbbing thumb. With a wide grin he leaned over to his bailiff, "I'll bet the two women who stood before old King Solomon didn't shake hands after *his* ruling!"

That evening, over drinks at Robinson's Tavern, the time had come for Charles and Thaddeus Mantooth to wrap up their business.

"I'd like you to compose a legal document that provides for Ophelia Royal to receive all rents on the Joy Street home for as long as she lives. Thereafter, if they survive her, the house is to become the property of Sarah and Sally Royal equally."

"Easily done," Mantooth said, placing his glass on the table. "Drop by my office anytime after eleven tomorrow morning. It will be on my son's desk awaiting your signature."

For Charles, that seemed to be the final loose end. Now just one item remained to be settled.

"Thaddeus, in all this time we've never discussed your fee."

"Ah yes! I hope you didn't think it slipped my mind. Or that my services would come cheaply.”

“Of course not.”

“Good! Well Charles, I’ve given the matter a great deal of thought. I have worked up a bill for you and I assure you I will settle for nothing less!”

Charles braced himself for the worst.

“The charge is *absolutely nothing*,” Mantooth deadpanned. “*And I must be permitted to pay for these drinks.*”

Charles was totally taken aback. “What?”

Mantooth smiled. “It is I who am in your debt, Charles.” He tilted his head back and sighed with satisfaction. “I’ve been caught up in the Cause since before the Boston Tea Party. You probably didn’t know it, but you’re looking at one of the founding members of the Sons of Liberty. When the Revolution finally arrived, I had to sit idly by because of this,” Mantooth tapped his crippled leg, “While others such as yourself carried the standard. I read all the accounts, Charles — the victories, the defeats, the terrible suffering of our brave lads in the field. I suffered too. For my own, personal reasons.

“But thanks to you, Charles, thanks to you I, who could do nothing, was at last able to do *something*.

“Do you understand?”

“I think so.”

Mantooth raised his glass to Charles. “Then you know why this day is a day I shall never forget.”

When Charles arrived home later that night he found Caitlin and Sarah waiting up in the parlor. Aunt Ophie had not yet returned from her regular Friday night civic club meeting and Sally was out on a date.

“I’m home,” Charles announced as he hung his hat and cloak on the peg in the hallway.

“Did you settle-up with Mr. Mantooth, Charles?” Caitlin called from the parlor.

“Yes.”

“Guess what, a letter arrived from Rake today.”

“Really! Where is he, back at Oakmont?”

“Yes. And by the sound of it he’s already itching to move on. Listen:

“‘Junius is doing a fine job running the old fiefdom. I’m pretty much in the way here, though he would never admit it.

“‘We had some trouble with a few of the local toughs who were harassing Junius, but I paid them a neighborly visit and impressed upon them the error of their ways.’ I can only imagine what Rake used to ‘impress’ them,”

Caitlin interjected with a wry grin.

"'With matters here at peace I am free to consider what new adventure I might undertake. I was enjoying an ale with some veterans of the Maryland Continentals the other evening and the opinion was voiced that we should travel to Europe together and try our hands at being soldiers-of-fortune. With this prospect in mind, perhaps you could teach me a sufficient amount of French upon your return so that I will be able to order about the soldiers on the battlefield and to charm the favors of the mademoiselles thereafter.'

"That's about it," Caitlin said, then added with a smile, "Oh, there's a postscript: 'P.S. If you haven't already left him for a better man, say hello to Charles for me!'"

Charles laughed aloud at that last comment. Vintage Rake.

"Your brother must be quite a character," Sarah said in amusement.

"You'd like him," Caitlin replied, then added, "And he'd like you."

Caitlin seized this unexpected opportunity to broach a subject that she and Charles had already discussed in private.

"Sarah, now that matters are settled here in Boston, have you considered where *your* future lies?"

She had, but her response was guarded. "Well . . . there is really nothing left in this place for me."

Caitlin grew instantly excited. "Then come with us, back to Maryland. Charles and I would dearly love for you and Sally to make your home there, where we could all be together."

"We'd be imposing. You and Charles have your own lives to live," Sarah protested weakly. Secretly, it was her heart's desire to sail off with them.

"We're *all* family now," Caitlin argued. "And this family has been apart for far too many years already. Please, say that you'll come."

"It's what we *both* want," Charles smiled.

Sarah paused, then burst out, "All right!"

Caitlin threw her arms around her sister-in-law and they embraced and laughed.

"Now what about Sally?" Caitlin asked. "Do you think she'll come too?"

Sarah shook her head. "Sally's heart is already anchored in Boston, I'm afraid."

"It wouldn't have anything to do with a certain *Thaddeus Mantooth* would it?" Charles asked with a knowing wink.

Caitlin appeared dismayed. "Isn't he a little . . . old for her?"

Now it was Sarah and Charles's turn to share a laugh. "Not the lawyer!" Sarah explained to Caitlin. "His legal apprentice son, Thaddeus, Junior."

Caitlin joined the laughter. "Thank God!" she muttered.

Chapter 33

T ime was growing short now before the return voyage home to Maryland. Caitlin and Charles sold the carriage and Caitlin donated the proceeds to the Boston Home for Wayward Children orphanage. They gave the horses to Aunt Ophie for her and Sally to use.

Maxwell Chessman promptly met all of the stipulations in Judge Bates's ruling. And in a gesture of reconciliation and good will, he offered Charles, Caitlin, and Sarah free passage to Maryland aboard one of his recently refitted packets that would soon be sailing for the West Indies.

While Caitlin and Sarah were off favoring the merchants of Boston with a final visit, Charles spent the day before their scheduled departure rummaging through some old family belongings up in the attic of the Joy Street house. Underneath some dusty drapes he chanced upon his father's old sea trunk. With his pocket knife he pried open the rusted latch.

Beneath some salty clothes was an old volume with a frayed leather cover. Charles recognized it immediately from his youth. It was his father's private journal. Inside the front cover rested a sealed letter on which was written the words: *To My Beloved Charlotte.*

Putting the letter aside, Charles settled back and cracked open the book. There were long gaps of time without entries. Charles was about to toss it back into the sea chest when his eyes locked onto the words written under the date: *July 4, 1745.*

> *I am arrived back in Boston now after the most fortuitous conclusion of my recent military excursion into the northern wilds. In addition to a share of the victory laurels which have earned me the grudging respect of the local snobbery and will undoubtedly open doors for me in the months ahead, I returned with the more substantial benefit of the French payroll that I intercepted purely by chance enroute to Louisbourg.*
>
> *With my personal finances now much improved, I intend to purchase a fine vessel and establish my own venture as a sea trader.*

"So *that's* where his fortune came from," Charles said aloud at the revelation. His father had absconded with the enemy's payroll.

Charles flipped through the old journal, but nothing else caught his eye so he put it aside. He stared at the mysterious letter, and then opened it on impulse. Charles's eyes widened and his heart began to race as he read its startling contents.

February 1, 1772

My Dearest Charlotte:

I know we agreed never to write to one another because of the possible dire consequences to Charles, but as I lie here feeling my body growing weaker by the hour, I fear that my eyes will never light upon your beautiful and kindly face again in this world. And so I break my own rule.

For more than eighteen years we have kept our secret — more painful, I know, to a mother's heart than I might ever conceive. And only you, my love, can judge the ultimate wisdom of our choice made so long ago.

Charles has grown into a free spirited young man. He is wild at times and needing focus, but I see in him the makings of a man of distinction one day. His place in society is assured, despite Robert's misgivings. I believe Robert has discerned the circumstances of Charles's birth — either by his own wits or through the spiteful tongue of Mrs. Royal. Their coolness towards him grows daily, though they know better than to voice their feelings. As long as I live, no scandal shall deprive Charles of his inheritance, or bring dispersions on the Royal name.

One day, when he has attained adulthood, I (if I survive) will explain all to him. And if he is willing, a reunion with you will be arranged.

My hand grows weak, my love, and I must rest. I shall place this letter in hiding until I can see to its discreet delivery to you. For safety's sake, you should burn it after reading it.

Forever Yours,

Joshua

Charles dropped the letter in his lap, thunderstruck, and stared blankly ahead. Then he picked it up and read it a second time. And then a third.

His thoughts tumbled one over another. Could it be true? Was this woman, this *Charlotte,* his real mother? Actually, it would explain alot. Particularly the hostility displayed by Robert and his mother — or the woman he *thought* was his mother — after his father's death. But why the secrecy? Why hadn't he been told long ago? He knew of only one person who could provide the answers.

Charles flew through the front door of Aunt Ophie's house so fast that it banged against the wall.

"Aunt Ophie! Aunt Ophie!" Charles yelled.

"What is it, Charles?" Aunt Ophie said rushing in. "What's the excitement?"

Charles held the telling letter before her. "Who is Charlotte?"

Aunt Ophie's face suddenly turned pale. "Step into the parlor, Charles. It's time we talked."

When they sat down, Aunt Ophie stared at the floor for a moment, collecting her thoughts. "Charles, this Charlotte woman, she was very special to your father. For more than twenty years he kept company with her."

"Is she my mother?" Charles asked point-blank.

"Yes."

"My God . . . why wasn't I ever told?"

". . . It was the times, Charles, the times. Your father was a married man, an ambitious man, consumed with the goal of becoming the richest and most powerful person in Boston. Charlotte . . . was a common woman. If news of their relationship — of your illegitimate birth — ever leaked out, the scandal would have ruined your father's plans and brought you and the rest of the family down with him."

"And my mother, or Mrs. Royal, why did she keep silent?"

"Out of shame. What did she have to gain by speaking out? Her place in society, which she coveted, plus the prospects for her own children by your father would have all gone up in smoke too."

"And what of this Charlotte — what possible reason could *she* have had for remaining quiet?"

"She was your mother, Charles. Perhaps she thought it would be best for you."

Charles stood and walked to the fireplace. He leaned on the mantel, staring into the flames. "Do you know if she's still alive?"

"Charles, it's been *so* many years. Why dredge this all up now?"

Charles repeated slowly, "Is she alive?"

". . . Yes. At least I think so. I heard she had taken down with consumption, and if that's true, well . . ."

"Do you know where I can find her?"

"Charles . . ." Aunt Ophie's tone was of a plea not to do this.

"Please," Charles said quietly.

". . . Go to a tavern on Water Street, the old King's Cross. For years she had a room upstairs."

Just as Aunt Ophie finished, footsteps could be heard coming up the snow on the front steps. Charles caught Caitlin by the arm on the porch and spun her about without breaking stride.

"Where are we going?" she asked in astonishment.

"To meet my mother."

At the tavern, Charles asked for the whereabouts of Charlotte. A gray-haired barmaid looked him over skeptically. "And who might you be?"

Charles replied, "Her son."

Charles entered the small, poorly lit room first, with Caitlin behind him. Two elderly women greeted their sudden presence with a wary eye. "You can't just barge in here, sonny. Have ye no respect for the dyin'?"

"It's all right, Molly," said an ashen-faced figure lying on the bed. "Step closer to the light."

Charles moved to beside the bed and looked down at the frail woman. She was indeed in the last stages of her battle with consumption. Death might be waiting for her just outside the door. Neither spoke. Nor did they smile. They simply stared at one another.

"Do ya know this young man, Charlotte?" the second woman asked.

She nodded then replied to Charles, "He's my son. Charles."

Molly motioned to her friend to step outside. "You'll be wantin' some time together. We'll be right outside in the hall if ya need us, dearie." They left and closed the door behind them.

"I just found out today," Charles said. "I was going through some of Father's old things and I came across this letter, addressed to you. I guess he never sent it."

Charles handed her the letter. She glanced at it, then placed it on the nightstand unread. It was her son she wanted to see.

"I use to watch you as a child, you know. Your father would tell me when he was taking you for a walk, and I would go down to the lighthouse. The keeper was a friend of your father's and me. I'd climb way up to the top and off in the distance I'd see you coming. Maybe gathering seashells. Or tossing pebbles into the harbor. And then when you'd get close, your father would have you stop and wave and smile up at me. You couldn't see, but I always waved back."

Charlotte struggled to bring her arm up. Charles lowered himself to meet it. She smiled ever so slightly, reached and gently brushed aside a strand of hair from his forehead.

"Mother, I would like you to meet my wife, Caitlin." Caitlin stepped forward and extended her hand. Charlotte took it, and nodded her approval.

Caitlin looked at mother and son. "Living in the same city, for so many years, and you never met?"

Charles and Charlotte gazed at each other with mutual acknowledgement. "Once," Charles said to his mother. "Briefly. One snowy night long, long ago."

It was time to go. Charles placed his hand gently on Charlotte's shoulder. "I've just come into a considerable amount of money. More than sixty-five hundred dollars. Whatever you need, whatever you want, just tell me. The money's yours for the asking."

Charlotte shook her head slightly. "What good would money do me now? Go, with your lovely bride. I am at peace."

The next morning Charles, Caitlin, and Sarah arrived at the dock early. They had said their farewells to Aunt Ophie and Sally back at the house. Everyone promised to write, and Sally agreed to visit Oakmont in the fall — with what she hoped would be her fiancé.

Maxwell Chessman's directions were right on the money. The refitted packet stood freshly scrubbed and ready to sail.

"What's that you're doing?" Charles called in a friendly way to a workman sitting on a scaffold as the passengers and baggage moved slowly up the gangplank.

"She was made into a British frigate during the war," the workman replied. "Renamed the *Vulture*. Now I'm returning her to her true identity." Charles watched as the workman carefully repainted the letters: W . . . E . . . S . . . T . . . W . . . I . . . N . . . D.

As they reached their turn to board, Charles paused. Instinctively he turned. He turned to face the distant lighthouse. He turned to face the distant lighthouse and wave. And smile. Caitlin, standing beside him, did the same.

"Cast off!"

Charles and Caitlin stood by the rail as the great ship pulled slowly away from the land.

"I guess this marks the end of our Boston odyssey," Charles said whimsically, gazing out toward the open sea.

"Oh . . . I'm not sure I'd say that," Caitlin replied. She took her husband's hand and pressed it against her lower stomach. Charles looked into her eyes, asking if it were true. The twinkling gleam of light he met there confirmed that it was.

Soon the *Westwind's* sails were billowing full of life and she glided gracefully out of the harbor. Out into the vast ocean. Sailing off to that distant line on the horizon where sea meets sky.

Author's Note

As you wended your way through the preceding pages, you may have wondered at times whether certain individuals were representative characterizations or actual historical figures. If so, the following should help.

Fictional Characters

Ben Bates

Boils

Celeste Bradford

Charlotte

Maxwell Chessman

Hebron & Isaac Cooley

Mrs. D'Angelo

Private Foley

Henry Fowler

Hans Haupt

Captain Jacoby

Ambrose Jenkins

Junius

Maggot

Thaddeus Mantooth

Angus McBride

Temple McVee

Montoga

Lieutenant Nicholson

Sergeant Novoski

Jonas O'Hare

Phillip Overton

Mr. Parsons

Perfesser

Captain Reynald

Mr. & Mrs. Robinson

Caitlin, Charles, Joseph, Joshua, Morgana, Ophelia, Robert, Sally & Sarah Royal

Rainbow Samuels

Judge Abraham, Nigel & Rake Serling

Dalton Seymour

Cicero Steele

Strawman

Reverend Stocker

Tilly

van Gist brothers

Colonel Wainwright

Samuel Waverly

John Wayland

Whistler

Whittler

Willow

Hattie "Fat Hat" Wylie

PATRIOT ROYAL

Nonfictional Characters

Sam Adams

Benedict Arnold

Adrienne d'Ayen

John Burgoyne

Henry Clinton

Lord Cornwallis

Guillame des Deux-Ponts

William Erskine

Benjamin Franklin

Horatio Gates

King George III

Lord Germaine

John Glover

Admiral de Grasse

Nathanael Greene

Alexander Hamilton

John Hancock

John Haslet

Richard & William Howe

Baron de Kalb

Thomas Knowlton

Henry Knox

Marquis de Lafayette

Charles Lee

Benjamin Lincoln

Betsy Loring

Robert Magaw

Francis Marion

Joseph Martin

Charles Mawhood

Daniel Morgan

Lord North

Charles O'Hara

Thomas Paine

Andrew Pickens

Asa Pollard

William Prescott

Israel Putnam

Johann Rall

Paul Revere

General Rochambeau

Daniel Shays

William Smallwood

John Stark

Baron von Steuben

Lord Stirling

John Sullivan

Banastre Tarleton

George & Martha Washington

William Washington

Anthony Wayne

Otho Holland Williams